M000170338

THE
DAGGER
AND THE
FORBIDDEN HEIR

THE FORBIDDEN HEIR TRILOGY | BOOK ONE

EMILIA JAE

EMILIA JAE
FANTASY AUTHOR
EM'S BOOKISH REALM

The Dagger And The Forbidden Heir | The Forbidden Heir Trilogy: Book One.

Copyright © 2023 by Emilia Jae.

All rights reserved.

No portion of this book may be reproduced in any form without written permission from the publisher or author, except as permitted by U.S. copyright law.

Front Cover Art By: Celia Driscoll

The Map of Velyra: Andres Aguirre | @aaguirreart

Editor: Makenna Albert | www.onthesamepageediting.com

Original Publication | October 2023.

Paperback ISBN: 979-8-9888968-0-7

Hardcover ISBN: 979-8-9888968-1-4

To all the readers that always felt
like a side character in their own
story, and were never brave
enough to stand up for
themselves, or be the hero.
Our time is now.
This is for you.

Dedication Continued

To Celia & Tory.
This never would have been possible without your constant,
unwavering amount of support. Thank you for never giving up
on me. I am forever grateful for you both.

& to my parents.
Who always encouraged my crazy imagination as a child, even
when the rest of the world tried to snuff it out.

Content Warning

Please note that this book is not intended for readers below the age of 18. This warning is due to explicit language, violence/gore, mentions of past child abuse, and mentions of sexual assault.

This series has multiple POVs, including the villains. Please note that these villains are true in their nature. They are wicked to their core and you will see inside of their minds, which can be disturbing to some readers.
Reader's discretion is advised.

Pronunciation Guide

Names:

Elianna (Lia) Solus: Ellie-Ana (Leah) Soul-iss

Kellan Adler: Kell-an Add-ler

Jace Cadoria: Jayce Ka-door-ia

Jameson Valderre: Jame-es-son Val-dare

Idina Valderre: Eh-deena Val-dare

Ophelia: Oh-feel-ia

Kai: K-eye

Avery: Ay-ver-ee

Finnian: Finn-ee-an

Lukas: Luke-us

Zaela: Zay-lah

Callius: Kal-ee-us

Veli: Vel-ee

Nyra: Near-ah

Matthias: Math-thigh-as

Euphoroot: You-for-root

Ruefweed: Roof-weed

Places:

Kingdom of Velyra: Vel-ear-ah

City of Isla: Eye-la

Ceto Bay: See-toe Bay

Ezranian Mountains: Ehz-rain-ian

Sylis Forest: Sigh-liss

Alaia Valley: Al-eye-ah

Celan Village: Sell-an

Vayr Sea: Vay-er

Prologue

The King

THE SCREAMS OF PAIN and agony could be heard from the farthest reaches of the castle grounds. Ophelia had been hidden within the healer's chamber of the castle while she prepared to give birth to our first child.

I had never seen anyone as beautiful as Ophelia in my entire four-hundred years of life. Her stunning, pale green eyes were in such contrast to her sun-kissed skin and flowing black hair. The moment my gaze laid upon her in the courtyard of the House of Healers over three centuries ago, I immediately knew she had to be mine. The only problem was that I had been promised to another upon my birth. Sealing the fate of the Kingdom of Velyra's queen.

I would've made Ophelia my queen, though. Gods if I could, I would have. This wasn't to say that Queen Idina wasn't beautiful as well, with her auburn hair and eyes of warm honey, but she wasn't my Ophelia.

Velyra had always put strong family ties first, and with Idina being the daughter of a powerful Lord within the city of Isla, and Ophelia born the daughter of a tavern's keeper, there would have never been a way to break my family's oath to Idina's father. We were to be married by the time we reached the age of one hundred and fifty years, and that was exactly what occurred. Only I never stopped seeing Ophelia. The ache in my chest wouldn't allow it, even when she tried to push me away, saying that the duty to my kingdom was far greater than our love.

The time had come to break the news to the queen regarding my actions. Ophelia wished to still remain a secret, but that was not the life I desired for my first-born child. The babe deserved everything I had been given and more.

Deciding that the fewer eyes on the situation at hand the better, I sent Veli, the castle ground's healer, home for the night. With Ophelia being a healer herself, she insisted that she could do this on her own, and she just needed me by her side for support.

"You are doing incredible, my love," I praised her in between her deep breaths of distress.

"I don't know if I can do this James, the queen...she still does not know of this. Of us. What will she do? If she is anything like her father, she will have me–"

"She is nothing like her father was," I cut her off. "Her father had a cruel streak in him, I have never seen anything like that in Idina."

"James, why are you speaking as if he is..." She paused for a moment. "Did...did something happen?" She asked softly with worry.

I loved how she called me that. Everyone else referred to me as King Jameson. Hearing her nickname always made my heart clench. "It happened just days ago," I whispered. "I did not want to worry yo–"

"Worry me?!" She screeched through her deep breaths as sweat dripped from her brow. "Her father is dead? What happened to him?"

I let out a breath through my nostrils. "Humans. Her father, brother, and their small fleet were trapped and murdered by a human colony outside of Ceto Bay."

I had just been informed the night prior by the queen. The timing of such an unfortunate event would make my betrayal to her much worse.

Her face paled. "...Please tell me this isn't true. She will make you go to war for this, James. Our babe will grow up in a broken world. A world full of bloodshed and loss. You know how I feel about war."

She was right. I knew my wife would force the declaration of war upon my hands due to the loss of her kin. I had been trying to avoid a war for decades now, but Idina's father had been reluctant to give up on not following through with one against the mortal race.

"And I feel the same way Ophelia, we will not go to war," I assured her. "Please do not worry, but I must go and find Idina before the birth and let her know what is happening here. I will take care of everything. Both you and our beautiful babe will be safe. You know of my personal guard, Lukas, and he is now aware of the situation at hand. While he has always advised against it, he knows how I feel about you, and about our child. He will stand guard at the door while I am gone."

I kissed her forehead and headed for the door of the healing quarters where Lukas was already waiting for me.

"This is not going to go as well as you are for some reason thinking..." Lukas greeted me on a sigh, as I quietly shut the heavy door.

"It's not as if I am delusional enough to think that Idina will not show any rage," I countered. "She has every right to feel the emotions she will. Her husband, her king, is in love with someone else. I have always been in love with someone else and that is at no fault of Idina. I love her as a dear friend and respect her. I am not looking forward to this or hurting her."

"I believe you give her far too much credit for kindness she has never truly shown," Lukas stated.

"Are you trying to tell me that you believe your *queen* to be unkind? I would love to be provided with any examples of this," I said, as I stared into his deep chocolate-hued eyes.

Lukas chuckled. "I cannot provide examples, my king. It's just a feeling that I and some of the other guards get around her. She does not radiate the warmness that you do."

"I do not have anything to say to you regarding Idina. However, I am trusting you to guard Ophelia while I go break the news to her in our quarters."

Lukas swallowed. "We have known each other a long time, and while you are my king, I will never not consider you a dear friend of mine."

"Lukas, you know I will also always consider you to be the same…" I went to turn away, but he grabbed my arm, halting me.

He cleared his throat nervously. "It is an honor, Your Grace. And while I respect you and what you are about to do…please tread lightly when speaking to Queen Idina. And I say this as your friend."

I nodded at him and walked up the spiral stairs.

I rounded the corner of the east wing and headed to our quarters. The evening came upon us but an hour ago, and the hallways were lit by torches that hung on either side.

Lukas couldn't be right. He seemed truly nervous—worried even. Of my wife? Were there things I had not noticed all these years while being wrapped up in Ophelia? I'm sure I had overlooked *some* things, but I would know if the female was as cunning and vicious as her father had been. I provided her with anything she could want. All the gowns, jewels, gatherings, horses…you name it. If she desired it, I made it happen. While it could've been for my own selfish reasons of distracting her from finding out about my affair, I truly believed her to be as just and selfless as I was when it came to our kingdom.

Had her father's influence tainted her beliefs so profoundly in his relentless hunger for war? I hated that I didn't know the answer, and the fault was my own.

The worst part of it all was when the queen expected us to come together in bed, as she desired a child, an heir, as well. Guilt always tore through me when I would be forced by duty to be claimed by her seduction.

I found the queen in her bedchamber, staring into the decorated mirror on her beautiful vanity. She always knew how to decorate a space. Tapestries and oil paintings hung from each wall, and extravagant chandeliers took up much of the ceiling space. "You look stunning, Idina."

She lifted her hand and tucked a lock of her fiery hair behind her pointed ear, and smiled at me through the mirror. It was a closed-lipped smile that did not meet her eyes. "Hello, Jameson. We have much to discuss regarding this upcoming war. I hope you have told Lukas to prepare his soldiers. I just sent Callius off a few moments ago. He will be readying the ships," she stated.

Callius. Now if anyone rubbed me the wrong way, it was my wife's personal guard, who also ran our sea fleet. Something had always been off about him, but he was appointed by her father, and she had always seemed comfortable around him, so I never brought it up in discussion.

"My queen, we are not going to war, but you are correct. We have much to discuss."

I could've sworn I saw liquid fire ignite beneath her stare. "Come again? Why would we not be preparing to go to war? My father and brother are *dead* due to the human filth that has tainted our realm. We need to be rid of them once and for all." Each word was more clipped than the last.

"Surely all humans shouldn't be held responsible for their deaths, Idina."

That was clearly the wrong thing to say.

Idina whipped around and rose from her chair, slamming it behind her into the vanity. "Jameson. You are a king. A *king*. And you will let the lesser beings of this world walk on you and murder members of our family and not retaliate? Is that the kind of message you wish to send?" she snapped viciously.

"Of course not!" I exclaimed. "We can absolutely send out soldiers and get rid of the colony that did this, but an entire war is too much."

"You are a fucking fool of a king," she shot back, as she sat back down in the vanity chair. My brows rose as I took a step back in shock. Queen or not, no one should speak to their king that way.

"Idina, we need to talk, and not about your father or a war," I said sternly.

She wouldn't even look up at me. "I am listening."

"There is no easy way to say what I need to, and I completely understand how you are about to feel..." Her head snapped towards me. That got her attention.

"I am in love with someone else. She is with child and is about to give birth. I have no idea what else to say, but I know

7

I need to start with I am sorry. I am so sorry for the deceit I have committed in our marriage." She stared at me as I continued to ramble nervously. "We can figure out the situation and the babe all together, but I would really love for you to meet her. It wouldn't feel right if you didn't. I have been living a double life behind closed doors for too long as it is. She may be giving birth as we speak."

About a minute of unnerving silence passed before she burst out in laughter.

"Oh my gods, Jameson. *Ha*. That is odd because for a second it sounded like you said you have been sleeping with someone else. Someone who is not your queen. Tell me, who is better?" If I thought she had a fire in her eyes before, that didn't even compare to how it radiated beneath them now. "Tell me, *husband*, who is this wonderful female you just confessed has claimed your love?"

I stood there frozen for a moment. I knew that this wouldn't go well, but I didn't expect the venom behind her words to strike so true.

"Ophelia. Her name is Ophelia, and she is a healer. We met before we were married, and the relationship should've ended. In fact, she tried, but I couldn't let her go. I was already promised to you, but that was from birth. I do love you, but she may be my ma–"

"So help me fucking gods if you say you think she is your *mate*, Jameson."

"It's just the–"

"The what?" she spat. "The truth? Please, I know you don't truly think that a king of the most solid bloodline in Velyra could truly be mated to some peasant healer. As if the gods would even consider such an absurd thing."

"Don't you dare refer to her as a peasant." I could feel the heat in my cheeks rising.

"Is that anger I sense? The 'kind and fair' king of Velyra is feeling anger? Are you serious? No, Jameson, that just simply will not do. The rage is mine to own in this situation."

I just stared at her as my chest tightened painfully by her reaction, but I knew she was right.

"Come now," she said, as she stood from the chair once more. "Let's go meet this precious little bastard babe."

The smile on her face was the most terrifying thing I had ever seen.

I anxiously led the queen down to the healing chambers of the castle. The sound of her heels clicking off the polished marble floor was the only noise to be heard. Once we turned the last corner, I saw Callius was now standing next to Lukas outside of the door that guarded Ophelia. What in the realm was he doing down here? Idina said he was leaving to ready the ships.

"Callius," Idina greeted them, not even acknowledging Lukas. "I see you must've heard the great news."

Callius raised a brow. "This is good news, my Queen?" he asked. "I could hear the screams from the chamber throughout the lower levels of the castle. I came down here to investigate when I found Lukas standing here guarding the door with no healer to be found."

She turned to me. "Where is our healer, Jameson?"

I cleared my throat. "Since Ophelia is a healer also, we decided it would be best to send any staff on this floor away due to the situation at hand."

She chuckled wickedly and turned back to Callius. "Don't be silly, you old fool. This is fantastic news!" My eyes grew wide, as did Lukas'. "The king has fathered a child." The tone of her voice sent a chill down my spine. I could not let her speak to Ophelia this way.

"Yes, my Queen. The babe was born not even ten minutes ago." Callius gestured to Lukas. "This one had to slice the cord with his dagger. She rests with the mother now."

"She. *What?*" I burst through the door, Lukas following closely behind me.

There, in the arms of my Ophelia, lay the tiniest little babe I had ever laid my eyes on. Her mother smiled so brightly.

"Looks like Father missed the birth of our little Elianna," she said teasingly. The name we chose for a daughter.

"Elianna," I whispered, as I slowly made my way to them. "My beautiful little princess." I reached out and gently took our child from her arms.

Ophelia's smile dropped quickly when she looked up at who stood in the doorway.

"Oh, don't stop the happy meeting on my account, Ophelia," Idina said, her words dripping with poison as she stepped into the flickering candlelight. "I was just told the amazing news and came to meet the female who somehow learned how to compel a king to stray outside of his marriage."

"Idina, don't be cruel," I hissed, as I stared at her from Ophelia's bedside.

"Please don't let her near our baby..." Ophelia whispered so low that even I could barely hear it. The scent of pure fear that now radiated from her threatened to clog my nostrils, and my own heart began to race as nerves took over me.

As I looked down, I noticed a bit of blood on the sheets. "Are you okay?" I asked. Idina snorted from across the room.

"Yes, I am okay, it's just from the birth and Lukas cutting the cord. I do feel very tired though," Ophelia stated calmly.

I looked into her green eyes and then down at my arms to see that our daughter had that same beautiful gaze. My heart fluttered in my chest as I kissed the babe's forehead, and then Ophelia's. "Of course, you must be exhausted. I will take Elianna and get her cleaned up while you stay here and rest." Truthfully, I had no idea how to clean a babe, but I could do this for her.

She looked hesitant at first, but then looked up at me with a smile full of love. "Okay." She paused for a moment as if she were still unsure. "I will stay here if you truly want me to."

Idina stormed out the door and left, her gowns flowing behind her. Callius followed closely after.

"That was awful. I feel like such a horrible being. She must hate me," Ophelia said, lip trembling.

I shook my head. "She will come around, she desires an heir. I believe that is where most of her rage lies. There has never been a love between the queen and I that resembles anything even close to what we feel for each other," I said, as I walked towards the door. "I will be back soon."

In the bathing chamber a few floors away from where Ophelia rested, I washed our daughter off in the bath. I had no idea what I was doing, but I was happy. I felt at peace and excited to see where this future in my hands was going to bring my family and kingdom.

Since the moment I found out Ophelia was bearing my child, my mind had raced constantly regarding what our youngling would grow to be to Velyra. She was of my blood, and in my mind and heart, Elianna would be my heir. Ophelia had been hesitant about the idea since it was first discussed, fearing that it would make Elianna more vulnerable to threats since a proper heir would be a child of the queen. The sweet babe in my arms filled me with a warmth that made the thought of anyone harming her unbearable, and knowing that she feared someone may try to set my emotions ablaze. I would never let anything happen to either of my girls.

Lukas ran into the chamber, chest heaving to catch his breath. "Your Majesty, I feel as if we need to have eyes on the queen and Callius. I do not trust them. Callius would not leave my side when the babe was born, and I didn't trust to leave him there with Ophelia alone to run and get you once the birth happened."

"Lukas, I know you think the queen is less than benevolent, but–"

"Far less than that, Your Majesty. You saw how she spoke in there. I still have a chill running down my spine. Her words were laced with a threat before she stormed off with Callius. You do not have any other heirs. She will see that babe not only as a constant reminder of what you have done, but also of what you did not give her. Your first-born child. An heir," Lukas desperately pleaded.

"If you truly think she would harm an innocent youngling and her mother, then you have truly lost your mind. The queen's anger is justifiable, it'll all simmer down over time," I said to him while smiling at my daughter.

A moment later, a loud, terror-filled scream erupted from the hallway, echoing from floors away. The queen.

Both of our spines straightened, and I was moving before I could even blink. I held Elianna in my arms, tucked tightly to my chest, as both Lukas and I darted down the winding hallways and stairs until we came face first with Idina, sobbing uncontrollably outside the healer's doorway. My stomach twisted in knots at the sight of her.

"There was nothing to be done, Jameson. Sh-she...she was gone when we got back here."

My heart leapt to my throat, clogging it. No. No, it couldn't be. I shoved Idina aside as I barreled into the room and stared at the empty bed. Empty...and covered in *blood*. So, so much blood. The air was ripped from my lungs.

"Where is she?! What happened? Where is Ophelia?" The rapid questions tore through my throat on a scream.

Callius walked in then. "I am sorry, my King. I did not think it was a sight you needed to see, so I removed her body. She began to hemorrhage and lost too much blood. She was gone before anything could be done."

"Bullshit," Lukas spat at him, his lips curled back in a snarl.

I couldn't breathe.

"You dare accuse Callius of foul play?" Idina shot back at Lukas, eyes narrowing in on him.

"Oh, never," Lukas retorted, his words cold as ice.

She said she wouldn't need a healer on site and that she could handle this all on her own—I was such a gods-damn fool. I had left not even thirty minutes ago. Not but a half hour and she was *gone*. She died alone and was probably terrified, and I had failed her. I had failed her as a lover, a partner...and, and a mate. My mate was gone.

"...My mate," I whispered.

"Oh, don't even start with that!" Idina hissed back at me, her tone full of rage.

Lukas just stared at us and the scene before everyone, eyes wide, unknowing of what to do or say.

I let out a monstrous roar of agony as I shrank against the wall with Elianna still in my arms, tears of disbelief pouring from my eyes.

Lukas gently placed his hand on my shoulder when he said, "Don't worry, Your Majesty, we will get this cleaned up and figure out *exactly* what happened here." He gestured to Callius as he shot him a warning look. "Help me grab all of this and get it out of his sight so he can have some privacy," he snapped at him, tone entirely different than when he spoke to me only a second before.

I stared at the bloodied mattress, rapidly shaking my head in denial, as I watched both Lukas and Callius pull the sheets up from the bed and silently walk out the doorway.

I almost forgot I wasn't alone when I heard the soft, malicious whisper of a voice that I barely recognized as my wife's, as she bent down to my ear, "You may keep your bastard daughter, but I will have my war *and* an heir of my blood. Mark my words, Jameson."

ONE

Elianna

137 years later...

THE GROUND HAD BEEN coated with the blood of humans and fae
alike. This was nothing new for the war we had been living in
for the last century. For most of the humans fighting, it was
the war that began with their grandparents. My father had
told me the war truly began the day I was born. That was the
day the queen decided to claim her revenge for the deaths of
her father and brother. At first thought, I couldn't blame her.
If someone harmed my own father, the king, I would want to
destroy everything in my path as well. It just never should've
gone to this extent.

One hundred and thirty-seven years, the realm had been
cursed with the blood of those who were not responsible for the
events that led to the death of the Lord and his son. The mortals
alive today should not pay for the sins of their ancestors when
they weren't even alive to commit these heinous crimes. The
queen's stance on the war would never change, my father had
told me time and time again. His compromise to the war was
that he was able to keep me—his "bastard" daughter, the queen

referred to me as, just never in front of a soul. In front of others, I was the "unfit" captain of the armies for her war.

Growing up within the castle walls, I never understood why the queen loathed me so intensely, but once I was in my second decade of life, the king told me everything. The tragic story of his true love, my birth mother.

I grew up without a mother's love, but luckily my father did his best to make up for it. It still never seemed fair; I spent my earlier years watching the queen with her own children, born years after me. I watched how she would gently brush their daughter's hair and rock their sons back to sleep after terror had found them in their dreams. It took me years to come to terms with the fact that she would never accept me for what, or who, I was.

Even before her children were born, I would receive nothing but doors slammed in my face, being forced to eat alone in my chamber or be reprimanded cruelly for little offenses, such as sneaking out into the gardens past dusk.

I would never forget when I was not but thirteen years of age and was caught sneaking into the queen's personal bedchamber. I just wanted to use some of her beautiful hair brushes. I sat down at her vanity, pulled the brush through my long, dark hair once, and looked up to find the queen glaring at me through the mirror with a scowl carved into her face. She then dragged me by the tip of my pointed ear all the way down to the stables. Once there, she had Callius, her henchman for all intents and purposes, take a whip to my back three times as punishment. The pain was excruciating, causing me to vomit all over the floor as the queen laughed. She later locked me inside my own chamber for two days without food and denied me access to a healer. That hairbrush was the same one I watched her brush through her own daughter's hair years later.

My father and Lukas had left Isla on business to meet with the Lords throughout Velyra. They never learned of what happened that day, but I still bear the scars.

Being fae, our heightened senses and rapid healing abilities typically don't arrive until the age of twenty-five. Before then, our bodies are nearly just as fragile as mortals.

I took in the sight of the battlefield before me and observed my soldiers as they searched through the bloodied bodies that were piled up on the terrain. I wiped the gore from my blade clean on the side of my pants and then sheathed it at my side as my eyes continued to roam our surroundings.

Lukas had become the commander of the king's armies when the war began, and I took over the position fifteen years ago. I had earned the respect of most of the males within my ranks, but of course not all. Some would never show respect for a female captain. Luckily, they knew better than to act out any idiotic thoughts they had about it. Lukas had taught me personally from the time I was able to lift a sword.

I trained as if I were a boy, day and night within the walls of the castle, and when I came of age, I began to attend lessons of battle strategy with the other males.

Throughout my years of training, I would always hear the whispers of disbelief and outright anger regarding a female practicing among them. I would constantly be shoved to the ground, ignored and mocked by my peers. I refused to let it bother me. I also refused to have Lukas handle the confrontation for me. The male trainees needed to know I was just as much a threat to them as they were to me.

The look on their faces when a female could kick their asses up and down the field would never get old. I could always tell that my father and Lukas felt the same.

My level of skills eventually earned me the respect I received when Lukas chose me as his successor, with the blessing of the king. However, there would always be those few who didn't even try to hide how they truly felt about being under my command. They felt as though I shouldn't be of higher rank than them, or even close to them, just because they believed that I was, for some reason, favored by the king...imagine their faces if they ever discovered that I was his daughter. A grin grew on my face at the thought. It was honestly laughable that they thought it was due to me being chosen by him when I worked my ass off and earned the title of "Captain" by sheer determination and skills alone. They just couldn't accept the fact that I was better than them.

"You going to stand there all day and smile about our victory or are you going to help load the wagons up so we can get back to Isla there, princess?"

I jumped at the word *princess*. Nobody truly knew that I technically was one. It didn't matter how many times Kellan, the male exclusively claimed to me, called me that. It always sent a bolt of nerves through me.

"Ah yes, Captain Adler! Is there a body count yet?" I asked, praying the number was low.

Kellan commanded the sea fleets while I led the land armies. We often joined forces together in battle.

He walked up to me and kissed my lips so fiercely that it caught me be surprise and caused me to almost lose my balance. Looking up at him, I noticed that the blue in his eyes were practically glowing in contrast to the dried-up blood splattered across his rugged, but handsome face. Blood and dirt also thickly coated his hair to the point where it appeared almost black, vastly different from the natural, dirty blonde it typically was.

"The men have counted seventy-two dead so far from your ranks, an unfortunate loss but not even comparable to the four-hundred and sixty-three human bodies found so far."

"Indeed," I replied dryly. "Any loss is too great."

"This is war, Lia. There will always be loss," he said, as he took my face in the palms of his calloused hands. "You take it too harshly. These males are prepared to die for their kingdom and get rid of the disgusting human filth that remains in this world once and for all."

"The human lifespan is a fraction of ours. These people fighting us were not even alive when this war began..." I said to him while holding his gaze. His arm dropped to my shoulder as he turned us around and began walking back to where the camp was packing up.

As I glanced around the battlefield and what remained of our men, I felt my heart clench. I would always take any loss personally, no matter how small. These were my soldiers. I led them here and now some would never return to their spouses and younglings.

Bodies lay sprawled on top of each other, arrows protruding from chests and skulls, limbs cut clean off from the freshly sharpened blades prepared for the battle. The flies were already flocking toward their next feast. The aftermath was always too much for me to stare into directly without feeling the utmost guilt. I observed my remaining soldiers as they moved to respectfully pile the bodies in preparation to burn them.

Kellan was quiet for several moments. "You should not speak with empathy for them. One might hear you and believe you to be a mortal sympathizer. They are a violent race that will try to kill us the first chance they get. Only the gods know why they were created in image of us." He scoffed. "Lesser beings with no magic or heightened abilities. They are wicked and are prepared to wipe themselves from the realm entirely with a wholly pathetic attempt to do that very thing to us."

"Has it never occurred to you that they feel the same about us?" I shot at him. "I'm not saying they do not hold blame, they were just born into this mess and now they will all pay with their lives." He continued to stare ahead in silence. "I guess I just have the same mindset as our king."

"Well, thank the gods for the queen, then," Kellan retorted. He removed his arm from my shoulder and walked towards his ship that was anchored in the sea beyond the battlefield. "I will see you back in Isla," he announced without looking back.

Peering around the battlefield wasteland, I could see that almost everything had already been packed up by the soldiers that remained. The horses had finished resting and eating, so it was time to head home to the city of Isla, where Kellan and I would need to report back to the queen regarding the results of the battle. Gods, I just couldn't *wait* to do that.

I rolled my eyes at the thought.

"Soldiers!" I yelled, my voice carrying through the open field. Everyone glanced in my direction. "You all fought bravely, and I am proud to command such fearless and powerful warriors. Now let's go home."

A short cheer echoed off the wind as I glanced back to the sea towards Kellan. We had never been on the same page when it came to the humans and the war. I just prayed to the gods that wouldn't drive a further wedge between us.

TWO

Elianna

IT HAD BEEN A three-day ride almost nonstop from the battlefield before we could see the gates of Isla. The soldiers were exhausted, along with me. Most of us had run into the sea before leaving to wash the blood and dirt from our bodies, but I was in desperate need of a hot bath. Preferably with bubbles.

We lost two more soldiers on the journey home due to blood loss. Each had lost a limb, and without a healer among us, thanks to the queen, the exhaustion that their bodies were put through made them unable to heal fast enough to survive. More deaths that I would forever feel responsible for, no matter what Kellan said. I could never understand how the queen justified her hatred for healers enough to refuse their care to her own armies. My anger toward the situation rose as my thoughts consumed me—their deaths were preventable, yet their blood now lay on my hands, instead of the queen's.

I stared ahead at our city from the hilltops a few miles outside of the gates. It was always a beautiful sight to see, especially after being away for weeks at a time. The sun shone down on the terracotta roofs of the homes of our people. The castle overlooked the entire city and the harbor, where Kellan's ship had already docked. I could even appreciate seeing the darkness of the slums on the outskirts of Isla...after all, I had heard from many of my soldiers that the slums were where the fun was to be had after returning from battle. Not that I could ever, or would ever, partake in such a thing. I promised my father I would never set foot there...as if I couldn't handle myself, but he would always worry about me. It isn't as if I would ever really feel the need to go to a brothel anyway, but the rowdiness of the taverns did seem as if fun could be had. However, my father had not been well for quite some time, so I made it a point to not add any more stress to him aside from riding into battle.

As my hips rocked painfully side to side to the beat of my horse's steps, I couldn't help but think about the king. Over the last few months, my father's health had been declining. Healers could not figure out what was wrong with him, and all he could describe was that his insides felt as if they were charred. I had never heard of such a symptom, and clearly neither had the healers. The queen had even been reluctant to let healers visit him as often as he requested, and the staff didn't understand why. I assumed they believed that she felt as if he was being dramatic, but I knew the true reason—my birth mother was a healer.

Over a century had passed and the jealousy and betrayal she felt was still right at the surface of who she was, and I assumed having me around didn't help the situation at all, either.

Gods, I hated her. I knew why she could never stand the sight of me, but the treatment of my father behind closed doors had taken every ounce of my being to not strike her down. Not only was I great with a weapon, but I could throw a mean punch too, thanks to Lukas. But alas, that would be considered an act against the crown, and king's bastard daughter and commander of the armies or not, that would be punishable by death. Another mischievous grin appearing on my face as I stared ahead at the city...she would have to catch me first, but once again, I could never put my father through that.

After King Jameson's betrayal of her with my birthmother, he gave her everything she wanted. Her war, her own chambers in the castle, and as many children as her body would allow her to bear, which turned out to be three.

Kai was born first, and he was just as rotten as his mother, perhaps even worse. Cruel to his core, he could almost always be seen taunting the castle staff, animals, a beautiful female he decided he was entitled to, and...me. He'd made it a point to consistently try to crawl under my skin. It took an immense amount of mental restraint from myself to not level that asshole out on the castle floor and teach him a lesson that's been needed for the last century.

Next came Avery, my very best friend, even though she came almost twenty years after I was born. She shared with me the kindness of our father, and it killed me that she could never know we were sisters. Since the day Avery was born, she had been treated like a true princess—acted like it too. I chuckled to myself thinking about it. With her stunning gowns that she loved to flounce around the castle in, to the gorgeous jewels and tea gatherings with the other Ladies of Isla, she was a true princess. Though treated greatly, she had always been very sheltered and kept within the castle's battlement, yet she craved adventure. Whenever I returned home from a trip, she begged me to tell her stories of the road and what I had seen. It was funny to think that sometimes we wished we could trade places with one another, but that could never work. I wasn't raised to be a princess—I was raised to be a warrior, and vice versa.

Lastly came Finnian, who had been a shy and quiet boy his entire life. He would keep to himself, and on the rare occasion that Kai would force him to join his menacing escapades, Finnian always looked uncomfortable and as if he immediately wanted to apologize on Kai's behalf.

After Finn was born, the queen was told it would be wise to not have any more children—by then I believed she had grown tired of trapping my father in her chambers anyway. It was extremely unfair that my mother, someone who loved helping people so much that she had become a healer, did not survive birth complications, but the queen was able to have not one, but three children and survive with them.

The gates of Isla opened as we neared and my soldiers and I were greeted with cheers from all citizens out in the street, some even throwing beautiful flowers into the air. This reminded me of why we did this; to protect the people, to see the smiles on their faces, and to know that they felt safe within the walls of our kingdom.

Of course, there would always be the part I dreaded about coming home, and that was meeting with the families of the fallen. Kellan always told me to just have someone of lesser rank take the burden of it, but my answer back had, and would always be, that it was my responsibility. It would never be easy, and I often would go back to my quarters, high up in one of the castle's towers, and sob for the remainder of the evening. Since the moment I became Captain, I felt that I owed it to my soldiers to be the one to comfort their families when hearing of their loss. Even though he believed it to be a waste, Kellan would accompany me to meet with the families of my fallen, even though he refused to even do it for his own. I wasn't naïve enough to not recognize that he did this to stay in my good graces, though.

Together, the two of us commanded the strongest warriors in all of Velyra. Once we claimed each other, there were, of course, whispers surrounding the reasoning, but the two of us together just made sense. Plus, we worked well together...most of the time. I would be lying if I said he didn't pursue me for years. He always trotted around so arrogantly and was, of course, popular amongst all the beautiful Ladies of Isla due to his handsome face and rugged persona. However, if Kellan was one thing...it was persistent. I dragged him along for a little while, and after I was promoted to Captain, I decided to give him the time he had begged for over the last few decades.

Lukas and my father were always wary of him, most likely due to the brutal methods he had shown over the years, but he had always shown loyalty to me. I never questioned that, which had given me at least some peace of mind. If there was anything that drove me insane, though, it was how he could never let me defend myself—he would always be the one to swing first and ask questions later. He would say it was to defend my honor, but he of all should know that I could swing for my damn self.

After I arrived back at the castle grounds, I decided to bring my horse, Matthias, back to the stables to make sure he received the extra love and treats he needed after such a hard couple of weeks beyond the castle's battlement.

The stables weren't far off from the gardens on the rear side of the castle. The walk was always a lovely sight, accompanied with being enveloped by its floral scents. Guiding Matthias through the garden, we passed through rose bushes, irises, and lilies, each section of the garden more breathtaking than the last. Even on the castle itself, wisteria vines had grown, winding up to the highest of towers on the southern wing. This truly was one of my favorite areas of the castle grounds.

On the rare chance I had any spare time, I enjoyed sitting down here on one of the stone benches while reading a book from the king's library. He said my mother loved to read, and it's one of the many traits I received from her without ever truly knowing her. It was an odd feeling to miss someone you had never met.

Once we reached the stables, I hung Matthias' reins on one of the door's hooks, but oddly, there was no one to be found.

"Hello?" I called out as I stripped out of a layer of armor and sheathed my sword in his saddle. I patiently waited for a response, but none came.

I walked around the corner and again, there was no one to be seen.

"It's Lia! I brought Matthias back and was hoping he could get a few extra treats and ear scratches for being such a good boy out on the road." I chuckled, thinking there was no way the stable keepers heard that from any of the male soldiers that boarded their horses here.

Still, no response had been received.

"...That is odd. Where is everyone?" I whispered to myself.

Suddenly, I heard a loud crash and the shuffling of feet echo through the stables from above, up in one of the lofts, followed by a lot of hushing.

Interesting. I grabbed one of the hatchets that had been hanging on the wall next to me and began to climb the ladder leading to the first loft.

"You know, if you're going to be sneaking around and be in an area that you shouldn't, you may want to start in the slums, and not in...oh, I don't know...the fucking castle grounds of the king of Velyra."

I was met with silence once more. This was getting aggravating.

Rolling my eyes, I hid behind a barrel of hay up in the loft, and after a few minutes, I began to hear murmurs again coming from around the corner, towards the back. "Caught you," I whispered.

Smirking, I ran out from behind the hay, hatchet held high above my head as I whipped around the corner and yelled, "Got yo–" I cut myself off.

Staring back at me, both as naked as the day they were born...was one of the stable keepers and...and *Finnian*.

The three of us all stared at each other in the most awkward silence I had ever felt. My jaw had dropped so suddenly that it felt as if it was hanging down at my feet. The hatchet slipped from my hand, that had been frozen in the air, and clattered onto the ground, startling all of us.

"Oh my gods, Lia! Lia, you shouldn't be here!" Finn cried, eyes so wide it looked painful, as he began stumbling and tripping towards me...still naked.

"Finnian, what the fuck! Go put some clothes on! This is so gross...and weird," I shouted back while covering my eyes.

"Well, that was...kind of rude Elianna, but yea, I will get right on that," he shot back at me, as he reached for his pants.

Ugh, right. To me, he was a little brother. To him, I was a friend who lived in the castle his entire life because the king did not want to see "the daughter of his favorite handmaiden who had passed in childbirth" go off to live in Isla's orphanage. Gods, the lies about me were spun so expertly that if I ever needed to prove who I truly was, it would be impossible. To be completely honest, I believed the plan was for me to never know who I was, but my father could not possibly keep that from me.

I took a deep breath. "Finn, I'm sorry, I didn't mean it like that...I think I am just in shock." I glanced over at the other male, whose cheeks were so red it looked like they were about to burst. I had definitely seen him before. He had been brought on about a year or two ago, if I remembered correctly. I never had time to get to know him, but Matthias liked him and, apparently, so did Finnian.

"How long has this been going on?" I asked.

"Two weeks!" Finn yelled while the other male shouted, "A year!"

Ha. Busted. I raised a single brow at them while smirking.

"Ugh, okay fine, yes it's been about a year," Finn said. He turned back towards the male. "And a wonderful year it has been, of course!" The male looked less than impressed with Finn's rambling as he finished buttoning up his shirt.

"Okayyyyy," I said, still staring at them. "Does lover boy have a name by chance?"

"Landon, Miss. My name is Landon. I'm so sorry about this," he stuttered. "All of this is my fault. Please do not blame Finnian and get him into trouble."

"Don't be a fool, Landon. You would receive a far greater punishment than I," Finn retorted back to him. I watched them bicker back and forth about whose fault being caught was. You would think they were younglings instead of lovers. "Oh no...Lia, you cannot tell Kai about this, please! Anyone but Kai. He cannot know about Landon," he pleaded to me, pure fear radiating from his eyes.

"I would never tell...anyone about this, Finnian. Especially Kai. If you thought you had seen cruelty from him before, I...even

I would be afraid of the aftermath if he received knowledge of this." I gestured to them. "However, I think it is beautiful if you two have found love with one another, and I'm very happy for the both of you," I said with a soft smile.

"Thank fuck," Landon whispered, as his head fell, hanging near his chest.

Finnian shot him a warning look and said, "Yea, don't worry, Lia is cool." He looked over at me with gratitude in his warm, honey-hued eyes.

"Yes, well, that being said..." I quickly kicked the hatchet up off the ground and caught it in my hand in one swift motion. I shot over to Landon and pinned him against the wall with the hatchet to his throat. "If you hurt him, Kai will be the least of your problems. You will have to deal with me," I said with a sweet venom lacing my voice as I chuckled.

Finnian began to rub his temples. "Okay, Lia, you made your point."

"Have I?" I whipped my head in his direction with the prettiest, taunting smile I could muster up.

Landon looked me in the eye. "You don't have to worry about that, Miss Lia. If anyone will be hurt in this situation, it will be me."

Well, *that* was depressing. I released his body that I had been pinning to the wall of the stable.

"Well, personally, I would prefer neither of you hurt one another." They just stared at me—this was getting awkward again, so I cleared my throat. "Okay, let's get you boys out of here before someone much less forgiving than I am comes in here and sees you two. And for the love of the gods, can you two *please* be more careful moving forward?! I could've been anyone!"

Neither of them responded to me, but I watched as they exchanged menacing smirks.

After we climbed down the ladder, I could see that the sun was setting outside of the stable doors. I would need to report to the queen soon with Kellan. I glanced over at the two males, and they appeared to truly enjoy each other. I watched as Landon picked little shards of hay out of Finn's shaggy, auburn hair while he fed Matthias a carrot—one of his favorite snacks. My brother and my horse were happy, so that meant I was, too.

"Alright Landon, while it was wonderful to meet you, I have a hot date with Finnian's mother that I am definitely not looking forward to, so I would like to get it over with." I grinned at him as he glanced over in shock. I walked over to them and awkwardly tried to put my arm around Finn's shoulders, forcing myself up on my tiptoes in the process. "Care if I steal your lover for emotional support?"

"You're keeping our love a secret. You may do whatever you want. As long as I get him back at some point," Landon stated, as he crossed his arms and smiled at us.

"Perfect, you can have him back later this evening if you'd like!" I said with a wink.

As we walked back towards the barn doors, Finn looked down at me, now wrapping his arm around my shoulder. "Thank you," he whispered.

"You never have to thank me for anything, especially this," I said softly, as we made our way toward the castle.

THREE

Elianna

WALKING BACK INTO THE castle with Finn was like a breath of fresh air. As the staff ran by us, we were greeted with a smile from each of them. It always made me feel extra grateful to come home to warm faces after being out on the road for weeks at a time. The castle's entrance was stunning as ever, per usual. Walking through the foyer I noticed the fresh flowers, most likely hand-picked from the garden that morning, and the ceiling was decorated with the most extravagant chandeliers that coin could buy. The candles that hung in them reflected off the spotless marble floors. The place looked immaculate and clean, a stark contrast to what I was.

Now I was *definitely* counting down the minutes until I could take that bath.

Finn started speaking as we neared the throne room, "Now tell me all about the past few weeks? What did you see? Did you kill anyone?"

Gods, I hated that question.

"Finn, you know that I don't like to disc–" I was cut off by a shrill screech coming from one of the side hallways leading into the foyer. My hand automatically flew to my hip, reaching for the sword I was no longer wearing since I left it with Matthias in the stables. Shit. I whipped around to the hall the scream echoed from and before I could even blink, I was tackled to the floor.

Panicking, my vision finally cleared to see Avery's freckled, smiling face hanging above mine with her long, beautifully curled red hair hanging down on the sides of my face. She was lucky I adored her.

"Avery! Are you out of your mind? I could've struck you!" I shouted in her face, trying to hide my smile.

"I mean yeah, but you didn't," she teased, giggling as she rolled off of me.

I looked down to see her lovely lavender gown was now speckled with dirt that had been on my armor. Serves her right.

"I just think it's funny how you all thought you could talk about your epic adventure outside of Isla without me present!" she sassed. "Now, where were we…ah, yes! What happened the past few weeks? What did you see? Did you kill anyone?" she asked with a wink.

Gods, these two.

"As I was just telling Finnian, I don't like to talk about *that*. You know this," I replied dryly.

"And why is that, Captain Solus?" I heard echo from the throne room doorway. The voice sent a shiver down my spine.

Solus was the surname given to all younglings orphaned at birth in Velyra. My father wanted me to possess the Valderre name, but the queen shut that down for obvious reasons. The truth was, I loathed my given last name. It just served as a constant reminder that I could never be recognized for who I truly was.

Glancing towards the doorway, I noticed Kai staring at us with a smirk plastered across his face. I felt both Avery and Finnian tense behind me.

"Kai, how are you?" I greeted, with the fakest, closed-lipped smile I could manage.

He stared at me for a moment. "It is Prince Kai to you, as you have been told numerous times before. Perhaps frolicking around with these two…" He gestured to his siblings. "Has made you once again forget your place here."

Oh, I had forgotten absolutely nothing. And I did not *frolic.*

"Apologies, Prince Kai." I would've loved to wipe the smirk off his face by dragging it across the spotless floor.

"Now tell me, why do you not like to discuss destroying our enemy? Your queen will be most displeased to hear that you are defending the humans. In fact, it would be considered treason if I am not mistaken."

His eyes were as cold and depthless as his mother's, even though they shared the same honey-hued tones as his siblings. It always bothered me that Kai acquired our father's dark brown hair, just as I had, while Avery and Finnian both shared the queen's auburn locks.

"I would never side with the enemy. Do not put words in my mouth, little prince," I challenged.

Kai looked as if he were about to lash out in anger when the king appeared behind him.

Putting a hand on Kai's shoulder, King Jameson looked at me from across the foyer and smiled brightly. Moving slower than I had seen him in the past, he aimed toward me. Meeting him halfway, I was greeted with the tightest, warmest hug I had received in weeks. An instant, genuine smile spread across both of our faces as we held each other's gaze, earning the usual intrigued looks from the surrounding staff.

He bent down, putting his lips near my ear so others could not hear, and said, "Your mother's eyes. I have missed you, daughter." My heart clenched, but I shushed him so others would not gain too much curiosity about what was said.

"We can talk in your chambers later," I said to him in a hushed tone. "First, I must report to the queen."

"Ah, yes," he said, as he wrapped an arm around my shoulder, and his other around Avery's. "Let's go, my favorite, beautiful ladies. You too, sons."

The cool stone floor of the castle echoed with the sound of our footsteps as we all made our way to the throne room.

Queen Idina stared down at me from the dais, sitting on her throne next to my father as their three children set themselves off to the side. Her eyes practically drilled a hole through my skull as we all waited for Kellan to arrive so he could be included in the debrief. I refused to break eye contact with her.

Her hair cascaded in waves down to her waist with fiery intensity, framing her face that resembled porcelain. Eyes that beamed of amber served as a window to her malevolent soul. It was so contradictory of the same gazes her other two children bore—while theirs held warmth, the queen's left anyone who dared to stare too long feeling unsettled by their ferocity. The bone structure of her face was sharp and consisted of high cheekbones that any fae would envy, paired with a crimson-hued tint painted onto her lips that were twisted into a grimace. She was the epitome of beauty that had been tainted by pure wickedness.

The throne room was always used for parties, balls, and any extravagant gatherings the kingdom held, but when it was not decorated, the room was bare and cold. Occasionally, Idina would hold punishment sentencing in this room for anyone who was caught being a mortal sympathizer. The results always ended in being hung by the neck until dead in the heart of the city. The bodies would often be left there for weeks at a time, being picked at by the crows until nothing remained but bone and scraps of clothing. The queen believed it would leave the citizens restless enough to never even consider committing that form of treason. A shudder went through me at the thought of it all.

I could see movement in the doorway and glanced over, seeing that Lukas had arrived and was standing guard by the door. I smiled at him—I was excited to see him, but also...where in the realm was Kellan? I knew he became aggravated out in the field thinking that I was sympathizing with the humans, but surely that wouldn't prevent him from coming here and announcing our victory. I even saw his ship in the harbor when I arrived not but an hour ago.

Callius appeared up on the dais and whispered in the queen's ear. This also caught the king's attention.

Idina cleared her throat. "It appears that Captain Adler will not be joining us." She glanced in my direction. "Unfortunately, this means we will have to take your word for how the battle went, Elianna." The king shot her a look of disappointment.

"Where is Kellan?" I asked immediately, taking a hesitant step toward the dais.

She could not have looked more unimpressed if she tried. "Oh, do you think due to your romantic relations with the sea captain that you are entitled to his location at all times?"

My eyes twitched in anger. "Of course not, Your Grace, it's just that—"

"Just. What?" she barked at me.

Oh yeah, she was ready for a fight. A fight she knew I could never give in front of the staff and guards stationed throughout the room. "It is just that I know his ship is docked in the harbor and I would love to know why it is acceptable for him to not come here and report on our victory."

She shrugged. "Ah, well, it appears he has been very preoccupied since his return, unlike you, who thought the best idea was to putter around in the garden and stables since you've returned. You also look..." She looked me up and down twice. "Filthy."

I quickly made eye contact with Finn, who looked as if he was going to puke at the mention of the stables. "I apologize, Your Majesty. I simply brought my horse to the stables and then came in here to report what happened. Which was a victory, by the way." I tried to tame the sass in my tone, but it was no use.

"Ah yes. Well, you are standing in front of me, so it would appear to be a victory," she replied, looking bored now.

I stared at her. "Indeed, of course, no battle comes without loss, unfortunately. We lost seventy-four in total, including the soldiers who passed on the way home due to you refusing us healers." My teeth clenched tightly on the last word.

Gasps of disbelief rang out from the corners of the throne room as a few of the remaining handmaidens moved quickly to exit, realizing that they had made it known they were listening to a conversation that they had no business being a part of. My stare shot down to the floor at my feet as I cursed myself for not being wise enough to hold my tongue.

"Healers would not be necessary if you trained your soldiers properly, Elianna. Consider their deaths on your hands," she retorted viciously.

I could feel the heat of my blood as it surged up my neck and to my cheeks. I quickly pivoted my body to hide my reaction from her and met Lukas' stare, seeing that his jaw was gaping open at the queen's words.

"That is *enough*, Idina!" the king snapped. I focused my attention back up to them as he leaned into her and began whispering something I couldn't hear. She rolled her eyes at him. At this point, my vision was blurred with red. I needed to stab something. Preferably her or Kai.

With the queen distracted, Avery rushed over to me from the dais and slipped her fingers through mine as my hands hung at my sides. She tugged at my arm and turned me around, away from the dais as the king and queen continued to bicker about her behavior.

She guided me back to the front doors of the throne room where Lukas stood, still in shock at what the queen had said. Once we passed him, she led me up the main staircase, and Finnian followed closely behind us in silence.

FOUR

Elianna

AVERY ORDERED THE STAFF to come and bring up hot water so I could bathe in her gorgeous porcelain tub that I had always been envious of. Her chambers were certainly fit for a princess. Pink tapestries hung on each wall, candles strung up in every corner, incredibly vibrant paintings, and a bed fit for three kings in the center of the room with a cream-colored canopy that hung down from both the ceiling and the bedposts. An intense difference from my plain chambers that were only a tower over, filled with only the necessities.

"Alright, the bath is ready for you, Lia, whenever you want. Just be sure to use it while it is hot," Avery said, as I admired one of the newer pieces of art on the wall. Flopping onto her enormous bed, she shot Finn a look. "You may leave now, it is time for girl talk." Then she glanced over at me, wiggling her brows repeatedly at a rapid rate.

Finnian headed for the door. "Don't have to tell me twice. I'll see you later," he said, as he exited her room.

I walked over to the bathing room and started removing what remained of my armor and fighting leathers. I forgot how stiff my body always felt after wearing the same gear for days at a time. Once completely undressed, I covered my breasts with my long, dark hair, that apparently still had sections of dried mud and gods knew what else in it, and I inched my way into the hot, steaming water.

"Oh my, this feels amazing," I called over to her, where she still lay on her bed. "I don't even remember the last time I was able to take a hot bath."

"Well, that's gross Lia," she teased.

"Hey! Listen, once you're the one out in the wilderness for weeks on end, surrounded by nothing but brute males, then you can come and talk to me," I shouted jokingly. I waited for a reply, but nothing was said.

I forgot how much it bothered her, that she had never been beyond the city gates after the queen deemed it unsafe due to the mortal threat. She would tell Avery that there was nothing more that she could possibly need outside of Isla—which only proved how little she knew about her own daughter.

"I'm sorry Avery, trust me, it isn't all it's cracked up to be. It's dangerous, and not just because of the human threat. There are wild creatures out there that are always hungry. Even the berries that grow beyond the gates are poisonous!"

She appeared then, leaning against the doorframe, crossing her arms. "What is it like to have a mate?" she randomly asked, causing me to choke on a rough laugh, which turned into an uncontrollable giggle. "I don't know why you would laugh at such a thing. You have a mate and I do not."

I calmed my giggles as I looked up at her. "Avery, what in the realm are you speaking of? I don't have a mate. I don't even believe in mates! They are made-up tales so females think they can find their one, true twin-soul." I started chuckling again. "I wouldn't even want a mate! It's just another excuse for the males to get even *more* territorial and overprotective than they already are."

"You must take me for a fool, then. If Kellan is not your mate, then what is he, huh?" she shot at me, a little fire in her eyes that normally wasn't there.

Was she joking? I honestly wanted to ask, but I felt as if I had accidentally struck a nerve already. "Avery...Kellan is not my mate. He is...he is a– " I didn't even know what to say. "A distraction? No! That is the wrong word." She raised a brow at me. Now I was the one rambling like Finnian had been earlier. "He is my partner. In both commanding our fleets and..." I paused. "Amongst other things." I gave her an awkward smile.

"So, a fuck friend?" she asked.

I audibly gasped. "Avery! Absolutely not, and who even taught you that phrase? I can't imagine your Ladies of Isla friends speak like that." I tried to hide my amusement with my gasping disbelief.

She chuckled. "You would be very surprised."

Well, damn. Ok Ladies of Isla, I guess maybe they *did* know how to have fun when they weren't sitting around at tea parties, gawking at the Lords as they sauntered by.

"Okay, well, I'm sorry to disappoint you, but Kellan is not a 'fuck friend' or my mate. We are claimed by each other, and that is all. We are exclusively together and I trust him to be loyal to me," I said right before I dunked my hair under the water.

"Will you ever marry him?"

For a second I thought I had water in my ears after I came to the surface, but she definitely just asked me about marriage.

"Perhaps, I'm not sure if either of us are the marrying type, but if it makes sense, then yes," I said softly to her, and also to myself. I had never thought of marriage. Of course I had a love for Kellan, but both of us had always focused on commanding our warriors first.

She stared at me while biting her lower lip. I reached for the towel that was hanging by the tub and lifted myself up to dry off.

Now I couldn't get this out of my head. Did I want a marriage with Kellan? Yes, actually, eventually I think that would make sense. Just not yet.

"Where is all of this coming from?" I asked her as she walked back toward her giant, comfortable bed.

"Oh, you know, I am just your typical princess locked away in a tower full of every beautiful item and artifact you could dream of. I will never get to experience what you do. I have no life outside of these gates. I also will never know the feeling of spontaneous love. I am eventually to be married off to some far-off Lord across the sea, never truly knowing if I have a mate out there, or if I could've loved without it being forced upon me," she explained to me, each word hitting me harder than the last.

I felt awful now because she was right. She barely had a life outside of the castle grounds, never mind the city gates.

"I'm so sorry, Avery. I clearly wasn't thinking. You are right. I just get nervous thinking of you outside the gates, but I know you could hold your own if you needed to," I whispered to her, as I twisted one of her curls around my finger.

I went to turn toward the door, but she reached out and grabbed my wrist to halt me. I turned back to face her and saw she was staring at my back with eyes that radiated concern.

"What's wrong?" I asked her softly.

"Your scars." She blinked. "I just always forget how horrific they are. I can't believe they're still so deeply imbedded from when you were a youngling." She broke from her trance and lifted her gaze to mine.

I gave her a gentle smile. "Well that's what I get for thinking I was talented enough to climb the highest wisteria vines in the garden!" I teased. "Trust me, the rose bushes I fell on looked far worse than I did." I gave her a wink.

"I don't believe you for even a second." She chuckled as she lifted a finger to wipe a tear that slid from her lashes.

My heart thudded painfully in my chest as I continued to feed her the same lies I always had regarding the whip marks on my back. The lie wasn't convincing in the slightest, either, but Avery wasn't accustomed to seeing gruesome wounds. I was forced to use that to my advantage.

"However, I do need to head off to my own bedchamber, I'm sure I will also need to do some dusting before my head hits the pillow," I joked again, trying to lighten the mood.

She patted the space next to her on the bed. "Just stay here tonight! We can have a sleepover like we used to. Mother will never know. I will send the staff away so nobody can run and report to her." She gave me an evil grin as she looked up at me through her brows.

I contemplated it for a moment, thinking of all the times we used to wander around the castle late at night and then ended up back in her bed before we were caught. "Sure, why not? Your bed is much more comfortable than mine is, anyway," I said to her with a grin.

I glanced out the window to see that the crescent moon was high in the night sky, it must be getting late at this point. We each walked around her rooms, blowing out the candles that lit up her space. Once finished, we both crawled into her enormous bed, facing each other. She took both of my hands in hers as she wiggled her way into comfort under the blankets. I could only see half of her face thanks to the moonlight peeking through the curtains.

With her eyes closed and head resting on the pillow, she sleepily said to me, "For most of my life I have dreamed of having a sister, but now I am thankful to have you instead."

I stared at her peaceful, resting face as my heart sank. There had been so many moments throughout our lives when I wanted to tell her everything, but that could never happen. So, I watched as sleep claimed her for the evening.

"Me too," I whispered on a quiet sob. And then sleep came for me as well.

FIVE

Elianna

I WOKE AS THE sky turned into what appeared to be hundreds of different swirling shades of pink. I glanced over at Avery, whose eyes were starting to flutter open.

"Good morning, sunshine!" I said to her.

Stretching her arms over her head with an extremely loud yawn, she replied, "You're awfully chipper this morning for someone who needs to go find Kellan."

Ugh. Not only would I be finding him and updating him on what he missed with the queen yesterday, but when I found him I would also be kicking his fucking ass across Isla.

"He will have to wait. I didn't get a chance to talk to Lukas yesterday and I want to see him. He has been taking care of Nyra for me, and I have been dying to see her."

Nyra was a wolf pup I found out beyond the gates about ten years ago. Her pack had wandered too close to the city and the majority of them were killed by farmers that were in fear of losing their sheep. The rest of the pack fled which led me to find Nyra abandoned in the woods a few days later. The queen threw a fit when she found out, saying that she would never allow a mutt to roam her halls. My father stood up for me and allowed her to stay, it also helped that Avery instantly fell in love with the little fluff-ball and begged her mother to let me keep her. Nyra was my favorite thing to come home to.

"Oh Nyra, I love that little, white-furred babe. You know, whenever she was walking with Lukas and came across Kai, she would growl at him? It was the funniest thing. He pretends he isn't terrified of her, but whenever she shows her teeth, you can see a shudder go through him." Avery chuckled.

"Good." I smiled as I stood up from the bed and made my way to the doorway. "Do you know where I can find them? I'd rather not wander around and risk running into Idina."

She stared at me and then looked towards the window to where the sun rose in the sky. "I would check the dungeons."

I blinked at her. "I'm sorry, what?" That couldn't be right. "Why the hell would he be there?"

"Probably to make sure Kai is behaving." She sighed.

"Ok, if Kai is in the dungeons, then this I absolutely need to see." I practically skipped the rest of the way to the door.

"It isn't what you think." She paused. "And unfortunately, I know you aren't going to like what you see. I just found out about it myself. Brace yourself, Lia."

That was odd. I had no idea what could be down there, but now I had a sinking feeling in my chest. "Ok, I will see you later."

She nodded, and I then I was out the door.

As I made my way through the castle, I did my best to not be seen, and walked to one of the outside courtyards that had a hidden staircase that led below the castle and into the dungeons.

I glanced across the yard to see Callius standing under a fully blossomed magnolia tree. We made eye contact, and he started to aim toward me. Great.

"Callius," I said coldly. A chill ran up my spine as the memories of the whip in his hand rushed through me.

He didn't speak for a moment. He then looked me up and down before stopping in front of me and began smirking. "Elianna."

An awkward silence passed. "Well, I will be on my way then," I said, moving around his enormous body.

"Have you spoken with Captain Adler?" he asked. I turned around to see his smirk had widened. I would love to smack it off of his face.

"Not that it is any of your business, but I have not seen Kellan yet, no."

He was no longer smirking. It had turned into a full-on feral grin. "Have a nice day, Miss Solus," he said, as he tucked his arms behind his back and walked away.

The *nerve* of this male.

Don't say it. Don't say it. Don't say it… "It is 'Captain Elianna Solus' to you and anyone else of or below your rank. Personal guard of the queen does *not* outrank a captain. You will do well to remember that!" I shouted at his back, which was pointless. I really needed to get better at not showing him, Kai, or the queen how easily they could dig their way under my skin.

He completely ignored me, but aggravation tore through me as I watched his shoulders bounce in a chuckle.

Now, back to what I came here for originally. I made my way to the hidden stairs behind a vine covered, iron rod door and began the descent down into the castle dungeons.

I hated it down here. The air was so stale it was hard to breathe, and it had a strong odor of musty water. The hallways were long and winding, with multiple tunnels that led in different directions. If any prisoner were to escape, it would be nearly impossible to find their way out.

After following the dimly torch-lit hallways, I had finally come to a stop next to a few cell doors. The bars were all rusted out, and they were vacant aside from the layers of black mold growing along the cracked, seeping walls, and the bones of the prisoners who had never left. These cells had not been used in decades since the queen had chosen a noose as her favorite form of punishment.

A shiver ran down my spine. Someone should've at least disposed of the bodies once they passed. Give them to their kin or have the decency to burn the bodies so their souls could rest amongst the gods. It was one thing I felt very strongly about, and I had always made it a point to find my soldiers that had fallen and burn their bodies before leaving the battlefield, so they could be at peace.

After walking for what felt like another ten minutes, a faint glow could be seen up ahead from an opening in the hall. That must be Lukas, but what could he possibly be doing all the way down there? I turned the cobweb-lined corner and came to a sudden halt as my eyes flared wide. I immediately ducked into one of the dark cells to avoid being seen.

What in the hell was going on?

Fire. All I could see was a massive wall of roaring flames that were slowly beginning to wink out. I could feel the heat on my face even while hidden and at least two hundred feet across the wide open space.

I blinked rapidly, as I couldn't believe what my eyes were witnessing as the fire faded out entirely. Standing on its hind legs, the size of at least four war horses, and a wingspan larger than most buildings in the slums, was a *wyvern*.

Awe and primal fear coursed through me, holding me in place as I gazed upon the incredible, unexpected sight. It was *enormous*. Its giant, blocky head was adorned with spiked horns and connected to its elongated neck. The gleaming, golden eyes that adorned its face could pierce even a soul of the gods with its stare. The beast had numerous rows of terrifying, dagger-like teeth. Its scales appeared to be a shade of onyx, but as it moved, the torchlight reflected a deep shade of amethyst. It was magnificent—beautiful, even. I imagined it would seamlessly blend in with the night sky, gliding through the clouds undetected.

I stood there staring into the cavern-like space with my jaw dropped for what seemed like an eternity, until a sharp, heinous laugh echoed across the room, twisting my stomach into knots instantly.

Kai.

He walked out into the open cavern, staring at the creature. "Looks like you used all of your flames in one shot yet again. Lucky for me, you really are just a stupid beast that will never learn." A deep growl rumbled through the dungeon, echoing from the wyvern's throat.

Wyverns were so rare to be seen, legends said that the species carried the magic of flame within them, but if spent too quickly, they could run out, and it took their bodies days to replenish that kind of power. Turns out some tales had truth behind them.

"Now, let's have some more fun, shall we?" Kai taunted, his tone dripping with malice.

Oh, no. Nope. Absolutely not.

"I hope that thing fucking eats you!" I shouted without thinking, as my lips curled back into a snarl. My hands immediately flew to cover my mouth.

Kai whipped around with panic in his eyes. "Who's down here?! I will have your head for this."

I rolled my eyes. He really was always one for the dramatics. I slowly tiptoed out of the cell, swinging my hips with as much swagger as I could muster up in this situation. I stopped a few feet from him and gave him a little wave with my fingers.

"You," he seethed. "What the hell are you doing down here, Solus? You just threatened the future king. Surely, being someone of your rank, you are aware that such a threat is punishable by death." His eyes glistened with challenge.

"I did not threaten you, little prince. I simply said that I hope that beast..." I pointed to the wyvern, which now had its full attention on me. "Eats you." I smiled.

"How about I feed you to it and call it a day?" he retorted.

I shrugged. "Well, I suppose I would be tastier, with you being just bones and all..." I crossed my arms as I finished speaking.

"Careful, Captain. There is only so much time your king has left. Eventually, *I* will be your king, and I have many plans for you." Hearing him say that about our father felt like a dagger to the chest, and I tried to hide my flinch. The wyvern started growling again at Kai.

"That is enough with the threats," a deep voice echoed from the hall I entered from.

As I turned around, I saw Lukas standing there with an enormous slab of raw meat slung over his shoulder, Nyra prancing around next to him. I was surprised she had barely any reaction to the wyvern. I had never been more relieved to see her.

"Prince Kai, your mother is looking for you," Lukas announced, as he approached us.

Kai didn't reply to him as I turned to find him staring me down, lips pursed in a scowl. "Count your fucking days, Elianna." He moved towards the exit and slammed his shoulder into Lukas as he passed, causing him to grunt. Kai then anxiously skirted around Nyra, who looked as if she was about to take a bite out of his ass, but luckily she behaved herself. Which was clearly more than I could say about myself.

Once I could no longer sense Kai was near, I dropped to my knees. "Nyra! Oh, I have missed you, sweet girl!" She trotted to me and started plastering my face with her kisses. "I hope you have been good for Lukas."

"She is about as well-behaved as you are," he teased, as he dropped the slab of meat right outside of the wyvern's reach. Once he turned back to walk towards me, the wyvern dragged its breakfast over to itself with the claw that mounted the tip of one of its giant, leather-like wings and feasted.

I smiled at her while scratching her fluffy, white ears. "Maybe a bit more behaved, actually."

He chuckled. "Maybe."

I stood, and he gave me a hug that could've rivaled the one I received from my father the day prior. Lukas practically raised me as his own, since no one could know who my true father was. He never married or had any children of his own, so he treated me as if I were his family.

"What is the deal with the wyvern?" I asked cautiously. I examined the beast as it finished the slab of meat he brought to it. Its eyes lifted to meet mine, and my heart nearly stopped in my chest as it curiously observed me, just as I had been. The wyvern didn't cower away or show signs of wanting to attack, but I was definitely thankful it was out of fire.

"I caught Callius and Kai coming down here frequently and one day, a few months back, I decided to follow them. Apparently, it has been down here for nearly two years."

"Two. Years?!" I gasped. That poor creature. It didn't belong down in the dungeons. It should have remained in the wild.

Lukas sighed. "I still haven't received a straight story on how or why it is here. From what I can sense that is the truth, Callius stumbled upon an egg up near the Sylis Forrest a few years back while out looking for mortal camps. He took the egg, and it has been here ever since."

That poor creature *hatched* here. It hadn't known anything aside from Kai's heartlessness. I glanced back towards the wyvern once more. One thing was for sure, it didn't seem nearly as tense as it had when Kai was here.

"I hate them so much." I sighed.

"Yeah, I know. Trust me, Nox does too, as you can tell," he said, as he wrapped his arm over my shoulders and guided me and Nyra to the exit.

"Nox? Is that its name?" I asked, as I turned my neck to look back at the wyvern that was now curled into a ball on the ground, finally looking at peace.

He nodded. "That's what I call him, anyway. I started bringing him leftover slabs of meat that the chef deemed not suitable to be consumed by the royal family. Before I stumbled upon this nonsense, Callius had been feeding him food that had turned rotten."

I wanted to stab Callius. Why did both he and Kai find such pleasure in being cruel?

"I really do hate them," I whispered.

"Me too, Lia. Now let's get out of this hell hole."

SIX

Elianna

As we made it to the top of the hidden stairs that led into the courtyard, I couldn't help but start to actually *worry* about Kellan. This wasn't like him. He typically would never miss a report to the queen, and for him to still not show up or even come and see me? Something didn't feel right.

"Do you know where Kellan is?" I asked Lukas reluctantly, as we walked side by side with Nyra trotting around our feet.

He eyed me in that father-ish way that made me feel as if I were once again a small youngling that was far too curious for my own good. It only made me feel more intrigued.

"I know of his whereabouts, Lia. I wanted to discuss this with you before I tell you where he is."

"What could possibly need to be discussed? Is he okay?" I asked nervously. "Did something happen on his journey home?"

He sighed. "Nothing like that. He is fine, at least until I get my hands on him."

Woah. Okay, something was definitely happening.

"I don't know what you could mean by that," I said, stopping in my tracks. He eyed me as he halted next to me, and the look in his eye made the nervousness I felt turn into anger fueled annoyance. "Where. Is. He?" I demanded, patience wearing thin.

He looked hesitant, his warm brown eyes, that matched his skin, narrowed in on me. "If I tell you, you need to promise me you will not run off and do something incredibly stupid."

My stance widened as I placed my hands on my hips. "You of all fae should know that I make no such promises," I said, each word more clipped than the last.

He chuckled. "Gods help me. Very well, Lia. He has been spotted just outside of the slums. He has been there since he returned, which was the day before last. He reported to Callius and then immediately went there with some of his crew, and they never left."

I could feel my cheeks heating as my eyes widened. "Why in the realm would they all be there for days? I can understand going to a few taverns and bars to celebrate the victory, but..."

"He was not seen in any taverns." Lukas paused, and for a moment, I didn't think he was going to continue. It definitely appeared that he had no desire to. He blew out a breath. "He has been spotted at The Evergreen Belle. I've had eyes on him since he docked."

He was kidding. He must be. I don't know why he would joke about Kellan being held up at Isla's most well-known brothel for *days*, but I most certainly was not in the mood for this.

I stared at him, completely unimpressed. "This isn't funny Lukas, I know you don't like him for some reason, but I'm not in a joking mood at the moment."

"Why would I make something like that up, Elianna? I have told you time and time again that the male is not deserving of you. He is as rotten as the firstborn prince, you just cannot see past what you wish to be there." He rubbed his temples roughly with his fingers. "I never wanted to see you get hurt. I have been trying to prevent it. The more I threatened him, the sweeter he would be to your face, trapping you more to him."

I couldn't breathe. "How long has this been happening?"

"The threats, or the cheating?" he asked, still refusing to look me in the eye.

"Both," I replied through my teeth.

He was silent for a moment. "...Since the moment you claimed each other."

Years. It had been years then. How could I have been so blind? My vision clouded with a haze of red as my hands balled into fists at my sides. "Let's go, Nyra."

I turned on my feet and headed towards the gate that would lead beyond the castle grounds and into the city.

"Gods help me with this female," Lukas grumbled. He caught up to me quickly. "Wait, I'm coming with you!"

"I was raised to never need backup. I can handle myself." I shot at him over my shoulder, offended he would think I couldn't handle this on my own.

A sharp laugh left him. "Oh, I know. Do you forget who raised you to be that way? I'm coming with you to make sure you don't kill him...even though I would love to see it."

A ghost of a smile cracked on my lips. "Very well, then."

And then we were beyond the gate.

On a normal day, I loved walking through the city, but under the current circumstances I felt anything but enjoyment. Isla constantly bustled with all of its citizens that were either out for a stroll or selling their goods. Every corner we turned smelled of unique aromas and spices from the food that was being served from restaurants and street carts alike. My favorite smell, of course, was the freshly baked bread from the bakeries. One thing was for sure, my thighs didn't get this thick on their own.

The Evergreen Belle wasn't exactly in the slums, but not far off. Wealthy lords, sailors, and merchants were often the customer base, yet sometimes a few drunks wandered their way in there. If they had the coin to be there, of course.

The brothel was run by Lady Lorelai. A beautiful fae, obviously, but as far as I was concerned, beauty was only skin deep. She was once a part of the Ladies of Isla, whom Avery now considered her friends. A few decades back, Lorelai decided that instead of being the prized possession of a rich Lord, she would try to become one herself. Unfortunately, she did this by exploiting the bodies of young girls that had nowhere else to go. Just thinking about it made me sick, but I wasn't going there for her or to destroy her despicable business. I was going there for Kellan.

Walking up to the giant oak doors of The Evergreen Belle, my breath caught. Hand on the doorknob, I closed my eyes for a brief moment as I took in one more shuddering breath of air. He really was in there, I could feel it in my bones. His scent even lingered in the archway.

"You know you don't have to do this, Lia. I know you feel anger right now, but it's okay to allow yourself to be upset and feel heartache about this...even though the bastard doesn't deserve a single tear shed in his honor," Lukas said to me in a voice so soft I barely recognized it as his.

I turned in his direction. "I know. There will be no tears shed. You're right, the fucker doesn't deserve them. I just feel like a fool."

He gave me a sad smile.

I looked down to see Nyra trotting up the steps behind us. "Stay here Nyra, we will be back soon."

Once inside The Evergreen Belle, I looked around the foyer to see that the walls were painted a dark green, most likely a nod to the name of the establishment, with curtains the color of onyx strung up and closed on each window. The only source of light was from the hundreds of golden candlesticks that had been lit. Some looked as if they had been placed on top of a previous candle numerous times, as hardened wax drippings appeared down their sconces.

A voice from a few feet away startled me. "Captain Solus! What brings you here today? Business or pleasure?"

I looked over to see Lady Lorelai was standing behind a desk towards the back of the room. Her golden blonde curls hung down to her waist, which appeared to be synched entirely too tight by her corset, pushing her pale breasts up to her chin. It was a miracle she could even breathe.

She gave me an incredulous look. Oh, she knew *exactly* why I was here. "Hello Lorelai, lovely to see you. Is it always so...dark in here?" I gestured to the surrounding walls. "You may want to consider redecorating. Not sure if you're aware, but it is daytime out there." I gave her a smirk.

Lukas tried to cover his laugh with a cough, but I could see the irritation written all over Lorelai's face behind her smile. "I don't think that will be necessary, Captain. The customers seem to like it. Wouldn't you agree, Sir Lukas?"

Lukas actually choked this time, and now I was about to gag. I peeked over at him, and his cheeks immediately flushed to a bright pink as he scratched at his neck nervously. Males.

He mustered up the voice to speak, "I don't know what you mean, Lady Lorelai."

"Interesting," she said, looking like she was about to throw us right back out the door. She turned to face me once more. "I will ask you one more time before I have you removed from my establishment. Are you here for business or pleasure?"

I looked at Lukas and saw that his gaze had lifted to the staircase that was hidden in the corner of the room. He turned back to me, teeth clenched, and nodded.

I threw a pouch of coins onto the desk in front of Lorelai. "Business. I'm here on business."

Her grin grew ear to ear as she snatched the pouch from within my reach. "Up the stairs, third door on your left," she announced, as she gave me a taunting, little wave with her dainty fingers. "Have fun."

SEVEN

Kellan

My head felt as if it was about to split in two. The amount of rum in my system was enough to kill a warhorse. A tiny sliver of light was peeking through the curtains that covered the room in almost complete darkness. I glanced toward the wall the bed was against to see a tanned, naked body with long black hair sprawled out across the pillows.

I smirked. The past two nights had been insane, filled with ale, brawls, and too many whores to count. The best part was that Lia would never know thanks to Callius covering for my whereabouts.

I gave the broad's tight ass a smack to wake her up, and she started giggling in her fake little voice that Lorelai had taught her, and all the others, so well.

She stretched out her arms and began crawling on top of me, kissing my lips and working her way down my neck and chest. She straddled me as tightly as her long, sleek legs would allow and sat up, making her tits perched beautifully in front of my face. I grinned wickedly as I secured one of her nipples between my teeth, but out of the corner of my eye, I saw movement within the shadows near the door.

When she saw my attention had wandered elsewhere, she turned around to see the shadow of a figure behind us and screeched loudly as she flipped off of me and onto the floor.

I grabbed the black curtains next to me and whipped them open, filling the room with the late morning sunlight. I blinked numerous times to adjust my vision to the blinding light, and was horrified to see that *Lia* was sitting on top of the room's table by the door, picking her nails with the dagger that I left there the night prior. She looked up to me, and as her green eyes met mine, she smiled and started waving the dagger at me in greeting.

Fuck.

"Ca-captain Solus! Wh-what are you doing here? Can I help you with something?" The whore stuttered.

Lia's eyes never left mine as I sat there frozen, rummaging through my brain on how to find an excuse to get out of the shit storm that was about to be unleashed upon me.

"Get out," she ordered, her voice cold as ice.

And just like that, Lorelai's favorite prize ripped the sheet off the bed, wrapped it around herself, and scurried out the door, slamming it shut.

I cleared my throat. "Hi princess, what are yo–"

Before I had a chance to blink, she was up and hovering over me, holding the dagger to my throat. "Don't you dare finish that sentence," she cut me off in a hiss.

Double fuck. I would kill Callius for this. I knew he loved to taunt her, but telling her I was here? Bastard.

"Don't you think this is a little dramatic, Elianna? Gods, I got a little drunk and I don't remember ending up here. It was an honest mistake. One I will be sure to never commit again." The lies slipped effortlessly through my teeth.

She stared at me for a moment. *That's right, believe what I'm saying to that pretty little face of yours.*

"You honestly expect me to believe that when you have been posted up here for *days?*" Apparently, the lies weren't as smooth as I originally thought. "You missed the report to the queen. You hung me out to dry when you know how she loathes me, and the entire time you were here..." She paused. "With your cock in another female's mouth!"

She pressed the dagger tighter to my skin and a bead of blood dribbled down my neck. "I don't know when you started using that kind of language, princess, but it is very unbecoming of a lady," I said.

"Do *not* call me princess," she seethed, eyes radiating with fury. "You may refer to me as Captain Solus, just as anyone else moving forward." She hesitantly removed the dagger from my throat and stormed toward the door.

I grabbed my pants and began pulling them on as I followed her, aggressively trying to button them as I chased her. "I don't know why I would call you that when we are claimed to each other." I was trying to save face, but I could tell it wasn't working.

She ripped the door open so violently, I thought it was going to come right off the hinges. Once I saw who now stood in the doorway, I felt just as much rage as she did.

"What the fuck is *he* doing here?" I pointed at Lukas, anger seeping from my pores.

Lukas raised a single brow. "I'm the least of your problems right now, boy."

Oh, I would fucking kill him for that. And for bringing Lia here. Callius had nothing to do with this. I could now see that this piece of shit guard had been keeping tabs on me still. I didn't like that one bit.

Lia took my dagger she had been holding and slammed the blade deep into the wood of the table she had been perched on only minutes before.

"We are through. I will see you on our next quest beyond the gates, Captain Adler," she spat at me.

And then they were gone.

EIGHT

Elianna

My head had been spinning during the entire walk back to the castle. I could barely even process the fact that Kellan had been sleeping with others behind my back, never mind physically seeing it for myself. Also, the fact that he looked me in the eye and tried to lie his way out of it...the situation was nauseating. My biggest concern was how the hell we were going to go about commanding our armies together after this. The gods knew he barely listened to me before when it came to strategizing for battles, and I'd be damned if he thinks I'll be obedient to what he tells me to do with *my* soldiers. This should be fun.

"How are you holding up?" Lukas asked, as he patted my shoulder.

I shrugged. "Oh, I will be fine. I am worried about how this will impact our soldiers, though."

"Your soldiers in your army are loyal to you." I shrugged, knowing that not *all* of them were. "If you and Kellan do not see eye to eye, do what you feel is best, and the ones who are true to you will follow," he stated.

Good point. "You're right." I smiled up at him. "I need to go spend some time with the king, though. I have barely seen him aside from the disaster in the throne room yesterday."

"I couldn't believe what Queen Idina said to you. It hasn't sat right with me. I hope you know it's not even close to the truth. She has refused the armies healers since the war began and we have been fortunate that our numbers have been on the lower end of the spectrum pertaining to lives lost." Lukas stared at me for a moment. "The queen has let hate decay her heart. The king still doesn't see her for what she is. I tried to tell him the night you were born."

I couldn't look him in the face. "Did you know my mother? Was she kind?"

"I never knew her personally, but your father loved her very much. I was with her the night you were born, I even cut your umbilical cord, but just in that short time, I could tell by the way she looked at you in her arms that she had a heart of gold, and she loved you endlessly." He sighed. "That night was not your fault. You were just a babe being brought into this world." I tried to blink back tears as he continued, "Your father is very proud of you and the fearless leader that you have become. As am I."

Now the tears were flowing. "Thank you, Lukas, for everything."

He wiped a tear with his finger as he said, "No need to thank me, Lia. You and your father are very dear to me. Even those two little redheads that the queen has somehow managed to not taint with her wickedness I have grown very fond of."

I smiled at him. "Yea, those two are okay, I guess," I said with a wink.

He let out a heavy chuckle as we strolled through the castle's entrance. "Go see your father. He has not been well, but Veli has been sneaking in and seeing him without the queen's knowledge. Hopefully, we should have some answers soon."

Veli. It wasn't very often I felt uneasy around someone, but her presence always sent a shiver down my spine. One of the most beautiful fae I had ever seen, but she always carried an other-worldly aura to her.

I also hoped he knew how ridiculous it sounded that the king had to sneak a healer into his own gods-damn chambers, just to avoid an argument with his wife.

Healers had become few and far between in Isla over the past few decades—ever since the queen shut down the House of Healers that once stood near the city square. The traditions of medicine were now passed down from parent to offspring in order to keep the knowledge alive. Whether the queen was aware or not, I had no idea, but I was glad the hidden remaining healers had taken matters into their own hands.

I gave him a nod and made my way up the stairs.

Thankfully, my father's quarters had been separated from the queen's since my birth. It wasn't very often she was in there with him, so fortunately, the odds of running into her today would be low.

I always wondered what the staff's whispers had been like that day over a century ago. A queen removing herself from the king's bedchamber permanently? It must have been quite the scandal.

I knocked on the enormous iron door that led into his bedchamber and heard a joyous voice advising me to come in. A smile instantly tilted my lips.

He was sitting at a table when he stood up and hurried towards me, greeting me with another loving bear hug.

He took my cheeks in both of his palms as he looked into my eyes, that were tearing up yet again, and said, "My Elianna has finally returned home. I have missed you, my sweet daughter."

"Hi, Your Grace," I greeted back to him. "I've missed you as well."

He laughed. "Lia, you know in here you do not need to call me that."

"Sorry, it's just a habit," I said, as I glanced around the room.

The chambers were built for royalty, with maroon and gold tapestries strung up along the walls, various magnificent weapons, such as swords and polished axes, hanging between each. The room was filled with sunlight, quite the opposite of The Evergreen Belle. I knew his favorite, personal touch was the mounted head of a black-coated stag that had been centered between his two bedposts.

"I wish you would get rid of that awful-looking thing." I pointed to the mount.

He gawked at me. "Now you know that was your grandfather's. He'd curse me from his grave if I even removed it from the center of the room!" he teased.

A slight smile crept up on my face. "Oh yes, I am sure *that* is the reason, and not the fact that you love it."

"I would be lying to you if I said that I was not a fan of having such a rare, magnificent creature, such as an onyx stag, posted up in my bedchamber." He chuckled at his own dramatics. "Come here, I have something I want to give you!" He gestured for me to follow him deeper into the room.

He opened a drawer in his nightstand with a key that had been hanging around his neck. Within the drawer was a long box wrapped in a red ribbon. My father handed it to me with a soft smile.

"What is this?" I asked with a nervous giggle.

He shrugged, his brown, shoulder length hair moving with him. "You'll have to open it and see."

I smirked at him and playfully rolled my eyes as I made my way over to the settee at the foot of his bed and sat down. While I was unraveling the ribbon, he began speaking, "I hope you know how proud I am of you, and not just because you are my daughter. You have grown into such a strong female, commanding our armies, and leading our soldiers back home from battle. It is not a simple task."

My breath caught as I peered inside of the decorative box to see the most stunning dagger I had ever laid my eyes on. The iron blade was black as night, and marked throughout it were swirling designs carved from polished obsidian. The shined hilt crafted with unbelievable detail and stained an emerald green so dark that it resembled the blackness of the blade until reflected in the late morning sun. The last feature I noticed made my heart almost stop in my chest. At the very top of the hilt, there was the head of a wolf carved from white antler.

"Nyra," I said in a shaky whisper.

He sipped from a goblet of wine that I hadn't noticed was on the table. "The bond you share with that pup doesn't go unnoticed. I thought it added the perfect touch."

"Thank you so much," I said, as I threw my arms around him and gave him a hug. "This is the most wonderful gift I have ever received. I will carry it with me always."

He grunted as he sat next to me. I could tell he was trying to hide the pain he felt. "Have the healers found anything wrong yet? Lukas told me that Veli had been sneaking in here to see you."

"He's always had a big mouth, that one," he said, chuckling.

I gave him a look. "Seriously, what's going on?"

The king sighed and then said, "Lia, Veli doesn't know. I have even been tested for every known poison. All have come back negative. At this point, I am beginning to think it is some unknown disease that will leave my insides a bit crispy."

I blinked at him. "Yeah, I'm not going to even entertain that shitty attempt at a joke," I replied, sounding as unimpressed as possible. "But if Veli can't figure it out then..."

"She has the magic touch you know." He looked at me and gave me a sad smile.

"Oh I know. That's your reasoning for trusting only her since I was born." I crossed my arms and gave him a small smirk.

Grief swallowed his features, and I almost winced, realizing that the only other healer he had ever trusted aside from Veli, was my mother.

"I'm sorry," he said after a few moments of unbearable silence. "I just don't have a single clue what to do. Every day it gets worse and I fear that soon I will not be able to leave my bed. In the morning when I wake up it is the worst. It's as if I swallowed a liquid blaze the night before."

This was so strange. "And nothing else has changed from your routine?"

"No, I will have my nightly glass of wine before bed, typically just one glass. It helps me sleep, but I have done that since before you were born."

"Yes, that I recall. Perhaps you should cut back," I said with a grin.

He didn't speak for a moment before he brought up what I had been dreading. "I apologize for the way Idina spoke to you yesterday. It was not right, and I want you to know that I spoke with her in private following the incident."

"There was no use wasting your breath, Father. She hates me and that will never change," I said dryly. "Her mind was made up the second you decided to keep me."

"There was never a moment in my life that you were not wanted, Elianna. I could not be prouder of you. It kills me every day to not be able to name you as my heir."

I choked on a sharp laugh. "Don't be ridiculous, I could never be fit to rule."

"You are more fit than anyone I know." He sighed. "Kai, even though he is my son, will not make a great king, and I fear for my kingdom every day once I leave this realm."

I just stared at him confused. He never spoke of Kai in my presence, which I never complained about because I rarely tried to bring him up.

He continued, "The male is rotten, Elianna. I know you recognize this and I should have voiced this sooner. I will never know where I went wrong, but reports I have heard of him since he was just a boy from Lukas are disturbing. I have even taken the liberty upon myself to watch his actions from a distance. If he has ever been cruel to you, I am so sorry, Lia. It is unnerving to be a king and know that three of my four children are kind-hearted, yet the one to be heir has a soul full of cruelness."

I was speechless. I couldn't believe these words were coming out of my father's, the *king's*, mouth.

"The queen is to blame for Kai's behavior. She has enabled him since he was but a youngling," I told him.

"Now, Elianna, I know that some of Idina's actions have been questionable, and a fair amount of them absolutely...cruel, but do not forget what I put her through all those years ago."

I knew I shouldn't say this, but I needed to let it out. "Father, I have heard rumors of the queen being malicious even before my birth. You have given her far too much leniency with her actions and she has dragged out a war, with countless deaths, due to the actions of a small group of mortals." I paused, but he let me continue. "She will not stop until every last human is gone and their race is extinct. It isn't right, they have their own lands. I am all for destroying the individuals who threaten our peace, but the humans alive today didn't even exist back when the war began. Their life spans are a fraction of ours."

I had always been aware that he genuinely wasn't fond of the queen, but for my sake, and the realm's, he kept silent. I hated more than anything that he felt forced to hide his true feelings behind a fabricated smile.

Sadness clouded his eyes. "This is exactly the reason why I wish I could go back in time and make you known to our world for who you truly are and were meant to be. It is, and will always be, my greatest regret." Tears slowly lined his eyes. "You would be a fair queen, loyal to your kingdom and any race that inhabits it."

My bottom lip began trembling. I could only ever be this vulnerable with him...well, and Lukas I supposed. "I love that you believe that, Father, but the people would never accept a bastard daughter as an heir."

"Never refer to yourself as that again," he snapped, and it caught me off guard. "You were brought into this world out of the most intense and beautiful love I have ever known. They would accept what I wanted, and if I had the courage to have named you my heir when you were born, things would be very different today." He sighed. "I believed your mother, Ophelia, to be my mate when everything happened, but mates have the ability to sense each other's pain. I felt nothing as she lay there, dying. And while deep down inside I've realized that she was not my *true* mate, for all intents and purposes, she was. And I will be in love with her until my last breath."

I gave him a soft smile and cupped his cheek in my palm. "That is all that matters."

He started wiping his own tears with a finger. "Enough of this talk, I am sorry to have brought this up. I just wanted you to be aware of how I felt regarding the ascension of the throne...what is new with you? Are there any adventures to report back on?" he asked.

Ha, might as well be honest. "Kellan's cheating on me," I said on a dry laugh, refusing to meet his stare.

Without skipping a beat, he replied, "Would you like me to have him hung in the city square?"

I nearly choked on the laugh I let out. "Who are you and what have you done with my father?"

Chuckling, he replied, "Your wish is my command, princess. I never liked that male, anyway."

Yeah, that seemed to be a common trait, apparently. Standing up from the settee, I kissed his forehead and said, "I have it covered, but I appreciate the offer."

"You always do," he said to me, as I walked toward the door.

"Also, you are the only one allowed to call me that."

"...Call you what?" he asked cautiously, while raising a brow.

"Princess. Kellan would call me that, and it never sat right with me," I answered.

His eyes narrowed as he combed his fingers through his beard. "I don't like that."

"Me either, but it will never happen again. He can address me as Captain from now on." I winked.

He stood and gave me one last hug before I walked out the door. "That's my girl."

NINE

Elianna

AFTER MY FATHER HAD gifted me the dagger, I left his chambers to pay my visits to the families of the fallen that I had lost in our most recent battle. All seventy-four visits ended in tears of devastation from the spouses and younglings left behind, and I always despised that I was forced to put on a brave face for them due to my rank. I wished so badly to cry with them, and sincerely show that I never considered a single soldier of mine disposable.

A few weeks had since passed since I returned home, and my days here were typically always the same. I would wake at dawn and go for a run with Nyra around the castle grounds and through the gardens. Following our run, we visited Matthias at the stables, which as of late had also included seeing Landon and even sometimes Finn if he deemed it safe enough to not be seen by too many curious eyes.

Some mornings I would even help Lukas bring Nox his breakfast. The wyvern seemed to deem the two of us worthy company when we arrived with a slab of meat, but I wasn't naïve enough to believe that if given the chance, he wouldn't bite our heads off. I have still yet to see a lick of flames come from him since the incident with Kai.

The afternoons I spent training with my soldiers. We would go over combat strategy, dueling, shielding, and my personal favorite, archery. I had always been great with a sword, but I never missed a target with a bow and arrow, even on horseback.

The most difficult part about training was avoiding Kellan. He would try to grab my attention daily, and had the audacity to believe that I was avoiding him because I was "still devastated." At least, that was what the rumors had claimed. The real reason was I just didn't trust myself enough yet to attempt a conversation with him that wouldn't result in taking my new dagger and burying it in his chest.

Once today's lessons were over, I decided to stick around a little longer and use my bow while the fields were empty.

I took a shot at the target and my arrow struck true in the center. Too easy. I then grabbed an empty rum bottle that was left out in the field, tossed it in the air, and took a shot. The arrow shattered the bottle into a million pieces and I watched as they all rained onto the grass below. I would need to talk to the males later about drinking while out in the fields...

Once I was out of arrows, I took the dagger sheathed at my thigh and started admiring the sight of it. I had never laid my eyes on anything like it before. The hilt reflecting emerald in the sunlight was entrancing, and the carved head of the wolf had a smile tilting the corners of my lips every time I lay eyes on it.

Now I would always have Nyra with me, even outside of Isla.

The sun was setting behind the hills in the distance, and I quickly whipped the dagger at the target with the arrows still protruding from it. My throw even surprised *me*. The blade effortlessly sliced right through the arrow in the center of the target and nearly cut through the other side. My grin was ear to ear.

I heard a slow clap in the distance, and as I turned around, I saw Lukas coming up the hill behind me. I jokingly began bowing repeatedly, causing him to let out a genuine laugh that echoed through the open field.

"You're still the best shot I've ever seen, arrows and now daggers," he announced.

I looked up at him. "Well, I guess I learned from the best. What are you doing all the way out here at this time?"

He followed me as I sauntered out to the target to retrieve the dagger. "The queen has summoned us for a meeting after the royals have their dinner tonight. I went looking for you and when I found Nyra in the gardens with Avery, I assumed you would still be out here."

I stopped bringing Nyra to the fields with me after she tried to bite one of the soldiers I was dueling with during practice. While I personally thought it was hilarious, the warrior on the receiving end of her fangs did not. Regardless, I loved that Nyra would watch over Avery when I wasn't around.

"Interesting. Well, we better head back then, wouldn't want to keep *Her Majesty* waiting, right?" I joked while ripping the dagger from where it stuck.

"Trust me, it is of top priority for me to not do that," he retorted.

I grabbed my ceramic canteen of water on the ground and tilted it to him. "Cheers to that."

We then began our trek back to the castle that sat off in the distance of the setting sun.

As we entered the throne room, I could see both the king and queen were already on the dais, with Kai standing next to his mother while Avery and Finn were huddled in the back corner of the room. Callius and Kellan were also already there, staring at us as we walked toward them all.

Something was happening, and with every step, my stomach turned. "Your Majesties, how can I be of service to you?"

The king gave me a smile as he was half hunched over on his throne, while the queen grimaced. "It has come to our attention that there is a mortal fleet that has camped along the coast of Ceto Bay. It seems as though they are trying to repeat history and destroy more of us where this all began with my own kin."

Oh, gods.

"Where have these reports come from?" I asked, trying to not sound as annoyed as I was at the situation. How was information of this magnitude not immediately reported to me?

Her eyes narrowed on me. "I have my resources."

I glanced over at Kellan to see him sneer, as he crossed his arms and rocked back and forth on his feet while staring at me. "And you wish for the both of us to go to this camp?" I asked her.

"I wish for you and at least thirty of your best sailors and soldiers to sail there and destroy them." My lips parted, but no words followed.

Kellan stepped forward. "I have just the group of sailors in mind. Thank you for trusting us with this, My Queen."

I was going to be sick. "Surely there is another wa– "

She cut me off, "Surely you do not see any issues with traveling and continuing to command our armies with your ex-love. I did not take you as a female that would jeopardize our kingdom for the sake of some mishap at a brothel."

Out of the corner of my eye, I could see Avery slap her hand over her mouth in shock. I hadn't given her many details regarding why I separated from Kellan.

The queen continued, "After all...that is the way of males." Her eyes narrowed in on me. "A truly committed female would have chosen forgiveness."

The king flinched at her words as my own eyes grew wide.

Kellan began looking around at everyone curiously, as if he were trying to decipher what she meant. Callius kicked the back of his calf to get him to focus.

"I will never have respect for someone that does not show it to me," I finally spoke, my eyes darting back and forth between

Kellan and the queen. "But I will do what is needed for the crown and the Kingdom of Velyra."

The queen pursed her lips and then said, "Very well, then. You leave at dawn tomorrow."

After the meeting, I went back to the stables to say goodbye to Matthias. Avery, Finn, and Lukas decided to join me, and we discovered Landon was already there. I had no idea how long this trip was going to last, but Ceto Bay was at least six days from Isla by ship, and that was if the waters of the Vayr Sea cooperated.

"I wish you told me about what Kellan did. You were right...he is definitely not your mate," Avery said, breaking the silence.

Lukas snorted. "Mate? Avery, you must not be able to hear yourself. Just because they claimed to be with each other, does not mean they were mates. That connection is rare to begin with, but someone like Kellan will never deserve to have one of those. And definitely not your si–" He cleared his throat. "Definitely not Lia."

My mouth dropped open, and I shot him a death glare, in disbelief that he almost said *sister*. Luckily no one else seemed to really be listening, and Avery's attention had already gone back to scratching Nyra's ears as she slept on a block of hay. Lukas gave me an apologetic look.

I huffed out a breath. "I just hope we can get along well enough to command the troop we are bringing."

"Just be sure to have your wits about you at all times," Lukas warned.

"Kellan isn't going to physically harm me, Lukas. The male is a lot of things, but he wouldn't do something like that," I said to him a little too harshly, but he didn't look entirely convinced.

Landon and Finnian were keeping their distance from each other, most likely because of Avery and Lukas, but I knew that neither of them would care about the situation between the two males.

I straightened and made my way around the room, giving hugs to each of them. "I will miss you all, but I should be back in a few weeks." None of them looked even remotely happy about what was occurring.

I then turned to Lukas. "Look after them for me please, even that one over there." I pointed to Landon, whose cheeks flushed.

He raised a brow but replied, "Always. And of course, Nyra and Matthias will be well taken care of as well."

I smiled up at him. "What would I do without you?"

He patted my shoulder lightly. "You'll never have to know, Lia."

The time had come for me to make my hardest goodbye. I reluctantly knocked on the king's bed-chamber door and was horrified that when the door opened, it was answered by the queen.

She had a small vial of red liquid that I could only assume to be some kind of rare wine half full in her hands. She then shoved past me. The abrupt movement was accompanied with an eye-roll as she stormed down the hall. My stare of confusion followed her for a few moments—I hadn't seen her near his wing in the castle in years.

"Come in," my father call out.

When I turned the corner, I saw him already in his bed with his nightly glass of wine.

I sighed. "You should really cut back on that." He began to open his mouth to interject but I continued, "Yeah, yeah, I know, it helps you sleep."

He smiled. "I will miss you. Please be safe on your journey."

"I always am, but I'm not worried about me...I'm worried about you. Should I send for Veli?" I asked, hoping my face didn't look as panicked as I felt at the sight of him like this.

He shook his head. "She was in here earlier and was nearly caught by Idina on her way out." I hoped he knew how ridiculous that sounded.

I nodded. "Very well."

"Do not worry about me, Elianna. I am looking forward to seeing you once you return home with yet another victory for the queen. Perhaps she is turning a new leaf." He shrugged as if he didn't even believe it himself. "Things could have gone much worse in that throne room today."

I scoffed. "The only thing that kept her tamed is that she accidentally almost let it slip that you stepped out on her all of those years ago."

He tried to hide his smile. "That she did...you know, a few months ago she started coming here to share a glass of wine at night. When it began, it was around once a week. Recently it's been almost nightly. I would like to think that she is finally trying to put the past behind us."

"Interesting," I whispered. That must've been why she was in here a few moments ago, but something about all of that didn't sit right with me.

"I will see you once you return, Lia."

Saying goodbye to my father was an emotional storm that threatened to engulf me. I looked into the kindest eyes the realm had ever known, and it left my heart heavy with a mix of sorrow and gratitude. I stood before him as he smiled at me with pride beaming in his stare, and I worked to memorize every feature of his face, just as I always had when called out to battle.

"I love you," I said, as I kissed his forehead. I then turned from him and quietly walked out of the room, swiping away the tear that slipped from my lashes with the tip of my finger.

TEN

Kellan

THE SUN WAS RISING, reflecting brilliant colors atop the calm waves of the Vayr Sea, and my sailors were making their rounds, checking that everything needed for the trip was secured on board. And Lia still wasn't fucking here.

"Still waiting on your beloved, Captain?" I heard a member of the crew call out from behind me. "Rumor has it that you spent one too many nights out at the brothels." Chuckles rang out across the deck.

My jaw ticked at their taunting. "It would be wise to mind your tongue," I hissed. "Before I cut it out of your skull." I patted the sword on my hip, and without even needing to turn to face them, the shuffling of boots echoed across the ship as they scattered.

I expected some pushback from Lia, obviously. She had the stubbornness of any male I had ever met, maybe even worse. However, we had not spoken at all since The Evergreen Belle incident, until I saw her in the throne room yesterday evening. I would be lying if I said the shock on her face once she saw me didn't bring me pure joy. She truly thought she could avoid me...as if my sailors and her army weren't a working unit together.

Laughable. Honestly, all of it was laughable because all she was doing was delaying the inevitable. We claimed each other, and nothing about that had, or would, change. The bitch was mine. She could hide all she wanted, but no other male with half a brain in this kingdom would even dream of looking in her direction without receiving the consequences.

At first, my chase of her was brewed out of boredom. I had made my way through the Ladies of Isla, and then some, but Lia was one that took a while to break. Years, to be exact. Once she was promoted amongst the ranks, shocking almost every soldier, I had to have her. It would never be acceptable to not claim her as mine.

She was the highest-ranking officer, aside from myself, and was one of the most physically attractive females I had ever laid eyes on. That mouth on her could use some work, but I just tuned her out most of the time, anyway. All of that aside, she was favored by the king, and that would come of much use to me.

One thing I could not get my brain to understand was her relationships with the king and queen. It had been obvious for decades that she was favored by the king and his moronic guard, but the queen...she acted as if Lia should be strung up on the noose in the middle of the city square. I had inquired about this to Callius, but his answer was always the same, which was no answer at all. He would either tell me to "shut the fuck up and worry about my own business" or he'd just grunt and walk away.

Anything that entailed Lia was my business, so the fact that I received not a single answer regarding the situation was rather annoying.

While staring out at the sea, as the sun was almost fully risen, out of the corner of my eye I noticed an hourglass figure with long, dark hair approach my ship. At a closer look, I realized that Elianna had finally made her grand entrance and was already barking at my sailors from the dock.

"...And that's an order!" she yelled up to the deck. I could already hear those aboard groaning.

"Princess," I greeted her, as she made her way onto the ship. She whipped around to me. A scowl etched into her features.

An abrupt laugh left her. "I see you're going to pretend as if nothing happened. Looks like I owe Finnian some coin," she said, as she crossed her arms. "And as I stated before, you may address me as Captain Solus." She looked back across the ship.

I reached out and grabbed a small lock of her hair and twirled it around my finger. "I do not like to hear that bets are being placed regarding my actions, but I will take the fact that you are actually speaking to me as a good sign. I am so sorry for my actions, sweet Lia."

She rolled her eyes so hard I thought they were going to get stuck in the back of her head. "Ah yes, speaking to me *is* a privilege. A privilege you no longer deserve. However, I will not have our fleets suffer due to idiotic actions committed by one of their commanding officers."

She started stalking across the ship's deck, and I followed. "You're in an excellent mood on this fine morning, I see. Very well, *Captain Solus*. But you might want to do yourself a favor and look around at who you are with for these next upcoming weeks."

The ship was cast off the dock and on its way to floating mid-harbor by the time I caught the look of horror as it spread across her face. I gave her a wink and made my way to the quarterdeck.

"Everyone to your stations!" I yelled down to the crew. "We have a long, bloody journey ahead of us."

Cheers could be heard across the ship, and I could've sworn Lia's face paled.

Elianna

This couldn't be happening. I underestimated Kellan, and truthfully I should've seen this coming. The entire crew on the ship was from his armada. Not a single soldier from my army was brought with us.

When I was promoted to Captain, there were definitely many who had reservations. Most of those soldiers transferred out of the land army and chose to sail under Kellan instead. Annoying, but it never truly concerned me. My warriors who stayed were loyal to me and that was all I cared about...until right now.

A sinking feeling fell in my gut as I glanced around the ship, realizing that the majority, if not every crew member, had previously been soldiers under my command. There was not a single soul aboard this ship that I could trust, and with Kellan playing his games already, this was not looking good for me.

No. No, I needed to snap out of this. Everyone here was loyal to the crown, meaning they were also loyal to me. I was of higher rank than any of the males, aside from Kellan. It would be considered mutiny for them to break that. They weren't that stupid, they couldn't be...

I kept to myself most of the day, pretending I didn't notice any of the looks the males on board gave me as I passed by. Sitting on the bow of the ship while watching the sunset in the distance, I heard footsteps approach from behind me.

"Captain Solus." The tone of his voice was of nothing but mockery.

I sighed. "Can I help you, Captain Adler?"

"Just wanted to see how your first day at sea has been, and if the sailors have been behaving," he said with a hint of teasing, but I was in no mood.

I looked over at him. "Is there a reason for you to believe they would not behave in my presence? Sounds like you need to run a tighter ship."

Any hint of the previous teasing was now gone. "Ah, well I figured I would check in since you know that most of the males aboard do not see you as a fit captain."

Heat rushed to my cheeks, and it took everything in me to not reach for the dagger strapped to my thigh. "Well, you made sure of that, didn't you, Kellan?"

The look on his face was unnerving. "Will you come with me? I would like to show you something."

He stretched out his hand, but I refused to take it as I jumped down. "Lead the way." I gestured to the ship's deck.

ELEVEN

Elianna

I FOLLOWED KELLAN THROUGH the space below the deck. Hammocks were hung throughout where the crew would rest, and there was a small kitchen in the back corner with a very questionable-looking stew brewing. The smell down here was also horrendous, reeking of body odor, piss and rum.

I came to a stop and crossed my arms. "What is it you wanted to show me, Kellan?"

"It's right through these back doors," he said, as he took a key tied to a string from around his neck and unlocked said doors.

Once I could see inside, I saw that these were living quarters, and to my surprise, they were actually suitable for living. A bed big enough for two sat in the center, with a few cabinets spread throughout the space and a small table in the corner with compasses and maps spread across it. Was he really giving me a room on the ship? I assumed I would be forced to bunk with the rest of the crew in the hammocks. Perhaps this trip wouldn't be as awful as I originally thought.

"Kellan, this is wonderful...tha–thank you for this," I reluctantly choked out.

He put the key to the room down on the table and made his way toward me.

"I'm glad it is suitable for you, prin–" I shot him a death glare before he could even finish the word. Clearing his throat, he continued, "I'm glad it is suitable for you, Elianna."

I blinked at him. That was strange. I was expecting much more of a fight, but he was trying to be sweet. I didn't know how I felt about it. Deciding it would be best to not take advantage of his seemingly good mood, I decided to not pick a fight about how he should be addressing me as Captain.

As I flopped down on the bed, that barely gave any bounce, I said, "It will do, I suppose."

He winked at me and looked around the room when I overheard some of the crew shouting in the hallway—my spine stiffened in response.

"Have you seen the captain?"

"I saw him heading into his quarters with Solus."

"Wow, that didn't take long. I will grab his attention later. I'm sure he has his hands full...if you know what I mean."

The laughter of at least ten of the males aboard erupted through the cabin.

I stood from the bed and glared at Kellan, who had the nerve to chuckle at the conversation that he also, very clearly, overheard.

"I am sorry, I'm sure I did not hear them correctly," I snapped at him. "Your. Quarters?!"

He looked at me as if he thought I was kidding. "What, did you think you would have the captain's cabin all to yourself? I forgot how funny you can be, Elianna."

I could feel the tips of my ears heat, and I wouldn't have been surprised if steam was shooting out of them. "What I *thought* was that this was part of your apology, and maybe that you had a room elsewhere. Over my dead fucking body am I sharing a space with you during this trip."

He sat down on the bed and gave the space next to him a pat. "Oh, not just a space, we will share the bed as well. We need to look like a united front for our fleet."

"...You are delusional," I spat, as I rolled my eyes.

Before I had the chance to blink, he jumped up from the bed in an instant and backed me into a wall, placing each of his arms on either side of me, essentially trapping me where I stood.

His face was not even an inch from mine. "Oh no, that is where you are wrong, little Lia. You see, if we want our armada to respect us, we need to at least appear as if we respect each other in front of them. Appear as normal in front of them. Fight me all you want in private. Shit, you know I like that anyway," he admitted, as he slowly licked up the side of my neck and all the way up my cheek. It sent a shudder down my spine. He then got close to my ear and whispered, "You will *always* be mine."

Nope, didn't like that. He leisurely pivoted his stare to face me once more, mimicking a predator circling its prey. I looked up into his sea-blue eyes and batted my eyelashes, distracting him. Before he had a chance to realize, I tilted my neck back and then head-butted him so hard that my own vision blurred. He stumbled back, yelping from the pain that now radiated in both of our skulls, and I reached out and grabbed the key he left on the table and shoved him further away. Luckily, this caught him off guard long enough that I swung one of my legs out and tripped him, forcing him out the door.

While he was stumbling around in the hallway and trying to find his footing, I looked him dead in the eyes and said, "I will *never* be yours again."

I then slammed the door in his face, locking it from the inside.

Kellan

This was getting to be fucking ridiculous. After Lia shut me out, I banged on the door repeatedly, screaming her name for over an hour, and the only answer I received was the occasional giggle on the other side of the door. My crew was having an absolute field day with this, and I didn't appreciate how this was making me look with her. That was the issue with Lia. She would always think that she was in control when the truth was that, as long as I was around, that would never be the case.

After spending my night in one of the hammocks, as if I was one of the shipmates, I decided to try again and get her the hell out of my room.

Knocking on the door softly, I heard the scurrying of feet over on the other side. "Come on out, Lia. You have been in there for over twelve hours, and I know you must be hungry." Still, there was no answer on the other side. "I brought you some leftover stew from last night."

The door slowly started to creak open, and I saw a single, pale green eye appear between the crack in the door frame. She then stuck her nose through and sniffed the air. "It still smells disgusting," she grumbled, and then she slammed the door back in my face.

Gods, this female was infuriating, but I needed to be back in her good graces if I ever planned to get anywhere closer to the king.

"Captain Solus, I know that the food on the ship is not up to your standards, seeing how you lived in the castle, for some reason, your entire life, but this is what we have. We are in the middle of the Vayr Sea. You will not survive another five days without food." I yelled back at the closed door, trying to tame my temper as much as possible.

The entire door swung open then, stopping the crew in their tracks behind me. "I am sorry, but did you somehow forget that I also spend days out on the road with my soldiers? That I sit with them day and night, cooking the food we have or find?" she snapped at me, as she started waving her finger in my face.

Got her. It was too easy.

"Not only do I almost never get to eat the same food that the royal family receives, but you *do* actually know why I grew up there." I definitely struck a nerve. Good. Her focus then went to behind me, to the thirty other pairs of eyes now on her. "There is *nothing* to see here. Now, back to your posts!" she ordered.

As the crew scurried around behind me, I met her gaze. "Why does the queen hate you, Lia?"

She looked frozen for a moment before she said, "That is none of your concern."

I leaned down to be at her eye level and then said to her, "That is where you are wrong, princess. *Everything* that involves you is my concern."

She stared at me for a moment and then slammed the door back in my face. All I could do was laugh. Taking a bite of the stew she refused, I made my way back up to the deck. If she wanted to do this the hard way, we could absolutely do that.

TWELVE

Jace

THE PLAN WAS WORKING. With our numbers rising, we may finally have a chance to win this war against the fae. For years, I had worked my way through the ranks. For years, I sliced through body after body on the battlefields, taking a piece from my soul each time. That didn't matter, though. Nothing fucking mattered besides winning this war and winning back the lands our ancestors had lost. I wouldn't stop until these lands were soaking with the blood of my enemy, instead of the blood of my brothers.

Villages were burned to the ground. Our women and children slaughtered. For decades, no matter what we did, the fae were always a step ahead of us. Until now.

I looked upon the maps that were sprawled out on the table of the tavern. We had hidden small camps spread throughout all of Velyra, and as far as we knew, all still remained undetected.

Most of the women, children, and the elderly had been relocated beyond the Ezranian Mountains. We also had hundreds of thousands of our men living beyond the mountains, guarding them. The fae believed our numbers were dropping drastically, when in reality we had grown.

Millions of angry men, women, and children that all had one common goal; win this war. And I would be the one to lead them to it. I didn't care who needed to be cut down. Anyone who stood in my way would face the same fate as any fae I crossed.

I scratched at my week-old facial scruff as the tavern's barmaid made her way over to me, swinging her voluptuous hips a little more aggressively with each step.

"Can I get you anything else, handsome? How about another ale?" she asked, batting her long eyelashes at me as she bent down at my table—her breasts now inches from my face.

The tavern's door swung open, and I immediately rolled my eyes at who stood in the doorway. "No thanks, love." I gestured to my half-filled mug, "I'm all set for now," I said, as I went back to looking at my maps.

"Suit yourself," she said, as she made her way back behind the bar.

A shadow then appeared over my shoulder, but I ignored it.

"Jace! Brother, did you not see me come in?" A familiar voice asked.

I smirked without removing my gaze from the parchment. "Oh, I saw you."

"Oh, and you just chose to ignore me? How typical of you," he said, as he pulled out the chair across from me and sat down.

Gage was my second in command. He ran the troops of our men when I couldn't or had to go off on other business. He was the only man I could ever fully trust. He was also my best friend, like a brother to me. And an absolute, giant pain in my ass.

Kicking up his mud-covered boots on the table, coating my maps in the fallen dirt, he grabbed the ale I had been drinking and finished it off.

"You owe me another ale, you asshole," I grumbled, sounding completely unimpressed.

He shot me a feral grin. "Oh, calm your tits." He whistled at the barmaid who had been here not even a moment ago and pointed to the mug. She looked reluctant to even acknowledge him, but started pouring another mug, anyway.

"Is there a reason you are here and not out scouting?" I asked, as I tried to regain my focus on what I had been trying to do.

"Our plan worked."

That got my attention. "And?"

"A falcon was just received from Isla. It carried a note from one of our scouts planted in the city stating that the king and queen heard of our plan to make camp at Ceto Bay. They supposedly sent both head captains and a crew of their finest soldiers to, and I quote, 'destroy us'..." The smirk on his face told me he wasn't taking this seriously.

"Is this funny to you for some reason?"

"I mean, kind of. One, they think they're smarter than us when they fell right into our trap. And two, they actually think they can just waltz in with a few of their men...or are they called males?" He paused for a moment and then shrugged one of his shoulders. "I don't know, either way they believe that we still aren't a threat and can easily be destroyed, when we actually will be the ones to end them instead."

I never liked the idea of having scouts in Isla, mainly because they were fae. However, it was far too risky to have a human amongst them—they would be spotted almost instantly. If the sight of them didn't give it away, their smell absolutely would. The fae had heightened senses, which certainly was not in our favor. Their bodies were also naturally leaner, and more agile—giving them yet another advantage.

Our scouts were supposedly called "mortal sympathizers." When sympathizers were caught, the king and queen of Velyra refused to even hold a trial. It would be an instant death sentence where they would be hung by the neck until dead and then left in the city square as a reminder to all its citizens. These creatures were fucking *barbaric*. So, due to the risks the sympathizers take, my men trusted them. Personally, I preferred to keep them at an arm's length, but sometimes they needed to be let in on plans so we could all communicate what was happening inside and out of their head city gates.

"That is good news, then," I replied.

Gage raised a single brow at me. "What's our next move then, Commander Cadoria?"

A faint smile grew on my lips. I unsheathed my dagger from my boot and slammed the blade down onto the map where Ceto Bay was sketched in.

My eyes met Gage's. "We teach them to never underestimate us again."

THIRTEEN

Elianna

THE PAST FOUR DAYS at sea had been nothing short of my own personal hell. Kellan constantly went from a teasing mood to actually making it seem like he *wanted* me to stab him. The situation was becoming increasingly tiresome and confusing.

The two of us fought over the captain's quarters nightly. I was able to hide in there for about a day and a half before I was ready to destroy anything in sight for just a bite of that horrendous smelling stew. I made sure to sneak my way back in there before him, but this morning I forgot to keep the key in my pocket when I left the room and the fucker managed to grab it.

Tonight should be our last night at sea, and I had no idea how I was going to manage to get that key back. Perhaps I should just let him have the room for the night since he had been sleeping in...actually, I had no idea where he had been staying.

Making my way to the deck, I passed by a few of the sailors lingering in front of the kitchen area, eyeing me as if I was the last piece of meat on this ship. "Can I help you? Surely there's work to be done."

The three of them approached me leisurely, their body language exuding dominance, but I stood my ground.

"Is there a problem, Captain Solus?" one of them asked.

Before I could notice, another one of them had slipped behind me under the cover of the shadows, and I was now trapped between the three males. "What do you think you are doing?" I demanded.

"It's not fair that Adler gets you all to himself. We all have needs, yanno." Each word was dragged out, and panic swelled in my chest, but I couldn't let that show on my face. "Surely, being the only pretty little thing to look at on this ship, you can understand how we feel."

This couldn't be happening, and there was nobody else below deck with us. I slowly gripped the hilt of my dagger. "Careful there," I spoke with a surprisingly steady voice. "You are threatening your commanding officer."

"There are no threats here. Only the threat of a good time, right, boys?" They all started laughing at me as they tiptoed in closer.

I tried to calm and steady my breathing when the one who had been speaking gradually leaned his face down towards my own, his lips only inches from mine.

Fuck. No.

I unsheathed my dagger from its belt and quickly made my move, ripping the obsidian blade across the top of his thigh, shredding through his flesh. While the other two were distracted by the agonizing scream that tore from his throat, I shoved him with all my strength and ran around them to go up the stairs.

I could have taken him if he was on his own, maybe even two of them. But not three. Not by myself. Lukas would be proud of me and my 'wits' today. The male's shouts of pain were music to my ears as they continued to echo from behind me.

The sunlight nearly blinded me when I reached the top of the stairs. I frantically glanced around the ship's deck to make sure I wasn't about to be attacked again. I locked eyes with Kellan, who was up by the ship's wheel. As his eyes lingered on me, I straightened my shirt and turned on my heel to walk toward the front of the ship.

As I stared out at the waves beyond, large footsteps sounded behind me. "Did something happen, Lia?" He actually sounded concerned.

I cleared my throat. "Nothing I couldn't handle."

He grabbed my arm and turned me towards him. "What the hell happened?" His eyes nervously searched mine.

"I don't know why you care. You have done nothing but try to make this entire journey miserable," I grumbled, as I shot him a death glare.

He kissed my forehead, sending a wave of surprise through me, and I would be lying if I said the gesture didn't feel sincere. "Come now, Lia. I thought we were just having a little bit of fun."

"Fun?!" I snapped, as I shoved him away. "Well, you should know that your sailors value very little of their lives because if it wasn't three against one, I would have fucking *ended* them for what they just tried to do. And they all *will* face consequences once we dock."

"What are you talking about?" I could see the rage building beneath his stare.

"As if you didn't know that three sailors, hand-picked by you to be on this trip, didn't just corner me below deck and threaten to assault me!" I spat back in his face.

He said nothing. No words left him as he turned on his feet and stormed towards the stairs that led below deck.

"Kellan, wait!" I rushed after him. I pulled on his arm, but he continued to move as if I wasn't even there. "I can handle myself. I do not need you to handle issues for me, and these males will *never* respect me if you do that." He grunted and ripped his arm from my grasp.

As Kellan stomped down the stairs, I decided to wait near the mast of the ship. Angry shouts rang out from below and all the sailors manning the ship quickly stopped what they were doing to watch the madness unfold.

Kellan appeared then, dragging all three of the males in his grasp up the stairs. It was honestly impressive to see. He then physically kicked them out into the middle of the deck. One of them already had a black eye and a bloody lip.

"Who's idea was this?" he shouted in their faces, his voice booming with fury. None of them spoke. "I think I can take a good fucking guess at who the ringleader behind this was." He glanced between the three of them. "...Last fucking chance. Who's bright idea was it to try to attack Captain Solus?" Again, nothing but silence.

A malicious chuckle rumbled from his lips. "Very well, then." Kellan then struck, sending his fist straight into the nose of the male who spoke the threat to me. The sounds of bone and cartilage crunching beneath his knuckles echoed across the ship.

The male let out a loud screech of pain and dropped back down to his knees on the floor beneath him. The others began to tremble with fear. "I can see she got you good herself, asshole." Kellan pointed to the man's ruined thigh. And now he had a face to match. I tried my best not to smile, but the corner of my lip tilted up.

"Let this be a reminder to all aboard this ship," he bellowed. "Captain Solus is above you all in every way, shape, and form. The next person to touch her, or even look in her direction for anything other than receiving orders, loses their miserable fucking life. This is your *only* warning. Do I make myself clear?" he spoke out to all aboard the deck.

Murmurs of agreement erupted across the space, and then Kellan waltzed back up to the male, who was now laying in a pool of his own blood, and violently sent his boot directly into his ribs. He then spat on the male's face and his gaze whipped to mine, searching for any sign of approval. All I could manage to do was give him a slight nod, and then he stalked back up to the ship's wheel as if nothing had just occurred.

I paced back and forth in the captain's quarters once the night had fallen. I hadn't seen Kellan since the incident earlier, which most likely was a blessing from the gods because I didn't know how to feel about how everything unfolded.

Kellan knew how much I loathed him stepping on my toes and "handling" things for me because he believed I couldn't on my own. But this felt different. This *was* different. One of his own sailors had threatened a captain, and he took action. That had to be done, right? He had every right to do that. Perhaps he felt more obligated to because of our situation, as well.

A friendly knock sounded at the door, and when I glanced up, I noticed him leaning on the door frame.

"How are you holding up?" he asked, voice abnormally soft.

"Fine." I cleared my throat. "I'm fine. Thank you for what you did earlier."

An abrupt laugh left him. "You don't need to thank me. Not one, but three under my own command thought it would be appropriate to attack you. Someone who is not only a captain herself but also claimed to me...or was anyway before I fucked up." I could see the sadness lingering in his stare from across the room.

I carefully approached him and took his hands in mine. "I don't forgive you for what you did to me." He winced slightly. "But thank you for what you did earlier."

He smiled softly, and kissed my cheek. "Would you like me to bring you any food left over from dinner?"

I turned my nose up. "Is it—"

"Stew? Yes, it is."

Ugh. "No, thank you."

He nodded and moved to turn. "Kellan?"

"Yes?" he asked, his voice nearly cracking with anticipation.

"Will you stay here with me tonight?" He looked just as surprised as I felt about the invitation that came out of my mouth. "If you try anything, I will stick my dagger into your gut, but I would feel better knowing you are guarding my back."

The sorrow behind his eyes slowly faded. "I would be honored," he responded, as he gently shut the door behind himself and made his way toward me.

Kellan

Staring at Lia asleep next to me was something that I honestly was beginning to think would never happen again. She had been much more difficult regarding forgiveness than I originally thought she would be, but I knew I could eventually carve my way back into her heart.

She refused to fuck me tonight but give it a few more days and she would be begging for it. She always did—just like they all do. I just needed to prove myself to her once more.

As I slipped quietly from the sheets, Lia stirred slightly before turning towards the wall. I pulled on my shirt and boots and left the room on silent feet.

I walked into the kitchen to see that most of the crew were lingering around and sipping their ales scattered throughout the space. I smirked once my eyes met a bloodied face staring back at me from the far corner. I made my way to him.

"Vin," I greeted, reaching out my hand to the male that I had publicly beaten the shit out of earlier in front of Lia and the crew.

He grasped my hand tightly and shook it in greeting. "Did it work?" he asked.

"You bet your ass it did," I responded. "Excellent work, my friend. She practically begged me to spend the night with her." I crossed my arms as a grin crept up my face.

Vin chuckled. "Well, after the show we put on earlier, I would be very disappointed if this didn't work. You owe me a new face, by the way...that wasn't part of the plan," he grumbled.

"I had to make it believable. Your nose will heal in a day or two."

Vincent was my unnamed Second. Lia never knew about him. In fact, most didn't. He always appeared as a working hand in the background. It came in handy that way. If I needed something done that I couldn't do at that exact moment, he was sent. It didn't matter how dirty or cruel the job was, Vin was always happy to oblige. Tricking Lia into thinking that some of my crew members had double-crossed me and went after her pussy was no exception.

He handed me a mug of ale and clinked our two cups together. "To the foolish females of the world."

"To climbing the ladder," I replied, right before I sent the entire drink to the back of my throat.

FOURTEEN

Jace

WE ARRIVED AT THE outskirts of Ceto Bay last night, and not a single man had rested as we all prepared for the arrival of the ship carrying the enemy fleet to our shores. Tents went up, fires had been set, flags raised, and all other necessary precautions to make the area look as if it had been inhabited by us for weeks.

"Scouts say they saw a ship not too far up the coast. They are estimated to arrive by morning," Gage said, coming up from behind me.

Excellent. "We will be ready."

"I'm still slightly confused about why this entire setup was necessary. Why did we need to waste energy and supplies to make it look as if we are actually here, instead of just hiding out and attacking?"

Sometimes I swear he just never listens to me. "We are not wasting energy and supplies, Gage. Look around!" His gaze swept over the beach. "The whole reason they are coming here is that they heard about a human war camp set up at Ceto Bay. If they arrive here, or even yet, see from their ship that there isn't even a single tent set up, they will know something is not right.

116

They may not even see a reason to anchor the ship and come to shore. We need to make this as realistic looking as possible."

He contemplated that for a second. "But when they come to shore, the beach will be empty, won't they know something is up then?"

"They may, but by then we will have the camp surrounded by our men, and it will be too late for them to retreat. We need to be quick and accurate, but the plan will work."

He nodded. "So we hide out in the trees and attack when they least expect it?"

"Exactly," I confirmed.

This was going to work. It had to.

My gaze wandered around to the far corner of the beach and I watched as my cousin, Zaela, finished setting up the last decoy tent. Her eyes met mine and she gave me a curt nod as she took a step in our direction. She liked to consider herself my *true* Second, since Gage could be an idiot.

"Is everything in place?" she asked, jogging up to us.

I was about to speak when I was cut off. "You have eyes, don't you, Zae? Take a look around and tell us," Gage teased, as he elbowed my side, making sure I knew that he was mimicking my earlier words to him.

Zaela looked up at him, batting her eyelashes, and without even a flicker of hesitation, punched him straight in the gut.

Gage let out a loud grunt and dropped to his knees in the sand.

She looked at me. "I don't know why we still bring him places."

"Sometimes I can agree with that," I choked out through a laugh.

"I'm still here, assholes." Gage flipped his middle finger up at us and climbed to his feet.

All three of us started walking towards the tree line. "Gage was just telling me that the fae's ship should be here by morning. We should all post up in our positions tonight just in case they make good time. I don't want any surprises."

She nodded. "I will take twenty-five of the others and take the west side of the bay. You take the south with yours, and Gage can take the north with his twenty-five. They will have nowhere to go. They will be surrounded by us and the sea. They will either be forced to die or surrender."

Seventy-eight against thirty. "We leave no survivors," I stated.

Zaela looked at me, her lips pressed with tension. "Jace, I know you want to destroy the fae crown, and all who support it, but–"

"But nothing, Zaela."

She looked perplexed. "Is that wise, Jace? We should leave one alive, maybe two. Even if we kill them later down the road. They could be useful."

"She has a point, brother," Gage chimed in.

My jaw ticked with tension as my eyes aggressively darted back and forth between them. "Let me make something clear to the both of you. They never would allow one of us to survive. Do you think they would bring a human in for questioning? Never. They kill first, and don't even bother to ask questions later. They are murderers. Conquerors. They will not rest until every last mortal is nothing but dust left in this realm, and I am doing everything in my power to make sure the exact opposite of that happens."

Zaela's eyes softened, a rare gesture for her. "Jace, if this is about your mother–"

"It's about all of the mothers!" I shouted at her. "All the mothers, daughters, sisters...*everyone*. Everyone who cannot protect themselves. We are doing this for them. If I need to bathe in the blood of my enemies to make sure my people are able to sleep soundly at night, then so be it. If you two do not agree with that, then you are in my way."

"We are always with you," Gage whispered, as he placed his hand onto my shoulder.

"Then let's get this done."

FIFTEEN

Elianna

I AWOKE TO KELLAN leaning over my body, lightly patting my arm. As my eyes adjusted to the darkness, I looked out through the tiny, circular window of the cabin and could barely differentiate the sea from the sky. It must've been the middle of the night still.

"Lia, dawn is not far off. We make our move now. You, me, and the majority of the crew will be coming from the back end through the forest. A smaller group will be taking the sails off of the pinnace and row towards shore."

My brows flew up my forehead as he announced his sudden change of plans. It was brilliant. While normally I dreaded what would come next, I realized that the sooner we finished here, the sooner I could get back home. "Well, what are we waiting for? Let's go!" I said, as I jumped out of the bed and laced up my boots.

I walked up to the deck, and once my eyes adjusted to the early morning darkness, I realized that we were about a mile offshore. "Where is the bay?" I asked him, as I finished strapping the last of my weapons to myself.

He pointed toward the land mass as he came up behind me and gently rested his chin on the top of my head. "Do you see that bend? There is another after that, and then Ceto Bay lies just beyond. About three miles on land from where we will reach the shore."

My brows furrowed in thought. "So, essentially, they will be expecting the rest of us to be on the ship, but we will be coming up from behind them unseen."

"You are correct, princess," he replied as he placed a hand on each of my shoulders from behind me and massaged them awkwardly. The urge to correct him nearly consumed me, but I knew he wouldn't stop calling me that no matter how many times I asked...or demanded.

I turned around to see most of the crew were standing behind us waiting for orders.

"Soldiers." Kellan's deep voice boomed across the ship. "The human camp is not but three miles away, and it was built for the sole purpose of harming our kind. Will we let them get away with this?"

"No, Captain!" The crew shouted in unison.

He shot me a quick smirk and it took every effort to not roll my eyes at his arrogance.

"Our queen has trusted me to pick my best soldiers to destroy this enemy camp before they have the chance to grow. Will we let her down?"

"No, Captain."

Kellan looked back at me once more, and his grin was ear to ear. "Then let's go have some fun, boys."

The crew immediately dispersed into different directions, headed toward wherever they had been assigned.

I stalked after Kellan and grabbed his arm as he headed toward one of the smaller boats to get to shore. "If there are any children, we leave them unharmed. If any surrender, we take them as prisoners."

He turned to face me and looked me up and down. "My intentions are to leave no one left alive that isn't of high importance, but we can discuss this when the time comes."

And then he boarded the pinnace.

Once on shore, we watched the ship as it sailed around the first bend, we needed to be quick if we were to make it to Ceto Bay on time.

"Alright, you all know the drill. We run into anyone who is not marked as a high-ranking officer, we kill them on sight. Anyone marked in a high rank we take back with us," Kellan spoke to his crew. I shot him a disapproving look, which made him grimace. "Unless, they surrender. Then we will hold them captive." He sighed.

The entire troop exchanged looks of confusion, and then entered the forest on silent feet.

The woods here were thick with willows, oaks and pine trees alike, which worked in our favor to provide camouflage. A small brook running between the boulders and trees provided the faint sound of rushing water to cover our tracks. I dipped down and stuck two of my fingers into the mud, smearing some across my face to help blend into the forest. Others followed suit and did the same.

The sun had risen fully by the time we had quietly marched two and a half miles toward the camp, and then my ears perked up.

While reaching for my sword with my right hand, I simultaneously raised my left, halting everyone behind me. "We are not alone out here."

SIXTEEN

Jace

EVERYONE WAS IN POSITION by dawn. We had men scattered throughout the forest, waiting for the signal from either me, Zaela, or Gage to move forward and storm the beach. The three of us were stationed on the ground, hidden between the shadows of the trees where the sand of the beach met the grass of the forest floor. Everyone else lay concealed behind us.

It had been almost an hour by the time we could see the ship making its way into the bay's harbor. Using my binoculars, I could see multiple members of the crew climbing down a rope ladder to board a smaller boat that would bring them to shore. Perfect.

I whistled out a sound resembling the call of a sparrow, giving the signal to the men that the ship had arrived.

As the smaller boat was pushed onto the shore, I noticed that there were only five males aboard instead of the expected thirty. The captain must have decided to check the situation out for himself before bringing his entire crew to the beach. This was not planned, and if we made our move against the five that now set foot on our shore before the others arrived, our element of surprise would be blown. Fuck.

On the other hand though, if that was the captain who was walking toward us now, and he only had four others to use as possible protection, we could take him down and send a message back to the crown. I didn't hate that last-second Plan B. If we took out one of their high-ranking commanders, not only would it send the message we were looking for, but it would also likely obstruct the setup the fae currently had within their ranks.

I made eye contact with Zaela and then the same with Gage. As I rose my arm to give the signal, I heard a loud thud sound from behind me, and then another. And another three seconds after that. The noises could only be described as resembling what bodies would sound like dropping to the ground. I whipped towards the trees behind me but nothing was there, when suddenly the next noise I heard was not the sound of flesh smacking into the forest floor, but a yelp of pain that was cut far too short to mean that whomever it came from was still living.

I frantically looked back up across the beach to see both Zaela and Gage had vanished. *Shit*. Were we tricked? I scanned the beach to see all five fae soldiers staring into the woods, all with sinister smiles spread across their faces.

I went to unsheathe my sword from my side when the cool touch of a blade was lightly pressed against my throat. Then the voice of a woman purred into my ear, "I wouldn't do that if I were you."

The sultry tone of my attacker's voice stunned me for a moment.

"What is someone with a pretty little voice like that doing out here?" I asked, trying to think quickly of how to get out of this.

That only caused her to press the blade to my neck harder. "Just working on thinking of how I should kill you."

"Well, you have a dagger to my throat, so I think your mind is made up there, Miss."

She hesitated for a fraction of a second, but that was all I needed. I stomped on her foot and as she yelped, I grabbed her arm and shoved it to the side while twisting around her body. I maneuvered my own arm around the bow that was strapped across her back, and had her neck pinched between my forearm and bicep, nearly suffocating her.

"Well played," she choked out.

I squeezed her throat tighter. "Who the fuck are you? How many others are there?"

Screams of agony began to ring out all around us. As I looked through the trees of the forest, I could see blood splattered throughout.

"No," I whispered to myself. She started laughing, making it clear that she was responsible and that she didn't fear death.

I heaved her up with my arms, and her feet were now dangling in the air, swinging back and forth, desperately searching for the ground. "Are you not afraid of this? Of the death I'm about to give to you for *murdering* my men?" I spoke hoarsely directly into her ear.

Before I could catch what she was doing, with all her might, she swung her leg back and forced the heel of her foot up into my groin, causing me to release her upon impact. She took off running between the trees the second her feet touched back down on the ground. I dropped to my knees, but I had no time to focus on the throbbing pain now radiating through my gut. I would kill her slowly for that, I didn't care that she was a woman. I forced myself to my feet, picked up my sword, and chased after her.

Blood was everywhere. Splatters of it were across the moss-covered boulders, the bark on the trees, and pools of it spread throughout the forest floor. Where were the bodies?! I needed to know if it was my men suffering or the ones accompanying her. The fae bleed the same color as we do, so it was impossible to tell whose blood now soaked the ground beneath my feet.

After still not being able to find anyone, I started yelling, "Gage! Zaela! Where are yo–"

Out of the corner of my eye I saw movement about fifty feet downhill. I couldn't believe what I was witnessing. One of the fae was now *dragging* the bodies of two of my men across the terrain.

While running as silently as possible toward the scene below, I lifted my sword above my head to strike, when out of nowhere a sharp, knee-buckling pain radiated through my calf, causing me to tumble down the small hill that I was just about to leap off of to attack. At the end of my fall, my head slammed off of a rock, blurring my vision.

I tried to look around but was losing consciousness rapidly, and the last thing I saw was a figure with long, dark hair leaping from a tree with a bow in hand. I glanced down to see the shape of an arrow protruding from my leg. And then I knew nothing but darkness.

Head pounding, I woke up from what seemed like a horrible nightmare, only to realize it wasn't a nightmare at all. It was real. I could feel that I had been tied to some kind of tree or post stuck in the ground. Blinded by the sun, I slowly opened my eyes and could not believe what what was unfolding before me.

Bodies. Piles of dead, bloodied, human bodies stacked on top of each other across the beach. I must have hit my head harder than I thought. This couldn't be happening. *How?* How could this have happened when we were so prepared? I thought out every plan, every detail, and my men that I brought here with me were all slain.

Just thinking of Gage and Zaela being amongst those bodies had me ready to vomit. All the faces I could see were so mangled, or covered in so much blood and dirt, that I couldn't tell who they were.

I looked toward the tree line and counted thirteen of my men lined up, bound by their hands and feet, and gagged. Walking toward me from where they were was the woman, or female, that had pressed her blade to my throat and then shot the arrow through my leg.

"Look who decided to wake up." She placed her hands on her hips. "How's the leg?" She glanced down and smirked at the arrow still sticking out of my ruined calf.

I bared my teeth at her. "What have you done?"

"The men by the tree line surrendered. They will be transported back with us as our prisoners, same as you, Commander."

I didn't realize I still had my badge intact on my armor. Forcing myself to look back up to the too few men who stood by the forest, a sinking feeling fell in my gut when I saw that Gage and Zae were not among them. They never would have surrendered anyway. They would have preferred to greet death in the face with a smile as they swung their swords high above their heads.

"You will pay for what you've done." She refused to look at me. "I will see to it that you personally fucking suffer for all the lives that were lost today, and every day since the war began." She started walking away when I shouted, "Cowardice, bitch!"

She whipped around, her hair flowing rapidly around her face from the beach's wind, and stormed up to me. She took two of her fingers as she glared into my eyes and lightly pressed down on the wound. Light or not, the pain made me feel as if I was about to lose consciousness again.

"Let me make myself perfectly clear, Commander." Her face was now an inch from my own. "You could have gone about your life in a manner of peace, but you chose to lead these armies. You chose to camp here and plot murder. And you chose to dedicate your short, mortal life to killing my kind. My loyalty is to the crown of Velyra, and anyone who threatens that is my enemy. My enemies are dealt with accordingly."

She then removed her hold on my wound and stormed off.

By the time night had fallen, I could tell my calf was getting infected. I could lose this leg if the arrow wasn't removed, and the wound treated.

The enemy fleet was gathered around the fire they had set earlier. I couldn't help but notice that the female was sitting on the lap of someone whom I could only assume was the captain. As I observed further, it seemed that he was holding her in place, rather than her willingly sitting with him. She was probably just the captain's whore who got lucky with her bow earlier.

"Captain Solus?" one of the males yelled.

Solus. That was the name in Velyra that was used for orphans...interesting that he would keep such a name while being in a high ranking position.

To my surprise, the person who I thought would respond didn't even acknowledge the call, but *she* did.

"I will be there in just a moment. Thank you," she called out to him.

Captain Solus? The female that held a dagger to my throat and shot me down only minutes later? That was...impressive. I would give her that. I watched her rise from the male's lap. He gave her ass a smack as she made her move away from him, and she seemingly laughed it off as she swatted at him. Who could that male be to disrespect a captain? Even a husband or wife shouldn't make a move as such in front of others when their spouse was highly ranked.

I glanced over to see most of my men that had been captured were asleep on the ground, still gagged and tied. I needed to come up with a plan to get all of us out of here alive.

I leaned my head back against the post I was tied to on the beach and closed my eyes as I listened to the waves rolling in and out, begging for sleep to come for me, but it never did. Every time I closed my eyes, all I could see were the faces of the men who would never return home to their families. And it was all my fault.

SEVENTEEN

Elianna

I AWOKE AT DAWN to see the sky was ablaze with hues of reds, pinks and sapphires. Another victory was won yesterday, and thanks to Kellan, we didn't fall into the trap set for us by the mortals.

The humans somehow managed to get word to Isla about a camp at Ceto Bay and lured us out here to fall into their ambush. The only logical explanation was that there were far more sympathizers remaining in Isla than originally believed. Today we would begin our journey back to the city with our prisoners, and I would get to reunite with my father, Lukas, my red-headed siblings, and Nyra...I was even looking forward to seeing Nox.

I was sitting in the sand, staring out into the sea when I felt eyes on me, as if they were burning a hole into the back of my skull. Turning halfway around, I noticed the human commander staring into my back, his features radiating nothing but hatred. I couldn't blame him. If almost my entire fleet were killed and I was being held captive, I would be a hell of a lot worse than he was being right now.

Kellan waltzed out of one of the tents and began buttoning up his shirt when our eyes met. He leisurely swaggered his way over to me.

"Are you ready to be on our way home, Lia?" he asked.

I nodded. "Of course." When I went to stand my knee buckled.

"Are you okay?" he asked.

"Yeah, my leg is just sore. I think I may have pulled a muscle in my calf when I leaped from the tree to take the commander down yesterday." He looked me up and down carefully and then turned when I grabbed his arm.

"Thank you for taking the humans who surrendered as prisoners."

He gave me a brief, unconvincing smile and was back on his way.

The morning was spent loading the ship up with all of the supplies the humans set up. There was no use in leaving it all here and letting it go to waste. Especially the food. Now, hopefully, I wouldn't have to force myself to stomach that stew another night.

The commander still hadn't said a word. I looked at his leg and could tell even from across the beach that it was getting infected. I made my way to him, our eyes locked on each other the entire time.

"Hello, *Captain Solus*," he hissed in greeting, and my brows furrowed in surprise. He must have heard the soldiers speaking to me last night. The wicked smile that stretched across his face did not meet his eyes.

"Good morning, Commander," I dragged out the word. "...I'm sorry I do not know your name."

"Don't say sorry as if you truly care. I will never give you my name."

This was going to be a fun trip home.

I stared at him for a moment, pitying him. "Listen, I came over here to see if you would like that arrow removed from your leg since it's clearly getting infected, and I really do not feel like dealing with that mess if it gets worse. However, if you are going to speak to the *captain* like that, and clearly you know that is exactly who I am, then you are a bigger fool than I originally took you for." I turned away to head back up the beach.

"Wait." He sighed. "Remove it."

I turned back to face him as I threw my hands down at my sides. "Excuse me?"

"Remove the arrow."

"I will do no such thing for some mortal, fool commander, who sounds nothing short of ungrateful," I snapped.

He was silent for a moment. "Please," he grunted out. "Please remove the arrow that *you* shot through my leg..."

I flinched, hoping he didn't notice. It had been years since we took a prisoner captive, so I wasn't used to keeping my mask of the "tough captain" on, considering conversations with the enemy were rare, to say the least. His eyes narrowed in on me as I bent down on one knee and inspected his leg.

"Shit, this is worse than I thought." He met my gaze. "I am going to have to rip this out as fast as I can and then apply pressure in case the bleeding worsens again, but we have to be careful, we don't want any of the outside puss to get into your bloodstream."

He nodded and I didn't miss the slight tick that set in his jaw.

I pulled out a tin of salve that I stole out of Veli's stash in the castle and placed it on the ground next to us to have at the ready. Before we left Isla, I snuck down into the abandoned healing chambers of the castle, which was where Veli liked to hide away supplies for those in need of it. It was a miracle the queen hadn't sniffed it out after all these years. I wanted to be prepared in the event that members of the crew became injured—even though these males were technically under Kellan's command. I refused to lose more soldiers in addition to what was lost in our most recent battle.

I grabbed his arm and ripped off a piece of his shirt for the wound. He eyed me, looking extremely unimpressed. "Sorry," I murmured.

"Let's get this over with," he said through his teeth.

"Okay, I will pull it out on the count of three. Ready?" He didn't respond, but his eyes never left mine. "Okay...one!"

I ripped the arrow out in one swift movement, and the commander's body jolted. I quickly applied pressure to the wound using the piece of his shirt.

"You said on the count of *three*. I don't know if you fae don't know how to count, but three comes after–"

"Two." I raised a single brow at him. "I'm aware." I looked at him for a moment and then patted the wound down and spread on the salve. "A thank you would be nice."

He snickered as he continued to look into my eyes. "I'm sure it would be."

Kellan

Red. All I could see was a fiery haze of red clouding my vision as I watched Elianna clean the human commander's wound from across the beach.

What the fuck was she doing? I would've left the arrow inside of him until his leg rotted off his body.

My teeth clenched as a growl rumbled through my throat at the sight of them. I was doing what she asked. I kept those who surrendered alive, but what good would it do? It made us look *weak*. She was making *me* look as if I had gone soft in front of my own crew by leaving survivors. And now she had the audacity to make a fool out of me and flirt with that human filth?

I spat at the ground, crossed my arms and then called out, "Vin!"

Vincent ran over from one of the far tents. "Take a look over there." I pointed to Lia, whose back was turned to me. "What does that look like to you?"

Vin scratched his chin. "It looks like she's helping the human? Why would she do that?"

"Exactly. But that simply just will not do, will it, Vin?"

The look he gave me could be described as nothing other than purely sinister anticipation.

Lia then turned around and smiled at me, which was accompanied by a dainty little wave. I was about to wipe that smile right off of her gods-damned face.

EIGHTEEN

Jace

WHO *WAS THIS FEMALE*? She commanded their armies, yet assisted their enemy with a wound that *she* inflicted. It made absolutely no sense, but I couldn't remove my stare from her as she did it.

She was stunning to look at. That was undeniable, but her beauty was laced with poison. While I was grateful for no longer having to worry about losing my leg, I still felt nothing but pure hatred for her.

My men were dead, their bodies still scattered across the beach before my eyes. She would pay for it. They would all pay for this with their lives, just as my men had.

"There, that should hold you over until we get back to Isla. I will check it in a day or two on the ship, but the salve is strong," she stated while dusting the sand from her hands, and rose to her feet.

I said nothing to her.

"Soldiers!" a powerful voice boomed from across the beach, causing everyone to look up, and Solus whipped around in the direction it came from.

It was the male that she sat with the night prior.

"Have we ever taken in those who surrender?" he yelled.

"No, Captain!" the crew answered in unison.

Wait. *Another* Captain?

"Yes, you are all correct!" He spun around, making sure all eyes were on him as he spoke. "And that is because it makes us look *weak*...now tell me, is that what we are?!"

"No, Captain!"

From the corner of my eye, I saw Solus take a hesitant step toward him.

Oh, no. No. No. No. What was he doing?

"Change of plans, boys! There will only be a single prisoner taken from this camp." He raised his sword and pointed the blade in my direction. "And it's their dearest Commander." He paused for a moment. "Kill the others."

"NO!" I shouted, as I desperately tried to break free from my restraints.

I couldn't stop screaming. Begging. Pleading for them to stop.

My eyes whipped over to Solus, who had both hands balled into fists at her sides, with her jaw hung open, but she said nothing—did nothing to stop what was about to happen.

Coming out from the tree line was a male that I had seen wandering around the camp all morning. I recognized him from his black eye and busted nose. One of my men must've gotten a decent swing in before he went down. Good.

The male then walked up to the first of my soldiers in line, pulled his head back by his sand-crusted hair, and slit his throat with a dagger he pulled from his boot. Blood instantly poured down his front, soaking him, and then the brute kicked him in the back, forcing his body to slam into the sand.

The murderer looked up and smiled at me. *Smiled.* And then went down my line of men and repeated what he had done to the first, over and over again. Until all thirteen were nothing but yet another pile of corpses.

I tried to force my body to stand up by using the pressure from the back of the pole I was tied to, but it was no use with my ruined leg.

"You motherfucker! I will kill you!" I screamed. "Every last one of you, I will send you back to Isla in pieces for what you have done!"

Solus looked back at me as if she cared. She opened her mouth to speak.

"Don't," I seethed. "Don't you dare say a word to me. I will have your head on a spike right next to theirs." My lips curled back at her in disgust.

She looked me up and down and hesitantly walked toward the sea in silence.

The male captain who gave the order then stormed his way over to me. Bending at the knee, he stuck his face directly in front of mine. "Hope you don't mind." He smirked. "We just needed to pack a little lighter for the trip home."

I spat in his face.

His smirk didn't budge as he pulled at the front of my shirt with both hands and wiped his face with it aggressively.

He then pulled his sword from its sheath and twirled the blade in the air. I waited for death to take me, but instead of plunging his sword into me, he slammed the hilt of it into the back of my head.

And once again, darkness claimed me.

NINETEEN

Elianna

I REFUSED TO SPEAK to Kellan after the shit he pulled on the beach. I couldn't. The look on his face was made of pure venom. He *enjoyed* the sight of their throats being slit, I could see it laid bare on his face. Not only did he order to have them all put to death, but the one who carried it out was the male he punished for trying to attack me not even two days ago. Something didn't feel right.

He agreed to keep anyone who surrendered alive. I knew they would eventually be put to death for their actions, but not at least until we brought them back to Isla for questioning, and I was going to petition to at least have them die with dignity. They surrendered. In my opinion, they deserved that. But Kellan went behind my back *again*.

I would never be able to get the sound of the commander's screams out of my head. Agony. I could feel the absolute anguish radiating off of him at the sight of what was done to his men. His face had turned red, and it wasn't due from the beaming sun, but from his screams. The veins of his neck visibly throbbed, and his body vibrated with fury. If his leg wasn't injured to the extent that it was, I honestly believed he would've found a way out of his bindings and attacked one of us—maybe even me. He threatened to have my head put on a spike right next to Kellan's. The look of hatred was permanently etched into his face until Kellan knocked him out again.

After we all boarded the ship, the male that Kellan had ordered to slit everyone's throats threw the commander into the prison cell below deck.

I avoided everyone to the best of my ability. It seemed like I would need to find a way to barricade myself in the captain's cabin once again the entire trip. I couldn't wait to be home. I didn't trust these males, and I also no longer trusted Kellan.

Gazing out at the sea, it seemed as if the wind had picked up and the waves became extremely choppy. We had amazing luck on our way here with the weather and sea—I could only hope we would be granted the same on the journey home.

Making my way below deck, I could feel wandering, curious eyes on me from every direction. I tried to hide my reaction to how I felt about what was done only hours ago at the bay, but clearly my thoughts on it had become well known to the crew.

Once I reached the captain's cabin, I grabbed hold of the brass doorknob and was surprised to find that it was unlocked, however, the room wasn't empty...

Kellan stood in the corner with his arms crossed, speaking once again to the male that had tried to attack me.

My ex-claimed looked at me and a soft smile appeared on his face. "You are dismissed, Vincent," he said to the male.

As he made his way to me, well to the door, Vincent's eyes locked with mine and a faint smirk grew across his lips as he passed through the doorway.

"You may close the door, Elianna," Kellan called over to me.

Was he serious? He really thought we were going to be normal after all that just occurred.

"Oh, may I?" I hissed.

He slowly leaned back on the wall and faced me. "You are angry with me."

I slammed the door shut behind me, rattling the room and furniture within it. "Do you think there is a reason I should not be?" I snapped at him.

"I think your anger is misplaced."

"Misplaced?!"

"That is what I said, princess, is it not?"

"Do *not* call me that."

He raised a brow. "We are back to this, I see."

"And what would ever make you think that we wouldn't be?!" I shouted, as I threw my arms out in frustration. "You went behind my back. Again. You went against what we both agreed on. You did not bring this to me. This was well thought out and executed without my knowledge purposefully. You knew I would be against this."

He took a step toward me but I held my ground. "What makes you think that?"

I rose my fist and pointed a single finger at his face. "Do not take another step closer to me, Kellan, or I swear to the gods that

I will gut you where you stand." He stopped where he was. Good, at least he took that seriously. "Do you think I am an idiot? That I wouldn't notice who it was that slit the throats of the men that surrendered?"

The corners of his lips twitched up. "He wanted a chance to prove his loyalty to me, Lia."

"Bullshit!" I spat.

"Bullshit?! Why would that be? He fucked up. He tried to touch and harm what was mine. He—"

"I. Am. *Not.* Yours!" I cut him off, my breathing turned ragged.

He looked angry now. Finally.

"This is getting old, Elianna...as I said before, we claimed each other, and that isn't going to change." All the features on his face tightened, he twisted from me slightly in an attempt to hide his wrath as it flooded his veins.

"I thought you punished him for trying to attack a captain, not because you thought you still had some kind of *claim on me*. The male should have been thrown overboard for what he had done, and I can't even believe I didn't realize that sooner!"

The chuckle he let out sent a chill down my spine. "Perhaps. However, he has been punished and is willing to prove himself. Here I was trying to prevent you from being irritated with me for killing a member of my own crew, yet here I am days later, being howled at over human *filth*."

"Oh my gods," I whispered, as my eyes grew wide. "That's why you did it, isn't it?" He didn't say a word. "You killed them because I helped their commander with his wound, didn't you?"

His lips pursed as he turned away from me. "The only reason he is not among those with their throats slit is because of his rank, and he will be brought in to be tortured and questioned before he is also put to death. The sight of you touching his skin..." He paused for a long moment. "And assisting the enemy disgusted me to my core." He pointed to his broad chest as his lips curled in revulsion on the last few words.

My eyes flew open as wide as they could. He did this out of *jealousy*?

"I will not apologize for touching the skin of a man that does not mean anything to me. I also will not apologize for assisting with a wound that was about to be ridden with infection. We do not have a healer among us, and that is something I didn't want to deal with. If he died on the journey home, we would have nobody to bring in to question regarding the other remaining human camps."

"I think you've gone soft, and it is quite concerning considering the rank you hold, *Captain*. How will the queen take it when she hears of you not only helping mortals but also taking salve from a healer?"

"That salve could have come in handy for anyone!"

He stepped out from the wall, and hovered directly over me. "Tell me, princess, are you a mortal sympathizer?"

"Of course not," I said through my teeth.

He grabbed my face with both of his rough, calloused hands and planted his lips onto mine aggressively. I repeatedly shoved at his chest with my fists to get him off of me, but his strength overpowered my own. Once he was finished, he threw my face away from his, causing me to lose my footing and stumble back.

I stared at him in disbelief as I stormed to the cabin's door and swung it open so hard that it put a small hole in the wall it crashed into behind it. "Don't you ever touch me again," I said sternly, as my stare bore into him. Then I slammed the door back shut.

With nowhere else to go and be alone, I decided to check on the prisoner and see if he had awoken in the cell.

His unconscious body still lay on the splintered wooden floor of the ship. There was no cot in the cell. Only nearly rotted wood, dirt, and rusted metal bars to hold him in.

I sighed and glanced around. Barely anything was down in the prison section below deck. Aside from the cells, there were a couple of extra barrels of supplies spread throughout, but that was it. While snooping, I found a dust covered bottle of rum tucked in the corner. I popped the cork off the top and gave it a whiff. Gods knew how old this was, but I decided I didn't care and took a swig from it anyway. And then another.

I crawled on top of one of the barrels and decided to just wait it out down here until both Kellan and I calmed down. I couldn't stand him, but arguing publicly in front of the crew wouldn't do either of us any favors. Mainly me. Would he really tell the queen that he believed me to be a mortal sympathizer? That couldn't be right. I knew we were on the worst terms in the history of our relationship, but surely he wouldn't risk my life like that. Or would he?

No. No, he wouldn't do that.

I slowly raised the bottle of rum in the air, toward the commander on the ground and chuckled. "To the two enemy commanders in Velyra being prisoners together," I said, and then I threw back another swig of the amber liquid.

TWENTY

Jace

MY HEAD WAS POUNDING again. The ground beneath me no longer felt as if it was sand. Which meant I was no longer on the beach of Ceto Bay, where the bodies of my men had laid before me. What had they done with their corpses? Were they buried? Burned so their souls could pass on to be with their lost loved ones? I doubted the fae even believed in such things. Which meant my men were left in the sand to rot.

I rubbed at my chest as nausea crept up my throat from those thoughts that now plagued me.

Groaning, I carefully began my first attempt to sit up. Thankfully, my leg was healing already, so I was able to apply slight pressure when adjusting my body. Sitting on my ass with my back pressed against the wall of the ship, I realized that I was in a dark cell. There wasn't any sign of light peeking through the cracks in the ship's boards, which led me to believe that night had fallen. How long was I asleep? Hours? Days?

I needed to think of an escape plan out of here, but I knew that wouldn't be possible until we docked in Isla. Then I would be in the heart of my enemy's land.

"Ah, there he is," Solus' voice echoed from the dark corner of the room outside of the cell.

Grinding my teeth, I bit out, "What are you doing here?" My eyes were able to focus and I could see she was hanging off of a barrel upside down, feet high above her head, resting on the wall, and her long hair hung down to the floor in a giant tangle. An empty, dust covered bottle lay beneath her on the ground. Was she...drunk?

"Oh, you know, just making sure you're still alive."

I scoffed at her. "And why would you give a shit if I were alive? You didn't care about my men that you slaughtered before you knocked me out again," I seethed.

She quickly twirled her body around and jumped down from the barrel. Nearly pressing her face through the bars of the cell, she whispered, "You know that I had nothing to do with either of those things."

"You didn't? Last I heard, you were the captain, are you not?" I retorted.

She was quiet for a moment, and her jaw slacked as her eyes glazed over in thought. "I do not command the sailors aboard this ship. Captain Adler does."

Adler, he must be the prick whose lap she was in last night...or however many nights ago that was.

She continued, "I command the land armies while he handles the sea."

"Interesting setup."

"Glad you think so," she snapped back at me, accompanied by an infuriating smirk.

I rolled my eyes and turned away from her.

She spoke again, "I need you to know that...*woah.*" She cut herself off as the room swayed hard to the left. She stumbled on her feet, and I was glad I was sitting down because I would have fallen on my ass with this leg still half useless.

"Drunk, Captain Solus? You look like you lost your footing there for a second," I snarked.

"No! You saw the barrels slightly roll." She hesitated. "Okay, maybe I also had some rum, but the ship hasn't rocked that hard since I've been aboard," she said nervously.

Again, the ship swayed hard, this time to the right.

My shoulder slammed into the pole beside me. "Shit, what is the weather like up there?!" I shouted at her, as the roar of the waves outside grew louder.

She sucked her bottom lip in through her teeth. "The waves looked like they were getting to be a bit choppy a few hours ago, but I have been down here since."

I blinked. "Exactly how long were you watching me sleep?"

She eyed me. "Don't flatter yourself, Commander." She looked to the stairs that I could only think lead up to the deck.

"Don't you dare abandon me down here, Solus."

"Oh, relax, nothing will happen to the ship, but I need to make sure all hands are on deck and the sails are brought in so they don't tear."

"I thought you didn't command these sailors?" I yelled over to her as she made her way up the stairs.

She halted her steps for a moment, as if realizing I was right. I thought she would say something back to me, but she then slowly continued her ascent up and then left my sight.

TWENTY-ONE

Elianna

CHAOS. THERE WAS NOTHING but absolute chaos commencing on the deck. I sobered up instantly as I was met with the sight of the intense, storming skies that surrounded us. The waves had already breached the sides of the ship and the water was halfway up my calf. The crew members were all screaming at each other as they scattered, and I looked up to see Kellan manning the ship's wheel as he barked out orders to get everyone in line.

I ran up the stairs to him, shouting over the intense wind and rain that was slamming down on us. "What do you need me to do?!" I asked, as I grasped onto the railing to hold myself up.

"Lia!" he shouted, sounding concerned. "Get in the cabin now!"

"You are a fool if you think I would do such a thing!"

The wheel was ripped from his grip as another wave slammed into us, sending me flying back down the stairs and landing in a pool of seawater, soaking me entirely.

This was not good.

I got up and ran back up the stairs. Kellan tried to pull the wheel to the left, but it was no use. It wouldn't budge.

"Fuck!" he roared into the storming sky above.

A loud tear sounded from the front of the ship and we turned to see one of the sails had been ripped free of its ropes and was now being torn apart by the intense gusts of wind.

"We need to get that sail back under control!" I made my way towards it, but Kellan grabbed my arm and pulled me back into him.

His eyes frantically searched my face. "Go inside. Now! It isn't safe out here."

I shoved him back. "How is it any different from out here?! I will be tossed around like a rag doll regardless! At least make me useful!"

"Well, if you are inside, you cannot fly over the rails of the ship, Elianna!" he boomed in my face.

"That would not happen!" I screamed, as another wave sent us toppling to the ground. Kellan's body caught mine before slamming into the unforgiving wooden deck.

I looked down below at the same moment a monstrous wave took three sailors, swooping them off the ship and into the dark, dangerous water below, causing me to gasp out in horror.

Oh my gods, this couldn't be happening.

"I told you! Get inside!" he screamed in my face.

I looked at him and unsheathed my dagger from my thigh—worry flashed across his face, looking as if he thought I was going to try to stab *him* with it, until I quickly leapt down the entire set of stairs and ran towards the sail that was being shredded apart.

The crew was getting smaller by the moment. Many had already been thrown overboard by the waves.

What I needed was more rope. I saw out of the corner of my eye a cluster of barrels holding supplies tied together. I ran over and quickly cut the rope free from them with my dagger and threw the rope over my shoulder before I made my way to the main mast of the ship.

Looking up into the sky, I could barely see the top of the mast thanks to the wind whipping my dripping hair around my face. Letting out a harsh breath, I carefully started to climb the ladder blindly.

As the waves rocked the ship, my body swung violently from side to side, repeatedly slamming into the mast itself with each toss. My fingers were already beginning to blister and bleed from holding onto the rope woven ladder for dear life.

Once at the top, I held onto the mast as tightly as I could with one arm as I desperately reached out for the sail's rope that was swinging around in the powerful gusts. The boat jolted, and I moved my other arm back to the mast pole, holding on as tightly as I could so I didn't fall to what surely would be my death.

I searched down below and watched as yet another wave swooped across the deck, this time taking Kellan with it. His body slammed hard into the rails.

"Kellan!" I screeched, but I doubted anyone could hear me over the roar of the storm.

I took a deep breath and quickly shoved my arm out and reached for the sail, shocking myself that I grabbed it on the first try. I pulled the sail into me and realized there was nothing left worth salvaging. After all of that, the sail had been completely destroyed in the wind. I screamed into the thundering clouds above out of frustration and fear. We were all going to die.

I saw below that Kellan was now stuck under the weight of the barrels that I had untied to steal the rope, angrily trying to wrestle his way out from under them. Oops.

My hands shook with nerves as I tied one end of said rope, that was still hanging on my shoulder, to the mast of the ship and the other end around my waist.

"You can do this," I whispered to myself, as my hair painfully whipped at my face.

Without another thought, I leaped out into the air, desperately clinging to the rope that was now swinging me over the entire ship while I was pelted by the rain.

Time froze as I swung midair, and if it wasn't for our impending doom, this would actually be kind of fun.

Surprisingly, I landed on steady feet as I untied the rope from my waist and ran toward Kellan.

I shoved a barrel off of him, as he was choking on seawater.

I reached for his hand and forced him up. "You need to get up! We need to take cover."

He gripped my wrist tightly enough to cause discomfort and pulled me down closer to him. "And go where, exactly?!"

Kellan looked out, and his eyes grew larger than I had ever seen. I followed his gaze to see a massive cluster of jagged rocks protruding from the water's surface, and the ship was headed straight for it.

He let out a loud, wicked laugh as he threw his head back. "I never thought that this would be how it would end," he said, as he connected his lips with mine in farewell. "Hold your breath, Lia," he whispered on my mouth.

My breaths became quick and shallow as fear completely took over me. I pushed away from him when I remembered that the last thing I said to the commander was that the ship would be fine. This was *anything* but fine. I took off into a sprint and made my way to the stairs, carefully running down the steps as seawater poured over them. I distantly heard Kellan shout at me from where he remained, but I was panicking too much to decipher what he said. I made a quick right turn, and glanced down the second set of stairs that led to the cells, where there was already at least three feet of seawater down there.

"Shit."

I jumped down them, and the water instantly filled my boots.

"Are you alive?!" I shouted into the room.

"Nothing is going to happen to the ship, huh, Solus?! I think the fuck not." I heard from the cell.

Rude. How was I supposed to know this was going to happen? I waded through the water. "Where are the keys so I can let you out?!"

"*You're* asking *me* that?!" he yelled.

Good point.

"Sorry," I muttered too low for him to hear, as I searched the walls for a set of keys.

I bent down and began to feel around on the floor in case they had fallen, but it was useless.

"I can't find the keys," I choked out, as he stared at me with a hint of fear in his eyes.

He pushed on the bars as if they would budge.

"Wait a minute, hold on!" I ran up the stairs, pushing through the force of the water that continued to pour down them.

I found a bench in the kitchen and forcefully kicked it back down the stairs, making a large splash as it landed.

"What are you doing?!" he howled.

I picked up the bench, flipped it upside down, and stuck its legs between the horizontal bars across the cell door. "Saving your life!"

I jumped up and put all of my weight on the bench, forcing the bars up and popping the door off its hinges. I then ripped the bench away, taking the door with it.

He stared at me for a moment, a single brow raised with his jaw slightly dropped open. "...Impressive, Solus."

"Thanks," I said reluctantly.

The ship rocked again, and my body slammed into his. We instantly both straightened at the contact, but still held each other for balance.

"Why are you doing this?" he asked, panting.

I looked up into his hazel eyes that I didn't want to admit took my breath away, but before I could respond, a thunderous crash halted the ship.

The rocks.

It happened so fast.

The boards from the wall of the ship crashed in behind him, sending gallons of water rushing through the now gaping hole.

I screamed as the water slammed into me and sent my body crashing into the opposite, back wall. Excruciating pain radiated through me upon its impact.

I sucked in the last deep breath I was able to as I began frantically swimming towards the stairs to climb up them completely underwater. The water was so dark, I couldn't see anything around me, including the commander, and had to rely on feeling my way up the ship.

I grabbed onto something that resembled flesh, and when I pulled it closer to me, I noticed it was a lifeless body floating in the water.

I let out a screech, wasting too much of the precious breath I took down in the cells. I started panicking and kicked off of a hard surface beneath me and swam up as fast as I could, kicking and wading through the strong current.

My lungs felt as if they were about to burst when my head finally broke free above the sea. I still could barely see anything aside from waves as they rose and crashed all around me, sending me with them.

Pieces of the ship were scattered in the water surrounding me.

"Kellan!" I screamed, and salty water poured down my throat.

Coughing uncontrollably, I could already feel I was losing my strength from treading and keeping my head above the rough waves.

I turned around in circles, desperately searching my surroundings and tried again, "*KELLAN!*"

I couldn't hear anyone or anything aside from the storm. Tears of horror streamed down my cheeks.

The seawater ripped me out into the current and sent my body spiraling and swishing around beneath the waves.

I forced my head to break the surface once more, right before I noticed the rocks the ship had hit appear directly in front of me right as another wave sent me hurtling into them.

I felt pressure first, and then intense, shooting agony throughout my entire body.

And then my vision went black.

TWENTY-TWO

Elianna

Sparrows. I could hear the distant song of the birds surrounding me. It sounded peaceful, like I was swept off into a dreamland. The next sense that returned was smell. The scent of pine enveloped me. I never thought the afterlife would smell of pine, but I also didn't believe birds would exist here, though I guess it made sense that they did. The afterlife had always been spoken of as being serene, and anything that particular soul desired it most to be. Suddenly, the feeling of excruciating pain rattled through my skull, forcing me to realize that wherever I was, certainly wasn't where I originally assumed.

I slowly creaked my eyes open, and was instantly blinded by the light that shone down on me, rattling the aching in my head even further. I cautiously blinked through the blurriness of my vision, and as it cleared, I saw the tops of trees swaying high above me. As my sight returned fully, a forest of lush greens presented itself. The ray of sunlight that had initially blinded me was peering down through the leafy canopy of the woods' trees. This place was beautiful.

As I straightened my back, a tight pressure dug into my chest. I looked down to see a rope tightly wrapped around me, securing me to the trunk of a willow tree.

"What the?" I whispered to myself, as I went for my dagger with my hands that were also bound tightly as they rested on my lap. Upon reaching for the sheath, a void met my touch, and a surge of emotions engulfed me as realization dawned that my dagger had vanished.

"Shit," I hissed, as I rolled my neck, cracking the stiffness in my joints.

"Looking for something?" A taunting voice called in the distance.

My head snapped up at the sound. "Who are you?" I demanded. "Release me at once."

A faint chuckle sounded. "Yeah, I don't think so, Solus."

My eyes widened. The commander. That didn't make sense. What the hell could have happened?

"You've had your fun, Commander. Now show yourself!" I snapped.

"You hit your head that hard, huh? Well, good, now you know how it feels. I was knocked unconscious twice, thanks to you."

I blinked repeatedly and peered around myself, confused. I saw a figure hidden by the shadows of the willow vines about fifty feet in front of me, leaning against a large boulder.

I huffed out a sharp laugh while trying to wiggle free from the ropes. "You clearly hit *your* head harder than I thought because what *I* recall is that you slammed your own head off a rock, and then Kellan is the one who knocked you out the second time. I had nothing to do with that."

"Kellan? Is that the sea captain's first name?" He paused for a moment. "Or should I say, is that your *lover's* name?" Mockery filled his tone.

I bit the inside of my cheeks so hard that I could taste iron in my mouth. "That is *none* of your concern. Now untie me!" I demanded, as I twisted in frustration, trying to loosen the ropes.

"Absolutely not."

"Why!?"

"...Did you untie me as I was forced to watch the remaining members of my men slaughtered?"

I flinched as an ache settled in my throat. "I am so sorry. They surrendered. I was told that we–"

"I don't want your fake apologies. However, things have clearly changed." He straightened his stance and walked toward me. "You are my prisoner now, and we are to head back toward Silcrowe, and then Ellecaster from there."

"Silcrowe? As in the city of ruins?" I raised a brow.

He sighed. "That is what we have renamed the entirety of our lands. The *human* lands. Ellecaster is essentially the headquarter city that stands at the foot of the Ezranian Mountains...where Silcrowe once was."

This was annoying.

"Well, *thank you* for telling me the secrets of your race, Commander," I hissed mockingly. "And what exactly do you plan to do with me once we get there?"

"After we get the necessary information from you, I assume, kill you." He shrugged. "Which is why the knowledge you hold of us won't matter."

I laughed. "Well, that is...rude. I appreciate the honesty, though."

He knelt down before me and held the tip of my own dagger to my throat. "It is what you planned to do with me, is it not?"

He got me there. "I suppose." I gave him a sweet smile as I tried to move my flesh away from the surface of the blade.

When he said nothing, I continued, "So where are we? What even happened?"

"Well, the ship was destroyed out at sea."

"Obviously," I said through my teeth.

"You and I washed up on shore close to each other. I believe we are a few miles north of Ceto Bay."

"North?! We were headed south..."

"I am aware of where Isla is. The storm was intense, and we were pushed very far by the waves, clearly."

How the hell did I not drown?

"Were there any other survivors?" I asked nervously.

"None that I saw, but they could have washed up anywhere."

I eyed him as he stuck my dagger into his boot. Brows furrowing, I said, "Now, tell me again how I ended up in a forest tied to a willow tree."

"I am sure you could guess yourself... I simply dragged your body, so we wouldn't be seen by any scouts possibly looking for you at sea and then obviously tied you to the tree using some rope that washed up with other debris."

Did everyone else really meet their fate at sea? Yet somehow the human had survived? Was Kellan dead, or had he washed up on another shore? I had so many questions and none of them would be answered while I was tied to this damn willow.

"How long have we been here?" I asked.

He looked to the sky. "The sun seems to be setting through the trees, so about twelve hours. We will camp here for the night and begin our journey to Ellecaster tomorrow morning at dawn."

Wait a minute. The forest that is beyond Ceto Bay is...Oh gods.

"You said we are north of Ceto Bay?"

"Correct," he said, as he started kindling a fire for warmth.

I looked around frantically. "Are you aware of what woods these are?" I whisper shouted.

He looked up at me then, his features looked as if they were made of stone. "The Sylis Forest." He then went back to kindling.

"I don't know if you humans are aware of what lies in Sylis Forest, but—"

He chuckled. "Surely, you don't believe in the stories you were told as a child, Solus."

"I have a first name, you know!" I didn't even want to give it to him, but anything would be better than being called by my given surname.

"I don't care." He didn't even look up at me.

I was about to lose what little patience I had left. "They are not just stories, and you are a fool to think so. The forest itself is said to come alive if it wishes! This willow..." I glanced up to the tallest branches. "Beautiful as it may be, could strangle us in our sleep with its vines if it decided to." I could have sworn the wispy vines danced around my face in acknowledgement as I finished my sentence.

I looked back over at him and realized that he still wasn't listening to me. "There are trolls, centaurs...wyverns!" I shouted.

His head snapped up then. "*Wyverns?* Are you mad? Those have not existed in centuries, and even then I doubt they ever had to begin with."

"I have seen one."

He looked amused at my panic. "In the forest?" He raised a brow with a smirk.

"In the castle back in Isla. It was stolen as a...actually, never mind." I said too much.

He continued to stare at me, amusingly. "Sure, Solus. You have a wyvern living with your precious tyrant of a king."

I shoved my body against the ropes so hard that for a moment I thought they might snap, freeing me. I wished they had, because then I could strangle the life out of this pathetic mortal. "Don't you *ever* say a word about my king."

"Struck a nerve, did I?" He grinned.

I hesitated for a moment before I softly said, "The king is not like that."

He stood over me then, his face only a breath's width from my own. "Your lies are like a siren's song, Solus. They roll off your tongue so sweetly, beautifully. Almost enough to convince me," he said in a low, alluring tone.

I bared my teeth at him as he turned to grab a fallen branch about the height of his waist and sat back down on the boulder. He pulled out my dagger once more to carve the tip of the branch into a point.

"What are you doing with my dagger?"

He let out a loud sigh. "You're a smart girl. I'm sure you understand that since this is the only weapon I currently have, I will need to create more. Mainly for hunting."

As he said that, my stomach growled. "I didn't realize that was all we had."

"We?" he laughed, "No, that is all that *I* have. You will not have a weapon."

"I am great with a weapon," I answered with a manipulative smile.

His eyes met mine. "I am aware," he grumbled, gesturing to his calf.

My eyes narrowed in on his leg. "Wait a second! How are you walking around on that leg? Humans don't heal quickly like that. At least, that is what is mentioned in our texts regarding your race."

"Texts?" he questioned, raising a brow. "Well, as you said earlier, the sea captain's relationship with you is none of my concern. I will say that the rate my body can heal is none of yours."

I watched him closely. Was he a halfling? Did those still exist? Any halfling that was known of back in Isla had been executed at the queen's command when I was just a babe. She convinced the citizens that halflings would be more likely to be mortal sympathizers and the risk couldn't be taken. It was barbaric. My father didn't even know of the act until it had been completed.

I looked at his ears—they weren't pointed like mine, but that didn't mean anything. Halflings often carried distinct traits from both the fae and human parent, making it hard to tell if they were of either race or just of whichever one they looked more prominently like.

"Very well, then," I said.

"I am going to find food. Stay put." He pointed to me with the spear he made.

I rolled my eyes. "You tied me to a tree. Where the hell would I go?"

He turned from me and walked deeper into the forest. I watched as his shoulders rose and fell quickly, caused by what I could only assume to be a chuckle.

I needed to find a way to get my dagger back and free myself so I could return to Isla.

TWENTY-THREE

Kellan

I COULD FEEL THE gritted sand between my teeth as I clenched my jaw. I opened my eyes, blinded by the sun peering down on my face. The sand was sticking between every crevice of my body. Sitting up, my body groaned as I looked around to see I was lying on a beach, the sound of crashing waves and screeching gulls filled the surrounding air, while my skin roasted in the blistering sun.

I glanced around and saw a few bodies of my sailors spread out along the coast. Debris from the ship still floated and scattered in the seawater.

Sighing, I called out, "Pulse check! Any of you fucks alive?"

Multiple hands went in the air as they all groaned and pulled themselves up. I counted eleven.

Not great, but could have been a much worse loss for a crew of thirty-two, including myself and Lia...Oh, shit.

I stood on wobbly feet too fast and made my way through the sand. Storming around, I violently tossed aside any large piece of debris I could find, searching for any sign of Lia underneath.

"Fuck," I whispered.

I looked down the beach to see Vin up on his feet and headed toward me as I continued to search.

"What is the damage, Captain?" he asked hesitantly, as he arrived.

Still glancing down the beach, I said, "I counted eleven alive so far, but no sign of Elianna."

He let out a quick chuckle as I whipped my head to him. "I'm sorry. Is something funny?" My head tilted to the side in question as I shoved at his chest so hard it forced his body to the ground.

Nervously, he leaned up on his elbows and waved to all of our surroundings. "Captain, look around! She most likely did not survive. It's a miracle we did."

I leaned down and punched him in the face, breaking his nearly healed nose once more. "She is alive, you idiot. I know it."

He stood up, wincing as he clutched his nose, catching the drips of blood that fell, and followed me as I walked down to the water's edge.

Gazing out, he said, "Don't tell me after all this time you believe she is your mate or some shit. You're acting like you actually care."

"No, she is not my mate. I just know she's alive. And we must find her before she makes her way back to Isla. If that bitch is one thing, it's persistent. She won't go out by drowning at sea."

He looked at me confused. "It's not exactly like she would have a choice in such a death, Captain. But I don't understand. Would you not want her to get back to Isla?"

I growled. "You don't know her like I do." I pointed to my chest as my lip curled back in a snarl. "She is onto us. She questioned me about you being the one to slit the humans' throats. I did my best to convince her why it was you and said you were trying to prove yourself, but she didn't believe it. She doesn't trust any of my sailors, and now I know she doesn't trust me, either."

I was an idiot lost in a fit of rage when I had Vin act on slaughtering the humans, I should've known she would've caught on. I would've been better off doing it myself.

"So?" he asked.

"So?...She is favored by the king, for only the gods know what reason. Her precious little Lukas has been searching for a way to relieve me as captain since I took the position decades ago. If she can convince them that I am not fit, everything we have worked for will be for nothing."

He continued to watch the waves as they rolled in. "Callius?"

"His protection only goes so far. However, if she does not return, then I not only command the sea but the land armies as well."

Callius had taken me under his wing when I was just a boy. My father was a pirate, one of the most well known in all of the Vayr Sea, and when he was finally detained and executed, it was by the crown. Since I was so young, they allowed me exemption from the noose as long as I proved myself to be an outstanding citizen and that my father's vicious mindset hadn't poisoned me. So that's what I did. I weaseled my trust into Callius and other commanding officers, proving myself time and time again until I climbed the ranks to become captain.

The truth was, I really wasn't anything like my father. I was smarter, more cunning and *patient*. He wanted all the riches of the world instantly. I knew that in order to achieve such, you had to play the long game. And that's exactly what I've been doing ever since.

He grinned. "You weren't looking for her to be alive. You were looking for a body."

"I was looking for her body, dead *or* alive."

"Were you planning on killing her on the ship, or if you found her here?"

I contemplated for a moment. "No, I would've had time to convince her that I can be trusted. Both claiming wise and commanding our armies. That's still the plan if she is found. We just must find her before she makes it back to Isla."

"Why would you even want to keep her alive at this point? She is nothing but a pain in our asses. And as you stated...in our way."

"Because you fool, if I appear to be close to her, and make my way into the trust of the king, and his heir, then we have our ticket in. Our influence on Velyra will then be unstoppable. We can bring back the position of The King's Lord once Prince Kai ascends the throne."

The position of The King's Lord had been lost in Velyra since King Jameson was crowned. He wanted no one else, trusted no one else, aside from Sir Lukas Salvinae, but Lukas refused the position like an absolute fool. He didn't desire power—he wanted to protect people. It was all so fucking pathetic.

Me though? I wouldn't take that lightly. Not only would I have full control of the kingdom's armies, but I would also have the influence to place laws on its citizens, and guide the king in whichever direction I deemed fit. Obtaining the role would be crucial to fulfilling what I desired most—extensive power and influence over the realm.

The corner of his lip twitched upward. "And if the sea took her life? We would have no way of knowing, Captain," Vin stated.

I gazed out into the unforgiving waters. He had a point, and she could be anywhere if she was still alive.

"Tell you what..." I gripped his shoulder. "We bring the survivors back to Isla, and we wait it out there. We keep guards stationed at every entrance post and gate within the city. If they see her, they report back to us immediately and we intercept her before she has time to meet with the king or Salvinae."

"Brilliant, and that way we are not out wasting time searching when she could be anywhere in Velyra."

"Exactly," I said to him.

Turning around, I faced my remaining crew. "We have a long road ahead of us. Let's go home."

TWENTY-FOUR

Jace

MY EYES OPENED as the sun's hues peeked through the canopy of the trees. The time had come to wake Solus up and make our way to Ellecaster. I didn't know what to expect, but what I did know was that this was *not* going to be easy. She would fight me every step of the way and make everything extremely difficult.

I saved her life, and now I had to pay the price of dealing with her.

I had not once been out at sea when such a storm hit. Never in my life did I think it would be possible to survive such an incident.

When the ship hit the rocks, and the seawater flooded the cells, I could barely see as Solus kicked off a wall and swam her way up the stairs of the ship. I followed her the best I could, but the force of the water pulling me down made it nearly impossible. By the time my head broke the surface, the ship was shattered into many pieces. I grabbed hold of a piece that seemed like it had once been part of a door and held on for dear life.

As I was riding out the storm, frantically looking around as I did my best to tread the waves as they crashed into me, I watched as Solus' body slammed into the cluster of rocks that caused the ship to wreck. I watched nervously, waiting for her to resurface...but she never did.

Cursing myself, I paddled as close as the waves would allow and dove beneath the water, searching for her. After having to come back up for breath three times, I was about to give up when I found her unconscious, with her foot stuck between a crevice in the rocks. I was losing the breath I had taken when I finally wiggled her foot loose and brought her head up above the water. I could barely keep us both afloat as I held onto her body when I luckily found a piece of debris floating amongst the waves that was large enough for the two of us. Once I was situated and found my balance, I pulled her body next to mine.

I held onto the makeshift raft for both of us as we rode out the storm. She was still out cold by the time I was able to paddle our way to a shore using nothing but my arms. I checked her pulse multiple times. I had no idea what to do with her.

I contemplated just killing her outright, but that didn't feel right since she opened the cell door to try to help me as the ship hit the rocks. She was also the only one who was willing to assist with the arrow...that she shot at me, but still. Then I thought of the fact that she commanded the enemy fleets. That could be useful.

Now here we were. Two enemy leaders stuck in the middle of a supposedly enchanted forest together.

I lightly tapped her leg with my boot. "Solus, wake up. It's past dawn and we need to get moving."

She didn't budge.

I moved to wake her again when she quickly lifted her bound legs and forcefully swung them under my feet, causing me to fall right on my ass. I looked up to see her stretching as far as the rope would let her, reaching for her dagger that was in my boot. I used that foot to kick dirt up in her face as I went to stand.

"Are you out of your fucking mind?!" I yelled.

She swung her legs out again. Apparently, she was.

"That dagger is *mine*," she seethed, out of breath.

I grabbed the hair on top of her head, and pulled her face to look up at mine. "Listen! You are not getting your weapon back. We need to get moving, and I need to trust that if I untie you from the tree and remove the bind from your feet, you will not attack me or run. Honestly, I'm not in the mood to deal with either." I released her hair.

She snickered. "It's adorable that you think I'm going to make this easy for you."

I dusted the dirt off of my pants. "Fine, I will leave you tied here to the tree as troll food."

Her eyes widened in panic and I turned around to move further into the woods.

"That isn't funny, Commander!" she called to me.

I turned my head back to her as I kept walking. "Who's laughing? Certainly not me. I don't even believe that the creatures you fear live within these trees exist anymore, but in case they do, hopefully they will take this lovely offering that I've left them and leave me alone."

I could hear her struggling to break free from the bonds.

"Fine!" she yelled out in a pout.

I stopped in my tracks and completely turned around to face her. "Fine, what?" I crossed my arms.

She huffed out a breath of frustration. "Fine, I will not try to harm you or run off."

"I don't believe that for even a second, Solus."

"Then what is the point of this?!"

I walked to her, removed the dagger from my boot, and cut the rope that held her to the willow tree. "I'm choosing to trust you here, which I will most likely regret within the next hour."

"Try twenty minutes," she mocked.

I tried to hide the fact that my lips faintly turned upwards into a smile. Why did my body try to react that way when she was being difficult and annoying? The last thing I needed her thinking was that I found her amusing.

I cut the binding on her feet and grabbed her arm to pull her up.

"What about my hands?" she asked.

I cocked a brow. "If roles were reversed, would you untie mine?" I watched her as she eyed me, replacing the dagger in my boot.

She looked up into the trees, ignoring my question. "How far are we from Ellecaster?"

"Difficult to say." I reached for the multiple spears I made the night before and tied them to my side. "I'm not sure where we are right now but by foot, I would say at least a two-week journey."

"Well, we better get moving then, huh?" she declared, as she stormed off in the wrong direction.

"Solus." She ignored me. "Ignore me all you want but judging by the moss on the tree next to you, you are headed south, not north."

"You're catching onto things, huh?" she sassed.

I ran to catch up to her. "What happened to not running away? You are delirious if you think I will let you just waltz out of here and back to Isla."

"Last I checked, you were about to leave me as troll food, so I don't know why it would matter if I went with you or not."

She was infuriating.

"I don't care how skilled you are in combat. With no weapon, and your hands bound, you won't last a week in the forest."

She stopped in her tracks and turned around. Storming past me and now headed north, she said, "Fine, I suppose dying with dignity to protect the secrets of my kingdom is better than being eaten by some beast among the wood."

I stood there speechless for a moment. I had nothing to say to that because she was right. Eventually, she would be put to death, and she knew that. The only reason she hadn't yet was because she held vital information that could help me win this war and free the mortals of the realm.

I watched her while she tried to find her balance with her hands bound as she climbed over the large roots that covered the forest floor.

Without another word said between us, I slowly moved to follow.

TWENTY-FIVE

Finnian

IT'D BEEN ALMOST TWO weeks since Lia left and everything had been falling apart since. I had barely been able to see Landon because I constantly felt as if I had eyes on me. The only times we interacted were when Avery was with me, but I assumed that she was also catching on. I could only make so many excuses to go visit the stables.

The king was getting worse as the days passed. He wasn't even able to make his way down to dinner the past three nights. Avery and I had grown very concerned, while Kai just seemed indifferent to the entire situation. He was probably thrilled, thinking he would get to ascend the throne sooner than expected.

I just hope our father survived long enough to see Lia when she returned. She cared for him so deeply, and I knew she would be devastated if his soul passed on without getting the chance to say goodbye. I imagine she viewed him as a father figure since he took her in against the queen's wishes when she was orphaned.

Our mother hadn't been seen much around the castle. Rumor claimed she was distraught regarding the state of the king, which made no sense to me. My entire life, I barely saw the two of them together. It was as if she hated him, and I wasn't entirely sure why that would be. The king was loved by all, always doing what he could for his kingdom. He also allowed my mother to continue on in this war. All over a grudge she held.

Tensions were running high between Callius and Lukas. The two constantly lurked about and followed each other. The most trusted guards of the crown had always been at odds, but since Lia left, it had been felt much more intensely. Two nights ago, I thought they were going to get into an all-out brawl in the east courtyard over something that Callius whispered to Lukas as he passed by.

I never liked that male.

Sitting out in the blooming gardens with Avery as she read her book, I scratched Nyra's ear as a deep growl grew in her chest.

I glanced up at Avery. She also seemed nervous by the noise Nyra was making. She never growled at us, only–

Kai stepped out from behind the pillars with five of his minions that belonged to The Lords of Isla. If you asked me or Avery, those Lords were just as corrupt as Kai. Avery rolled her eyes as she stuck her nose back into her book.

Nyra was then on her feet, her lips curled back, showing her sharp canines. Her eyes fixed on the group as they approached us.

"I think it is about time this vicious mutt gets put down, wouldn't you agree?" Kai spat at us, as the group behind him burst into laughter.

Avery met his stare. "The only thing out in the garden that is vicious is *you*, Kai."

My jaw dropped. That line was something straight out of Lia's mouth. I was jealous she had been brave enough to say that. That was until I peeked up and saw the look on Kai's face.

"I can't wait until Mother sells you off to the highest bidder, *sister*," he snapped at her.

Avery's bottom lip trembled slightly, and for a brief moment I thought she was going to lose her shit on him. Instead, she slammed her book shut and dramatically stormed out of the garden, Nyra followed closely behind after she tried to snap at Kai's ankle.

Kai turned back to the Lords and they started talking amongst themselves, making fun of Avery.

I rose to stand quietly to make my way out of the gardens when I heard Kai speak. "Where are you going, Finnian?" I stopped in my tracks. "Surely not to run after our dearest sister?"

I reluctantly turned to face him, and nervously cupped the back of my neck. "Was just going to head back up to my chambers, Kai."

"Nonsense, come with us. It has been too long since we had our fun together." The look in his eye made me feel as if I didn't have a choice, so I reluctantly walked back over to him and the Lords.

In unison, they all started to stroll toward the stables. My stomach dropped. What did they want to do in the stables?

"Wh-why are we heading to the stables?" I stuttered out.

Kai's steps didn't falter, his hand glided over the roses on the garden's bushes, ripping them out as he passed. Without looking back, he replied, "Just showing my friends around the castle grounds."

That didn't make sense. These assholes were always wandering around here with him, taunting the staff and Ladies of Isla.

He shoved the barn doors open, startling the horses inside.

My stare locked with Landon's from across the room. Both of our eyes went wide. We instantly knew nothing good was going to come from this.

"Stable Keeper, you are dismissed," Kai said to no one directly, but he was referring to Landon.

My eyes pleaded with Landon to make him obey, but his jaw locked as he slowly shook his head at me.

"I am sorry, Prince Kai, but I cannot do that. I cannot leave the stables unattended until I am relieved of duty by the next keeper coming in for their shift."

I closed my eyes tightly, knowing how well that was going to go over with Kai. All the Lords let out wicked chuckles.

Kai's head cocked to the side curiously as he took a step in Landon's direction. "You dare disobey your prince?"

"It is not a matter of disobeying, Prince Kai, but a matter of duty that I have made promises to keep," Landon answered proudly.

"Do you think I am here to harm the horses?" Kai asked mockingly.

Landon's eyes peeked up at me, and then back to the prince who was now in his face.

Kai glanced back at me for a moment, eyes charged with realization. While the act of Landon looking to me was brief and small...he noticed.

"Of course not, Prince."

Kai's focus narrowed in on him. "Excellent, because that would be a very foolish thought to admit." He paused for a moment. "Now tell me...which horse belongs to the lovely, and ever so disrespectful, Elianna Solus?"

I quickly shook my head at Landon. If Kai harmed Lia's horse, she would kill him.

Landon's lips parted and closed quickly over and over. "I am not sure, Prince."

Kai promptly backhanded Landon across the face hard enough to send him to the ground. The sound of flesh on flesh echoed through the stable.

I audibly gasped, catching everyone's attention.

Kai's left eye twitched as he stared me down. He pushed his fingers through the tangles of his black curls. "Let's try again, shall we?" he said, as Landon slowly got to his feet, using the stable wall as support. "Which horse is Elianna's?"

Landon raised a shaking hand and pointed to Matthias.

Kai walked over and opened Matthias's pen gate. He slowly circled the horse, making him uneasy. "No Velyran brand marks this horse. Why is that?"

"Ca-captain Solus doesn't believe in brands. She doesn't want any physical harm to come to her horse. Th-the king respected her wishes."

Kai sucked on his tooth as he stared at the warhorse. "Well, that just won't do," he said, as he stormed away and reached for the branding iron with the Valderre Crest that hung on the wall across from Matthias' pen.

Landon stepped forward. "Don't!" he screeched.

Kai whistled and gestured to Landon using his chin. Two of the Lords moved next to him and secured him by his arms to keep him in place.

"Kai, don't do this," I whispered.

"Shut the fuck up, Finn!" he snapped, nostrils flaring as he pointed the iron in my direction.

Like the coward I was, I did as he said.

Kai stuck the branding iron into the small fire that was roaring next to the stable door. He smiled back at us. He was actually *enjoying* this.

Once the brand was hot, he walked back over to Matthias, and without hesitating, he stuck it into the horse's side and held it there for far too long. The horse thrashed and loudly neighed, the sound ending in a whimper of pain while stuck in his pen.

"NO!" Landon and I yelled in unison.

Kai released his grip, and when he removed the iron from Matthias, his skin was sizzling.

My head instantly sagged between my shoulders. "Alright Kai, you had your fun," I said, as I let out a breath. "Now let Landon go."

My eyes flew wide open and my lips parted in fear from the information I had just realized that I had accidentally given out. To the one person who could never know the truth.

Landon straightened—he knew too.

Kai pointed the iron brand in Landon's direction. "Ah, so the stable keeper has a name? Interesting that my brother knows it so well." He looked back to me. "You may release him, Lords."

The two males let go of Landon's arms at the same time. Landon straightened his shirt as he stood tall.

"I don't want any trouble, Prince. I am just trying to do my job," he said, voice steady.

With eyes locked on each other, Kai took a quick step toward him again, and tauntingly said, "Me? Trouble? Never."

It happened so fast.

Kai shot forward and pressed the blazing hot iron into Landon's chest.

I went running toward them as I shouted for Kai to stop, but the Lords stepped in front of me, blocking my way, and held me back as Landon screamed in agony.

Kai's lips tilted up as he then pressed the iron so hard into Landon's chest that he was pushing his body against the stable's wall.

After what seemed like endless minutes of torture, Kai eventually whipped the branding iron behind him, making me and another Lord dodge out of the way from it's path. Landon dropped to the ground as his wound was sizzling and bleeding as intensely as Matthias' had, maybe even worse.

Kai bent down and grabbed his face with one hand, pulling him up as close as possible. "If I find out you send for one of those traitorous little hidden healers, I will personally come back and kill you myself."

He then spit on Landon's face and threw him back to the ground. I flinched as his body hit the floor with a loud thud.

I was going to be sick. I was paralyzed where I stood in disbelief. I couldn't believe that just happened.

Kai twisted his neck side to side until it cracked, and then marched past me, grabbing my arm as he dragged me out of the stable with him and the others.

Landon refused to look up at me as I was forced to leave.

TWENTY-SIX

Elianna

IF THE COMMANDER THOUGHT I was going to make this journey easy for him, he had another thing coming. Why did I have to wash up on the same shore as him? Better yet, how did he wake before I did? Ugh, I couldn't remember anything after I caught a quick glimpse of the rocks that the storm's wave sent me flying into.

Things would be quite different if I had woken up before he had. *He* would be the prisoner, as he originally had been, and we would be headed south to Isla, instead of north.

I had never heard of Ellecaster. I assumed it made sense that the humans would give names to their lands beyond the Sylis Forest.

How had he never heard of the legends that called these woods their home? He laughed at me as if I were a child repeating a scary story our parents told to encourage good behavior.

I guess, in a way, I was doing just that. However, I knew the legends weren't myths at all. They were real, and Nox was proof of that.

Callius had found the wyvern's egg within these very trees. There's no telling how many other creatures there were, and they could be hiding in plain sight at this moment, watching us.

With my hands still bound, stepping over the roots protruding from the forest floor had been my own version of hell.

The commander wished to kill me once I told him and the remaining humans the secrets of the Velyran Crown. He expected me to break, but I would gladly die with those secrets if they would keep the king and my other loved ones safe.

The king. I wish I could send a falcon message to Isla to let him know I was okay, Lukas, as well. With my father's health still declining, I was terrified that my longer-than-expected absence would worry him further and cause his sickness to worsen.

We had been walking through the Sylis Forest for hours now and we had not spoken a word to each other since we left the willow tree. The only sounds aside from our footsteps were that of the buzzing insects, and the wind as it rustled through the treetops. I was walking several paces behind him, but he kept looking over his shoulder to make sure I was still following and not trying to run off again.

For a fifth time.

I took a deep breath. "So, are you going to tell me your name now?" I asked.

"Nope."

"Why not?"

"Because names aren't necessary for this situation, Solus, and the less talking you do, the smaller my headache will be."

So. Rude.

I stormed up to his back and kicked a small rock at his leg, almost losing my balance in the process. "See, that is the thing, though! You know part of my name, and you keep saying it as if it holds power here. I hate to break it to you, *Commander*, but it doesn't."

He whipped around, his face not even two inches from mine. "How about you ask the names of my men that you slaughtered?" He smiled, but the look in his eyes promised death. "The men that your precious *Kellan* had ordered to be executed and left in the sand. Their bodies are likely still lying there, and being picked apart by the gulls as we speak."

My mouth kept opening and closing, but words refused to come out.

He grimaced. "I didn't think so."

He turned around and continued through the trees.

I huffed out a breath and ran past him, stopping right in front of him. He looked down at me with his gold specked hazel eyes.

"I truly am sorry," I said softly. "That was not my call. Kellan and I had agreed to take any who surrendered back to Isla."

"Yeah, you said that already, but that didn't happen. Regardless, they would've been executed in Isla anyway." His voice then rose, "And for what crimes exactly, Solus? For fighting back? For trying to fight for a future of their race that you and yours are so set on destroying? To fight for their children and grandchildren?...Those men deserved to be buried or burned. Their souls will never know peace now because of you." He shouldered past me and sat on a large root next to an enormous pine tree.

"You're right," I breathed.

He chuckled maliciously. "Don't try to save face now."

"I am doing no such thing." I strolled up to him and sat down a few feet away on the ground. "I don't expect you to believe me, but I have been begging the queen to end this war for decades. She carries nothing but hate in her heart for your kind because mortals murdered her father and brother." I sighed.

"And how many fathers and brothers have been killed for her revenge?"

I snickered. "I have spoken those same words to her many times, and all it has done is threaten my rank. There have been whispers of me being a sympathizer, but luckily the king demands I stay in this position, and that is why I am still here."

He eyed me from where he sat. "Do not sit here and tell me the king does not want this war."

"Would you even believe me if I told you he doesn't?"

"Honestly, no."

"Then I won't waste my breath." I picked up a stick that lay on the ground beside me and awkwardly attempted to draw circles in the dirt with my bound hands.

Neither of us spoke for several minutes. All that could be heard was the birds calling to each other throughout the treetops.

"So you will die for the secrets of a queen you do not respect?" he asked, as he looked over at me.

"No." I paused and my stare slowly rose to meet his. "But I will gladly die protecting the few individuals that I do."

He quickly looked away from me as he clenched his jaw. "I can respect that, Solus."

"Elianna."

"What?" he asked, brows furrowing.

"That is my name. It is Elianna." I rose to stand. "My friends call me Lia, but well...you're not my friend. So Elianna will do." I gave him a wink as I waltzed past him and continued onto our path.

He stood and followed me. "My name is Jace," he revealed with a sigh, as if he accepted defeat in his own exhausting game of hatred for me.

"I don't care," I mimicked his words from hours earlier with the smallest tone of teasing in my voice.

I heard his footsteps falter for a brief moment before his pace picked back up.

I could've sworn I heard a whisper of a chuckle.

We walked until dusk had fallen and found an open area among the wood to camp. Not that we had any supplies to make camp with.

"Are you sure it's wise for us to be just...out in the open like this?" I asked, glancing around into the trees.

I thought I heard something move behind me and I jumped, whipping around in that direction.

"Are we really back to this?" he judged.

"Well, *this* never really went away. It is just easier to sense or see things in the daylight."

He threw a bunch of small branches down and began to kindle a fire. "Are you mad?!" I whisper shouted at him, as I stormed over to where he knelt. "A fire will attract all the beasts!"

I went to kick dirt at the fire but he instantly caught my ankle with his hand and looked up at me unimpressed. "How else are we supposed to cook the rabbits I caught earlier? We need to eat. Or I do anyway. I don't really care if you do."

I ripped my ankle from his grasp. "Charming." I continued to glance around our area. "Fine, but we need to put the fire out once it's completely dark."

"Gods." He rolled his eyes. "We will freeze."

"That is better than being eaten!"

He turned his attention back to the fire and worked on skinning the rabbits.

Once we ate, I kicked over as much dirt as I could and then stomped out the remnants of the fire. Jace watched me from afar.

I threw my bound hands up to one side in frustration. "Thanks for the help!"

"But you were doing so well," he said sarcastically, as he picked dirt from his nails. "Didn't look like my assistance was needed."

"Are you going to untie my hands now?" I asked, as I threw them down to one side.

"Not a chance in this realm."

Jackass.

He went to lie down under a tree and when I walked over to an oak across the area, he sat back up. "What do you think you are doing?"

"...Laying down?"

"Yeah, I'm going to need you to come over here. Much closer, so I can keep an eye on you."

"Are you trying to flirt with me, Jace?" I batted my eyelashes mockingly at him.

He let out a growl of frustration. "Just trying to make sure you don't do anything stupid. Like run off. Again."

"Are we really back to *that?!*" I threw his own words back to him again. "I thought I had proven to you that I am willingly going to Ellecaster. I'm not going to try to run off...again." I then laid down on the rocky, uncomfortable ground about ten feet from him.

"Fine, but your hands stay bound." He turned his body away from mine. "Just because I trust you not to run off, doesn't mean I trust you to not try to kill me the first chance you get."

I didn't have anything to say to that, so I kept silent. The bastard was snoring within minutes.

I sighed. There was no way I would be able to get a good night's sleep out here. Not when every rustle of leaves in the distance or tiny sound elevated by my fae hearing made my body jump out of fear by what could have caused it.

I looked up at the sky that I could barely see through the thickness of the trees' branches and wished that I was back in Isla, cuddling with Avery in bed again and talking about mates. I wish I hadn't told her the truth about not believing in them. She had every right to wish for someone to love her the way she desired and deserved. I could only hope that whatever Lord she ended up marrying treated her that way.

I glanced at the commander's back. He was the reason that I would never return to Avery in Isla. Or to Nyra, or Finn and Lukas. My father.

But how many men had died by the hand of my sword or arrow? How many humans would never return home because of me? To their families, spouses, and children? Hundreds, if not thousands. And that was just by my hand alone.

My time had come and I would gladly accept that if it meant keeping them all safe. I just wish I could have gotten the chance for a proper goodbye, but I supposed nobody really received that luxury in such circumstances.

Tears blurred my vision as I slowly closed my eyes and finally fell asleep.

TWENTY-SEVEN

Jace

THE PAST FEW DAYS had been a living hell. Elianna and I barely spoke to each other, and on the rare occasion she opened her mouth, I found that I wished she wouldn't.

Tensions between the two of us were running high, and I'm sure the lack of food we had been finding was a massive contributor to that. With essentially no supplies, barely any food and only being able to sip water from the forest's streams we found along the way, I started fearing that we may have sealed our fates by journeying through Sylis Forest.

We were heading north, but not all the trees displayed moss, so I started thinking that we had ended up going in circles. We should've reached the end of the forest by now.

I've considered untying her hands for the past two days, however I still couldn't trust her. That's the thing with the fae, they could *never* be trusted. It didn't matter that I actually believed the words she spoke about her wanting the war to end—she had seen all the bloodshed and effects of it firsthand. However, I refused to believe that the king also felt that way, and that this war was solely fueled by the queen's need for vengeance.

And what did she mean by the king protecting her position? That didn't make sense at all. I found it odd that a woman, or female, was running the fae's armies, but I didn't know their customs. For all I knew, that could be normal.

Regardless, if she was favored by the king, that meant she may have even more information than a captain typically would. That could be useful, and something I would need to keep in mind once we got to Ellecaster, and it came to extracting the information from her.

"Jace, there's a stream up here!" she called from ahead.

Jogging up to her, I bent down on my knees and splashed the cool water up onto my face. We hadn't come across any water since midday yesterday.

"Drink up, Solus," I said, as she rolled her eyes at me. I hadn't called her by her first name since she told me what it was. It felt too personal.

"We don't know how long it will be until we come across water again."

I felt her eyes snap to me as I continued to sip the water. "It has been days. We have been wandering around the forest for *days*. How much farther until Ellecaster?"

I glanced in her direction and raised a brow. "I told you it could be around two weeks. In a rush to surrender the truth of your kingdom?"

She let out an abrupt gasp in anger. "You are insufferable. We are lost, aren't we? Do you not think I know we have been going in circles all day?"

Dammit.

I looked up into the trees, it appeared to be in the middle of the afternoon judging by where the sun sat in the sky above. "It appears that much of the moss has been removed from the trees," I grumbled.

She chuckled. "Yes, well, the stags do love to shed their antlers with the assistance of tree bark. Do you know nothing of nature? You have been relying solely on moss!?"

"Well, it isn't like I have a fucking compass, Solus!" I yelled in her face.

She let out an obnoxious breath and stormed away from me, climbing onto and sitting on a giant boulder across from the stream. "We're going to die out here."

"No, we aren't," I assured her.

I watched her as she fiddled with her bindings.

"Relax, it's just really...itchy," she said, as her concentration remained entirely fixed on trying to wiggle her fingers around to itch the spots on her wrists that were exposed from the rope.

As I walked around the open area in the woods, a bright violet color caught my eye within the shrubs. I strolled over to it and realized it was a bush full of vibrant berries.

My mouth instantly watered as I fell to my knees and started plucking the berries one by one into a pile on the ground.

"I wouldn't do that if I were you..." she called over to me, each word dragged out.

I half turned my body back to her, annoyed by her statement. "And why is that?"

"Honestly, the more I watch you, the more apparent it is that you have no fucking clue what you are doing out here." She paused, but I had nothing to say. I had nothing to prove to her, and I was starving. "Those are velaeno berries. They're extremely poisonous. You'll be dead within minutes," she said, as her focus returned to itching her wrists.

"Sure," I mumbled.

I went to raise a fist full of berries to my mouth when she screeched, "Are you insane?! I know we're starving, but put those damn berries down!"

"Why don't you go back to focusing on your bounds!" I snapped.

She leaped down from the rock and stormed over to me. She lightly kicked my hand, which sent the berries flying from my grasp.

"Look down," she demanded.

I was losing my temper as I reluctantly glanced down to see the leaves on the ground that I had rested the berries on were beginning to *wilt*. I quickly wiped my hand in the soil I knelt on as I felt a small sting spread across my fingertips that touched the berries.

"...What the?"

"Exactly. Believe me now, Commander?" she hissed, as she turned back on her feet and wiggled her way back up onto the rock she originally sat.

I approached her slowly. "How did you know those berries would do that?" I asked her, half expecting her to bite my head off.

She sighed. "How do you think the humans who murdered the queen's kin weakened them? They dipped the heads of their arrows in the juice from velaeno berries just like that. While not enough to kill them, it was enough to bring them down and weaken them long enough to be captured, and eventually killed. Traces of the berries were found in their wounds once their bodies were discovered by our scouts days later."

I blinked. How had information so valuable been lost over the years? Something like this could've helped us significantly in the war.

I walked back over to the stream and sat down, cupping small amounts to my mouth to help try to quench my thirst.

My ears perked up when I noticed that the forest had gone...silent. Completely quiet and still. Not a single bird chirped, nor could I hear the faint buzz of insects hovering through the air. Something felt off.

I whipped my head back to Solus to see if she felt the same. She had also gone completely still. She could tell something was wrong.

I slowly rose to my feet when my eyes wandered slightly below Solus' boot to see a giant, yellow eye wide open and staring at me.

Oh, gods.

"Solus," I whispered softly. "You need to get down from that rock. Slowly."

She looked panicked as her skin flushed, and with wide eyes she nodded her head gently.

The second she moved, the rock she sat upon began *rumbling*. Her eyes snapped back to mine as the boulder rose from the ground...but it wasn't a boulder at all. It was an enormous forest troll, camouflaged as one.

"Fuck. Elianna, jump down, *NOW!*" I shouted, as I ran toward her.

She didn't waste a single second—she jumped from the troll, tucking and rolling once she hit the ground.

I pulled her to her feet, and got in her face. "We need to run. Come on!"

She shoved away from me. "You think *we* can outrun *that?*" She pointed with her chin to the troll that was now on its feet and staring at us like we were its next meal. Breathing heavily with fury.

It was atrocious to look at. Standing at least fifteen feet tall, the gray-toned troll was covered in moss, further helping it blend in with the forest. Its teeth appeared as if they had been sharpened into points, and they were just as yellow as its enormous eyes that were fixated on us.

I was frozen where I stood. The troll then ripped a thin birch tree from its roots in the ground and hurled it toward us.

"Look out!" Elianna screeched, but I couldn't move.

She tackled me to the ground, no doubt saving my life, as the tree whipped above our bodies, taking out everything in its path.

She was on top of me, breathing roughly. "Give me my dagger."

I grabbed her arms and flipped her over, my body now on top of hers. "Absolutely not!"

She threw her bound hands around my neck and pulled my face down forcefully into her shoulder as a rock skimmed by my head, just missing me again.

She shoved me off of her then. "I just saved your useless life *twice* within minutes and you are going to deny me a weapon to defend myself against a troll?!"

"A dagger isn't going to do shit to that thing!" I ran to the spears that I placed next to a tree when we arrived at the stream not even ten minutes ago.

I handed her one, but she laughed. Picking up a rock that clearly wasn't going to do any damage, she threw both arms behind her head and heaved it directly at the troll's face.

The sound the troll let out rattled the forest floor, causing the both of us to drop our spears and cover our ears from the deafening roar.

"*There's no such thing as trolls, Solus!*" she mocked at me. "What the fuck do you call that then, huh?"

I sucked in my bottom lip, biting down in anger. "Fine! You were right, are you happy? Now, how do we kill it?"

She began running right at the damn thing. "Aim for the weak spots!"

"The weak spots?!"

She aimed and awkwardly threw the spear with her bound wrists at the troll, but it was easily dodged. "Belly or throat! I read it in a book once!"

She couldn't be serious.

The troll then swung at her with the back of its hand and sent her body flying through the trees. I heard a loud thud echo across the area as she landed.

"Elianna!" I howled.

The troll's attention was then snagged on me. "Come and get me you ugly bastard!"

The troll charged at me and swung his hand down the same way he had with her, but I was able to dodge it, barely. With a deep yell, I lifted my sharpened tree branch spear and slammed it down with all my strength into the troll's foot.

It let out a roar of pain into the sky, allowing me time to run off into the trees to look for her.

I was running in the direction I saw her body fly when two arms stuck out from one of the trees and violently ripped me to the side.

She slammed my back into the tree, and when I opened my eyes, all I could see was the intense, bright green of her own shining through the mud splattered across her face.

She put her lips to my ear, freezing me where I stood. "I am going to take my dagger from your boot and you are going to stay the fuck out of my way."

I opened my mouth to tell her no, but in one swift movement, she released my body and brought her arms down on one of her knees so hard that the rope binding her wrists effortlessly snapped and fell to the ground.

I was staring at her in awe as she then ripped the dagger out from my inner boot and took off, running headfirst back in the direction of the troll.

I bent down, swiping up the rope she dropped and ran after her, practically tripping over my own feet in the process.

When I arrived back at the small clearing, I saw the troll was still glancing around, searching for us. Elianna had her back up against a large tree and was staring at me. She silently lifted her pointer finger to her mouth, telling me to be quiet.

As if my plan was to do anything but that...

She placed the blade of the unique dagger between her teeth and began crawling slowly along the forest floor, halting any time she sensed the troll was looking in her general direction. She was still covered in mud, so to the untrained eye, she was essentially invisible when she wasn't moving.

She picked up another rock and whipped it in the opposite direction of where she was. When the troll's stare followed the rock, she quickly, and expertly, climbed up the branches of an ancient, giant oak tree. She halted on a branch that was nearly as tall as the troll itself.

The troll then stormed back to that tree after it found nothing in its search, and each step it took rattled the ground beneath its feet. Its eyes were then leveled with Elianna and where she stood on the branch. It noticed her then.

It roared directly in her face, covering the entire front of her body in its disgusting, thick saliva, and the wind of its breath sent her hair flying behind her.

Gods-dammit.

"Hey!" I shouted. It looked over at me, and I shot her a look, unknowing of which one of us it would attack first.

I picked up one of my spears that was lying on the ground near my feet and sent it flying toward the troll, with a smile forming on my lips.

The spear bounced off of the troll's arm.

My smile instantly dropped.

Luckily, that split second of a distraction was all that was needed.

With a loud battle cry, Elianna sprang out from the enormous tree, holding the dagger high above her head with both of her, now unbound, hands.

The troll turned its body ever so slightly toward her, and just in time. The dagger pierced its flesh right at the troll's sternum, and Elianna held on tight as she forced her body down, ripping the dagger through its entire torso and spilling its putrid guts all over the terrain, and herself.

Stumbling back, the troll hastily tried to pick up its guts that were still falling from him and hold them in place, right before his legs gave out and sent his body crashing backwards down to the ground, taking multiple trees with him.

I couldn't believe it. There was no fucking way that just happened.

"Yes!" I cried, shouting into the air, and letting out a rough laugh. "Holy shit," I whispered to myself.

The dust in the air started settling when I noticed that Elianna was still laying on the ground. Unmoving.

"Solus?" I spoke out from across the clearing.

Nothing. Her body didn't even stir. Shit.

I ran over to her, the stench of the troll's insides much stronger where her body lay covered in it.

"Elianna?" I whispered to her back. Still nothing.

I dropped down to my knees and turned her body over. Pulling her up into my arms, I lifted her chest to my ear to see if she was breathing, when I felt a sharp point against my neck.

A small giggle left the chest I was holding so tightly to my ear. I lowered her body down to see a mischievous grin spread across her filthy, infuriatingly beautiful face, and the dagger held in her hand, pointed directly at my throat.

I angrily shoved her back down to the ground, using the momentum to stand up. She then bursted out into an obnoxious, loud belly laugh.

"Oh, this is funny to you?" I spat at her. "Pretending you're dead after we barely defeated a troll. You think that's funny?"

She slowly sat up and leaned back on her elbows. "One, *I'm the one* who beat the troll. That thing would be picking us out of its teeth by now if I left you in charge. Two, I wasn't pretending to be dead. My body aches from its lovely maneuver that sent me flying through the trees. And three...yes. Actually, I think this is hilarious. That's the most fun I've had in months." She continued giggling.

Unbelievable.

"I'll take that dagger back now," I said through my teeth, as I reached out my hand.

She pointed the blade at me, all signs of laughter removed from her features. "Over my dead body." She showed her teeth like an animal, revealing her slightly sharper canines.

I curled my lip back in disgust. "Whatever. Get your ass up and rinse off what you can in the stream. We're losing daylight and you stink."

I could hear her snicker behind my back as I stormed off, away from her.

TWENTY-EIGHT

Elianna

HE CALLED ME ELIANNA. It had been days since I told him my first name, and what I would prefer to be called, but he refused to acknowledge it. He had barely spoken to me at all, but if he was forced to, he would still refer to me as "Solus." I was grateful he never seemed to notice how much it bothered me. I loathed my last name, it represented everything the queen punished me for my entire existence. My father always said that while I could not properly bear his last name, I would always be a Valderre.

The way his voice cracked when he screamed my name...it sounded like he was concerned. Worried, even. But why? Why would he be worried about someone he just planned to kill? Was it because he needed me to die at the right moment? He didn't want me to die before I gave up the secrets of Velyra? Which I would never do.

I had so many questions.

I cleared my throat. "Since we are lost–"

"We aren't lost," he cut me off. "We have just taken a few accidental detours."

I arched a brow and pursed my lips. "Riiiight, well these few 'accidental detours' have seemed to cost us daylight, maybe even days of it. So, why don't we just follow the stream? Most streams lead to at least a body of water."

He sighed. "Rivers, Solus. Rivers lead to bodies of water. Not streams. This could be left over from rainfall for all we know."

There's that name again. "Well, it's the only lead we have, and I'm going to go with that. Also, it hasn't even rained." I shot forward.

He went to open his mouth, likely to scold me for the millionth time today. "Look..." I pushed my fingers lightly into his chest, making eye contact. "I am following the way of the stream pointed north." I gestured to the moss. "So you can relax now."

"I don't relax."

"No shit."

He let out a grunt as I proceeded forward again. "What I mean is, I won't be relaxing until we are back in Ellecaster and I have a better idea of what to do with you."

What the? Did he no longer plan to kill me?

He clearly could sense where my thoughts were going and changed the subject, "Come on, we will need to make camp within the next couple of hours. I'm not trying to run into another massive creature, so you better keep that loud mouth of yours shut."

I snickered. "Yes, sir!" I called out mockingly.

He peeked back at me, looking annoyed per usual, and then began his trek down the small hill, following the stream.

Night had once again fallen when we decided to make camp beneath the trees. He eyed me as I kindled a small fire.

"Not afraid of the trolls and wyverns anymore?" he mocked, with a small smirk twitching the corners of his lips up.

My eyes locked with his. "I told you they were real. You didn't believe me."

He huffed out a breath through his nostrils. "You're right. They apparently do still exist."

"Andddd?"

"And what?"

I crossed my arms. "No apology from the commander?"

"Why in the realm would I apologize to you?"

"Oh, I don't know...because you made fun of me for fearing things that very obviously should be feared..." I replied dryly.

He rolled his eyes so deeply, I thought they were going to get stuck in the back of his thick skull. "Fine, Solus. I apologize."

My eye twitched. "Why do you keep calling me that?" I snapped at him from across the fire.

"Your name?" he smirked.

"You know my name."

"I do, and I choose to use a different part of your name to address you. No need to make it more complicated than that."

Ass.

I scowled at him as I picked up a stick and started poking the fire.

We sat in silence for several minutes when I stood up and walked around the outskirts of the camp. "Where are you going?" he asked on a sigh.

"Just checking our surroundings."

"I will need that dagger back at some point!" he called over.

"Keep dreaming," I whispered to myself, knowing he couldn't hear me.

As I was about to turn back around, I noticed a tiny shimmer on the forest floor, reflecting off the moonlight.

"Ha, no freaking way!" I whispered excitedly, as I bent down and ripped the twinkling green ferns from the ground.

As I began running back over to the fire, Jace went on alert. He shot up and threw his hands out in defense, his neck craning from side to side as he peered around warily.

"What?! What is your problem?" I asked.

He eyed me suspiciously. "You are running at me, coming from between the dark trees. You are holding our only actual weapon..."

I scoffed at him. "You thought I was randomly going to attack you?"

This was getting so old.

"No, actually, I thought you were running *from* something else and we were about to have another troll situation on our hands."

Oh.

"Nope! Not a troll!" I paused for dramatic effect, but I could tell he was just getting increasingly irritated. Or maybe that was just how his face permanently was. I threw down the ferns I had picked at his feet. "Ta-da!" I half sang.

"What do you want me to do with a bunch of leaves?" He raised a brow.

"Leaves?" I frowned. "Do you know what that is?"

He chuckled as he picked up a single fern and twirled it between his fingers, the leaves shimmering in the firelight. "Euphoroot."

"Exactly," I said softly.

"And what exactly do you want me to do with the euphoroot, Solus?"

"Commander, I knew you were a bore, but you didn't strike me as the type to not dabble in the wonders that nature has to offer," I teased.

He tossed the fern back down to the ground. "We are not smoking that," he grumbled.

"Fine, you don't have to." I picked up a couple of the ferns and started rolling them into a cone shape with my fingers. "But I will be." I sat down, scooting my butt across the ground to get closer to the flames.

"You can't be serious." He started rubbing his temples.

"Have you ever known me to not be serious?" I gave him a taunting grin as I stuck the tip of the rolled fern into the fire.

He didn't say a word as he watched me place the opposite end of the leaf between my lips and inhale the glorious, fruity-smelling smoke.

I held that smoke in my lungs for as long as my body would allow before I blew it out, and right at him.

He began coughing up a storm as the smoke hit his face. "What the fuck, Solus? Cut it out. At least one of us has to be alert out here."

My eyes went to look at him, but my vision slowed down to practically a halt. I smiled at him widely as I said, "You called me Elianna today."

"What? No, I didn't..." Gods, he gets so defensive.

I nodded and pursed my lips. "You did. Three times."

He chuckled. "I didn't take you for a lightweight, the way you lit up that fern. Clearly, the euphoroot has taken effect already because I definitely did not."

A faint pink color blushed across his cheeks—he knew he did it. And he also knew that he did it out of being concerned, but I'd let him live in his little imaginary world.

The flames of the fire began to dance in various colors, forming a prism like effect. Blues, greens, reds, and intense yellows all curved with the wind, making my body want to respond and dance with them. The trees surrounding us swayed and the rustling sound of the leaves became a song. I felt so *free*.

I went to touch my face, but realized I couldn't feel anything once I did. Giggles escaped me uncontrollably.

"Gods." Jace got up and grabbed a fern, working to roll it.

My gaze shot to his, or at least I think it did. "Are you going to–?"

"Well, I don't feel like dealing with this situation sober, so why not have a little fun?" He grinned, and it made my heart flutter in my chest.

What the hell? Oh, I was *definitely* high.

My jaw dropped open as I watched him light his leaves in the fire and inhale the smoke even deeper than I had.

"Finally," I whispered, while covering my mouth with the tips of my fingers, trying to hide my smirk.

He blew out a cloud of smoke up into the direction of the sky, and when he looked at me, he *smiled*. I had never seen him smile so genuinely before—maybe at all. It was absolutely beautiful. His features seemed lighter, softer. He looked *happy*.

My lips parted as I stared at his handsome features.

Gods, no Lia, snap out of it. This was the euphoroot talking.

We had been sitting for hours, filling the surrounding area with thick clouds of smoke, the smell of citrus, and the sound of continuous laughter. I glimpsed over at him and somehow never noticed when he ended up right next to me, our hands resting on the ground next to each other, practically touching.

I couldn't even remember what we had been saying or doing this entire time to cause such nonsense to be happening between us. But for the second time today, I was having fun. I forgot what this felt like.

"Okay," he said through a chuckle. "We should probably put the fire out and get some rest."

"You're right," I agreed, as we both rose and started stomping out the remaining flames.

On my last stomp, I lost my footing and tripped, falling directly into his chest, but he caught me. His muscular arms wrapped around my entire body effortlessly. We slowly pulled apart and as my eyes met his, the golden flecks shone in the moonlight. I hated how it took my breath away.

He cleared his throat. "Are you okay, Elianna?"

"Yes," I said hoarsely, trying to bring my thoughts elsewhere as my heart skipped a beat once again at the sound of my name on his lips.

He released his grip on me and brought himself down to the ground, and I then laid a few feet away from him, making sure to keep some kind of distance between our bodies. My eyes fluttered shut.

"Goodnight," he said softly, sleepily. "I'm glad I saved you," he continued on a yawn.

My eyes flew open and I watched as he drifted away to sleep. What the hell could he have meant by *that*? Certainly not the troll. My eyes roamed over his resting body for a few moments. "Goodnight Jace," I whispered.

And for another brief moment of insanity, I felt like I didn't want this distance between us at all.

TWENTY-NINE

Elianna

My head was pounding, no doubt from the euphoroot we found last night. I couldn't say I regretted it, though. Smoking the fern and discovering that the ever-so-serious commander knew how to smile, and even *laugh* was kind of priceless. I felt a small smile form on my face as I continued laying on the hard ground.

"Why are you smiling in your sleep? It's creeping me out."

Any sense of peace I just felt disappeared at the tone of Jace's voice.

I sluggishly opened my eyes, as the sun peeking through the trees blinded me. "Have you never had a pleasant dream before, Commander?"

"I have had plenty of good dreams," he said matter-of-factly.

"Yeah, sure." I sat up and leisurely peered around the area.

"Get your ass up, Elianna. I'd rather not sit here all day," he stated, as he picked up the couple of makeshift spears he had left. He looked back down at me and saw that I was trying to hide a smirk by biting my bottom lip. "What?"

"You called me Elianna again."

He began walking towards me. "Well, that is your name, isn't it? You've only pointed it out hundreds of times."

"Well, excuse me for wanting to be treated with respect," I mocked him, as I stood up on surprisingly steady feet.

He took another large step forward and his body was so close to mine now that our chests were nearly touching. I could feel his breath on my nose as he leaned over me. "Is it respect you want, Elianna?" he asked, his tone alluring and wicked.

The way he said my name sent a shiver down my spine. My eyes darted across his face. "On most occasions," I answered in a soft, submissive voice I barely recognized, refusing to break his stare.

We stood in that exact stance in silence for a few moments before a soft growl rumbled through his chest and he turned away from me. I didn't think a human could make that sound.

I released my breath and watched him curiously as he made his way back to the stream.

After hiking for a few miles in silence, I thought it would be okay to try to make conversation. "So where have you smoked euphoroot before?" I asked, the question ending with a snicker.

He eyed me for a moment. "What, do you think I don't know how to have fun? That I wasn't a stupid teenager once and did everything my mother told me I shouldn't?"

"It's just hard to picture such an intense man having fun and letting loose is all," I replied, holding my arms out for balance as I walked along a giant root twirling up from the ground.

He chuckled. "I wasn't always like this. Knowledge and responsibilities will do that to anyone."

I halted my steps for a moment. "I suppose you're right."

He started walking backwards, facing me as he talked. "What about you? It's not every day you see a female or a woman as a captain, never mind one that barely takes anything seriously and apparently smokes hell's fern."

"Hell's fern?" I raised a brow.

"Like I said, my mother tried to ward me away from it." He laughed.

"She sounds funny," I said with a breathy chuckle.

"She was."

My eyes flew up, but he was no longer looking in my direction. I could feel the ache in his words. When had she passed? Was it by the hands of the fae? Was that why his hatred ran so deep?

I cleared my throat. "And your father?"

"Never met the bastard."

Ah.

"I didn't grow up with a mother's love, eith–"

He immediately cut me off, stopping in his tracks, forcing me to almost lose my balance and fall off the root. "I never said I grew up without a mother's love. I was loved very much, though I cannot fathom why."

"I'm sorry, I just assumed," I stuttered out.

"Well, don't assume."

It was awkward for a few minutes while neither of us spoke up, continuing on our path. I decided I should just give him my reasoning for chiming in. "My mother passed away in childbirth. Giving birth to me."

I thought he wouldn't respond when I heard him softly say, "I am sorry to hear that."

I was about to speak when a faint noise in the distance caught my attention, halting me once more.

"What is it?" Jace asked, as his concerned gaze whipped to me.

"Shh!" I hushed him, and he didn't look pleased.

"Do you not hear that?"

"I think we have already established that your hearing is far better than mine."

Right.

I jumped down from the overgrown root and took off running, following the noise.

"Elianna!" he called. "What in the realm are you doing?"

"Come on! Move those legs, Commander!" I yelled back, refusing to look at the irritated facial expression I'm sure his face wore.

It was about two miles before we came to a stop in front of enormous bushes and leaf covered branches, forming a wall-like structure. The noise that drew us here was close and sounded like rushing water.

Jace finally caught up. Completely out of breath, he put his hands down on his knees. "What the hell is that noise?" he asked.

I smiled at him as he stood up straight. I pulled a fern that was about twice my height to the side and was awed by the sight hidden behind the foliage.

My head snapped back to him. "Look!" I practically yelled in his face, as I pulled the entire plant to the side, exposing a massive, gorgeous waterfall.

The falls were at least fifty feet high, surrounded by hundreds of boulders, slippery from the mist in the air caused by the falling cascades. The grass bordering the pool of turquoise below the falls was lush and a green so vibrant it looked as if it had been planted directly from the hands of the gods.

"Holy shit," Jace whispered, as he pushed past me, walking up to the unbelievable view that had just unfolded in front of us.

I ran past him, straight for the water's edge. It looked as if it was shallow for about ten feet and then there was a drop, but it didn't make the water any less clear. Peering out, I could still see the sand and rocks covering the lagoon's floor.

I dropped to the ground and ripped off both of my boots.

"What do you think you're doing?" Jace asked, coming up from behind me.

"What does it look like? I'm going swimming, obviously."

He chuckled. "I mean, I assumed, but you don't think there could be any creatures in that water? You know, ones with razor-sharp teeth and scales the size of your body?"

"You are so dramatic."

He gasped. "*I'm* dramatic? Who was the one worried about a troll?"

I looked up at him. "We *did* run into a troll, that was hardly dramatic to think about it being a possibility..." I paused. "And that troll would probably be shitting you out as we speak if it wasn't for me."

I began to wiggle out of my pants.

"*Elianna!*" he screeched. "Don't you dare take your clothes off."

I smirked. "Don't flatter yourself there, Jace. But I won't be walking around the forest with soaking wet clothes after this. I'll keep my undergarments on."

I smothered a grin as I watched his cheeks flush like they had the night prior while I slid my top off, revealing my breast restraint that fit slightly too small.

I dipped my toes in the water to feel that it had been unnaturally warm for the time of year.

I looked up, my gaze tracing up the wall of flowing, shimmering bright blues and silvers.

Making my way to the rocks, I heard Jace call to me, "Please don't tell me you're doing what I think you are."

"If you're too chickenshit to do it, then stay down here, Commander," I teased, as I started climbing up the rocky ledge.

When I realized he didn't respond, I looked back to see a shirtless Jace kicking off his boots. The wind from the falls whipped my long, tangled hair around my face, but even from this distance, I could see how thickly toned his body was under the disguise of those clothes.

"Gods-damn," I said to myself as I shook my head, continuing my way up the slippery ledge.

The view was nothing short of breathtaking at the top of the falls. I could peer downwards and see all the way to the bottom of the pool or look out into the distance and see the treetops of Sylis Forest for miles.

Jace made his way up surprisingly fast. "You first, Elianna."

"Ladies first, how gentlemanly of you." I winked at him.

His smirk quickly dropped, and he looked like he was about to say never mind and go first himself before I gave him a taunting salute and ran as fast as the short distance would allow and dove out beyond the cliff's edge.

The freefall was indescribable, feeling as if it would last a lifetime. My stomach dropped halfway down and the roar of the water falling alongside me was deafening. I hit the water suddenly, and I could instantly feel the pressure of the liquid form to my body. I didn't swim up immediately. I opened my eyes in the lagoon to see many small, bright-colored fish swirling around me, and leisurely swimming throughout their home, unbothered by me interrupting their peaceful lives. I lazily swam up to the surface once my lungs tightened, making me realize my breath of air was about to run out.

As my head broke the surface, Jace's body slammed into the water beside me, splashing me, and plunged down to where I had just been.

His head appeared next to mine a few moments later with his thick brown hair slicked back, and the pool's water beading off of his dark eyelashes.

I tilted my body onto my back and began floating. "See, wasn't that fun?"

He glanced back up at the top. "Definitely, but I didn't appreciate being called a chickenshit."

"Hey, it got you to do it, so mission accomplished if you ask me," I said, as I closed my eyes, enjoying the warmth of the sun beaming down on my face.

"Do you think the sea captain is looking for you?" he asked quietly, as he floated a few feet away.

My eyes flew open, and I began treading water as I met his stare. "That was incredibly random."

"Are you going to answer the question?"

I let out a short, hateful laugh. "I honestly doubt it. And that's even if he is still alive."

"Why would you doubt that? Are you not together?"

"Why are you prying?" I snapped.

He shrugged. "Who knows if we will ever find our way out of here."

He had a point.

"We claimed each other, or I believe you humans would describe it as being exclusive, some years ago..." I paused.

"Recently I have had my reservations due to his actions, and he is well aware of them."

He watched me closely but didn't interrupt.

I continued, "We were supposed to report back to the queen together." I hesitated, knowing that he realized what we would've had to report back on. "Anyway, he never showed. I was worried about him, but turns out he was just out on a multiple-day bender at one of Isla's brothels."

He choked out a rough laugh. "Gods, you're kidding, right?" When I didn't reply he spoke once more, "Asshole."

I lazily began to swim around. "Yeah, he is an asshole."

"I'm just surprised he lived to see another day."

I chuckled. "Trust me, he almost didn't. I was being supervised for that very reason."

A faint smile appeared on his lips. "Why am I not surprised by that, Solus?" His eyes widened slightly, realizing what he had called me. "I know you said you grew up without your mother, but what of your father? Do you bear the last name Solus due to being raised by neither?"

It was like a dagger to the chest, having to deny that I had a father. "I was raised within the walls of the castle in Isla. My mother had been employed there and when the king learned she had died in childbirth, he decided I would be raised there by the staff, and not be forced into the already overflowing orphanages."

"And that is why you are favored by the king?"

I sent a small splash in his direction. "So many questions today. How about a question for a question?"

"Fine," he huffed out.

"Why do you hate the fae so much?"

His face dropped. "Next question."

I stared at him, still treading the warm water. He let out a sharp breath. "Your kind has been terrorizing my race for centuries, as I am sure you're aware." I went to open my mouth to speak, but decided against it. "My mother was one of hundreds, if not thousands, to be raped by the males of your kind, and left for dead. Brutally assaulted, laughed at, tortured. All for a bit of fun," he said through clenched teeth, as the veins in his neck popped out. "They come through in the dead of night, burn our villages and homes to the ground, slaughter the men, and assault our women for sport."

My heart began to race in my chest as a heavy sense of shock rushed through me, leaving me nearly speechless. There was not a chance in the realm that the queen or Kellan did not know this was happening. Before I took over the land armies, they were left under the command of Lukas. He would never allow such horrible actions to occur under his watch, and neither would my father. Callius, though...I had never known Callius to be anything other than cruel and devious. He ran the sea fleet before Kellan, and they were often sent out at sea to handle issues if it could be handled by a small group. And after my own experience aboard the ship with Kellan's handpicked crew, there was not a single doubt in my mind that these horrendous acts had occurred under the crown's watch.

I could feel a stinging feeling gathering behind my eyes as my vision blurred with silver. "Please tell me you didn't witness this as a child," I croaked out.

A closed lipped smile formed on his mouth, but it did not meet his eyes. No, his eyes were filled with nothing but *fury*. "I was not there. But I am the result of it."

My jaw dropped, and I quickly slammed my palm over it. I went to speak, but nothing would come out. I could feel the tears streaming down my cheeks. "Jace," I whispered, closing my eyes tightly.

"Save it. I don't, nor would my mother, want your sympathy. She was a strong woman until she was claimed by illness five years ago."

I took a few deep breaths. "I just want you to know that not all fae males are such brutal, heartless monsters. Just as I have always believed that all humans are not the same as the ones who murdered the Lord and his son, resulting in this war." Now I was thinking that the queen's father and brother more than likely deserved the fate they received. Gods knew what they were doing all the way in Ceto Bay in the first place all those decades ago.

"Your description of the sea captain has me doubting that."

I thought of Kellan and Kai, how cruel and reckless they both could be. And then I thought of my father, Finnian, and Lukas. How kind and trusted those males were. What they meant to me.

"As I said, not all males are like that," I said to him, starting to close some of the distance between us in the lagoon.

"Well, forgive me if it does not change the side I am on in this war, Elianna," he said, almost sadly.

"I know," I whispered.

With the tension in the air growing rapidly, I turned to swim back to a pile of rocks on the water's edge. The echo of a strangled growl had me turning back to face him.

"What is that?" he asked sternly.

Confused by his question, I looked around, but when I saw nothing, I cocked my head to the side as my eyes met his.

"*Who did that to you.*" His tone seeped with rage.

Not a question, but a demand.

I faced him fully, my hair floating around me in the water. "Excuse me?"

"The scars. On your back."

I let out an uncomfortable giggle. "I have many scars. You're going to need to be more specific."

"The three whip marks."

I flinched. Fuck. Not even Kellan had ever asked about those. He probably just assumed it was from training or I was nicked in battle...or maybe he just never cared, because the scars truly were brutal.

I continued to swim up to the rocks, and when I lifted myself up and sat, his stare was boring into me.

"I am waiting, Elianna."

I ignored him.

"Consider it my question in your little game you started," he said, as he followed the rippling path in the water to where I now sat.

"I don't like being told what to do as an adult, so I am sure you can imagine me as a youngling. Trouble found me quite frequently," I said without looking in his direction.

"Once again, you lie to me so beautifully."

"And why do you believe that?"

"Even though I have known you for a very short amount of time in your unfathomably long lifespan, I know you well enough to know that you would brag if you felt as if the marks were earned or deserved." He continued when I didn't respond, "Also, you admitted it happened when you were a kid. The king took you in and you seem very fond of him, so I am intrigued to know who thought they had the fucking right to do that to a female, especially as a child."

A single tear slipped from my eye, and I tried to hide the fact that his words rocked me to my core by biting my bottom lip, but it did nothing to ease the trembling.

"Why do you care?" I was barely able to get the words above a whisper.

He gently placed his calloused hand on my knee. "...Because maybe I am starting to realize that just because you are not human, doesn't mean you haven't suffered at the hands of horrific kinds of fae and humans alike. And that being said, I know that someone who has taken a whip to her back multiple times by someone I'm assuming she trusted, then leads the armies of warriors that don't respect her, and yet *still* keeps the secrets of her kingdom to protect the ones she loves..." He paused for a moment. "Is someone I would want on my side."

My eyes darted back and forth while staring at him. Did he really just say that? Had he meant it? Was the euphoroot still in his system? It must've been.

"I need to take a walk," I said, as I got to my feet and nearly ran back towards the cliff we jumped from when we arrived at the waterfall.

Once at the top, I tried to empty my mind. Why was I letting the words of someone who should be my enemy affect me so deeply? I had never been a crier. I've always refused to show my vulnerability. It was practically beaten into me by Lukas at a young age, so I would have a fighting chance at being a female in an army full of brutes.

The wind grew strong at the top, whipping my hair around to the point where it was nearly dry again. Between the wind and the sound of the falls, I barely heard him walk up behind me.

"Elianna, I'm sorry if I upset you," he shouted over the gusts of wind.

I turned to him. "I'm more upset with myself in this moment than I am with you."

He cocked his head to the side as he took a step toward me. "And why is that?"

"I don't know." And I didn't. I truly didn't know what was coming over me. I was loyal to the crown. To the Kingdom of

Velyra. To my king and the citizens I swore to protect. So why did it suddenly feel wrong?

"I think I know," he said, as he carefully inched his way closer. "You're slowly finding out the truth of the grotesque acts that have been done by your kind. While I have always believed that all of you fae were monsters, you are proving to show me differently. We are both realizing the truths that we chose to be blind to throughout our lives."

He was right, it wasn't that it felt wrong protecting those I loved and cared for. It was the fact that I was being forced to fight for the wicked queen and her revenge in order to do it.

"I'm sorry for what happened to your mother." I hesitated for a second before I continued, "And I'm sorry for the part that I played in what happened to your men. Your *friends*. This needs to end. Things have gone too far."

"They have," he agreed, our faces now mere inches from each other.

My lips parted slightly, and I opened my mouth to speak once more when he cusped the back of my neck with his hand, pulled my face to his, and fiercely pressed his lips to mine.

My eyes flared wide in shock. The force of his steps he took into me caused both of us to lose our balance and slip over the waterfall's edge.

His lips never left mine, and as we were free-falling through the air, it felt as if time had ceased. There was nothing else in the world. The war did not exist, nor did our hatred for each other.

The only thing felt was the fluttering in my gut, and I would be lying to myself if I said that it was from the fifty-foot drop.

Even as our bodies slammed down into the pool of water below, his grip on me never loosened. I opened my eyes once more to see the bright, colorful fish circling us, along with the rising bubbles caused by our fall. He broke off the kiss as we continued floating under the water. Jace looked into my eyes as he brushed his thumb across the swell of my bottom lip before he made his way swimming up to the surface.

Once my face was above water, I was terrified to look in his direction. He kissed me. The rude, arrogant and...extremely attractive commander *kissed* me.

And I enjoyed it. Wanted it even. *Gods, Lia, what the hell have you gotten yourself into?*

I didn't know what else to say to him, so when my gaze found his I blurted out, "The queen."

"What?" He tilted his head to the side in confusion while treading the water.

"The queen. She is the one who had me whipped as a child. The king still doesn't know of it to this day. Now the only person with this knowledge aside from myself is you. Well, and her guard that handled the whip."

Jace glided over to me effortlessly. "Then mark my words, Elianna, no matter where our journeys take us...if you desire it, *that* killing blow is yours."

The grin that slowly grew on my face while I stared into his eyes felt treasonous, but infinitely right in the same moment.

"Lia. You can call me Lia."

His answering smile made my traitorous heart skip a beat.

THIRTY

Elianna

THE PAST FEW HOURS laying on the lush grass at the foot of the lagoon with Jace felt as if I was floating within the clouds. Who knew such a hard ass could be fun sometimes? Or even charming.

The sun shining down on him as he smiled made the tiny gold flecks in his hazel eyes radiate. It took everything in me to try to focus on anything but that.

"Why are you staring at me?" he asked in an amused tone.

"What did you mean last night? About saving me?"

The question must have shocked him, because his eyes flared in panic. "What are you talking about?"

"As we were falling asleep, you said you were happy that you saved me. What did you mean by that?" I tried to hide my smirk.

He looked away from me and focused up at the sky for several moments. "We didn't wash up on shore together." He cleared his throat. "I saved you from drowning."

My heart stopped as I gasped out, "*What?*"

"When the ship crashed into the rocks, I tried to follow you through the water, but it was too dark, and the waves too strong.

When I came up for air, I watched your body slam into the rocks that the ship had hit." I was too shocked to respond. "I dove beneath the surface and brought your body up with me. I pulled you onto a piece of floating debris and we rode out the storm. When morning came, land appeared in the distance, so I paddled us to it."

I blinked. "And?"

"And you know the rest," he said with a sigh.

I sat there in pure disbelief. He must be lying. There was no way he saved me. "Why would you do that?" I was expecting him to say to get information from me regarding the crown.

"You saved me first. Twice. You salvaged my ruined leg and then you came back down to the cells to free me, so I would have a chance of not going down with the ship. It was the right thing to do."

"Thank you," I said in a hushed tone. "I'm not even confident that the crew would have done that for me. Definitely not the one I was with, anyway."

"As I said, it was the least I could do."

But it wasn't. Not in my mind, anyway. He easily could've let me drown when the only reason he was on the ship to begin with was because of me.

Trying to change the subject, I asked, "You said you were friends with some of your men you commanded? What was that like?" He didn't respond. I noticed a small wince at the mention of them. "Once again, I can't apologize enough, but it's just very foreign to me to believe you have formed friendships down your ranks."

The corners of his lips tipped up softly. "I am a well-respected commander from working my ass off nearly my entire life and fully dedicating myself to the cause, and I am sure the same goes for you." He hesitated. "My second and third in command were the closest people to me. They were both lost in Ceto Bay."

I sucked in a sharp breath as he said that. I went to open my mouth, but he held up a hand, stopping me.

"Gage, my second, was my best friend since I was a small boy. He was definitely the most adventurous of the two of us, always getting the both of us into trouble. I trusted him with my life, though." He let out a sad chuckle and looked out to the water. "Zaela was my third in command, but if you were to ask her, she was my *true* second, or 'the better second' as she would say." He laughed genuinely this time. "She was also my cousin. Very bossy, but a badass, nonetheless. She could hold her own with any man. You would've liked her."

"It sounds like I would have," I said softly.

"She probably would've slit your throat the second she saw you though."

"A few days ago I probably would've done the same," I said, as I pursed my lips tight and closed my eyes. That was definitely the wrong thing to say, considering that is most likely how she met her fate.

He cleared his throat. "Her father commanded the armies before I had. He stepped in as a father figure for me when my mother had no one else. My uncle took care of his family above all and was the kind of man I aspire to be. When he was killed in battle, the troops voted me in as commander. I was shocked, to say the least, and of course a few of the older soldiers weren't very keen on it, but that changed quickly. At only twenty-two years old, I was considered very young for the position, but I was hungry for blood. I've commanded my armada just as he had before me, although my temper has proven to cloud my judgement occasionally."

How could he even stand to look at me? Never mind *save* me. The fae had taken *everything* from him. If roles were reversed, I would've slaughtered him where he stood the first chance I had. Did he feel the same pull toward me that I did with him? Or has being stuck together, lost in the middle of the most dangerous forest known to both of our kinds, made us completely lose our minds?

Something had drastically changed in our dynamic, but I couldn't pinpoint when it happened.

"You say you have no friends, Lia, so who were you smoking euphoroot with?" he teased, and I was grateful for the change of subject. "Surely you weren't out smoking by yourself." He raised both of his brows with a smirk.

"I never said I didn't have friends. I said I didn't have them within ranks below me. There's a difference."

"Semantics," he countered, waving a hand at me.

"Well, the queen made it her goal to ruin my own childhood, so I felt as if it was only right to corrupt her children in theirs," I said with a wink.

He let out a sharp laugh. "The princes and princess? They had three kids, right? At least, that's what our reports say."

I rolled my eyes at that. "Well, Princess Avery, at least. The youngest prince, Finnian, was always too afraid to be caught. Once Avery had reached her second decade of life, we became very close. She has a good heart, as does Finn, but Avery has always craved adventure." I smiled. "We used to sneak out of the castle together and explore the gardens at night. Sometimes I would bring back euphoroot I found while out scouting during my training and bring it back to her. We would hide out in her chambers late at night and stick it in her fireplace. It's amazing we were never caught. Our giggles alone could probably be heard from floors away."

"Leave it to you to corrupt a *princess*," he muttered, but there was amusement in his tone.

I laughed. "Avery would've corrupted herself. I like to think I supervised for the first few years. I showed her all the secret tunnels hidden within the castle walls. It's how I got around most of the time without being seen. Or if I wanted to sneak out at night just to get some fresh air before I became captain."

"Secret tunnels?"

"Oh yeah, there's many of them, hidden right between the walls. I don't even think the king and queen know of them all. Some lead straight to personal chambers, others to the library or the dungeons, and some even go beyond the castle gates. I spent much of my childhood exploring them." I knew I was likely sharing too much with him, but at this point, my fate had been sealed with that damning kiss.

"That must've been terrifying if you got lost."

I shrugged. "Eh, I always brought a torch with me when I didn't know where I was going. And being lost felt better than risking the threat of the whip."

He looked at me with sadness in his eyes. "What about the other prince?"

My jaw clenched at the mention of Kai. "He is as rotten as his mother. Maybe even worse."

He scratched his facial hair that had grown since the shipwreck as he watched me. "And this is the heir to the throne you wish to protect?"

"I try not to think about that part," I whispered.

"Is it true the king is deathly ill with the root of the cause unknown?"

My eyes snapped to his. "How do you know about that?"

"We have eyes and ears throughout Isla," he admitted.

I snickered. "Sympathizers...It's impressive the queen and her loyal dog haven't sniffed them all out yet."

"Why does the queen treat you so poorly, Lia? How could she ever justify having you whipped as a child?"

I was stunned silent for a moment, taking in the fresh air and the calls of the birds singing to each other within the trees. "Excellent question," I said, as I rose to stand. "I'm going to go to the bathroom over beyond the cliff, what do you say we just camp here since the sun is setting?"

"Way to dodge the question," he murmured, as he sat up, holding his weight up on his elbows.

"Relax," I called back to him. "I'll be right back."

I looked back at him a few times on my way to find some privacy to see he watched my every move. Was this out of lust, or lack of trust? What would happen once we left this lagoon? Would it go back to how it was? With me once again being a prisoner with the information he needed, or would everything change?

One thing was for sure, if I ever made it back to Isla alive, I would do everything in my power to end this war, starting with heading straight to the king and telling him of all the treacherous acts done right under all of our noses.

Turning the corner, I found a small cave hidden within the rocks that built up to the cliff that held the waterfall. Deciding that this spot would be as private as any, and hoping it wasn't the home of a wyvern, I crawled in to do my business.

The cave was damp and the stench of mildew was overwhelming. I peed as fast as I could and brought my undergarments back up to get the hell out of here. The crevice I originally crawled through looked a little trickier to get out of than it was to get in, so I maneuvered my right leg through the thin gap first, and then my left. Arching my back, I bent backwards, moving my torso through the tight space, feeling the rocky granite scratch my skin on areas it touched. When I finally had most of my body out of the cave, I dropped down to my knees, slowly turning my neck and head to get out. "Phew, that was a little too tight for comfort," I whispered to myself.

Pushing up on one knee, I rose to stand when I felt a hand clasp tightly around my throat and send my entire body slamming back into the rocks next to the mouth of the small cave. Intense pain shot through my skull and down my entire back, as the jagged points in the rock wall sliced into my skin.

I tried to open my eyes as the tightness around my neck began blocking even more of the air that I was already barely able to get in, but my vision was too blurry to see anything or anyone clearly.

"Fuck," I said hoarsely.

"Oh, you're fucked all right," I heard a feminine voice speak sinisterly directly into my ear.

The person then slammed my head back against the surface of the jagged rock wall and my vision went completely black.

THIRTY-ONE

Finnian

IT HAD BEEN DAYS since the incident in the stables happened with Kai and Landon. I had barely seen either of them since, and Landon wouldn't even look in my direction if he knew I was near. And maybe the only reason why I hadn't seen Kai was because I had been hiding out in Avery's quarters whenever she wasn't out with her Lady friends.

Pretending to read a book while sprawled out across her enormous bed with Nyra, I silently watched Avery as she brushed through her long, auburn hair that was nearly blinding in the light that cast from the setting sun coming through her windows.

"How many times are you going to brush that one section?" I asked sarcastically, as I turned a page that I definitely didn't read.

"How many more days are you going to hide in my room to avoid your little unclaimed, unmated male friend?" she retorted sassily without even looking at me through the mirror.

My jaw opened and closed rapidly, shocked by what she just revealed that she knew. "I don't know what you're talking about."

"Oh save it, Finn. You're a terrible liar and even worse at sneaking around. Perhaps you should've hung out with Lia and I when we were younger a little more. You'd probably be better at both by now."

My jaw dropped. "How did you find out?"

"You mean when did I notice the two of you eye-fucking each other in the stables? Probably within the first twenty minutes of us all hanging out there. I mean, you should've realized I thought it would be weird that you *wanted* to be in the stables when you had never shown interest before."

Gods-dammit. She was right. I was terrible at all of this. "Fantastic," I mumbled, as I slammed the book shut.

She half turned her body in the chair to face me. "So why are you avoiding him, anyway?"

I let out a loud sigh. "I'm more avoiding Kai than I am Landon."

"But why? Kai, I understand, but I know you, and you never hang out with me like this anymore. Not unless you're avoiding something bigger than just Kai's antics."

I closed my eyes tight and rolled over, grabbing one of her pillows and smothered my face with it. "Kai is evil, Avery."

She snorted. "Well, we know that."

I removed the pillow from my face. "No, he is worse. So much worse than he used to be. The other day in the gardens...after you stormed off—"

"Did something happen?!" she squealed, worry evident in her tone. "Did he find out about you and Landon?" she gulped.

"Not purposefully." I sighed. "After you walked away with Nyra, he practically dragged me into the stables with the Lords. He wanted to torment Lia's horse." Her hand flew to cover her mouth nervously. "Landon was in there. He tried to stop him, but..."

"What did he do, Finnian?" she asked in a hushed whisper.

"He branded Lia's horse, and when Landon went to stop him, Kai noticed my reaction and then branded Landon across his chest as well. Told him that if he sought out a healer that he would kill him himself." She looked absolutely horrified. "There was nothing I could do, the Lords held me back. I haven't seen Landon since. I'm afraid if I go there it'll draw too much attention...and I doubt he ever wants to see me again anyway."

Her eyes lined with silver. "Oh, my gods."

"Father is not well, Avery," I said, trying to hold the tears back myself.

"I know," she said gently, wiping away the few tears that slipped through her kohl lined lashes.

I let out a large breath. "Kai is the future king. I am...terrified of where he will lead Velyra."

"As am I," she stated.

A soft knock sounded at the door, and both of our spines straightened immediately. We fixed our faces to look like anything was happening in here besides the tears that were flowing.

Avery cleared her throat. "You may come in."

The door opened slowly, revealing Lukas' head as it popped through the doorway. He looked worried.

"Hey, you two, I have been looking for you everywhere in the courtyards." He gave us a soft smile. "The queen is requesting your presence in the throne room."

Avery and I quickly made eye contact and then looked back to Lukas.

"Do you know what about?" she asked him.

"Captain Adler and the crew have arrived back in Isla, and he is about to report on his findings."

I raised a brow. "And Lia?"

Lukas sucked in his bottom lip through his teeth and closed his eyes as he shook his head slowly.

Oh, no. Not Lia. Something couldn't have happened to her, right?

"Lukas, what are you saying?" Avery chimed in, voice shaking with worry.

"I am saying that we need to all go down there immediately and find out what the fuck happened."

The throne room was dark, the sun was nearly set now, and the staff had lit candles throughout the room to provide some form of light, but all it did was make this entire scene before us seem eerie and cold.

"Mother," Avery spoke from the doorway as we entered. "Where is Father?"

"The king is too ill to join us tonight," Callius answered for the queen, as he stood beside her while she was perched on her throne.

I looked around the room and found Kai, Kellan, and another male, whose stance oddly resembled the sea captain's, off to the side of the dais. The only ones in the room now were the three males, Callius, the queen, and now the three of us.

Walking up to the dais, Lukas finally spoke up, "We are all here, Your Majesty. The captain may report on the journey now."

The queen gestured to Kellan. "You may speak now."

"Thank you, Your Highness. As you can see, we have arrived home in much fewer numbers than we originally left with."

Avery instantly burst into tears beside me, and I grabbed her hand to comfort her the best I could in this situation. Our mother gave us a scowling look.

"The humans. Have they been dealt with?" she inquired.

"Yes, My Queen. The humans have been disposed of in Ceto Bay. We ran into some...difficult weather and were shipwrecked. Most of the crew, along with Captain Solus, have been lost."

"You speak *lies!*" Lukas' voice boomed across the room, his face burning with crimson in anger.

The queen pointed at Lukas. "One more outburst like that and I will have Callius remove you from this room. Am I understood?"

Lukas gave her a single nod as he clenched his teeth so firmly I could've sworn I heard one crack.

"As I was saying," Kellan said insultingly. "Many lives have been lost. Some may still be out there, as the ones we brought back with us washed up on shore near where we had. Elianna, unfortunately, was not one of them, but I don't necessarily believe she is dead."

"If they are mates, he would know if she was alive!" Avery said to Lukas and I in a hushed tone.

"He is *not* her mate," Lukas quieted her.

"On our journey back to Isla, we ventured through a village, and a few of its citizens had been kind enough to lend their sea captain a few horses for my crew that remained." Kellan added.

"Ah, what a shame it is to hear of Captain Solus," the queen stated. It seemed as if she was practically foaming at the mouth with sarcasm. "We will proceed on with our days as if she is deceased as well, then." A small smile tilted up at the corners of her ruby painted lips.

Lukas' entire body vibrated with rage next to me.

Even Kellan looked surprised at her statement. Kai was picking his nails, looking bored to tears, but I could've sworn I saw him mouth the words "good riddance."

"Captain Adler, you will run both fleets in the meantime."

"That is exactly what the bastard wanted," Lukas stated. "He never gave a shit about Lia."

"You are all dismissed," the queen announced. "And Sir Lukas..." He met her stare. "I do not want a single, able-bodied soldier wasted on looking for Elianna beyond the city wall. Do I make myself clear?" Her voice echoed in the otherwise silent throne room.

"Crystal," he replied, irritation dripping from his tone.

I squeezed Avery's hand once again, and she immediately squeezed it back. I looked into her honey-hued eyes that were identical to mine, to our mother's—only they were now red and puffy from holding back tears and frustration.

We both knew nothing was ever going to be the same again.

THIRTY-TWO

Jace

LIA HAD BEEN GONE far too long to just be relieving herself. Did something happen? Did she fool me just enough to get the chance to run off?

I glanced down at the obsidian dagger near her clothes. No, she wouldn't run off without clothes, and *especially* without her dagger. Worry took over me.

I let out a sharp breath. What the fuck was I doing? Kissing my enemy? Why did I feel this way so suddenly over a female I met only days ago? It felt right in the moment, and it still felt right now. If only Zaela and Gage could see me now.

I pressed the backs of my palms into my eyes and rubbed them in frustration. What the fuck was I going to do with her once I got her back to Ellecaster with me? I couldn't exactly hide her. I didn't think I had it in me to kill her anymore.

Actually no, even the thought of that made me want to vomit everywhere. Fucking gods, how did this happen?

I have lived my entire existence hating the fae. I dedicated my life to destroying them the way they have us. Why did I have to meet one who had similar views as me? Who was willing to give her life just to protect the few people she cared about?

And she's fucking gorgeous. My heart sped up in my chest as I thought of those gorgeous green eyes.

She really should've been back by now. "Elianna!" I called out, my voice echoing through the air, but was lost in the roar of the falls.

Nothing.

"Where could she have gone?" I said to myself, as I got to my feet. "Elianna, this isn't funny!"

Storming off in the direction that she went, a sinking feeling fell in my gut, and an intense, sharp headache began brewing as stress took over.

Coming around the corner to the back of the cliff that led up to the falls, I noticed a small cave. She must be hiding in there. "Elianna, honestly is everything a joke to you? You scared me for a second."

With still no response, as I approached the cave, I saw streaks of a deep, bluish red smeared across the rocks. Walking up to it completely, I swiped my fingers across it and realized it was fresh blood.

"Fuck," I whispered.

I whipped around on high alert and couldn't see anything in the trees. The birds were still singing, and the world didn't seem to stand still as it had with the troll, but I felt as if I had eyes on me.

"I don't know who is out there, but you better release her at once!" I announced, mustering up the most powerful voice I could. The voice of the commander.

I went to take a step when out of nowhere I could hear a whooshing sound coming from behind me, resembling a whip. When I half-turned my body mid-step, I was too slow to notice the bolas aiming directly for my ankles.

My body slammed into the ground hard as I hurriedly tried to remove the rope from my legs.

"Holy shit! It's Jace!" I heard in the distance.

What the fuck.

My head snapped up in the direction of the familiar voice. Standing not even twenty feet from me...was Zaela, and then Gage appeared, running up from behind her.

"Gage. Zae! You're *alive?!*" I shouted into the air as I began fumbling around, trying to release myself from the trap that she expertly whipped at me.

I taught her that damn trick.

She started laughing as she slowly made her way to me. "Us?! What about you? How the hell are you here?"

Gage ran past her and then tackled me fully back down to the ground, locking my head between his elbow and embracing me in a suffocating bear hug. "You stupid bastard, we thought you were captured, or dead."

I ripped his arm from around my throat to try to get some air as Zaela knelt down beside me and started helping me out of the entwined bindings. "I thought you guys were killed! The fae piled up all the bodies and captured everyone who surrendered. The bodies were too mangled to tell who from who. I assumed the worst. How the hell did you escape?"

"We hid in the tops of the trees," Zaela said softly. "We watched as they tied your body to a post. Once it became dark, we crept down, but there were far too many of them for the two of us to handle. We went back to our original camp to gather supplies and attempt to find more help, but by the time we made our way back, you had vanished. We assumed back on their ship."

They were alive. Both of them made it out. My heart was racing impossibly fast in my chest, and I could feel my blood pumping into my ears from the sudden burst of relief and shock. I could barely hear what they were saying, but it didn't matter. They were here. Alive. And safe.

I then reached up, grasping the back of both of their heads with my palms and pulled their foreheads into mine. "Thank the gods you're both alright."

Zaela pulled away first. "That's more than I can say for all of our men. It was a fucking massacre, Jace." She nodded at Gage. "Gage was crying."

Gage knelt up on both of his knees. "Was not!"

She lifted a brow and eyed him humorously.

"Okay, maybe I did. But the entire scene was gruesomely brutal. We had a set plan, a good one too. It was shocking, and not only did we lose all of our men with us, but we thought we lost you, too..." He paused, and jokingly placed a hand over his heart as he looked into my eyes. "It's not my fault your cousin is heartless."

Zaela punched him in the chest so hard he fell back on his ass.

I instantly threw my head back and bursted into a deep laugh. "Gods, I missed you two and your obnoxious bickering. Who has been in charge since I've been gone?"

"Me." They both said in unison.

Oy.

"Typical." I chuckled.

Zaela got to her feet, and extended out her hand to lift me up. "You were about to be captured again, you moron. We trapped one."

"Trapped one?"

"One of the fae, we even recognized her as one of the ones that caught you in the first place. She must've been on your trail with that fae nose of hers," Gage chimed in.

Oh, no. *Elianna*.

I looked between the two of them multiple times before responding, "Is she alive?"

"For now," Zaela said, as she started making her way back to the trees. "Come, we will bring you to her. If anyone deserves to claim her death, it's you."

Oh, gods, what was I going to do?

I followed her. "Is she hurt?"

She snorted. "I mean I slammed her head on that rock wall back there to knock her out, but I'm sure it didn't do nearly as much damage as I was hoping."

That *was* Elianna's blood. Fuck.

Zaela came to a stop after walking about two hundred feet into the woods. She looked at me and smiled. "Here she is." She pulled back a branch and I saw Elianna strapped to a willow tree—unconscious, bloodied, her body nearly naked and appeared broken. The scene looked too familiar, and it made my heart ache.

How can I play this off so she wouldn't be killed? There was no way I could tell them what had happened a few hours ago at the falls.

"I don't know why she was naked, or mostly naked. I'm assuming she was going to try to seduce you once she found you. Disgusting fae whore," Zaela spat with hatred.

"I doubt that," I stated.

"It's not like that would've worked anyway, Jace won't even talk to a human woman, never mind a fae. He'd kill her before she even had time to say hello," Gage said, nudging me in the back. I eyed him, hoping he could tell I was annoyed.

"You've heard the stories!" Zaela threw up her hands. "While their males rape our women in the night, the females seduce our men. Legend has it, they were gifted that ability from sirens thousands of years ago."

A deep, throaty, painful chuckle echoed on the wind. All three of us looked to the willow tree to see Elianna laughing at us, smiling with blood staining her teeth.

"That may be one of the most ridiculous rumors I have ever heard," she announced.

"It's the truth," Zaela said through her teeth, gripping her sword's hilt.

Elianna glanced over to me, and then back to Zaela. "Has it ever occurred to you that we do not need the art of the sirens to seduce your men? And perhaps they just get tired of you and welcome us into their beds willingly?"

Fucking *gods,* I knew if these two ever met, it would be a scene. I just didn't think it would be possible.

Zaela immediately was in front of the willow as Elianna finished her taunting retort and punched her directly in the side of her face so hard that I practically felt it myself. "You speak when spoken to, fae whore."

She met her stare and just smirked at her. Why did I find it so attractive?

"Okay, that is enough," I said, stepping between the two of them.

Zaela looked at me, confusion etched into her features. "Why? You want all the fun for yourself?" She unsheathed a small dagger from her hip and handed it to me. "By all means."

"Sure wish I thought to bring my dagger back there. This situation would be very different right now. And your throat would be slit." Lia said cynically with a cold smile.

"Elianna, that is *enough,*" I whispered, as I whipped my face down to hers.

"Elianna?!" Zaela barked at me. "I'm sorry, but since when are you two on a first-name basis? Or any kind of basis at all?"

I could feel her anger brewing beneath her skin.

"Yeah, Jace. What the hell is going on?" Gage asked from behind us. I forgot he was even here.

I rubbed my calloused hand down my face. "Alright, everyone, calm down. There is a lot we need to talk about."

"Yeah, let's start with you being a fucking traitor?" Zaela spat.

Elianna watched her intensely.

"I am not a traitor," I said, raising my voice to bring a sense of authority. "In an extremely twisted turn of events...she is my captive."

I glanced down and watched as a flicker of sadness flashed across her eyes, it was so quick that I almost missed it entirely.

"Then why was she snooping around the back of the falls?" Gage asked.

"As I said, we have much to talk about. However, we will be bringing her to Ellecaster for questioning and take things from there."

Zae looked between her and I warily and finally released the hilt of her sword. "Can't wait to hear this. But I don't want to hear it from you. I want to hear it from her." She pointed down to Elianna aggressively and sneered.

This was not going to end well at all.

THIRTY-THREE

Elianna

WHO THE FUCK WERE these people? Whoever they were, they seemed to have enough power to cause Jace to forget about the past few hours together at the waterfall entirely. Everything about this situation was...aggravating. Also, my head hurt. Bad.

For the last ten minutes, all I did was watch the three of them mingle and bicker with each other. Mainly about what to do with me. It made sense though, I didn't know who these humans were, and I also still had no idea what Jace planned to do with me.

The other man reminded me so much of Lukas, with his rich, tawny skin and friendly demeanor. It was clear he didn't run the show.

The blonde-haired female, on the other hand, I didn't like her. She had been trying to boss Jace around about what to do with me. Swaggering her ego around like it'd do anything. She got a lucky shot in. The element of surprise was on her side—that was it. Otherwise, I would've wiped the forest floor with her.

And now she was staring at me, waiting to hear about our journey and how we got here. How I became the captive, and Jace the captor.

Then it clicked.

"Well," she snapped at me. "Let's hear it then, *Elianna*."

I stared at her for a moment, then glanced up at Jace. The face he was making at me looked as if he was about to get down on his knees and beg me to not include the last few hours.

"Nah," I said, grinning. "I think I'll just let your imaginations run wild like they had earlier about the sirens."

She unsheathed her sword impressively fast for a human and tipped my chin up with the tip of the blade, forcing me to look up at her. "It was not a choice."

"For fuck's sake, Zaela, stop it!" Jace yelled to her, his lip curling back into a snarl. Now *that* was not very human of him to do. Also...Zaela. That was the name of his cousin. Oh, shit.

My eyes focused back on her. "Hello, Zaela. It's lovely to meet Jace's cousin, considering we presumed you to be dead."

Her smile dropped, and her head flew to Jace. "What the fuck have you told our enemy, Cadoria."

Not a question. I also just realized I never knew Jace's last name.

"Oh, I've been told enough. He also thought you and I would be friends, but that clearly is out of the question at this point." She looked too stunned to speak, so I continued, pointing to the other man as my hand rested on my lap since my arms were bound tightly with my body, "You must be Gage. I like you quite a bit more than I like Zaela. You and I can be friends if you'd like."

He giggled. A grown man giggled like a small girl at my shitty joke to just piss her off. I definitely liked him.

Zaela looked at Jace, her stare boring into him. "Who are you? What the hell is this? None of this makes sense. The Jace we know would've ended her the second he could've and you're...stalling her death?"

Jace looked mortified, and now I felt kind of bad. Gods knew if I was caught in the same situation, then I would need to save face, too.

"He isn't stalling." All three sets of eyes were now on me. "He is bringing me back to Ellecaster for information regarding the fae and Velyra. Then he plans to kill me."

"Is this true?" Gage asked, looking back and forth between me and Jace.

Jace went to open his mouth, but I cut him off before he got the chance to bury himself into a deeper grave. "It's true."

"Excellent, now how about you start your story with how you slaughtered all the humans that surrendered?"

I flinched at her words, and I could tell she noticed. Fuck.

"She had nothing to do with that," Jace chimed in, but Zaela's eyes never wandered from mine.

Looking directly into her stare, I began, "I did not command the crew on my own, as another captain was among us. However, I had orders out to them to not harm any humans that surrendered. At first, it seemed as if they obeyed my command, but the following morning, their throats were slit against my wishes. I did not know they were planning to do that until it was already done."

"I'm sure they gave you a reason why they did such a monstrous thing like that. Now tell me, will you lie to my face and say my men decided to fight back? Or was it for sport?"

I quickly glanced at Jace, and now he looked intrigued as to why it happened as well. I no longer saw a reason to protect Kellan. "It was out of jealousy." Jace's jaw dropped. "It was out of jealousy because I assisted your commander with his injury, that I caused, with my stolen salve."

"Adler killed my men because you helped me that day on the beach?" Jace whispered, as his eyes darted back and forth between my own.

I just nodded sadly in response.

Zaela's eyes softened, but I knew it wasn't because of me, but because of the guilt she knew that Jace now felt.

She finally sheathed her sword back to her hip. "What else happened?"

"Long story short, we were shipwrecked. Your commander and I..." I looked back to Jace and saw the panic remained in his stare. "We washed up on shore together. He woke up first, and tied me to a willow tree." I saw her brows slightly furrow at that. "I know, weird isn't it? Guess that runs in the family." I started laughing at my own joke but nobody else seemed to appreciate it. "Anyway, we have been wandering around for days, and now here we are. I was off trying to go pee in a cave when you bashed me over the head and knocked me out. Nice tactic, by the way, I'll have to remember that one."

Jace's jaw ticked. It seemed as if he was contemplating telling her anything else.

"Why were you practically nude?" Gage asked, eyebrows fluttering up and down at Jace. Zaela didn't notice, but I had to force myself to smother a smile.

"We were bathing in the lagoon. It's not as if she could've gone very far without any supplies or clothes, so I trusted her enough to walk off a little for some privacy."

It felt as if he took my dagger and buried it deep in my chest, but his lie seemed to relax Zaela.

"Very well then." She turned to both of the men. "Jace, I am so relieved you are alive. We will commit to your plan of bringing her back to Ellecaster for questioning. Also, may I recommend sending her head back in a box to Isla? She is a captain. It will make the statement we need."

I gulped at the sound of her new plan. Death? Sure, I was prepared for that. But sending my severed, bloody head back in a box to the king? To my *father?* Gods, this bitch was crazier than I was.

"That will not be necessary," Jace spoke in a deep voice radiating authority.

"You're no fun anymore," she whined. "Alright boys, let's set up the rest of camp. Ellecaster is only a three-day journey from here. We'll be out of the forest by dusk tomorrow if we leave at dawn."

Both Jace and Gage fell asleep a few hours after the decision was made to head to Ellecaster in the morning, but Zaela was making it clear that she didn't trust me enough to let her guard down to sleep.

She stared at me from across the dying fire.

"You know, I'm tied to a gods-damn tree. I won't be able to attack you. You can get some rest."

"My cousin may be falling for your fae tricks, but I will do no such thing."

I laughed at her. "Do you hear yourself? I know you hate my kind, and I truly don't blame you. Not for a single moment. But what do you really think I could do to you while I am naked and bound, with no weapons?"

Her head snapped up. "What did you do to him? Is it some form of fae magic or sorcery? This is not the Jace I grew up with."

I chuckled. "A fae having magic is very rare. That is for the witch covens hidden throughout the realm." She continued to stare at me. "Ugh. No, Zaela, I do not have magic, nor did I do anything to him to keep me alive this long. I don't know why he did this either. I've told him time and time again I will not reveal Velyra's secrets."

"Then why is he protecting you?"

"I wish I had an answer. I am curious myself."

She eyed me as she put her head down, resting on the forest floor. "Whatever. I will figure you out, eventually. I'm a light sleeper, so don't try anything stupid."

"Wouldn't dream of it."

And with that, we both closed our eyes.

THIRTY-FOUR

Jace

I OPENED MY EYES to see Lia was still asleep, attached to the tree. I completely forgot to get our clothes last night that we left by the falls. She must be freezing.

Gage and Zaela were also still sleeping a few feet away from me on the ground. Now was as good a time as any to take a walk back to where we were before our little reunion yesterday.

I stood up slightly too fast, causing me to stumble faintly from dizziness. Yesterday's headache was clearly lingering.

I quietly made my way back through the trees, hoping that no forest critters ran off with what little supplies we had left there.

What the hell was I going to do? I was still in shock that both of my friends were alive. They could never know of what happened yesterday between Elianna and I. Truthfully, I wasn't even sure what happened, but it could never occur again. One thing I knew for sure now was that I didn't think I would ever be able to live with myself if she was killed by my hand, or at the hand of my men.

The way Zaela looked at me yesterday...pure disgust lined every feature of her face. She was upset with me, and she had every right to be.

Elianna could have told them everything, yet she didn't. She could've told Zaela and Gage that I let her walk around the last two days with her own weapon when I had a shitty, makeshift one. That I told her what happened to my mother, which before now, only the two of them knew. And that I had kissed her.

For fuck's sake, what had I gotten myself into?

Making my way into the clearing, I could see our clothes were still piled up at the water's edge. Thank the gods.

I pulled my own shirt over my head and began picking up Lia's clothes and her dagger that she had left stuck in the ground.

I hadn't really looked at the unique weapon until now. Blades crafted with obsidian were rare, and extremely expensive. At first glance I thought the hilt was made of the same material since it was nearly black, but as I turned the dagger, the early morning sunlight began reflecting off of the hilt, casting an emerald green sheen. Now *that* was different. It reminded me of her eyes reflecting in the firelight. The tip of the hilt had the head of a wolf carved into a hard, white material that resembled bone. I didn't think the crest of Velyra's royals contained a wolf, so I wasn't sure what that meant or if it held any significance at all.

I heard footsteps coming up from behind me, and I whipped around with the dagger in hand to see Gage stop in his tracks a few feet in front of me. "Gods, you scared me," I growled.

"Since when are you so jumpy?"

"Since the shit I've run into within these trees. Are we really only a day's hike out of here?"

"Just about," he said, as he came up to me and clasped my shoulder. "I've missed you, brother. Zaela has too. Don't let her bitch act fool you."

I let out a small cackle. "It never does."

"She cried too, by the way. You know...when we thought you were dead."

"I know." I smiled faintly. My heart thudded in my chest as I realized that I hadn't even had a moment to properly grieve them. I was surrounded by the fae on the beach, and then I awoke in my cell with Lia already there. I had essentially been with her ever since.

He looked up at the waterfall. "How fun would it be to jump off that, huh? We should try before Zaela comes and drags us out of here by our ears."

I followed his gaze up to the peak of the cliff that I had both jumped off and fallen from yesterday.

"It's higher than you think," I said, pushing him along, guiding him back to the trees.

He stopped in his tracks, pulling my arm and forcing me to face him. "What is really going on with you and that fae? Did something happen?"

"I don't know what you're talking about."

"She just..." He paused. "She knew about us. She knew our names. That could only mean you told her. What else does she know?"

"Nothing," I snapped, and a flicker of disappointment flashed across his features. "We had just been wandering around lost for days. At some point, we stopped arguing and just started talking. It doesn't change anything."

He gave me a knowing look as he began walking again in the direction we came from. "Whatever you say, Commander."

"Exactly! Whatever I say." I went to trip him jokingly, but he dodged it. "You have had a few days off from my command, so now it's time to whip you back into shape."

He laughed. "Oh perfect, see, this is the real shit I missed," he joked, as we arrived back in the area we camped.

Lia was awake now, and Zaela had packed up the supplies they brought. I threw down Lia's clothes at her feet as I got down on my knees and began untying the rope.

"Thank you," I whispered to her.

She wouldn't look up at me. "For what?"

"You know what."

Her eyes, full of sorrow, met mine then, and I wish they hadn't. "Don't mention it. We are just back to your original plan after a brief moment of insanity."

She was right, and to my own surprise, I hated that she was.

"I have your dagger," I said to her. "They will never let you carry it, but I will hold on to it."

"When she sends my head back, can you just make sure the dagger is in there too, as my only request? Actually, I have two. Please do not address the box to the king."

I looked at her, confused for a moment. She was truly ready to knowingly walk right to her death, and her only fear was who would see the aftermath of it. "We are not sending your head to anyone."

"Well, thanks for that then," she said flatly, as she reached for her clothes and began tugging them on.

Zaela walked up to us then. "Bind her hands. I am not taking any chances with her."

I raised my brow at her as she walked back over to Gage. Turning to Lia, I began to open my mouth to speak, but she held up her hands in surrender.

"No fighting back this time?" I teased.

She grinned wickedly, but I could see right through her mask. "In this moment, I am outnumbered and without a weapon. I'll just go along with her little plan for now."

"A wise decision, for once."

She let out a sharp laugh, causing Gage and Zaela's stares to land on us.

"Let's get out of here," I said to no one in particular.

The past five or so miles were walked in near silence, when Gage finally opened his mouth.

"So, anything crazy happen to the two of you in these woods? The Sylis Forest doesn't have the reputation that it does for nothing."

Lia spoke then, surprising me, "So you mortals *have* heard of the legends." She chuckled. "Jace here tried to tell me I was crazy for being wary of running into wyverns and trolls."

Zaela rolled her eyes. "There are no such things as either of those creatures. Just bedtime stories told in the night to keep children from getting into trouble."

I chuckled. "I said the same thing,"

"Yea, he did. And guess what? We ran into a troll," Lia announced.

Zaela and Gage stopped in their tracks.

"What?" Zaela cried.

"No fucking way! That is awesome. What happened?" Gage boomed in excitement.

Lia turned to me. "I really do like this one."

I tried to hide the fact that my lips were curling into a smile from Zaela.

"You really want to know what happened, Gage?" I said.

Lia let out a loud laugh, cutting me off. "What really happened is that I saved his ass from being troll food."

Now I was rolling my eyes.

"And how exactly did you do that as a prisoner?" Zaela countered.

Lia started to kick a rock along the path with her feet in each step. "Well, after I tackled Jace to the ground when he was almost wiped out by a tree the troll whipped in his direction, I snapped the bindings on my wrists down on my knees to free myself and killed the troll."

"Yeah, how *did* you do that, by the way? With the bindings?" I asked, realizing I had meant to ask this much sooner.

"Oh, that was easy, and I can't believe it took me so long to try to do that. I could do the same thing right now with these, but your companions prefer to be in the comfort of the illusion that I am entirely confined in these," she taunted.

Zaela's eyes went wide.

"Anyway," Lia continued. "I took my dagger back from your commander's boot and ran after the troll. Climbed a tree and then jumped out to pierce the troll's torso with the blade. Then I ripped it down its entire body."

"Holy shit," Gage whispered.

"Would've been a lot quicker too if I didn't have to make sure Jace stayed alive with his stupidity driving his actions."

"I saved your life, and you saved mine. We're even."

We weren't even close to even. She had technically saved my life three times now, and I saved hers once when she had been drowning.

"So, Zaela, to answer your many concerns about me retaliating and trying to kill you all in your sleep, I very easily was able to break free of my restraints and steal back my dagger within a few seconds. Only I did not attack your commander. I saved him."

Zaela didn't respond to her.

"Speaking of your dagger," I chimed in, breaking the awkward silence. "I was looking at it earlier this morning. It is unique. What is with the wolf's head on the hilt?"

For a moment I thought she wouldn't respond as she continued to face forward, twisting her lips as she thought of how to answer. "The dagger was a gift from someone very special to me. The wolf's head is carved from the antler of a white stag. It's modeled after my wolf back in Isla. Her name is Nyra."

"You have a wolf as a pet?" Gage asked.

"She is more of a companion than a pet, but yes. I rescued her when she was just a pup years ago. I believe her mother and part of her pack were killed by farmers that feared for their livestock. I found her and took her in."

I watched her as she said this. All the features on her face looked lighter, and happy.

I glanced over at Zaela to see that she was eyeing Lia intently. "Last night, you spoke of using stolen salve on Jace's wound," she cut in, changing the subject. "Why would a captain need to steal salve? Why not just provide your fleet with enough for assumed injuries that would occur?"

When she didn't respond to her after a few moments, all three of us were looking at her. Zaela continued, "Well, Miss Elianna? Are you going to tell us why, or was that just another lie in your web to try to get us to trust you? Making us think you helped Jace against your beloved's will, when in reality you probably sent the order to have our men killed."

I didn't say anything because I needed to hear how she would explain this.

"It's none of your concern," was all she said.

Zaela ran up behind her and forcefully shoved her body to the ground. "Lies. Everything regarding you, your tricks, and what happened to our men is *all* of our concern." She paused as Lia turned her body around on the forest floor, now lying on her back, looking up at Zae. "The truth. Now."

Lia's eyes met mine, and judging by the way she was staring at me, I knew this concerned one of the secrets of Velyra she planned to never discuss, but I needed to know.

"Tell us, Solus," I demanded.

Her lips parted slightly. "No," she whispered.

Zaela swung out her boot and kicked Lia in the ribs the second her response left her lips, leaving her to curl up on the ground in pain.

"Gods, Zaela, *enough!*" I shouted.

I reached down to help Lia up, but she pushed my hand away as she lifted herself up, shooting me a look full of revulsion.

I looked at Gage, and he just slightly shook his head.

The four of us then continued to make our way through the trees in silence.

Elianna

Gods, I hated Zaela. I was expecting Jace to start acting differently toward me again, but I wasn't fully prepared for him to call me "Solus" again.

I knew I spoke too much last night about bringing up the salve. I could never let the enemy know that we were forbidden to travel with healers and that I felt forced to steal from the supply in Isla to bring with us against the queen's orders. It would give the humans an upper hand that we couldn't afford for them to know.

The past few hours of walking for miles in silence, all I could think about was just telling his two friends that I also wanted to end this war, but I could already tell that *she* wouldn't believe me. Gage might, but not her.

"Won't be long now, the end of the woods is just about a mile ahead," Gage finally broke the incredibly tense silence.

I looked at him. "Are we near Ellecaster?"

"Not Ellecaster, but Celan Village. There are a few taverns and inns located there where we can rest for the night before we borrow horses to ride to Ellecaster."

I had never heard of Celan Village, but then again, I didn't realize the humans had their own names for cities and towns they had formed. All I could think about was finally being able to sleep in a bed, instead of on the hard, unforgiving forest floor.

"We are going to have to hide her identity once we are there," Jace cut in.

Zaela grunted. "And how do you expect we do that?"

He looked at her for a moment. "Does your cloak have a hood?"

"Yes?"

"Then you will give her your cloak. We just need to make sure nobody sees her ears," Jace decided.

"Her eyes aren't exactly subtle," Zaela snarked while staring at me.

"That is not a fae trait. I was just born with my mother's pale green eyes. I will keep my head down so nobody sees them, just in case."

Jace looked at me curiously, probably wondering how I knew what my mother's eyes looked like.

I couldn't believe we had finally reached the end of the forest. Not even two days ago, I assumed we would die in here, but we made our way out.

Zaela slugged the pack of supplies off her back and threw her cloak at me. "Dusk is upon us, so the darkness will be on our side. Just don't speak to anyone and do not, under any circumstances, take off your hood. Do you understand?"

I looked into what resembled a pair of familiar hazel eyes, but they were filled with displeasure. "Perfectly," I said to her, as she cut the rope binding my hands.

I pulled on her cloak, covered my face, and in tandem, the four of us made our first few steps beyond the barrier of Sylis Forest.

THIRTY-FIVE

Avery

THE PAST FEW DAYS had been unbearable since learning of the disappearance, and presumed death, of Lia. Even Nyra had been moping around, refusing to leave my side as if she understood what we had learned in the throne room.

The fact that my mother put out a direct order to not have even a single scout out looking for her told me all I needed to know regarding how she truly felt about my best friend. The queen hadn't paid enough attention to me since I was a child to even realize that Lia and I were close.

Once I would be sent away to my chambers for the evening, Lia would always sneak in through her numerous secret tunnels throughout the castle walls and we would get into all kinds of trouble together. I would never forget the first time I finally convinced her to show me her tunnels and where they led. I could almost never remember which route led to where, but she always did. I loved sneaking out into the garden at night and watching the fireflies light up along the wisteria vines that climbed the exterior castle walls.

Luckily, we were only ever caught by Lukas, thank the gods. He would always hide out, lurking in a corner unseen, and would reveal himself in the last moment. The first time he caught us I was about to beg for him to not tell the queen, but when I looked up into his kind, chocolate-colored eyes, I knew he was more out there to make sure we were safe than to ruin our fun.

Once Lia had been promoted to captain, I remember crying for days, without her knowledge. She was going to get to see the world. I was so excited for her—it was everything she ever worked for and wanted, but I was terrified that everything was going to change and I would never see her anymore. Luckily, that wasn't the case and every time she came home, we spent almost every free moment we had together. Now she was gone, possibly forever, and I could feel my chest tighten at the thought.

Thinking of all this made me want to get up and explore the old pathways throughout the castle walls in honor of my fearless best friend.

I looked to Nyra. "Come on girl, do you want to come?"

She just lifted her tail and gently placed it over her eyes, thinking I couldn't see her if she couldn't see me. Silly pup.

I sighed. "Fine, stay here. I will be back soon."

I glanced out my window to see the sun was setting, so I grabbed onto one of my lit sconces to bring with me.

Quietly slipping past my chamber door, I peered around the corner to see two guards were standing in the hall where one of the secret doors stood behind a massive tapestry. I knew that was the one that led down to the gardens solely because it was the main passage Lia and I used decades ago. The scenery that was woven into that tapestry was of hundreds of different kinds of wildflowers, which I thought was a nice touch.

The moment I stepped out into the hallway, the guards' gazes immediately snapped up to me. "Good evening, Princess Avery," one of them said.

"Good evening, sir. I am glad both of you are here." They both looked at each other in a state of confusion. "The queen requests your posts be moved to the lower floors."

The one who greeted me cleared his throat. "Why would Her Majesty do that? We have been posted here for the remainder of the evening."

"I believe there has been a bit of commotion, and Callius is tied up. She sent me up to my chamber and said once I see you both, I am to let you know that you are to change posts down toward the old healing quarters." Both of them looked hesitant. "Don't say I didn't warn you," I whispered while leaning into them.

Both of their backs stiffened, and they nearly ran toward the spiral stairs at the end of the hallway.

I chuckled to myself. "That was too easy."

Glancing around the hall, making sure nobody else was lingering around, I quietly pulled back the old, dusty tapestry that I hadn't touched in years and revealed the giant wooden door. A smile instantly formed on my face as I thought of all the old memories.

The knob turned easily, and the door creaked slightly too loud for comfort as I gently pushed it open. I was thankful for the candle I had since the passageway nearly resembled a black abyss. I quietly closed the door behind me and made my way through the winding tunnel. It was frigid, dark, and damp. Just how I remembered it.

While walking down the passageway staircase, I passed by many openings that led into different halls. I strictly remembered that the garden was a straight shot. Thank the gods, because I would absolutely get lost down here. I couldn't believe Lia always managed to find her way out.

Once I met another large wooden door, I placed my candle on the ground and began to push it open very slowly. I met a slight resistance on the other side, but once I got it open just wide enough to pass my slim body through, I managed to climb out of it.

White wisteria vines had grown over and covered the door completely, disguising it to blend in with the remainder of the wall. I glanced around and noticed Kai in the distance, his back faced me as he gazed at the fountain that lay in the center of the blooming gardens.

My dress got caught on one of the vines and I accidentally ripped the bottom of it while trying to crawl through them. Keeping my head low, I walked to a corner where fully bloomed yellow rose bushes cradled a wall of the castle and crouched down.

"Prince Kai," Callius' voice boomed from the courtyard's door. I ducked my head down even further to remain unseen. "The queen requests your presence immediately. It is about the king."

I watched through the bush, struggling to make out more than just their forms as he turned to face Callius. "Immediately? Has something happened?"

"I am afraid so, Prince. She wishes to speak to you about the fate of Velyra."

My brows flew up. "Father," I whispered to myself. Oh gods, he couldn't be gone too. I couldn't lose both him and Lia.

"What of Avery and Finnian?" Kai asked, and it surprised me that he even bothered to think of us.

"This will be a private meeting with you and the queen," Callius replied.

Why wasn't our mother summoning all of us? I had a sinking feeling in my gut.

"Avery, what are you doing?" A voice spoke much too loudly behind me.

I whipped around to see Finnian staring at me with his brows furrowed. I reached up, grabbing his wrist, and yanked him down to the ground with me behind the rosebush.

I placed my pointer finger over my lips, making sure he knew to stay quiet. He then heard the tail end of the conversation happening at the fountain.

"Where did you even come from?!" I whisper shouted.

"I was working up the courage to try to talk to Landon when I saw you crouching behind here. What the hell is going on, Avery?" he whispered, as I turned back and watched Kai follow Callius back into the castle.

"We need to move. Now!" I said, as I pulled his body up with my own and dragged him back to the secret door.

I started peeling back some of the vines when he grabbed my shoulders with both of his hands and forced me to look at him.

"What is going on?!"

"Something happened. I think to our father." I paused. "Mother is summoning Kai up to her chambers to speak with him about it. I just heard Callius tell him that it is to discuss Velyra's future. Why isn't she summoning us with him, Finn? Something doesn't feel right."

"Gods, you're right. That doesn't make sense. Is Father okay?"

"I don't think so..." I whispered, as I closed my eyes tight, my throat clogging with grief.

"Why are you ripping down the vines?"

My eyes widened, and I slowly rotated to him. "I am about to show you my secret tunnel."

He laughed in my face. "Avery...we aren't younglings. What are you really doing?"

I pursed my lips in annoyance at him and put pressure on the hidden door so it creaked open, letting out a small burst of stale air.

"What the hell?" Finn said to himself.

"I will explain later, lets go!"

Forcing our way through the small opening, I picked up the candle that I had left on the ground and stormed down the winding path.

"Lia showed me these passageways when we were younger. We used to sneak around the castle at night using them."

"*That's* what you two would do? Gods, I knew I was wise to not participate in your shenanigans."

I gave him an incredulous look. "Yeah, well, those *shenanigans* are about to come in handy now, aren't they? Come on, we need to move quickly."

Finnian

I couldn't believe I just stumbled upon this disaster. I was just making my way through the gardens to head to the stables. I finally gathered enough courage to go and see Landon after everything, and then I saw Avery sneaking behind a rosebush. Now she was dragging me through a tunnel full of cobwebs and gods knew what else.

How long had she been coming down here? How many more were there? Did this lead somewhere I knew of?

We came to a door at the end and she slowly opened it and pulled back a corner of a tapestry to reveal we were in a hall outside of her own chambers.

Avery kicked her shoes off and slid them under the tapestry on the floor. She gave me a look as if she was expecting me to do the same.

"You're kidding..." I huffed, rolling my eyes at her.

"Does it look like I'm kidding? We need to be as quiet as possible."

I sighed and began taking off my boots. "You know, they may be searching for us as it is."

"I doubt that. Now let's go. They were to meet in the queen's chamber."

So, on silent feet, that's where we ran.

THIRTY-SIX

Avery

PEERING AROUND THE CORNER, I could see Callius' back as he escorted Kai into our mother's chambers and closed the door behind himself.

"Shit," I whispered. "There must be another passageway around here."

"There was a tapestry hung on a wall behind a table. The hallway before last. Could there be one behind there?" Finn asked.

Genius. My little brother was a genius. I didn't reply to him as I grabbed his wrist and headed back the way we came.

How had I never noticed this before? Granted, the tapestry was very old and gray, blending in with the stone wall rather peculiarly. In front of it sat a small, thin table with a vase containing flowers from the garden and a few candles.

"Move the table," I said, as I grabbed one end, and Finn to grabbed the other on instinct.

We quietly moved the table to the side, and I had to peel the ancient tapestry from the wall, but we were in luck because behind it revealed yet another wooden door.

"Well damn," Finn gasped. "I am assuming you've never been in this passage before, right? How will we know where we are going?"

"Shh," I hushed him, as I snuck through, grabbing a candle from the table we just moved.

Finn followed, and as he quietly shut the door behind us, I realized there was no one to replace the table back where it had been. We needed to be quick to make sure nobody noticed.

This passage was different, and I doubted anyone had been in here in centuries. The walls and ceiling were covered in cobwebs and a thick coat of undisturbed dust collected along the floor.

"We are never going to find our way around in here," Finn whispered.

"Let's just follow the wall from which we came." With that said, I took a sharp left.

After walking about thirty feet, I could hear voices coming from one of the small crawl spaces veering off in the passage.

"That must be them!" I said, as I ducked down and made my way as close as I could. At the end of the crawl space, the ceiling rose slightly, just enough for a full-grown male to stand, and then I noticed that there was another door.

"Oh, my gods, this leads right to her room!"

"No way!" Finn said, as he crawled faster to catch up. We both barely fit in the space in front of the door and as I went to crack the door open, Finn gripped my wrist tightly. "Are you mad!? You are going to get us caught!"

"Relax," I whispered. I *very* slowly began to crack the door open, just enough to be able to hear their conversation clearly. This passageway was hidden behind one of the extravagant paintings in the queen's chambers—I doubted she even knew this awaited beneath it.

I turned back to face Finn. "I can't move the painting, it's blocking the doorway, but I can make out the silhouettes of their bodies from the shadows the fire is casting. Come sit closer to me."

Finn scooted his butt across the floor and we sat so close that our knees were touching, our bodies filling the doorway, and we listened.

"Kai, my dear, what I am about to say to you may come as a bit of a shock," our mother said.

"Father is dead, isn't he?" Kai asked in an uncaring tone.

"Yes, he is, Kai. Only a few hours ago. Does that upset you?"

My stomach dropped and tears suddenly started pouring from my eyes. Finnian grabbed my hand and squeezed it tightly. The *three* of us lost our father, so why was she only telling Kai?

Kai's shadow shrugged. "In a way, but we never exactly had a relationship. He was closer to his precious Captain Solus than he was to me."

I could hear Callius let out a low chuckle, as the queen said, "Yes, well, *that* we will also get to shortly." She sounded disgusted at his statement.

"What could she possibly mean by that? Why is Lia involved in this at all?" Finn whispered in my ear.

"I have no idea."

"What is going on, Mother?" Kai asked.

"What's going on, my sweet boy, is that you are now to be crowned king. Since I am not of the Valderre bloodline, I am not to sit upon the throne for longer than a month's time by Velyra's law since we have an heir of his blood. We will need to set a coronation for you upon choosing your bride and future queen. But first, I must teach you the ways of our world, the true ways. Not the way your father had ruled. Honestly, the male was many things, but I will put the title of 'fool' at the top of the list."

"Why don't you sit down, Prince? She has over a century's worth of information to share," Callius suggested.

My brows flew up at that. What could he mean?

I could see the shadow of Kai as he sat down on a settee near Mother's bed.

I watched the queen lift a glass that most likely contained her favorite, imported wine, as she began to speak, "Where shall I begin? Well, as you know, I was promised to your father at birth. We were promised to each other due to my own father, gods-rest his soul, being one of the most powerful Lords in all of Velyra. As tradition stated, we were married once we reached the age of one hundred and fifty, and crowned shortly after the king at the time had passed. It didn't necessarily begin as a hateful marriage, but we definitely did not spend much time together, and we most certainly did not love each other. However, that was typical of most arranged marriages."

"What is with this history lesson? Is there a point?" Kai interrupted.

If Finnian or I were to have said that to her, it would result in a smack across the cheek without the removal of her rings.

"Of course, there is a point, darling." She sipped her wine once more. "One hundred and thirty-seven years ago, your father told me he was in love with another."

"So? It's not like you loved him."

"She was with child. His first child, to be exact."

My eyes grew so wide it was nearly painful, and out of the corner of my vision, Finnian's jaw dropped.

"What the fuck?" Kai shouted, as he stood up from the settee.

"I am glad I now have your attention. Anyway, your father decided that we would all raise this youngling together. Me, himself, and his chosen love, *Ophelia*. She gave birth to the babe that very night. A little girl with pale green eyes that matched her mother's." The queen snickered. "I had never seen the king as happy as he had been at that moment. Never before, and not ever again after. Even when I gave him three beautiful babes myself."

"Lia," I whispered, as a vision of her eyes flashed before me. "Lia is our...*sister?*"

"He even went as far to consider that this Ophelia was his mate, which was absolutely absurd." She paused, and chuckled wickedly. "But they were not mates, for he did not feel her pain."

"Pain?" Kai asked curiously.

"What you will come to learn once you officially ascend the throne is that threats will present themselves in the most peculiar ways sometimes. And those threats need to be dealt with." She took yet another sip of wine. "Your father took the babe to get her cleaned up. He had sent Veli home for the night since the ever-so-lovely Ophelia was a healer herself, and your father was devastated when that did not matter in the end."

"What is she saying?" I whispered to myself. "She couldn't possibly mean..."

"Your father came running when he heard my scream echo throughout the castle. Him and Lukas came to find me distraught in the hallway outside of the healer's chamber. Luckily we had enough time for Callius to remove the body and all evidence."

"Evidence of what?"

The queen cackled once more. "You see, my dear, I could accept a few unknown bastard children lying around the city, but not one he loved. Not one he *wanted*. And most certainly not one who could take claim to the throne. I had no children of my own yet, no rightful heirs. This child was made with *love*. It was a betrayal to not only his queen, but his kingdom. It had to be done. The healer had to be dealt with."

My heart was racing and I couldn't catch my breath. I was in shock by what I was listening to, something that we never would've heard if I hadn't been eavesdropping in the garden not even an hour ago.

"I slit her throat." She sipped her wine. "Not Callius. I did it myself. And I would do it again. Ophelia knew it was coming too, and I looked into her haunted, enchanting eyes as I watched the life drain from them. That is what I see every time I look at Elianna."

Kai laughed. He *laughed*. "Well done, Mother."

She stood from where she sat and walked over to the settee. Cupping his cheek, she said, "I knew you would understand. Of course, your father was devastated at the news of his love passing away from birthing complications while he was off washing the babe. I took the opportunity to initiate the war on the humans that my own father was desperate to have before his untimely death."

"So, you let him keep the bastard babe alive to start your war?"

"Precisely. And it kept him occupied for a while too until recently. Of course, I knew Elianna was going to continue to be a problem, but we let her become too powerful by letting her slip through the cracks and obtain the highest rank in our army. She has been in your father's ear for years about ending this war. *My* war. And I will be damned if this war ends before every last mortal soul is wiped from this realm."

"I've heard enough, Avery, I can't listen to this anymore," Finn said, as he tugged on my shoulder.

"Are you insane? Sit the fuck down and shut up. This is horrifying, but we will never know anything else if we leave now."

Kai scoffed in disgust. "It all makes sense now. Why Father treasured his precious Solus so gods-damn much. That bitch constantly flaunted around her ego, *knowing* that she was the king's daughter. No wonder why the little cunt was so brave...but she doesn't have her precious king to protect her anymore, now does she? Of course, that's if she is even still living herself."

The queen's voice radiated with spite, "You are correct, my son."

Kai snickered. "Father didn't have an illness, did he?"

"Smart boy," Callius chimed in.

"I am *not* a boy, you brute." Kai snapped at him.

"Now, now, you two. Calm down. Where was I? Oh! Yes. You are familiar with the wyvern below the keep, yes?" the queen asked. Kai's shadow nodded. "Our lovely Callius found it as an egg within the Sylis Forest and brought it back to me, and what a lovely gift it has been. Kai, do you know what the blood of a dragon or wyvern will do to flesh once exposed?"

"Can't say I do." He sighed, starting to sound bored.

"It melts flesh within seconds, far too quickly for even the fae to heal depending on the depth of the wound without the assistance of a healer. A human would merely become a puddle of blood and bone if exposed to the substance. Nobody knew what was going on with your father because I was quietly slipping three drops of the wyvern's blood into his nightly glass of wine for months. It finally caught up to him. The blood was slowly and painfully melting him from the inside out."

I went to move to charge into the room, but Finn grabbed me by the waist and shoved me down, covering my mouth with his hand so no one could hear the scream of agony I was desperate to let out.

"Gods, that is a little brutal, even for you," Kai said to her.

289

"Brutal, but necessary. The key to this death was to have no foul play suspected, including poison. It also couldn't be a known illness that a healer could treat. I knew Jameson would sneak Veli in here against my will, knowing how I felt about healers, and she had always been the very best of them all. If anyone would be able to detect an illness or poison, it would be her."

"Is that why you hate healers? Because Father was fucking one behind your back? I applaud your pettiness." He let out a sharp laugh, but before he could finish, the queen stormed over and smacked him across his face—the sound echoed through the chambers.

Apparently, that was the line he needed to cross.

"You may be next in line for the throne, but I am still the queen, and your mother. You will respect me." I couldn't hear a reply from Kai, when I heard the queen speak up to Callius, "Go and find Captain Adler, our first order of business is to relieve Lukas of his duties to the crown and appoint Kellan to his position immediately."

"Of course, Your Majesty," Callius said, as I heard the click of a door.

"Shit! We need to move. Now!" I said slightly too loud, as I grabbed a hold of Finn's arm and dragged him back through the crawlspace.

We ran through the passageway and back out the door we had originally found. Completely out of breath, we were adjusting the table back into place when Callius turned the corner.

"Prince Finnian and Princess Avery, what are you doing in this wing at this time of night?"

Think, Avery, think.

"We were just going to visit Mother in her quarters. We haven't seen her much lately and decided to visit."

He looked down at my dust covered dress and the tear that had happened in the gardens, then eyed us warily. "The queen is not in her chambers," he lied so smoothly. "But if I see her, I will let her know you were looking for her."

"Perfect, thank you!" I said, my voice slightly cracking.

I didn't take another breath until he disappeared down the stairs at the end of the hall.

THIRTY-SEVEN

Elianna

AFTER WALKING FOR ABOUT three miles outside of Sylis Forest, the faint silhouette of a small town appeared on the horizon in the moonlight.

"I'm assuming that is Celan Village?" I asked, trying to make conversation.

"Nothing gets past you, huh?" Zaela snarked.

Gods, what I wouldn't do to punch her in her mouth.

Making our way up to the village gates, I noticed that the town was filled with humans in the streets. Bartering and selling goods, dancing to the street performers that played their instruments in front of the little shops that lined the cobblestone sidewalks, some even seemed to just be out for a stroll.

Everyone seemed *happy.*

"There is an inn at the top of the hill," Gage said to no one in particular. "I will go check and see if there is any vacancy."

"Thank you, Gage," Jace said, as he clapped him on the shoulder.

I glanced over at Zaela to see she was off handing coin to one of the street performers that had been taking a break when I turned to Jace. "She hates me."

"She does," he answered without meeting my eyes.

"And you?"

He went to open his mouth and hesitated for a moment, his jaw ticked. "To be determined."

"Charming." I rolled my eyes and began observing the bustling streets around us once more.

Gage came running back down the hill a few minutes later. "They have two rooms available for the night," he said, out of breath. "Looks like we're bunking up like the old days, bud." He elbowed Jace.

Which meant I would have to share a room with...

"I hope you know you'll be sleeping on the floor," Zaela said to me, coming up from behind me.

I was clenching my jaw so tightly I thought my teeth were about to shatter, when Jace said, "I will be sharing a room with Solus." All three of us stared at him, unblinking. "I don't trust you two to not kill each other in the night." He moved to make his way up the hill to the inn.

"It's insulting to me that you think she would be even capable of such a thing!" Zaela called after him.

Jace spun around. "Trust me, I am *very* aware of what she is capable of." He eyed me then, looking my body up and down leisurely, making my breath catch.

Uncomfortable with the tension floating in the surrounding air, I looked at Gage. He just shrugged and put his arm around Zaela's shoulders and said to her, "Hope you don't mind a lot of snoring."

"You say that as if I haven't dealt with it in the woods the last few days," she said with a laugh.

The three of us then followed Jace up the hill.

The inn had a tavern on the bottom floor, serving a small menu of food and ale. We sat in one of the tables in the far back corner, nearly hidden by shadows to try to not have my hooded appearance draw too much attention.

The barmaid had brought us each four rounds at this point and I could tell that Gage was ready to pass out already on the table.

"Another round?!" he shouted at us, as he stood up on his feet, his words slurring.

"I think you have had enough," Jace said with a laugh.

"Perhaps you are right," Gage answered, as he lost his balance and fell down, back into his seat.

I giggled at his antics. There's no doubt in my mind to where if the circumstances were different, Gage and I would be very good friends.

Zaela and Jace each took one of Gage's arms and holstered him up, dragging his half-limp body up the stairs. Once Zaela got the door open to their room for the night, I waited out in the hallway and Jace plopped Gage's body on the bed with a loud thump.

He walked his way back out to me when Zaela appeared back in the entryway, leaning her body against the doorframe. "You sure you'll be okay?" she asked him, concerned.

I raised a brow at her.

"I will be fine. Get some rest. We will see you in the morning," Jace said to her.

She eyed me warily and then shut the door.

"Our room is right up the last flight of stairs. It's the loft," Jace said, as he guided the way.

We arrived at the door at the top of the stairs. It seemed as if there was only this room up here, and no others.

He wiggled the key in the lock multiple times before the door finally gave way and opened. As my eyes focused on the room, I noticed at the same time he did that there was only one bed.

"Uhhhh," he blurted.

"I will sleep on the floor, don't worry," I rushed out, shoving past him.

"Don't be ridiculous, Elianna," he said, as he slammed the door behind him in frustration.

"Oh. So *now* I am Elianna again? Make up your fucking mind, asshole."

He sat down on the bed and placed his face into his hands, as his elbows rested on his lap. "I don't know what you mean."

"Are we really going to play this game? Now your friends are gone, you think we are going to go back to what happened at the waterfall?!"

He lifted his head and his eyes focused on me intently. "What happened at the falls will *never* happen again. It can't. Do you understand?"

"No shit," I spat at him, refusing to blink.

"It was a brief moment of insanity and loneliness. May have even been caused by lingering euphoroot. Nothing more."

My heart painfully stuttered in my chest. "Couldn't agree more."

His eyes softened, but he didn't say anything further.

The room went silent, and the atmosphere grew more uncomfortable as each second passed.

I cleared my throat. "Even though they clearly hate me...I'm glad they are alive. For your sake."

He chuckled. "Gage definitely doesn't hate you."

"Good, because that would probably make me cry if he did." I said, as the corners of my lips curved up slightly.

"You? Cry over an opinion? I doubt that."

I snorted in response and then smirked at him. "So, now I know why your leg healed so gods-damn fast. You're a halfling."

Any form of kindness that had been in his eyes vanished in an instant. "Do *not* call me that."

"But it is what you are. I understand not wanting to acknowledge who you truly are. I feel the same way, believe it or not. And I don't blame you for not wanting to claim your fae heritage due to whoever sired you, but that is your truth. It is what you are."

"I will never acknowledge such nonsense," he said through his teeth.

"Do you know anything about the fae aside from what you hate? Do you know anything regarding halflings?"

"There is nothing I wish to know."

Gods, he was so damn stubborn.

"Halflings are few and far between now in Isla, thanks to the queen. However, there are many still alive in secret, hidden throughout Isla and the realm itself. Halflings can gain many traits from both the fae and humans. Some are born with pointed ears, while others are born with round, taking after their mortal side. Almost all of them have some form of fae abilities, whether that be heightened senses or healing capabilities. Typically, all of them have a significantly longer lifespan than the average human. The oldest lived to be twelve-hundred years old."

His eyes grew wide as he shot up from the bed. "Again, your lies are alluring and beautiful," he said in a venomous tone.

"I'm not lying. It's the truth."

He snickered as he walked over to the window and gazed beyond into the streets below.

"How old are you?" I asked sternly. "Because you don't look more than a day over your twenty-fifth year of life, which is typically when the fae's aging process slows down significantly."

"I am twenty-nine years old, Elianna." The way he said my name sent a shiver through me. "And how old are you? I highly doubt you look your age."

I cleared my throat. "I am one hundred and thirty-seven years of age."

He was silent for a moment. "I cannot even fathom living that long."

"Well, you better start processing it soon, because unless you manage to get yourself killed, you will be living this long, and even further beyond that. The fae aren't even considered to be fully mature until the age of one hundred and fifty."

"...That explains *so* much," he said with a teasing grin.

I pulled off my cloak and shoved it at him as I tried to hide my smile forming.

"What happened to the halflings in Isla?" he asked.

I shut my eyes tight, as I prepared myself to say, "Not all of them were executed, but if they were unfortunate enough to carry the trait of rounded ears...it didn't end well for them." I opened one of my eyes into a slit to see his reaction and saw he had moved closer to me. I opened my eyes completely to look up at him. "I want you to know that I do not agree with what she did...and the majority of the hangings were when I was just a babe."

"They were hung just for having rounded ears? Because it gave them away for not being full-blooded fae?"

I nodded. "Known halflings that resembled the fae were executed as well. Her reasoning was that she thought anyone with ancestral ties to the mortal race would more than likely become a sympathizer."

"Bullshit."

"I agree, Jace," I whispered.

"And how is the king not one in the same as her, huh? How can you defend him? What has he done to stop any of this? *Nothing!*" he said, his voice raised.

I could feel a stinging in the back of my eyes, and I started to blink back the tears that were forcing their way to the surface. "The king was...occupied," I answered, my voice hoarse.

"That is no excuse, Elianna. It doesn't even make sense! The queen started a war. She didn't just act against the individuals that committed the crimes. A. War. One that has cost *thousands* of lives on each side. And you stand here and say the king was too occupied to notice what was going on around him? What the fuck could he have been occupied with?!"

The tears began streaming down my face as he was standing over me, shouting these words in my face.

I didn't mean to say it—I didn't want to. I couldn't stop the word from coming out. "*Me!*" I shouted back at him, and he immediately froze where he stood. "He was occupied with me."

THIRTY-EIGHT

Jace

"WHAT THE FUCK DOES that mean, Lia?" I whispered, as she met my stare.

"I am one hundred and thirty-seven years old, Jace." She continued to stare at me. "The same age as the war. Down to the very day."

My eyes grew wide. "What are you saying?"

"Just forget it," she said, turning her body away from me.

I reached out on reflex and grasped her arm, forcing her to spin back around. "Oh, I don't think so! What do you mean by all of that?"

She shoved my hand off of her. "It is none of your concern."

She was infuriating.

"Since this apparently is connected to the war that I have dedicated my life to, I would say yes. It absolutely is my concern." I paused. "Why are you favored by the king, Lia? Why do you protect his name and integrity? Why was he occupied with you?"

Her face turned a bright red as she looked away from me. "I am his *daughter*. His firstborn child, if you want to get specific."

What. The. Fuck.

"So that makes you–"

"A bastard child," she cut me off.

"So that is why you hate the queen?"

"No," she said sternly. "I hate the queen because she is wicked to her very core. My father is too kind for his own good. Before I left on this trip, he told me he was aware of the mistakes he has made, but it has gone on far too long to be fixed now."

I stared at her as I desperately tried to process what she was saying. "So, you are the true heir."

"I am no such thing. I am not a child of the queen."

"Why does that matter?"

"Because it does! Okay?" she shouted in my face. Her breathing became heavy as she lowered her voice, "My father told me he wished he named me heir the day I was born, but since I was not a child of the queen, he couldn't risk it. He refused to risk my life in that moment after he had just lost his true love. Not to mention that the kingdom quite literally has no idea that I exist, in that way anyway. They would never accept me as the heir." She paused to catch her breath. "I don't want to be anyway. Too much politics." She waved her hand on the last word as if to just brush it off.

"You could end the fucking war, Elianna."

"Don't you think I have tried? I have been in my father's ear for decades over it and he has not been able to convince the queen. And now he is dying. He is very ill, and nothing will be able to be done aside from the queen's evil, firstborn son ascending the throne."

"You command their armies, the soldiers...your soldiers should follow you," I said after a long silence.

"They are loyal to the crown. Not me."

"Who's to say that won't change once the tyrant prince takes the throne? They could choose to follow you!"

"And risk being tried for treason? For mutiny against their new and cruel king? I wouldn't risk my soldiers or their families like that."

"Well, you are a fool for not trying." I tried to remove the anger from my tone, but it was no use.

Her head snapped up. "Go to hell."

She got up and stormed for the door.

"Where the hell do you think you are going?" I snapped.

"For a walk, and don't you worry I will be back here to play prisoner by morning."

"Elianna, cut the shit." I got up and ran to the doorway, blocking it with my body. She tried to race past me, but somehow I was quicker than she was. "*Stop*." I breathed in her face, which was now barely an inch from my own. Her enchanting stare froze me where I stood.

She brought her lips to my own. "Never," she whispered onto them, and a moment later she kneed me in the stomach so hard that I dropped down to my own knees with a grunt, allowing her to shove past me and out the door.

Elianna

I stomped down the wooden stairs of the inn, making sure every single step was felt within the walls of the building, and stormed out the front door, back into the streets that were no longer bustling with life.

I couldn't believe I just revealed that to him. My enemy. Why did I even give a shit about what he thought? Perhaps because deep down, I knew that he wasn't my enemy at all. He was right, in a way.

No, Lia, don't think that way. There would never be a way to prove who I was, even if the citizens of Velyra would listen. Nobody would ever risk being tried, and inevitably hung for treason, or for being connected to a sympathizer. Which I was slowly beginning to realize that that was *exactly* what I was.

I walked around the corner of the inn to see there were more streets lined with stores and merchant carts that had long since been emptied for the evening.

The sky started drizzling, and when I went to pull up my hood, I realized I had left my cloak in the room at the inn. I fluffed out my long hair to try to hide my ears as I made my way up the quiet, lonely street.

Walking along the road, I noticed bakeries, salon parlors, blacksmiths and more lined the streets of Celan Village. It reminded me of a tiny version of Isla's center. The humans really weren't much different from us at all.

Glancing back from where I came, the inn seemed to be about a half mile off. I sat down on the damp sidewalk and looked up at the dreary sky.

"What the hell did I just do?" I mumbled to myself, as I placed my face into my hands and rubbed my temples.

I heard footsteps coming up to me, and without lifting my face I said, "Gods, can't you just let me have a *single* moment to myself?"

My hearing then picked up multiple footsteps.

"What do we have here?" A deep voice carried to me on the wind.

My head snapped up, and looking through the hair that was now sticking to my face from the rain, I counted five sizable men standing before me, surrounding me, and nearly cornering me into the building to my back.

I cleared my throat and smirked. "Whatever you males are planning to do, I am going to warn you that it would be very unwise," I advised, while getting to my feet.

"Males?" One of them snapped at me with a laugh.

Shit.

Out of the corner of my eye, I saw one lunge toward me—I dodged his hand, but not fast enough. He managed to catch a part of my hair through his fingers and pulled it away from my face, revealing the pointed tip of my ear.

"And what's *this?*" The one that lunged at me said.

"A fae? That isn't possible. How did you sneak in here and remain unnoticed until now?" the third man on the corner asked.

"What makes you think I didn't waltz right through the front gates?" I gave him a wicked grin.

"A feisty one. Looks like we have a real treat for the night boys, you've heard the rumors of fae women and the prize between their legs."

They all laughed. Gross.

I slowly pointed at each of them down the line as I counted out loud, "One, two, three, four, five..."

"It can count. How lovely. Tell me, fae whore, are you counting how many cocks will be inside you by the end of the night?"

I giggled. "Hardly. I am just counting to have you realize how incredibly unfair it is to have five against one."

"Unfair?" He raised a brow.

"When I kill you all within the next few moments."

All five of the men started laughing again, and I took the opportunity to turn back and run at the building behind me. I leaped up, kicking off of the door and flipped over the man closest to me, the one who had revealed my ear, and landed directly behind him. I then took his head between my two hands and snapped his neck in an instant.

The remaining four gasped and went for their swords. "I should've clarified that it would be unfair to you," I said, as the, now very dead, man's body dropped to the ground. I reached for my dagger, which was typically strapped to my thigh, on reflex and realized Jace still had it.

Fuck.

"You got lucky there, *princess*. You won't get that lucky again with the four of us."

That. *Word*.

Absolutely not.

I then dodged and rolled my body out of the way as the one who was talking took a swing at me with his sword. Now on the ground directly behind him, I swung my legs out tripping him, bringing his body to the ground next to my own with a loud thud.

Another man then launched at me from a few feet away, and I lifted up the sword that the one that I had tripped had dropped and blocked the blow with it barely in time.

I managed to get to my feet and twirled around, slicing the sword directly through the man's gut. Blood instantly poured from his stomach as he looked at me completely shocked. I lifted up my leg in one swift motion and kicked him in the chest, sending his body flying back. He was dead before his back hit the ground.

I waltzed back over to the man that I had tripped, who was still on the ground, unconscious from slamming his head on the cobblestones. "You were saying?" I asked, as I raised the sword's hilt above my head with both arms and plunged the blade down into his gut, ripping it across his body.

The cockiness cost me.

One of the remaining two men tackled me, slamming his body into mine, and pushed me back up against the building with his sword to my throat. "Fuck," I grunted out.

"You stupid bitch, I will gut you right here once I'm finished with you," he whispered maliciously in my ear. He then pulled my hair down by the nape of my neck and tilted my chin up toward him, exposing my throat even more to his blade.

I was looking into my attacker's eyes when, out of the corner of my vision, the other remaining man's body dropped to the ground. With the rain growing heavier, the human must not have noticed or heard the sound.

And another second later, a shimmering blade of night appeared across my assailant's throat.

A blade of obsidian.

My dagger.

A mischievous smile crept up my lips.

The man's eyes widened in horror. "Whoever you are, this doesn't concern you," he called over his shoulder. "This *fae* just killed all of my friends, unprovoked. She will be taken into custody."

The hooded figure behind the man then moved his face in closer, just to the man's ear. I then saw a familiar pair of hazel eyes shining in the dim moonlight that peeked through the clouds, staring at me as he spoke, "What makes you think that doesn't concern me? Drop your weapon. Now." His voice was full of authority, and an intense heat rushed between my thighs from it.

The man dropped his sword from my throat, and Jace immediately grabbed him by his cloak and whipped his body across the sidewalk, causing him to stumble.

Once the man found his footing halfway across the street, he looked back over to us. My body was still pressed against the building, frozen by the awe of Jace coming out of nowhere and saving me.

"Co-Commander?! When did you arrive?!" the man stuttered out. "She attacked us! I swear it! Just look at the bodies lying around."

I rolled my eyes and let out a hushed chuckle.

"On the contrary, sir, but I believe it is you all who attacked her," Jace answered, twirling my dagger between his fingers in the moonlight.

The man looked horrified, his eyes so wide I thought they might pop out of his skull. "Commander, she is a *fae*. She is clearly dangerous. Just look at what she did due to us questioning why she was here!" he pleaded.

Jace unsheathed a sword from his hip and pointed it at the man, my jaw hung open slightly, as my eyes started to dart back and forth between the two men.

"You antagonized her." He took a step closer to the man. "You attacked her when she was no threat to you until you forced her to become one."

"Please..." the man begged, voice trembling.

"And then you touched her." He let out a breathy laugh. "You will die for that."

Jace was now not but three feet in front of him with the tip of his sword resting on the man's sternum. "I know you are now clearly well aware of what she is capable of, and that she could kill you faster than you could blink, however, you pissed me off. So, your kill is *mine*."

In the blink of an eye, Jace lifted his sword and effortlessly sliced through tissue and bone, severing the man's head clean from his body.

The head fell to the ground with a loud, fleshy smack, my eyes looked up to Jace as he sheathed his sword back on his hip and rushed over to me.

What in the realm just happened?

He then grabbed my face intensely with both hands, his eyes darting back and forth between my own. "Are you hurt?"

"No," I whispered, for some reason feeling out of breath.

"Thank the gods," he said, as he let out a large sigh.

A moment passed before I shoved him off of me. "And I had that!"

He rolled his eyes. "You most certainly did not!"

He was right, and I was far too exhausted to argue with him, so I paused for dramatic effect and looked away from him. "...Whatever."

He chuckled, but it sounded more fueled by anger than an actual laugh. "Listen, you were fine until you were not. I was coming after you to apologize for how I acted and then came across this scene." He gestured to the bodies. "I watched him grab you and hold the blade to your throat. I wasn't willing to take the chance."

I blinked at him confused, not many people would've done that for me. "Thank you," I whispered to him so softly he may not have even heard the words.

"I need to get this cleaned up before anyone sees. Go back to the room and wait for me there. I will be back as soon as I can." He started shoving out of his soaking wet cloak. "Take this, and don't let anyone else realize what you are."

I nodded at him as I took the cloak from his grasp. Without another word, I slipped the drenched hood over my head and made my way back to the inn.

THIRTY-NINE

Jace

As I INSPECTED THE bodies of the five men who attacked Elianna, I noticed their armor...they were *guards*. My guards. Technically men under my own gods-damn command.

"For fuck's sake," I grumbled to myself, as I made my way to the small village gate we had passed through earlier in the evening.

Walking up to the seemingly unguarded gates, I pivoted toward a small building lit by candlelight off to the side of it. Once I got up to the door, I knocked three times before opening it and inviting myself in.

Four sets of eyes met mine. Each of the men had a mug of ale and looked to be lounging around, half drunk, when they should've been out guarding the village.

"Gentlemen," I greeted sternly. Each of their backs stiffened, and they all stood at attention at once.

"Commander Cadoria! I had no idea you were in the village. When did you arrive?" The one who had his boots up on the table asked as I approached. Irritation grew within me as he just unknowingly admitted that the gates to the village weren't being guarded properly, considering they hadn't realized anyone new arrived—especially their own commander.

"Yes, well, I was just passing through with Gage Davies and Zaela Cadoria and we decided to stay for the night. I wasn't considering doing a check in until now."

"Commander, with all due respect...why would you conduct a check-in when it is the middle of the night?"

"Because a woman was just attacked." All of their faces paled. "Who else is on duty?" I demanded.

"There are five others out on patrol tonight. We take turns since the village doesn't typically get rowdy," one of them spoke up. "I can go out and get them."

I held up my hand, halting him. "That won't be necessary. They are dead."

All four of the men gasped in shock. "What do you mean?" He reached for his sword. "Are we under attack?"

I grinned at him. "No. We are not under attack. The only one who was under attack tonight was the woman I had to save from *your* five men." I looked around the room slowly, meeting each of their stares. "I heard them myself plot out loud to rape and kill her."

"Fuck, surely there has been some mistake or misunderstanding," the mouthy one chimed in.

"You doubt what I heard with my own two ears?"

"N-no, Commander. That is not what I meant."

I took a step toward him and cocked my head to the side. "Then what is it that you do mean?"

"I...never mind. I think I am just in shock by your claims," he stuttered.

"As am I," I replied through my teeth. "If I ever hear of something so heinous happening under my command again, you will all meet the same fate they had, which you will also see, since you are now tasked with cleaning up the mess before the streets are once again filled with civilians at dawn. Have I made myself clear?" I shouted at them, as I slammed my fist down on their table, cracking the wood.

"Yes, Commander," they said in agreement, as they jumped back from my outburst.

"Excellent, now get the fuck out of my sight," I ordered, as I nodded my head in the direction of the door.

They all practically shoved each other out of the way to exit the cabin.

As I crept back into our room at the inn, I realized Lia was asleep in the bed, so I quietly shut the door behind me. I tiptoed across the small space and pulled my boots off, attempting not to wake her.

How could this have happened? They committed an act that I have hated her kind for my entire life—for what they had done to my mother and so many others...my own men were about to do the same to her. And not just one man, but five. And not just any men...*guards*. Sworn in to protect the people in this village. I didn't give a fuck that they saw she was a fae. I watched the entire scene unfold. All she did was sit down on the sidewalk, to which they approached her and attacked unprovoked. I allowed her to handle the situation on her own until she couldn't any longer.

I wish I could bring them back to slaughter them all over again myself.

My breathing turned heavy with anger as I peeled my soaking wet clothes from my body, and turned around to see her eyes wide open, and staring at me.

"Gods, Lia! I thought you were asleep!" I gasped.

"Sorry." She giggled.

"Why is that funny?" I smirked at her.

"Because you're practically naked."

I could feel the heat flushing my cheeks. "I, uh, I will sleep on the floor."

Her lips parted, and she looked as if she wouldn't say anything for a moment. "I can make room. The bed is large enough."

I froze, staring at her nervously.

"You look freezing, and your clothes are soaked." She gestured to the pile of them on the floor. "Just climb into the bed." She smiled mockingly at me. "I will behave."

Yeah, *she* might. But I didn't trust myself, to be honest. I sighed. "Okay, Lia," I said, voice heavy with mirth.

Her eyes lit up at the use of her nickname as she scooted over to the wall on the opposite side of the bed and I crawled in next to her, keeping as much distance as the confined space would allow.

I blew out the candle on the nightstand, darkening the room almost completely, aside from the tiny bit of moonlight peering in through the dispersing storm clouds.

"Thank you," she said softly, breaking the semi-awkward silence. "For what you did back there."

"There is nothing to thank me for. Those men attacked you and planned to..." I couldn't even bring myself to say it without feeling nausea climb my throat. "They planned to do unspeakable things to you. I would never allow that to happen."

"To anyone," she whispered almost sadly, as if she wouldn't have expected me to save her.

"To anyone, and especially to you," I answered, watching her eyes slightly widen at my admission.

"Why do you keep saving me?" she asked, and it caused my chest to lurch. "The ship and now this, it doesn't make sense. I know who you are. I know you would never typically do something like this, so why do you keep saving me? Is it just to bring me back as a pawn?"

I stared up at the ceiling, unsure of what to say exactly. "I couldn't let you die. Even that first night on the ship. I thought about letting you drown, but I couldn't do it. The thought of you even being injured...I can't explain it. It feels as if flames ignite within my very veins and light my entire existence on fire. It's not an option I was willing to accept. Nor will I ever."

"You are one of the few," she said after a moment.

My brows furrowed slightly as I turned on my side to face her. "Surely that awful brute you used to be with wouldn't let anything like that happen to you either, Elianna."

She let out a quiet laugh, that almost resembled a sob, as she looked into my eyes. "I can't prove it, but I am pretty sure he ordered an attack on me by his own men while we sailed to Ceto Bay."

My entire body stiffened. "What."

"Like I said, I can't prove it...but we had been fighting the entire time. It was a constant power struggle. The last night before we arrived at the bay, a few of his men cornered me on the ship and..."

"What did they do, Elianna?" My voice was low, resembling a growl that I barely recognized as something I was capable of.

"Nothing, thank the gods. I was lucky enough that they had distracted themselves by talking amongst each other long enough that I was able to grab my dagger, so I sliced through one of their thighs to make my escape. When I told Kellan what had happened, he made a huge show of it, but the punishment that was dealt out wasn't nearly good enough for an attack and threat on a captain. It didn't even register to me in the moment. I was just in shock. Then two days later, the same male that I had cut, and that Kellan had beaten, was the one who slit all the throats of your men that had surrendered. I watched him as he looked at you and *smiled*. I will never forget the look on his face. From that moment, I knew."

I flinched at the mention of my men. "You knew what?"

"That the whole thing was a show, a setup. I was surrounded by a crew that was not under my command, males I never felt comfortable with, and Kellan knew that. He had personally handpicked them for the journey. When we got back onto the ship to sail back to Isla I questioned him on it, but he came up with excuse after excuse." She hesitated. "I didn't believe him for a second, and I think he realized that. We have known each other for a long time, and we know each other's ticks."

A slice of fury cut through me at the thought of another man knowing her so well, better than I did, and using it against her.

"He should die for that," I said through my clenched teeth.

"He should die for many things, I am sure," she murmured.

She inched her way toward my body and snuggled up next to me. I could feel the warmth of her on my skin, sending a jolt through me. I took her chin in my fingers and lifted her gaze to mine. "From this moment moving forward, you are no longer my enemy or my prisoner. Members of each side have committed acts of extreme cruelty and horror. That no longer speaks for the entirety of either race. We are going to figure everything out. *Together*."

"Together," she breathed onto my lips, as her eyes glistened in the moonlight.

I couldn't hold myself back even a second longer. I leaned into her, taking her tender, lush lips with my own, and sealed the words we had just promised each other.

Elianna

His kiss ignited a blaze within me. In my very being—my soul. A powerful wave of heat rushed through my entire body at the feel of his lips on my own. A feeling he swore not even a day ago that I would never feel again.

A rush of emotions fluttered in me. Pleasure, heartache, joy, and I was waiting for the regret to sink in, but it refused to come. I was sure it would arrive for both of us by morning.

He lightly pushed down on my shoulder, guiding my body to be flat on my back as he straddled my thighs with his own, kissing down my neck in slow, teasing movements.

I could feel his length harden against my leg as he began kissing and licking from the nape of my neck, down to my chest. My nipple peaked out from the undone buttons of my shirt and he gently caressed it with his thumb as he continued to feel his way around my body.

"Gods," I breathed into his ear.

He slowly lifted his head. "I'm so sorry." He took a few deep, heavy breaths, "Do you wish for me to stop?"

I answered him by forcing my mouth back up onto his. His lips parted, allowing my tongue to slip inside and explore.

His scent of arousal enveloped me as he let out a rough moan of approval, and broke off the kiss, using his tongue to slip down the center of my throat and body until it found my exposed nipple.

I let out a quick gasp for air, as his fingers then explored beneath my waist.

I grabbed him by his hair, forcing his eyes up to meet my own. "Is this what you want?" I asked, as I tried to steady my breathing.

He smiled at me, his face blossomed into pure perfection as his hazel eyes seemed to radiate in the moonlight. It made my heart skip a beat and an intense sensation of heat flow down to my core in the same moment. "I think the answer to that is quite obvious, but of course only if you want to."

I could tell he meant that.

I smiled back at him and nodded. That was all he needed before he ripped my pants down my legs completely and I felt his hardness enter me as he once again claimed my mouth.

I could taste his need. Feel it with every fiber of my being as it lit up my soul. His demand. His want. For *me*. He was drowning in it, and I would gladly drown with him.

I allowed myself to get lost in him, as he did with me. Nothing in this moment existed aside from this, aside from *us*. He claimed my body as if he wouldn't accept a single inch of it to go unexplored. Every dimple and ripple of skin he kissed. Every scar that his fingers or mouth came across was worshiped as he would thrust deep into me.

He pulled out of me, and I immediately missed the sensation of him. He smoothly flipped my body over, and wrapped his hand around my throat, gently pulling me up so my back was flush with his chest. "You're so beautiful," he whispered onto the sensitive tip of my ear, as he nibbled on it delicately and entered me again from behind. He held me tightly to his body for a few more moments, lightly blocking my airway. It made each plunge feel more vigorous than the last.

As he removed his grip from my throat, he gradually moved his hand around my shoulder and down my back, carefully forcing my torso back down toward the bed as he kept his movements steady. His fingers lightly traced the scars on my back, *the whip marks*, sending a shudder through me.

"Lia," he groaned. "You're perfect."

His words of praise sent us both tumbling over the edge. We panted in unison as his body collapsed next to my own. He looked into my eyes as he removed the strands of hair that scattered over my face. "Together," he said on a breath, right before he cupped my cheek and kissed me softly once more.

I felt nothing but bliss.

FORTY

Jace

WAKING UP TANGLED IN Lia felt nothing short of surreal. I had obviously bedded women before, but I had never felt anything for them. I refused to let myself. If anything, they were just a distraction. A distraction I never truly needed when my primary focus was, and always would be, winning the war. They were also few and far between.

Gage had always mocked me for refusing to involve emotions in any situation regarding a woman. What good would it have done? Every second of my time had been consumed already. Why should I ever subject someone that loved me to wonder if I would ever come home from battle? The thought just never sat right with me. Until now, for she wouldn't be at home waiting for me to return—she would be right next to me on the battlefield, which both excited and terrified me.

Lia's hair was sprawled out across both of our pillows, enveloping me in her scent, a field of gardenias with the sweet essence of vanilla. I noticed the smell of her the day she shot me to the ground with her arrow, and I remember thinking that a creature born from such wickedness shouldn't smell so enticing. Or look it.

But I was wrong. She wasn't evil, or cruel at all. She was not this vile, wicked being that I had convinced myself she must have been. She was kind, smart, beautiful, and oh-so-fucking stubborn. She was also funny, but I could never let her know that. It would go right to her thick skull.

The only question now was, what would we do? With Lia being the rightful heir, we may actually have a chance at winning this. We just needed to get her back to Isla so she could try to convince her father, and if that didn't work, she would need to claim what was rightfully hers by birth.

It shouldn't matter that she was not the child of the queen. She was born first, and she carried the blood of the king in her veins. If he wished to name her heir now, he should be able to do just that. I didn't know much of the fae's politics, but wasn't that the point of being king to begin with?

Lia began to stir in my arms as she looked up at me with blinking, tired eyes, "Good morning," she whispered on a stretch, her legs still intertwined in mine.

I kissed her forehead, and she eyed me warily, like she wasn't expecting it. Truthfully, I wasn't expecting to do it either.

"How did you sleep?"

She giggled. "Peacefully, for the first time in...honestly, I can't even remember." I smirked, and she sat up. "Don't let that go to your head." She pointed in my face.

"Would never dare," I teased. "So what is the plan?"

Her magnetic eyes met mine. "How do you communicate with the sympathizers in Isla?"

That was random. "Typically by falcon."

"I would like to send a message to a few that I trust."

I raised a brow. "Is that wise?"

"At this point, they are most likely assuming that I am dead, which may come in handy for some circumstances, but I cannot sit here and willingly know and allow my loved ones to think my soul has left this realm."

I cupped her cheek. "Then we will send a falcon to Isla." She smiled at me. "But first, we need to talk to Gage and Zaela."

Her smile dropped. "Is *that* wise?"

"Well, we can't just have them assuming you are still a prisoner being taken in for questioning. They need to know that things have changed. The entire plan has changed."

"We don't even have a plan yet, and I cannot have more people know who I truly am."

She was clearly stalling. "That will be unavoidable moving forward, but I will keep it to just us four for now. Deal?"

Her jaw ticked. "Jace, I'm just warning you that if she tries anything or attacks me again, I will not hold back."

I chuckled. "Trust me, she won't either. I won't even know which one of you to bet on."

She punched me in the gut, a little too hard to be considered playful. "You will learn to never bet against me," she said sternly, but I could tell she was trying to hide a smile forming.

"Would never dare," I whispered on her lips, as I pulled her body beneath my own and took her as mine once more.

Walking down the steps of the inn, I started to get the sinking feeling that Lia was right, and telling Zaela would be brutal. Gage, I wasn't worried about. I never had to be with him.

Turning the corner of the creaking stairs, I could see the two of them already sitting in one of the booths near the kitchen. Gage waved to me, and Zae's head cocked to the side as she saw Lia standing directly behind me.

"Still think this is going to go well?" she asked, barely above a whisper.

"Let's just get this over with," I said, as I stalked across the floor to their table.

"Why isn't she wearing a cloak?" Zaela demanded as I approached.

I turned to Lia, her hair was down and her ears weren't noticeable. "As long as her hair covers them, she's fine."

Gage groaned as he rubbed his temples. "Remind me to not drink that much ale when I have barely eaten." Lia giggled next to me, and I tried to hide my smirk. "How did you two sleep last night?" he asked.

Lia's face turned a bright pink, and I could feel the heat rushing to my own. "Fine," I said, hoping he would drop the subject as I slid into the booth across from them, Lia close behind me.

"Who took the floor?" Gage asked innocently.

My eyes widened slightly. "I did." Both Lia and I said simultaneously. She kicked my foot under the table.

That got their attention.

Zaela's eyes snapped up to mine, a scornful look etched into her features. "Was there no bed?"

Luckily, I didn't have to answer as two of the cooks walked by, talking rather loudly to each other about rumors regarding the deaths of five guards the night prior.

"Did you hear that?" Gage nearly shouted. "Five guards dead? What the fuck could have happened? Gods, I know I was drunk, but I don't think I would've slept through an attack..." he said, as he leaned back and crossed his arms.

"Did you hear about this?" Zaela asked me, concerned.

My jaw locked as I nodded. "It's been taken care of."

Lia squeezed my knee from under the table.

"What happened? Did you hear something last night and leave? I had no idea something happened."

"They attacked someone last night," I said gravely.

"The guards?!" Zaela gasped. "Like a civilian?"

"Not exactly," I replied dryly.

Gage looked between all of us nervously. "Who did they attack? Was it a man? Woman? An intruder? I don't understand how all *five* of them could've ended up dead."

"Me," Lia stated calmly, causing the two across from us to look her way cautiously. "They attacked me. I had to defend myself."

Fuck.

"Excuse me?" Zaela spat with pure venom. "And why weren't you in your room?"

"We got into an argument and she took a walk for some air," I mumbled.

Her jaw dropped. "You let our *prisoner* go for a *walk* by herself? Who are you?!" The look of betrayal her eyes pierced my chest.

"Information was given to me regarding the Velyran Crown, and we did not see eye to eye regarding it," I said in a hushed tone.

I looked at Lia then, and she had nothing but wrath written across her face that I had already said something about what she had told me.

"And by that he means he was being an inconsiderate jackass and not thinking entirely clearly," she seethed without breaking eye contact with me. She turned to them. "I was minding my own gods-dammed business when five men approached me on a sidewalk. One pulled my hair, revealing my ear, and they threatened to assault and kill me. I don't know what else you expected me to do."

"How about not fucking kill our men?" Zaela hissed.

"She didn't have a choice," I said through my teeth. "In fact, she was almost killed. My blade is the one that finished off the last two." I couldn't let her take the fall for all of them. "I then sent Elianna back to the room and took care of the rest myself. I paid a little visit to the guard's quarters outside of the gate and told them what their men had done. They cleaned up the mess."

"So, they know she is fae?" Zaela asked.

"No. They think their men attacked a woman."

She scoffed at me. "So you will let the names of good men be poisoned by the world thinking they were hurting a woman?"

"No." My hand balled into a fist as I slammed it down onto the table, rattling the silverware and causing her to jump in her seat. My patience was entirely gone. "They were clearly never good men if they could execute a plan together, within minutes, to rape and murder an innocent person sitting on a sidewalk minding her own business." Zaela's eyes bulged in disbelief. "I don't give a shit that they found out she was fae. I saw the entire thing. This was at no fault of Elianna. Those men were clearly no better than the males of her kind that come through and do the same to our own women."

Lia gently placed her hand on top of my fist, in an attempt to calm me. "I will tell you two everything." She looked to Gage and Zaela. "But we need to get out of earshot of others. No one else can know what I am about to tell you."

They both nodded as we all stood from the table and aimed for the door.

FORTY-ONE

Elianna

I COULDN'T BELIEVE THIS was happening. As the four of us walked out the front door of the inn, I started to panic. I didn't even mean to tell Jace who I was. It just came out in a giant ball of word vomit. And last night? I could barely even process what we did...and then again this morning. I could feel the corner of my lip tip up at the thought.

Would we tell them about it? Was it something he regretted? I don't think he regretted it by the way he acted, and then reenacted the events this morning. But when we came down to talk to his two friends, neither of us admitted to anything happening between us. We both said we slept on the floor for gods' sake.

I could feel Zaela's eyes on me as we walked the streets of Celan Village in silence, aiming for the fields beyond. She was never going to trust me, this I knew, but I would try to gain her trust, for Jace's sake. Playing nice was never my strong suit against someone who refused to play nice first, but if we were to continue to be forced to work together, then I would need to do my best to bite my tongue.

"Well, I think this is as good a spot as any. Would you all agree?" Jace chimed in, breaking the awkward silence once we were about fifty yards into a hilly field full of wildflowers.

I nodded as I sat down in the grass, folding my knees in close to my chest as I looked up into the sunny sky. The birds were chirping around us and for a moment, everything seemed peaceful. That was, until Zaela once again opened her mouth.

"Ok, Elianna, you lured us out here to tell us your secrets. Now talk."

So much for holding my tongue. "You will speak to me with decency, or you will not speak to me at all," I retorted sternly.

Gage physically froze, and Jace's hand flew to cover his mouth. Whether he was trying to hide a smile or he was just surprised by my reply, I wasn't sure.

Zaela looked at me with challenge in her stare, but she calmed her tone. "Very well. What is it that caused you to get into an argument with Commander Cadoria?"

I almost giggled at her use of his title. I stretched out my legs and leaned back on my elbows as I met her eyes. "What I'm about to tell you...nobody knows. I can count on one hand the number of souls with this knowledge." She just blinked at me, and my eyes flashed over to Jace. He gave me a quick nod, so my focus returned to the others, and I told them everything about my true lineage.

It was silent for a few unbearable moments as they stared at me unblinking, and then both Zaela and Gage burst into tears with uncontrollable laughter.

I rolled my eyes in annoyance and turned toward Jace, gesturing to the two of them. "See?"

He let the laughter continue for a few more seconds before he cut them off. "She is serious."

"How? How is such a thing even possible or believable to you?" she asked, as she wiped a tear that slipped from her lower lashes.

"I believe her. I have no reason not to, judging by the way she reacted once she told me."

"Oh, and what was that reaction? Was it her begging you, 'please don't tell anyone'...honestly, did it never cross your mind that she probably said that because she was *lying?*"

Jace looked back at me, and for a moment my heart stopped, thinking he was about to play into her bullshit.

"I believe her. This changes things," he admitted.

"The only thing that this changes is that we have the king's supposed secret child as a hostage."

"Zaela, for once in your life will you shut the fuck up!" Gage snapped at her, shocking all three of us into silence. Zaela's mouth opened as if she was going to say something, but to my surprise, and I assumed theirs as well, she listened to him.

"I am on your side," I said while clearing my throat. "I have been for a long while now...I just couldn't bring myself to say it out loud. I already had a few individuals that suspected me to be a mortal sympathizer, my ex-claimed included." I saw Jace's jaw tick at that. "I have been trying to end this for decades. Jace seems to think that we can put an end to this war if I can somehow convince the kingdom of who I truly am, of the blood that flows through my veins. He is convinced that they will follow me, instead of the nefarious prince who plans to ascend the throne."

"So, your brother?" she asked.

"Half-brother," Jace chimed in, and I was thankful for it. "And he does not know who she truly is, either. While she is the daughter of the king, she is not that of the queen. That is why she wasn't named the heir."

"So, if she isn't the true heir, how does that help us?" Gage asked curiously, and honestly, I was wondering the same still myself.

"The true royal blood of Velyra is that of the Valderre line. That is the blood that flows through Lia's veins," Jace answered. "She is his first-born child. Rightfully, that makes her the true heir. The king even told her before she left on the journey to Ceto Bay that he wished he could change everything he had done, and name her his successor. Isn't that right, Lia?"

I could see Zaela blink confusingly at his use of my nickname. "It is," I muttered.

"Where do we go from here?" she asked, and I was surprised there wasn't even a hint of disdain behind her tone. "It is not as if we can all just waltz into Isla and demand the king announce his change of heart. All over a bastard child, no offense."

"None taken." I paused. "But you're right. All of us can't go back to Isla. The three of you would be slaughtered on sight. That is why it must be me."

"Lia, no," Jace nearly shouted at me. "And that is not due to a lack of trust in you, but a lack of trust in the fae that lurk behind those gates."

He was right. "Then we'll proceed with sending a letter by falcon. We will have the few that I trust plan to meet us in one month's time to come up with a strategy. They may be able to sneak all of us in. And once I feel it is safe enough to reveal you all before the king, we strike then. Show everyone that this cannot carry on."

"I'm sorry to chime in here again, but I will not allow you to bring more fae to our lands," Zaela stated quietly but firmly.

"I agree," I said. "We can't risk the civilians here." Her brows flew up at that. "We will have them meet us where it all began. Back at the bay."

Once I finished writing my letter to Lukas, I took a deep, nervous breath as Jace retrieved the falcon from the village post. I couldn't believe any of this. I was praying to the gods that this plan worked, and Lukas would be able to sneak out beyond the gates with a few of my soldiers to meet us.

I turned to see the falcon perched on Jace's shoulder, its sharp talons nearly curling into his shoulder's armor that he wore specifically for the bird. "Ready?" he asked.

"Not really, but I don't have a choice now, do I?" I mumbled, as I crossed my arms.

He pinched my chin between his fingers and tipped my face up toward his. "While I know we are running out of time due to the king being ill, we can try to think of another way."

We couldn't, though, he was right—we were out of time. This could be our only chance of ending all of this bloodshed. "There's no going back now, let's do this," I said, as I lifted the wrapped parchment paper up to the stunningly fierce bird atop his shoulder.

It immediately took it between its talons and shot off into the sky. "And now we wait," he said, still looking down at me with pure lust in his stare.

"And now we wait," I repeated, as he gave me a quick peck on the lips, surprising me.

Out of the corner of my eye, I saw movement on the ground next to the building and heard a quiet, eerie murmur coming from beneath the figure's cloak, "Beware of the day the pillar falls…"

What the? I looked at Jace, and he eyed me at the same time. We looked down to find a crone of a woman sitting beneath a large, hooded cape leaning up against the building.

I bent down, placing my hands on my knees as I tried to look into her eyes. "I am sorry, but were you speaking to us?" I glanced down to see a chipped, old mug lying at her feet with a few coins tossed in.

"Beware of the day the pillar falls, for an heir will rise of blood and malice..." she started saying again, now loud enough for us to understand the words she spoke, but I definitely wasn't comprehending them.

"Ma'am." Jace bent down toward her. "I'm the commander of the soldiers throughout Silcrowe. You should not be here like this. Please let me help you up," he said, as he went to stick his hand out to her.

I shoved his hand down and shushed him.

I nodded at the crone to continue. "And when the moment comes that the enemy weeps, a stranger of kin shall forge the way for the one who was promised."

My mouth popped open. What in the realm could that mean? She was speaking in riddles. "Are you a seer?" I asked in a soft whisper.

While giving me a bone-chilling smile, the crone finally locked eyes with mine, and what I gazed into were the darkest irises I had ever seen. They were a depthless onyx and ringed with the thinnest band of gold, followed by an outer strip of crimson. I leaned back with a gasp, almost losing my balance.

"Let's go, Lia," Jace said firmly, as he pulled on my arm.

I whipped my body fully towards him. "What does she mean?"

"How am I supposed to know? She's probably just drunk or spitting out bullshit for some coin." He laughed as he pointed to the mug, but I didn't find any of this funny.

"What if she is a witch?!" I anxiously whispered. "It could mean something,"

He pursed his lips at me in annoyance. "Don't be rid—" he cut himself off as he glanced back down to the ground, his eyes widening. "What the hell?"

I followed his stare to find that the woman and her mug of coins were *gone*. Vanished from thin air. We both looked around the streets wildly through the people bustling around the village, but she was nowhere in sight.

"Do you remember what she said?" he asked quietly.

I slowly nodded. "We better get back to the inn."

FORTY-TWO

Jace

Walking back into the inn and up the stairs, we found Zaela and Gage waiting back in our room. I was surprised to find them in here instead of their own, but it was also typical for them to invade my space.

"It smells like sex in here," Gage said through a chuckle, as he was sprawled out on our bed, flipping through an old book he found on the nightstand. Lia and I both froze. "Just kidding," he continued.

I glanced over at Lia to see her face had flushed once again, and I sensed that mine matched.

"That is disgusting and not even funny. Don't joke about that being a thing," Zaela said, while looking out the window. She turned to face us and cocked a brow. "Um, why do you two look guilty? Did something happen?"

Gage sat up from the bed abruptly and was staring at us, smirking at her words.

"Letter has been sent!" Lia interjected, luckily changing the subject as she casually pushed Gage's legs off the bed as if *she* was the one who had known him for years, and sat down, making herself comfortable.

"And what did it say exactly? Jace, did you read it?" Zaela's tone was a little harsher than I thought she meant it to be, but I could tell she was trying.

I gave her a knowing look. "No, I did not. I was selecting the falcon at the post when she wrote it."

Our gazes wandered back to the two on the bed.

Lia shrugged as she playfully ripped the book from Gage's hands. "It basically said that I am alive, and we can't have many knowing. And to meet us at Ceto Bay on the next full moon."

Gage reached back out to try to snatch the book back from her, but she quickly caught his wrist and forced it down on the bed as if he were a child.

"Gods, she is stronger than she looks," he hissed through his teeth, as he struggled to pull away from her grip. Lia just giggled in response.

A smile tugged at my lips. "Lia thinks we just ran into a witch."

"Well, I don't know what else that crone would have been! You saw her eyes. They were as dark as night, with rings of gold and a deep red. I still have goosebumps from it, and witches of the realm, while rare, are known to practice the dark magic of the gods!"

"Are you sure her eyes weren't just bloodshot?" Zae sassed, as she let out a short cackle.

"Positive," Lia growled. "She was speaking in riddles. Like a prophecy or something."

Gage raised a brow. "You fae believe in prophecies?"

"I mean, not really. But it was just creepy. What she said and the way she spoke. And then she disappeared from our sight! After the last few days I've had, I think I will believe in anything being possible!" she shouted, trying to convince them she wasn't crazy.

To save myself from the headache of them all bickering about false witches, I changed the subject. "We need to tell her our secret now."

All three of their gazes whipped to mine, each looking more confused than the other.

"Secret? What secret?" Lia asked curiously, as she threw the book back at Gage, causing him to huff out a grunt.

"Jace…" Zaela whispered concerningly, nervousness etched into her face.

"She told us her secret. It is only right that she knows exactly what she is getting herself into with us."

"What the hell are you guys talking about?" Lia demanded.

I let out a deep breath. "Obviously, she is serious about helping us. She wants the same thing we do." I paused, but Zae just turned away from me.

"I think it makes sense," Gage said.

I locked eyes with Lia. "What do you think the mortal population number is?"

She sat up straight. "I am not sure. Back in Isla, I believe their estimate is around only a few hundred thousand of you left."

I smiled at that, that meant our plan had worked over the last few decades. "That is precisely what we wanted you to believe." Her brows flew up her forehead. "We have millions of civilians in hiding beyond the Ezranian Mountains."

"*What?*" she gasped.

"A few decades back, before my time, the human race began plotting on how to keep everyone safe, especially women and children. They ventured beyond the mountains to find Alaia Valley. We have been colonizing there ever since."

"How is that possible?" she whispered more to herself than to me. "There is nothing inhabitable beyond those mountains."

"Oh, but there is, and we have done everything we can to make sure the fae did not find out what lies beyond them."

"How? It has always been known as a wasteland."

"Humans traveled beyond the mountains decades ago to find that was no longer the case. It is the one thing the gods have seemed to place on our side," Zaela answered for me.

Lia looked like she was in shock, and then she started chuckling. "I'm sorry," she said through her giggles, and I raised a brow at her in question. "It's just honestly kind of hilarious...and amazing, that you have been able to keep this from the fae. From the queen and her spies. It doesn't even sound possible." She looked around at the three of us. "Why are there so many people *not* behind the mountains? Why even risk living out here?"

"Many people did not want to uproot their lives entirely due to the war. Nobody really thought it would continue to last as long as it has. My mother was one of them." I paused. "After what happened to her, she was transported beyond the mountains. I was raised there."

Lia's eyes widened.

"The majority of our people have been moved to Alaia at this point. The bulk of those who remain are in our villages that we have hidden within forests and mountain terrains, and also in Ellecaster. Celan Village is one of the few that was built in an open field, and is used mainly for agriculture purposes. Many people on this side of the Ezranian Mountains are soldiers guarding the gates, and their family members who refused to leave them behind." Gage interjected.

"Along with quite a few who are still too stubborn to leave." Zaela crossed her arms. "And by a few, I mean thousands that still reside in those villages and in the city at the foot of the mountains."

"We also couldn't have the fae get wind that all the humans were gone. They would've immediately known something was up. So we dwindled down over the years, slowly, to make our decreasing numbers more believable. Especially between battles."

"Holy gods," Lia breathed. "You're all a bunch of fucking geniuses."

"We also have an entire army beyond the mountains. The numbers are in hundreds of thousands in addition to our civilian numbers. And none of that includes the thousands roaming *these* lands."

"And you command all of those men?"

"I do," I answered proudly. "They will follow me wherever I ask." I hesitated for a moment. "And that includes supporting you and your claim to the throne." Zaela grimaced in the corner while Gage looked as if he was ready to run through the wall with excitement. Lia looked...terrified. "Is that okay with you?"

She hugged her body with her arms and refused to meet my stare. "It's just a lot to take in." She took in a deep breath. "You have to realize that I never expected this, or even wanted it. While my father believes I am fit to rule, that doesn't necessarily mean I am convinced of it myself."

I shrugged. "Well, one thing is for sure, I am willing to bet you are much more fit than the queen and her wretched son."

Her eyes finally looked up at me with a smirk. "Maybe." There was a moment of silence. "I've already commanded the mass of Velyra's armies, how hard could the rest of the kingdom be?" She laughed nervously.

"Are we still going to Ellecaster?" Gage asked.

"Not necessary. It would be a waste of time to travel all the way there and then all the way back when we need to be back at the bay in a month's time. We will stay in Celan Village and help out around here in the meantime."

The room went quiet, but while glancing around to each of them, I could see a faint sliver of hope in each of their gazes.

This was going to work.

It had to.

FORTY-THREE

Lukas

IT HAD BEEN A week since I learned of the passing of my dear and truest friend. The moment I heard the whispers of it amongst the halls of the castle, I knew I had to make myself scarce. The queen had been waiting for the day she could relieve me of my position, but I wasn't ready to leave yet. Even if they had already promoted someone else to fill it, I had not been told, so in my mind I had every right to do what I planned. Something didn't feel right about any of this, and I promised Lia I would look out for Finnian, Avery, and Nyra. And, for some reason, that stable hand.

The royal family had a private service for King Jameson, one I was purposefully not invited to. It broke my heart to not be there honoring the greatest male I had ever known. I couldn't be there for him, or Lia. Gods, what the fuck had the realm come to?

There weren't many left that I trusted in this gods-forsaken city, so I had been spending my nights at The Evergreen Belle, quite literally paying off Lorelai to keep my stay there a secret. She believed I was keeping one of her females she assigned to me in my bed, but I could never do that again. Not after the way Lia, who was practically a daughter to me, looked at me with a face full of disgust the last time we were here. So, I was also paying the girl to keep quiet about me refusing her nightly offers.

I had decided that I should try to check in on Avery and Finnian, since I had not seen them since their father passed. Cloaked, hooded, and armed to the teeth, I made my way through the city and around the back of the castle battlements.

Not many knew of the few bricks that were loose along the wall. In fact, it may only be Lia and I who had the knowledge. I caught her one day back when she was young, trying to sneak off the grounds at night. I never had the heart to seal it on her, and today I was grateful for that.

After wiggling through the space that was entirely too small, I found myself behind the stables in the garden. Pushing my way to my feet, I could see two very familiar redheads in the open window of the structure and made my way over.

As I was walking up and about to open the door, I heard them whispering, along with a third voice.

"Landon, I know it has taken me weeks to talk to you, and I'm sorry. I'm so sorry about everything. All of it. Please forgive me," Finnian begged.

Why would he be apologizing to the stable hand? Finnian couldn't hurt a fly. I would know. He would screech as a youngling, demanding I killed the bugs for him.

"I am sorry to hear of your father," Landon said in a tone that definitely was not suitable to be towards a prince.

"Landon, please listen to him. Kai is awful. We know this. We are both so sorry for what he did to you, but you must listen to us. Lia is missing, possibly dead," Avery's voice cracked on the last word, causing my chest to ache. "And our father, the king, was *murdered*."

What the fuck?

I immediately ripped open the door handle, making them all scatter and yelp in surprise. Avery tripped over a stack of hay, and flipped over it backwards, while Finnan was half-way up the ladder before he realized it was me who rushed through the door.

"What. Happened." I said through my teeth, realizing that my anger was not towards them, but I couldn't bring myself to calm down.

"Lu-Lukas!" Avery stuttered loudly before she began to whisper shout at me, "Where the hell have you been?! We have been looking for you for days! If Callius or Captain Adler finds you–"

I held up a hand. "I will deal with them. I was just coming to check on you all when I was outside the door and heard what you said. Explain everything. Now." I knew better than to make demands of the prince and princess, but they both seemed eager to tell me what was happening.

Finnian blurted the words out first. "Avery was spying on Kai in the garden when Callius approached him about Father's death. I saw her and we both followed them through the castle. Avery apparently knows about secret passageways hidden within the walls, so we crawled around in them until we could hear the conversation between Kai, Callius, and the queen."

I noticed he didn't refer to her as his mother.

"Lukas, it was horrifying. Father wasn't sick this entire time. He was being killed. Slowly. Painfully. Suffering due to some ancient, jealous rage Mother has felt. And Lia!"

"Woah. Stop right there," I said to her, my vision blurring from my temper. "What did your mother do?"

"Wyvern's blood! She has been putting three drops a night into the king's wine. It melted him from the inside out. She used it because it was essentially untraceable to a healer."

That vindictive bitch.

I cleared my throat. "What else do you know?"

"Lia is our sister. Well...half-sister," Finnian chimed in. "And all of this started because our father loved someone else. She said that Lia had nearly convinced the king to end the war, and she knew the only way she could stop this was in death."

I couldn't believe what I was hearing. After all this time, they finally knew who and what Lia truly was.

"She sent Callius off to relieve you of your position," Avery interrupted. "We thought we would never see you again either. They cannot find you! You need to get out of here. There are talks of a coronation, but luckily I don't believe it will happen right away due to Kai not taking a wife."

"He has his eyes on Lady Florence," Finnian said. "I have been meaning to tell you. Her family is practically ready to throw her at Kai since he will be ascending the throne."

Florence Nilda was the daughter of one of the older Lords in Isla, Stanley Nilda. His family had owned the spice trade in the city's port for centuries. Avery had been her friend since they were younger. Florence wasn't like the other Ladies.

Avery looked distraught at what Finnian had disclosed. "Flo has always gone out of her way to be sure she is never around Kai. She knows something is off with him. She would be devastated if that happens!"

"Her family obviously won't be giving her a choice in the matter," I muttered.

Landon was just staring at the three of us now, eyes flared.

"Is there a passageway that you know of that could lead to the king's private chamber? There is something I want to check." I went back to the original topic.

Avery nodded as she turned to Landon and Finnian. "Can the two of you stay here? I will be back soon."

"Prince Finnian may stay," Landon rushed out. "My shift is about to end. I will finish my duties and head home."

Hurt flashed across the prince's eyes. "Landon, I–"

"Please save your words, Prince. Unless it is by order, I do not wish to hear them."

Avery's hand flew to cover her mouth, and my eyes bulged in disbelief. What in the realm happened between the two of them?

Finnian cleared his throat. "Very well. You may leave once your duties are completed." His tone was saturated with sadness.

The stable hand nodded and returned to his work.

I turned to face Avery. "Come on, Princess. We better get moving."

"What is it you wish to see in Father's chambers?" Avery whispered to me as she slowly peered around a hallway, making sure it was clear.

"Well, I want to see if it has been cleared out yet, but your father kept many prized items in his room. I would like to get them before Kai takes over that entire wing of the castle and disposes of them."

"It's clear, we just need to make it up the staircase and there should be a tapestry around the bend of his wing. We may be able to sneak in through there."

Gods, she sounded like Lia. "Lead the way, Princess." I motioned with my arm.

She immediately took off in a sprint on silent feet, stunning me for a brief moment before I took off after her, not nearly as quiet from the rattling of my weapons.

As we turned the corner at the top of the stairs, sure enough, there was a very old-looking wall hanging draped down to the floor. Avery did one more quick glance around the hall and pulled back the fabric, revealing a door. Honestly, how many of these were around here?

She fearlessly opened the door and ran through. There was nothing I could do but follow.

"Father's bedroom chamber is a few halls down. As long as we follow the passageways in the same direction, we should be able to find it."

Sure enough, after following her lead, and taking quite a few wrong turns, a door revealed itself. She pushed it open gently, along with the fabric blocking us on the other side, and revealed the familiar chamber I had spent many nights with my old friend, drinking and laughing until we nearly passed out. It was so rare he forced me to remember my duty to him. I would forever be grateful for the kind of male he was.

"What exactly are you looking for?" she asked, and to be frank, I wasn't entirely sure what I could manage to sneak out of here. So, I shrugged.

Walking around the massive room, my eyes landed on his nightstand. He always kept it locked, but when I walked over to his bed, I saw a tiny key on a string hanging from one of the bedposts.

"What are you doing?" she asked.

"I am surprised this room hasn't been torn apart yet," I stated. "Your father always kept this key around his neck. I'm assuming he took it off only to sleep."

"It's possible."

I took the key and pulled it from the post. It fit perfectly in the keyhole of the nightstand's drawer, and once the lock clicked, the drawer popped open. Revealing nothing but a small, leather-bound book.

I picked it up and slowly flipped through the pages.

"What is that?" She asked.

I blew out an exasperated breath. "It appears your father has kept a journal. For a very, very long time."

"A journal? That seems a little odd for him."

I typically would agree until I started to skim the first few pages. "It seems as if he only wrote in it on days when events occurred."

"What kind of events?"

"Births." I eyed her. "Deaths, tragedies in the war." I flipped to the back. "And...holy gods."

Her head snapped up. "What?!"

I began to read the passage aloud.

Tonight the queen is to send Elianna off on yet another hunt to end the mortals, only she is sending her with a crew full of males that lack the respect she deserves. Idina believes me to be blind to her wicked ways when, truthfully, I have been keen to them since the night of Elianna's birth. I just could never give up my daughter, and the queen has punished the realm for it since.

I wish I was a better, stronger male. One who had the courage to stand up to her that night all those years ago, and not cower away as the subtle threat against my daughter's life left her ruby-painted lips. I lost the way of being an honorable king when I tried too hard to appear as a doting husband to the scornful wife I betrayed over a century ago. I've looked past her lies, I've defended her heinous crimes against my own civilians, and I've allowed her to deny my kingdom the heir they deserve.

The mistakes I have made will haunt my soul in this realm and beyond. Elianna should, and would, be an incredible queen. I wish more than anything to publicly name her as my heir, or that I could find a way to prove to the realm that she is my firstborn and carries the Valderre blood within her. She would bring peace to Velyra, just as she has brought peace to me since the moment she took her first breath.

But alas, I am a dying male. And I'm still consumed by the fear that if I were to name her heir now that it would put a target on her back the moment I pass on. Or that I would be taken as being senile in my final days. With the queen coming to my room nightly now to share a glass of wine, I believe she knows my time is near. What started off as what I could only assume was to make amends, has turned into a goodbye. I am sorry, Lia. My sweet and fiery Elianna Valderre. I will be with your mother soon now, where I belong.

Please forgive me.

I blew out a breath when I finished, and looked up at Avery, who had tears flowing down her flushed cheeks. "He blamed himself for this mess," she whimpered.

I sighed. "That he did. However, this proves who he truly wanted as his heir. It may prove useful."

"How? If Lia is dead..."

Hearing those words rocked me to my core, but she had a point. "Just hold on to this, anyway. There are entries from the nights of all your births, his true feelings regarding the queen, and so much more that we haven't read. Keep this close. You said Callius has been looking to relieve me of my position. I cannot be in possession of this in case something happens to me."

"Don't speak such things into the air," she said, as she hesitantly took the journal and tucked it close to her chest.

"It is just the truth," I assured her. "Now let's get out of here before someone comes in and sees us sneaking around."

She nodded, and I followed her as she aimed for the hidden door we used to come in.

Avery decided to bring the journal back to her chambers to hide it before meeting Finnian back down at the stables. The girl was a lot brighter than she appeared.

I made my way down the spiral stairs as silently as possible and felt lucky when I noticed there still wasn't any staff moving about down there.

Walking through the castle courtyard outside, I was about to make it to the gate beyond the grounds when a shadow appeared between two pillars.

"Lukas. How wonderful of you to appear! It seems as if you have not been at your post for a week now." I could recognize Callius' voice anywhere. "How odd of you," he said, as he widened his stance and crossed his arms.

Fuck. I almost made it out of here. I was so gods-damned close.

"Yes, well, excuse me for mourning the king's death in private," I said, as I half turned my body to him.

He stepped towards me and began waving around his finger. "You see, though, that is just the thing. Like the fantastic partner that I am, I went to check on you in your room in the castle. You haven't been there either. So, tell me, old friend, where have you been?"

"We are not, and have never been, friends," I seethed.

"Semantics," he said, as he waved his hand. "Where have you been, Salvinae." His tone turned demanding.

"Around," I answered through my teeth. I wasn't going to make this easy. I would go down fighting, that's for damn sure.

"Well, while you were 'around,'" another voice chimed in from behind me. Heat rushed to my cheeks as I turned around to see it was Adler. "We received a letter for you by falcon." He held up a rolled-up piece of parchment.

"How kind of you to bring it to me," I said with a mocking smile.

"I hope that you don't mind that I took the liberty of reading it, since you were nowhere to be found." I honestly didn't even know who the letter could be from, so I just stared at him. "It is from our darling, missing, Captain Elianna Solus."

My face dropped, and my heart pounded painfully in my chest.

"Would you like to hear what it says?" he asked, as he pulled open the paper and started reading.

Lukas, I hope this letter made its way to you. I don't know how to start this off, but I will start by letting you know that I am alive. The ship was destroyed at sea and I washed up on shore with the human commander we took captive from Ceto Bay. In a twisted turn of events, I ended up as his captive, and to get even more twisted...I am no longer that. I am safe inside a village beyond the Sylis Forest. We can end this war, and I think I know how. I believe I'm finally ready to be what the king has always wanted me to be. I need you to meet us with a few of our trusted soldiers back at Ceto Bay on the next full moon, which is a month from the day that I am writing this to you. As much as it pains me to say this, please do not tell anyone that I am alive. Even the king. In order for this to work, we need as few people as possible involved.

Also, you were right about Kellan.

All my love,

Lia

My eyes went wide, and I desperately tried to steady my breathing. I couldn't fucking believe this. Lia was alive. She was with the humans, and she unknowingly just exposed herself as a mortal sympathizer.

"Now tell me, Sir. Lukas," Kellan began. "What ever could she mean by being what the king wanted her to be? I am quite curious. Surely the king wasn't a sympathizer like our lovely little traitor."

I glanced over at Callius to see he looked away from us, pretending that there was something very interesting on the

353

ceiling of the outdoor hall. Kellan didn't know who Lia really was, and it seemed as if Callius didn't plan to tell him.

"I don't know what you mean."

Kellan rushed me then and forced his face to be merely an inch from my own, but I didn't back down. "You have been in her pretty little pointed ear about me for *years*. You couldn't just mind your own gods-damn business, and while I always suspected it, it is written, clear as day, in her letter to you." His breathing became rapid. "You will tell me what you fucking know about her and what she is planning to do, and then I will kill you." He placed the tip of his dagger between two of my ribs as he spoke the threat.

"We may need him," Callius chimed in while still staring at the ceiling, looking bored. "Once we get Solus back here, we may need him to persuade her."

Fuck. I will force them to kill me before I let them use me against Lia.

Kellan let out a loud grunt. "Fine, lock him up beneath the castle," he said unblinkingly, as multiple guards that I had commanded for decades rushed me, coming out from the shadows.

They cuffed my hands behind my back and began dragging me away as Kellan turned to Callius. I craned my neck to watch them and witnessed Callius slip a vial of some sort into the pocket of his successor's shirt.

Kellan smirked. "Let's go get our girl, shall we?" Each word sounded more cruel than the last.

FORTY-FOUR

Elianna

TWO WEEKS HAD PASSED since I sent off the message to Isla. I never received a letter back, but it was possible he didn't want to risk being seen sending anything out. I wished he returned something though, letting me know how everyone was doing, especially the king.

Celan Village and its people had grown on me. My ears had managed to stay hidden, just so we didn't freak out the villagers. I was sure it would be a lot to take in for them. Jace wanted everyone here to know who I was, but I wasn't ready for that. Zaela shockingly agreed with me, but I wasn't naïve enough to believe it was for my own sake instead of her people's.

Jace was right though. If the circumstances were different, Zaela and I could've been friends in another life. I didn't entirely blame her for being the way she was toward me. If roles were reversed, I cannot confidently say that I wouldn't have flat out killed her the first night...or throughout the first week after we had met.

Just *thinking* about Avery or Finnian teaming up with someone who had been considered an enemy had my blood boiling, but Jace and I were far from enemies now.

What killed me the most was that I had no idea where the two of us stood. We had been staying in the same rooms at the inn this entire time, enjoying each other's company, and bodies, nightly. The thought of it sent a fluttering feeling through my stomach. Thinking about the road ahead, though, had me absolutely terrified. What would become of us once this was finished? Would he still want me in that way? Or was I just a body to pass his time, considering he was only affectionate behind closed doors? Thinking of that made me nauseous. I never felt anywhere near this way about Kellan, but I could never tell Jace that. Too much was at stake, and I couldn't allow him to become distracted. Granted, with him being half fae, his healing abilities would come in handy during battle, but even if he were full-blooded, he would never be invincible.

When we weren't helping out the little shops along the small cobblestone streets, the four of us had been training. Not with the guards within the village, considering they still had no idea who, or what, I was, but with each other. Some days, we would walk a few miles out in the fields, beyond sight, and train for hours. Gage had even gotten better with a bow, thanks to me. That little shit had become my greatest friend outside of Isla.

Reading a book from the village's tiny library while out in the field of wildflowers, I noticed the sun was setting in the distance, casting the sky above in deep hues of violet and fuchsia, when I heard a voice call my name from the distance. I sat up to see Jace jogging in my direction.

"There you are! I've been looking for you everywhere. I should've known you'd be out here," he said, almost out of breath.

I shut the book. "Do you know almost every book in this village is about how much the fae suck? Honestly, couldn't your human authors write some romance or something? I mean, I understand why, but it's boring."

He chuckled as he sat down next to me. "Most of the books here are about war strategies."

"So I've noticed," I said with a sigh.

He kissed my cheek, making them both blush. "I'll make a mental note to make sure wherever we stay has some dirty romances for you. How's that?"

Now I was *really* blushing. "That is not what I meant."

"Sure," he said with a huffed laugh.

"Where are Zaela and Gage?" I asked, considering normally they're up his ass from the moment they wake up.

"Back at the inn. I'm assuming Gage is probably driving her crazy, per usual."

"Have the two of them ever?" I dragged out each word.

"Gods, I hope not." His eyes flared. "I think Gage has been pining after her for years, but she has tried to make it clear that she isn't interested."

I was silent for a moment, trying to come up with a reason why anyone wouldn't adore Gage. He was hilarious, and had the warmest brown eyes, but then again, this was Zaela we were talking about.

"I wonder why."

"It probably has something to do with the fact that whoever Gage beds, he is promptly in love with them."

I burst out laughing at that. "Are you serious?"

"Does that surprise you?"

I thought about it for a second. "I guess not."

"Honestly, I don't think I have ever seen Zaela interested in any of the men that have approached her. Perhaps she is just extremely sneaky about it. Probably doesn't want to deal with the teasing from us." He shrugged one of his broad shoulders. "Come on, the sun is setting so we should probably head back and get dinner at the inn."

Gods, if I had to eat another plate of eggs and unseasoned meat, I might vomit. That inn served its purpose for sleeping, but their menu needed work, to say the least. "Why don't we go to one of the small taverns in the village tonight?"

He stood up from the ground and held out his hand for me. "Okay, I will let the other two know."

I mean, I definitely just meant the two of us since the only time we were alone together was behind our locked bedroom door late at night. I forced myself to hold in my sigh. "Perfect." I smiled up at him as I pettily refused to take his hand for help. "I'll race you back!"

"As if that's fair..." he surmised.

"One, two, three, go!" I said so fast he barely comprehended it, as I took off into a sprint, forcing him to chase after me.

Our laughter flowed on the wind that rustled the flowers beneath our feet.

As the four of us walked along the cobblestone street, we decided on an adorable little restaurant about three streets up from the inn. When we arrived, the owner offered us the best table in the building, saying it was an honor to host Commander Cadoria and his "lovely friends."

The table she brought us to was up against the large, open window in the front of the establishment, it felt as if we were sitting outside in the street, which was a refreshing change from the stuffiness of the inn.

We sat and talked for hours, eating the delicious food the cook made for us, and drinking an abundance of wine and ale. The room was starting to spin slightly, but I couldn't stop giggling. Every once in a while, Jace would trace his fingers playfully up and down my thigh, causing my thoughts to travel to wicked places. I had to resist the urge to kiss him every time he met my stare.

"So, we leave in three days' time for the bay," Gage said, snapping me back somewhat into reality.

"It appears so." I sighed.

"Do you actually believe they will allow all of us aboard their ship?" Zaela asked me.

I sucked in and lightly bit down on my bottom lip. "I know Lukas, and he understands me better than I do myself. He will go along with the plan once we convince him it will work. The tricky part will be hiding all of you in Isla once we get there. Once I set up a meeting with the king, I will bring you three out so you can tell your stories and all the horrors that you have faced as a result of the war." I ended the last word with a yawn.

"It's getting late," Zaela said. "I think I will head back to the inn now. Do you care to join me, Elianna?"

I looked up at her, confused that she civilly invited me to come with her. Out of the corner of my vision, I could see Jace nod in approval.

"Sure, why not. You boys have fun. Don't do anything I wouldn't do!" I said with a wink, as I stood up from the table and followed Zaela to the door.

Once out in the street, her pace picked up, almost as if she didn't plan to walk with me at all. I caught up to her easily enough, but she still didn't speak to me, so I walked a step behind her in silence.

After we made it to the inn, I followed her up the stairs, and nearly passed her as she put the key into the door of her and Gage's room when she finally spoke, "What is going on between you and Jace?" she asked out of nowhere.

"Uh." I looked at her. "That was incredibly random."

"Only it wasn't." She gave me a mocking grin. "Do you think we are blind?"

"No, I never said that."

"Then what is going on with you two?"

I *really* didn't want to discuss this with her before I even had the chance to with him, but she wasn't giving me a choice. "I am not sure," I whispered harshly, narrowing my eyes at her.

"Well, it is clearly something."

"I suppose it is."

Her eyes thinned into slits as she leaned her body against the doorway. "Tell me something then, Elianna. Do you love him?" She crossed her arms. "My cousin has barely taken an interest in women until you came along. He thinks we don't notice the way he looks at you."

My heart was racing so fast I thought it was about to burst out of my chest, and a fraction of a smile creeped up my lips. "Goodnight, Zaela," I said, as I turned away from her, ignoring her incredibly invasive question.

"Don't hurt him," she called up to me, as I was almost at the top of the stairs that led to our door. I turned back to face her. "Whatever you do," she continued. "Whatever the outcome of all of this is...just please, don't fucking hurt him."

"I won't," I promised in a hushed whisper, as I turned the key to my room and gently shut the door behind me once inside.

Jace

The night was beautiful, and a small breeze came through the giant, open windows of the tavern. I looked up at the night sky, filled with stars, and then I looked over to Gage sitting across from me. I couldn't remember the last time I was able to enjoy a few ales with my best friend, and we were able to pretend as if our lives weren't an absolute shit storm. He would always say I never let loose, and he was right. And to be honest, I barely knew how to.

"So, Lia," he said with a feral grin. "Brother if you don't bed her soon, I most certainly will."

I started choking as I took a swig from my mug. "You will do no such thing." I met his stare, and his eyes were filled with challenge, replicating back to when we were young boys out for the chase, and not adults with responsibilities. "And what makes you think I haven't?" I raised a brow jokingly as I sipped once more.

"I knew it!" he shouted, causing all the other eyes in the room to fly in our direction.

"Gods, keep your voice down," I grumbled out.

"Sorry." He didn't look remotely sorry. "When? What is happening with you two?"

I blew out a breath. "Not sure, Gage. And it is absolutely none of your business."

"Will you become king?"

My eyes flew open wide at his ridiculous question. "No, Gage, I don't even know how she feels about me. We've just been...having fun."

"Having fun?"

"Yeah, isn't that what you've always wanted for me?" I shot back.

"Brother, I would like to think that I have had a decent amount of 'fun' in my days, but whatever the hell is going on with the two of you...that is not...fun, at least not in that sense." I shrugged in response. "Why have you been trying to hide it?"

I laughed. "Have you met Zaela?"

"True. Your cousin is terrifying."

"Then there you have it," I said, as I gulped down the last sip in my mug.

"Do you love her?" he asked warily, causing me to spit out the ale that remained in my mouth.

My jaw dropped open in disbelief at his question, but before I had time to even think of a response, a loud scream echoed across the village, making both of us shoot up from the table.

Glancing around the street through the enormous, open window, a wall of flames could be seen in the direction of the village gate.

"No," I whispered, as more desperate, terrified screams ripped through the air.

EMILIA JAE

"Everybody out. Now!" Gage roared, and everyone in the restaurant with us scattered.

"It could be a house fire," I said to him, while I threw coin down onto the table for the owner.

"That is no house fire, brother," Gage answered, appearing stunned where he stood.

I looked back out to the village to see the flames had grown taller, and the streets were now frantic with those that called Celan Village home.

"We need to move. Now!" I said sternly, as we both gripped our swords and ran out the door.

FORTY-FIVE

Jace

THE VILLAGE WAS NOTHING short of chaos. Flames could be seen all throughout the distance, and the thick clouds of smoke were climbing through the streets. The only sounds heard aside from the roar of the flames were the screams of terror echoing around us.

"Shit, where are the girls?!" Gage frantically yelled in my face. "Do you think they made it back to the inn?"

"They've been gone for at least an hour. They definitely made it back, but I wouldn't be surprised if they were already out here amongst the madness," I answered.

I turned my body around in circles, overwhelmed with where to even begin. The fires were spreading. Fast.

"We need to get everyone out of here, Jace! We need to evacuate the village."

I nodded at him. "You take the western end, I will take the east. If you see the girls, tell them that's the plan. We need to get everyone out of here as soon as possible."

Off in the distance, I could make out the silhouettes of a crew of men. At first glance, I assumed it was the village guards coming to assist with evacuating everyone out, but as they made their way closer to us, I froze where I stood.

They took torches to every building they walked past, and cut down anyone who dared run by, even if they were trying to flee and beg for mercy.

And that was when I realized they weren't men at all. They were *fae*. And it wasn't just a random crew of them either. Kellan Adler led the way at the front of the lines.

"You're fucking joking," I said, as I unsheathed my sword.

"How the fuck is this happening?! How did they find us?" Gage shouted, as he matched my stance.

"Either Lia was betrayed, or she betrayed us," I said through my teeth.

His gaze whipped to mine. "Surely you're not truly thinking that second option..."

"I don't know what to believe right now, Gage! Get everyone the fuck out of here! The plan stands. We can't take them on without risking the lives of the civilians. Stay hidden and out of sight. Move. *Now!*" I shouted, as he took off in the opposite direction that I did.

Elianna

Shortly after falling asleep, I heard a commotion coming from outside. I gradually blinked my eyes open to see a bright orange hue coming through the window.

"It can't be dawn already," I whispered to myself, as I got up from the bed. I peered around and saw Jace hadn't come back from the restaurant yet.

Something felt off.

Once I got to the window, my eyes widened at the horror unfolding before me. "Oh, my gods…" My hand flew to my mouth in shock. I sped across the room to pull on my boots and grabbed my dagger and a few other weapons Jace had left lying around.

I swung the door open and leaped down the flight of stairs. I aggressively banged on Zaela's bedroom door. "Zaela, open up! Some of the buildings outside are on fire! We need to go help them."

She swung the door open, looking just as disheveled as I felt. "I can hear the screams, they just woke me up. Let's go!" she said, as we both ran as fast as we could down the stairs. "We are going to need to evacuate the village if the fires continue to spread, I'm sure the boys are already trying to do that."

I nodded in agreement. "Just let me know what you need me to do."

Her eyes met mine. "Just don't get killed and save everyone you can."

As we opened the front door to the inn, horror struck us both.

It wasn't just a fire.

It was an *attack*.

Bodies lay sprawled across the streets, some of them missing limbs, pools of blood beneath them. The scent of iron and smoke enveloped the air around us. The only sound that could be heard were the screams of terror and agony.

"What the hell is happening?" I asked, stunned where I stood.

"I know exactly what is happening." The tone of her voice was filled with fury, and then she *laughed*. It sounded nearly as wicked as the queens. "You know, I almost believed you, Elianna, I really did!" She began to back me into the corner of the room next to the door. "You fucking betrayed us. I *knew* one of us should have read that letter you sent with the falcon, but no. Jace trusted you enough to send it off. And *look*. Look where it got us!" She pointed out the door. The features of her face contorted into an unrecognizable beast of rage.

She moved to swipe her dagger at my face and I almost wasn't quick enough to block the blow with my own. My grip was shaking as I pushed her dagger back, away from my face. "Zaela, I swear to you...I didn't do this!"

She leaned into me, her face now so close to my own that I could feel her heaving breaths on my face. "Liar!" she screeched, as she kneed me in the gut, forcing me to grunt and lose my breath as I fell to my knees.

"Go with them and leave, or you will die amongst them!" she shouted on a cry. "I need to get our people out of here first before I deal with the likes of you." And then she ran out the door.

I couldn't catch my breath. Everything was crashing down around me. Had Lukas' letter somehow been intercepted by someone else? What in the fuck was going on?

I crawled to my feet as I rushed back to the door and quickly ducked back down around it when I saw who was now standing not even ten feet from the doorway.

"Shit!" I shrieked, as my breathing turned into rapid pants.

I tried to peer around the doorway but heard his steps getting closer.

I quickly looked around the room and saw a trunk in the corner across from where I hid. I rapidly crawled across the floor, and to my surprise, the trunk was unlocked. I crawled inside, contorting my body to fit around the items it held, and silently closed the lid as Kellan stepped through the doorway.

I desperately tried to will my breathing and heart rate to slow, but it was no use. He was here. He found me. And now he was going to make every single person in the village pay for what I had done.

I watched him through the keyhole of the trunk. He slowly made his way through the room, picking up cups on each table and smashing them on the ground, peeking underneath every table and chair as if he were looking for something. Or someone.

The male that tried to attack me on the ship all those weeks ago appeared in the doorway then. "Anything, Captain?"

Kellan picked up another glass and whipped it at the wall as he roared with anger. "Nothing," he snapped, as he rubbed the back of his neck. "But she is here. I can fucking smell her."

"We'll find her," the male replied.

"We will, Vincent," he said through his teeth, as he turned around to stalk back out the door. "Light it up. I want this entire village burned to the ground. Kill the men. Take the women for whatever you and the crew want. The children...I don't really give a fuck." My eyes widened in fear for all of the innocents he just spoke of. I was going to be sick.

I did this. This was entirely my fault.

And then he was gone. The male, Vincent, then took his torch and began to place it upon every table and wall within the inn.

The building was up in flames in only a few moments. I watched as he gave a nod of approval to himself as he admired his work and exited the inn.

I threw the lid of the trunk open and immediately choked uncontrollably on the thick smoke that was now filling the room. I looked to the doorway, and it was up in flames. I couldn't take the risk of running out there in case they were still standing in the street.

I glanced across the room and saw a window towards the back and sprinted over to it. I stuck my head out to make sure no one was behind it and dove through, landing straight on my stomach on the hard, unforgiving ground.

I heard the terrified scream of a woman come from a few buildings over and I was up on my feet and running before I even had a second to think. I burst through the door of the establishment, and saw she was cornered by a male I recognized from Kellan's ship. He was one of the three that cornered *me*.

The woman's frightened eyes met mine and widened slightly, but I placed a finger over my mouth to tell her to remain quiet as I snuck up behind the male.

As I got closer, I could see that he had his face buried into her neck and had her body pinned to the wall using one hand as the other slid up her dress.

Oh, fuck no.

I took one giant step forward and gripped him by his hair, ripping his face away from her. My dagger was pressed to his throat as he struggled against me.

The woman was panting as she stared at me. "Are you okay?" I asked her, and she started rapidly nodding her head up and down. "Good." I smiled at her and nodded toward the door. "Now get out of here, you need to evacuate!" I watched as she ran from the corner and out the door.

I then brought my lips to the male's ear. "Didn't your mother teach you that it isn't polite to force yourself onto a female?"

He chuckled as he tried to swing his arm back at me, but I just pulled his hair harder and applied enough pressure on the blade for a drop of blood to fall. "Fuck you, Solus." He sniggered. "How does it feel to be a traitorous bitch? You're next. Your beloved is ready to tear apart the realm to find you. We could scent you the moment we arrived."

A wicked smile appeared on my face. "He'll have to catch me first," I said, as I ripped the dagger across his throat, spraying fresh blood all over the wall the woman had just stood in front of. I didn't drop his body to the floor until I heard the gurgling stop.

Where the hell was Jace? Did he think I caused this purposefully as Zaela did? I needed to find him as soon as possible.

I checked the rest of the building to make sure no one else was in there before I ran back out and began going door to door to get people out. Any time I came across one of the fae, one that used to be one of my own soldiers, I plunged my sword through their bodies, killing them where they stood.

Out of the corner of my eye, as I was running down a street, I noticed a few people huddled between two buildings. I rushed over to them, and they were shaking with fear. "Please, don't hurt my family!" the man shouted. I counted him, a woman that I could only assume was his wife, and three little ones. "Take me instead, but please, please, I beg you, let my family go!"

My heart was snapping as I saw all their gazes upon me, horrified, thinking that I was here to hurt them. "I am not here to harm you or your family. I am here to help you." I tried to assure him.

"*Those* say otherwise." His trembling hand rose and pointed to my ear that I hadn't even thought to cover.

"Sir, I promise you I am here to help," I said with my hand reaching out to them, as I took a step forward. But he didn't believe me.

"Run!" he screeched, and his entire family turned from me and ran full speed to the opposite opening between the two buildings, right out into the open.

"No!" I screamed as I ran after them, but I was too late.

I skidded to a stop as I heard yelps of pain, and screams cut entirely too short as they filtered through the air. I peered out from the shadowy alley to see they ran straight into seven of Kellan's crew members. They were slaughtered the moment they left the alleyway.

My eyes burst into tears and my body slid to the ground against the side of the building. I tried to save them. I tried to help them, but they saw my ears and assumed I was one of the attackers. One of the horrible fae who came in the middle of the night to destroy their village, their home, and family. If I covered my ears, his family may still be alive.

I heard orders being shouted in the distance, but it was a familiar voice. One I wasn't running from. Jace's.

I was up on my feet instantly and ran toward him. "Jace!" I yelled as he came into view. Once I got to him, he looked anything but happy to see me. "Thank the gods you're okay!"

"Is that so?" he snapped without looking at me.

Did he *really* think I did this?

"Jace, I had nothing to do with this. I swear to you, please." I grabbed his arm, forcing him to look at me. "You must know deep down that I could never, would *never* do this!"

His features softened. "This is bad, Lia."

The tears welled in my eyes again. "I know." My chest shook on a sob. "I don't know what to do. I've been telling everyone to evacuate."

Every building around us was up in flames. The screams that had been haunting the air were now few and far between, and I truly hoped that was because people got out, and not due to them being massacred.

"Fuck!" he shouted, as his gaze was focused out into the distance. "Zaela went into that building to check for anyone left behind." I turned as he pointed to the two males that ran into said building.

I took off running toward them. "Find Gage! I think we got most of the survivors out. We need to leave!"

"Lia, no, don't!" he screamed, but I didn't stop. I couldn't. I couldn't have him lose Zaela. I didn't care that she'd rather see my head on a spike than work with me.

I burst through the burning door and instantly made eye contact with one of the males. "There she is!" he shouted, as I ripped my dagger off my thigh and expertly threw it directly into his chest—his heart. The male's body crashed down to the floor. The other one then had his bow aimed directly at my face, and I somersaulted out of the way as I heard the arrow whoosh by my cheek.

That was *rude*.

"I'm going to kill you," I hissed at him, making him laugh.

"Gods, you always were a pain in the ass, Elianna, but now look what you've done. Kellan's been very, *very* worried about you." He grinned.

My brows furrowed as I lunged for my dagger, still in the other male's chest. The one who had just tried to shoot me then kicked me directly in the back, sending my body tumbling across the room and slammed my head onto the floor. My elbow was nicked by the outskirts of the flames, causing me to yelp.

"I have her in here!" I faintly heard him call out, while my blurry vision tried to focus on him as he walked out of the building. Shit.

I never saw Zaela get out of here. She must be upstairs still. I forced my body up, peeling myself from the floor as I retrieved my dagger and ran as fast as I could, now with a minor limp. I forced my body up the stairs that were now encased in flames, burning my legs with each step.

"Zaela!" I called out, hoping I could be heard above the roar of the fire. "Zaela, where are you?!" I said through rough coughing, as I was forced to inhale the swirling, black smoke.

"In here!" I heard her call from the next room over.

I forced my way through the hall, watching each step I took on the creaking floor. Some parts of the boards had already been reduced to ashes.

I saw her then, standing on a ledge to a side of the building that had completely collapsed under the blaze. I forced my way to her.

"What are you doing?!" I yelled.

She looked at me, nervously. "There's no way out now, we have to jump."

I peered down at the distance. I would survive it, but she could break bones. "We can make it through down the stairs." I grabbed her arm. "Let's go!"

As I said the last word, a loud crashing sound rumbled as we watched a majority of what remained of the building fall, just as the wall had.

"Fuck!" I yelled as I looked back at her, sparks and embers flying through the air.

"What are you even doing here?!" she snapped in my face.

I looked at her dumbfounded. "Is *now* really the time to be pissed about this?! I am trying to help you!"

"I don't want your help!" she shouted over the flames, coughing with every other word.

She tiptoed back over to the edge, and I looked across the way to see that the male who had kicked me across the room below was now on the opposite side of the street from us—an arrow nocked into his bow and aimed directly at Zaela.

Time slowed as I watched him release the arrow. She was completely unaware, readying herself to leap out to the street below.

"No!" I screamed, as I jumped, face first in front of her, halting her from leaping off. A moment later, I felt the arrow tear through flesh and bone, right through my side.

My face was flush with hers, my bottom lip started to tremble from the pain. "Shit." I uttered at her, glancing down at the arrow's tip that was now protruding from the side of my stomach.

"Oh, my gods, Elianna!" she howled in my face, eyes flaring with terror by what had just occurred. I went to take a step back from her, forgetting about the gaping hole in the building directly behind me. She reached her arms out toward me, but not in time to stop me as my body plummeted to the ground below.

FORTY-SIX

Jace

THE SECOND ELIANNA RAN off, I heard screams in another direction and forced myself to turn away from her and go help the others, telling myself that she could handle herself, as she had proven time and time again.

Dawn was now approaching on the horizon, causing the tones of the sky to nearly match the low flames still ablaze on the ground. I continued stalking around the village, forcing myself to carry on through the exhaustion and intense pain that radiated through my body. I just didn't remember taking any hits from our attackers. I was too focused on moving everyone to safety.

I peered around the corner to make sure the coast was clear, and as I ran back toward the building that Lia had entered to help Zae, I saw that it had collapsed entirely .

"Mother of the gods!" I gasped.

"Jace!" I heard a soft shriek to my left. I whipped around to see Zaela creeping down, hiding behind a barrel. "Where is Gage?" she asked, as I made my way to her.

"He is with the others, leading them far out from here. Where is Lia?!" She closed her eyes extremely tight and bit her bottom lip before she looked back up at me again. My heart stopped. "Zaela. Where is she?"

Her voice began to shake, a reaction I had never seen from her my entire life, "Sh-she fell." She slowly raised a trembling finger and pointed to where the building had stood.

"What do you mean she *fell?*" I raised my voice, standing over her as she remained crouched down, making her shrink even lower.

"The building was collapsing. Jace, I'm so sorry!" She paused, and while I knew she was upset, my patience was wearing thin. "One of the fae saw us as we were about to jump, because it was the only way out. The stairs had turned to ash at that point. He shot an arrow at us...well, at *me*." My brows flew up my forehead. "She must've seen him because she jumped in front of me and took the hit of the arrow. It went through the side of her stomach." Her voice cracked on the last few words.

I couldn't breathe. My vision was blackening around me, and I had to force my next words out, "Is she alive?"

"I think so. She fell backwards from the second floor, but I think she was unconscious when she hit the ground. I jumped down from the building a moment later, but the fae men saw me and aimed arrows at me again. I had to run."

My eyes snapped back to hers. "*You. Left. Her. There?!*" I screamed in her face as my arm swung out and pointed in the direction they had been.

"Jace, I'm sorry, there was nothing I could do." She was talking so fast I could barely understand. "Once I was out of their view,

I peeked around from where I hid and watched them drag her body away. I'm not sure where they went."

My jaw ticked, and I bit down on my inner cheek so hard I could taste the blood as it trickled into my mouth, I extended my hand out to her to help her up. "You will find Gage, and once everyone is settled a few miles from here, come back. I need to keep track of them in case they leave."

"I am *not* leaving you," she said, as she stood up, refusing my hand.

"You will do as I say, Zaela." Her eyes lined with silver at the tone of my voice, stopping her dead in her tracks. "That is a fucking order." She continued to stare at me. "If they take her, they will kill her, and I refuse to allow that to happen. It isn't a fucking option. I promised her, Zae. I *promised* her that!" I admitted, as I stormed off in the direction she had pointed.

It didn't take long to find them hiding out beyond the, now burned down, gates of the village. I hid and ducked down amongst the debris left from the collapsed buildings.

The sun had risen, revealing the true damage of the attack. Nausea built up in my throat. Bodies lay everywhere on the ground. Men, women, and children alike. Lives lost on yet another senseless act—one that could've been prevented. We were planning to leave Celan Village in only three days to head towards Ceto Bay. If only they were a day or two behind, or if we had left yesterday morning instead, we may have been able to catch them outside of here and none of this would have occurred.

Peering through the wreckage, I could see Lia's body was tied standing up to one of the outside posts. She appeared to still be unconscious. Captain Fuckface was standing in a circle amongst his fae men, laughing about the events of the night.

I would kill him for this. Mark my fucking words. If he wouldn't die for all the monstrous ordeals he put Lia through, he would die for *this*.

After a few moments, he walked away from the circle and made his way to Lia, and my heart began to race. He picked up a bucket of what I assumed, and hoped, was water and dumped the liquid over her head, causing her to jerk and stir to consciousness. The look in her eyes regarding the scene that lay before her told me everything I needed to know—she truly had nothing to do with this.

I slowly, and as quietly as possible, started to inch my way forward through the debris.

"There she is." Kellan chuckled mockingly in her face. "My beautiful little traitor finally awakens." She stared at him through pinched brows, breathing heavily. "I'd love to say you look wonderful, *princess*, but honestly you've seen better days." He leaned in close to her and sniffed. "You reek of that commander's cock," he said in disgust, as he turned towards his crew that now gathered around the scene. "Not only is she a sympathizer, boys, but it also appears she has been fucking the leader of the enemy!"

A roar of laughter erupted from the fae men, Kellan included. Did he know she was a princess? She didn't react when he called her that. But how could he know about...*us?* The fae's senses must be significantly stronger than I originally believed.

He turned back to her and got in her face. "You've been so bad, my Lia."

Hearing him call her *his* sent my blood boiling even further. He then grabbed her face and squeezed her cheeks in his hand, bringing his own down to hers and ran his tongue from the tip of her jaw up to her brow bone.

Without hesitation, she spat right in his face. "Go fuck yourself," she seethed, her lip curling back in an animalistic snarl.

Now that's *my* Lia.

He then grabbed her by the hair and wiped her phlegm, that now dripped down his cheek, from his face with it, and then slammed her head back into the pole, and I winced as she grunted out in pain. The scene felt too familiar, replicating only two months ago when I was in her position.

My body instantly jerked—I wouldn't be able to hold myself back much longer. All I could do was pray to the gods that Zaela and Gage got back here quickly.

Then he did the unthinkable. I didn't even notice the arrow was still sticking out from her side. He took her by the throat with one hand and then took the tip of the arrow between two of his fingers on the other and began to *twist* it inside her body. My jaw dropped in horror as the scream of agony she let out tore through the morning air.

I was up and running to her before I even had a plan.

I unsheathed my sword and promptly severed the head of one of the crew members that had been on the outskirts of the crowd, and then another. Before anyone could react, I started slicing through everyone I could.

"Jace, no!" I heard Lia cry out, but I didn't care. I wouldn't stop. I couldn't. They hurt her, intentionally. Not only that, but they enjoyed the sounds of her screams. They would pay for that with their lives.

I had cut down six of them before I felt the force of a boot to my back, nearly cracking my spine as it sent me flying across the space, and face first into the dirt.

I waited for the inevitable, deadly blow to come, but it never did.

Instead, I was ripped up from the ground by the back of my shirt and disarmed. They bound my limbs so quickly I didn't even register it was happening until I realized I couldn't move my wrists or ankles.

Kellan stood before me. His stance was wide, with his arms crossed. The smirk etched across his lips made me want to carve it off his face with Lia's dagger.

"Well, well, what do we have here? A rescue attempt?" Laughter sounded throughout the crew once more. He walked over to me, his body not even three feet in front of me now. "I can respect the bravery, or in this case stupidity, but take it from me. She's not worth it." He began to laugh again in my face.

"You have never known her worth, and you were never deserving of someone like her," I said through my teeth.

"Oh, and you are?" he taunted, all signs of laughter gone. I struck a nerve. Good. "Tell me, Commander, what was it like when you finally got her to spread those thick, pretty legs of hers?" I could feel the blood rush to my ears. "How did her pussy feel?" He paused. "Well, I know how good she feels, and I hope you enjoyed it, because it will cost you your worthless, pathetic, mortal life for touching what's mine."

Out of the corner of my eye, I could see Lia flinch at his words. "She will *never* be yours again!" I barked at him.

He chuckled again, but the crew was silent. "That's where you're wrong. She will *always* be mine, as I have told her many times." Our eyes were locked on each other's as my body radiated with fury. I could feel the veins ready to burst in my neck as my teeth clenched harder as each second passed.

"Please, Kellan, just let him go!" Lia shouted through tears. "You have me. You got what you came for. Just let him go. You can do whatever you want to me. Just *please* do this one thing."

He whipped to her. "Shut your fucking mouth. I'll deal with you later."

My heart was racing to the point where I thought it may explode in my chest. She was trying to sacrifice herself to get me out of here. Knowing all the things he could, and would, do to her once back in Isla.

His eyes found mine once more, darting back and forth. "She actually cares for you," he said in a confused whisper. His jaw locked then, and he stormed over to her.

"No, wait. Don't you fucking touch her!" I yelled, as his crew held my body back, but he didn't even spare a glance at me.

Once he made it to her, he grabbed her face with both hands and aggressively shoved his tongue down her throat. I was forced to watch as she jolted around, desperately trying to get away from him.

He then reached down and violently unsheathed the obsidian dagger from her thigh, slicing her leg open in the process. She yelped in pain as blood began to run down her leg.

"Vincent, get the vial," he ordered, as one of his crew members walked over to a sack sitting on the ground and pulled out a vial of what appeared to be a thick, red liquid.

Once Vincent handed Kellan the small bottle, he dumped it onto the blade of the dagger. Kellan gave her a quick glance. "Lia, I hate to be the one to tell you this, but your darling king is dead."

My eyes flew open in horror at what he revealed. Lia was just staring at him in shock. "You lie!" she shouted.

He sent her a wry grin. "Oh, but I do not. He passed on a few weeks ago." Lia instantly burst into tears. "My condolences, of course. Kai will be officially crowned once he takes a bride."

The king was dead. The wretched prince would now ascend the throne and our entire plan just went to shit. There would be no winning this war now. No way to convince the realm of who Lia truly was and was meant to be.

"Anyway, I know you are familiar with the wyvern below the dungeons of the castle," he said to her.

Her breath caught. "Nox," she forced out through sobs.

"Sure..." He held up the, now empty, vial. "Tell me, Elianna, are you aware of what the blood of a wyvern can do?" She said nothing. "I didn't think so." He held up her dagger, the blade now dripping with what I assumed to be wyvern's blood. "It melts. Mimicking the fire it wields within its breath, their blood can melt through flesh and bone."

"Kellan, whatever you're thinking of doing with that blade..." she rushed out.

"A fae would have a chance of surviving it. It would be a bitch to heal, but a flesh wound would not kill one of us, unless cut deep. A mortal, on the other hand..."

I knew exactly what he was getting to, but I refused to show him even an ounce of fear.

"Kellan, don't you *fucking* touch him with that!" she seethed in a tone that promised death, as she frantically tried to twist out from her bindings.

"See, Elianna, but I must. Because he touched what is mine and dared to try to claim it as his own," he said with a wicked smile, as he approached me.

"Kellan, *don't!*" she screamed, but it was too late.

He lashed out at me, swiping the blood coated blade across my face, narrowly missing my right eye.

I heard the sizzling of my skin melting away first, and then felt the excruciating, unbearable pain that followed. A fire ignited within my veins as my own blood felt as if it were bubbling beneath my flesh.

FORTY-SEVEN

Elianna

I WATCHED HELPLESSLY IN horror as Kellan ripped my dagger's blade across Jace's face. The screams he let out once his skin made contact with the wyvern's blood rocked me to my very core, the sight of it making me vomit all over the ground.

Breathing heavily, I forced myself to look back over at Jace, whose body was now twisting on the ground in agony as he tried to hide how much pain he felt.

Then I realized it was how much pain *I* felt.

I felt *his* pain.

"Mother of the gods..." I whispered.

"The gods aren't going to help him now, princess," Kellan said to me, but I didn't acknowledge him. "Alright crew, round everything up, let's get the hell out of here," he barked, as they all began to scatter.

I fearfully watched Jace's body as his movements slowed, no longer contorting around in the dirt.

This couldn't be possible. The only way you could feel another's pain...their *true* pain, physical and emotional, was if you're their...*mate*.

Mate. What I refused to believe in my entire life due to the impracticality of it. I believed it to be a fairytale for young girls who dreamed of finding their one true love. The other half of their soul. Their equal. Their twin-flame.

My mate. Someone who had been my enemy, that I could never find a reason as to why I felt drawn to him so intensely. No matter how badly I wanted to hate him, I never could. The emotional pull I felt when he projected his devastation over losing his small army that day in the bay.

My leg...on the beach. I thought I had pulled a muscle leaping down from the tree, but really the pain I felt was his. From my own arrow I shot at him.

The pure euphoria I felt when we finally came together that first night in the village. The *magic* I felt occurring between us as it unknowingly locked that bond in place.

"My mate," I whispered to myself.

"What should we do about him?" I heard Vincent ask Kellan, snapping me out of my stupor.

"Don't you touch him, you bastard!" I viciously retorted.

Vincent observed Jace then. I could see his chest moving as it slowly rose and fell, confirming he was still alive. "His face isn't nearly as melted as I thought it would be, Captain."

"Give it time," Kellan said to him without looking in his direction. "Just leave him there to rot. The blood will demolish his body over the next few hours."

He sounded unsure, giving me hope that he was wrong. He also had no idea that Jace was a halfling, and the only fae quality we even knew he possessed so far was that he could heal abnormally fast. Well, that and now a mating bond, that I had no idea if he also felt...or even *wanted*.

I sent up a quick prayer to the gods that I was right, and he would survive this.

Kellan wiped the blade of my dagger with a cloth, as he approached me once more. "Now, we can do this the easy way, or the hard way, and knowing you, I'm assuming I should just brace for the hard."

I cackled wickedly. "You can brace yourself for whatever you see fit. But mark my words, you will die for what you did today. You will die for the havoc and devastation you caused this village of innocents. And you will die for harming what's *mine*."

Any hint of amusement he had fell from his face. He then took my dagger, placed the tip of it into the dirt on the ground, and stomped down directly on the blade, snapping it clean off of its hilt.

I gasped out in devastation. "And I will fucking *destroy* you for that too, you piece of shit!" I screamed so loud that the birds in the far-off trees flew off into the morning sky, fleeing their posts.

My dagger, the only thing I had left of my father, whose soul had left this realm and I never knew. My favorite weapon, my most treasured gift and reminder of who I truly was, gone. Destroyed out of spite in only a second of time.

Kellan went over to Vincent, who finished loading up their small wagon, and was handed a small bottle of amber liquid that resembled tea.

He stalked over to me with the bottle in hand. "Open your mouth," he demanded.

"Absolutely the fuck not."

A fraction of a moment later, he ripped the arrow completely out of my gut, causing my body to convulse and my legs give out. I was now only being held up by the rope that secured me tightly to the pole.

As I let out a loud cry, he poured the entire bottle into my mouth and placed his hand aggressively over my lips, forcing me to swallow the mysterious liquid.

Once he let go, I began coughing uncontrollably. "Ruefweed is one hell of a substance there, love." He laughed out as he cut the rope, making my aching body crash down onto the hard terrain.

I tried to push my body up, but the feeling in my arms was already diminishing. My muscles felt weak, as if they were made of liquid.

I forced my neck to look up gradually towards Jace, who was now unconscious only twenty feet from me. His eyes were closed and I could see the massive gash sliced across his beautiful face.

My vision started to blur as someone tugged on my boot, and then I noticed I was getting further and further away from my mate. I was being *dragged* away from him.

I was barely able to turn my torso as I saw Kellan's back, watching him as he pulled my limp body to the wagon. I hissed at him as he bent down to me.

"Oh yeah." He smacked the side of my cheek a few times, but I couldn't feel it. "Won't be much longer now. She'll be out for at least a few days."

I could hear his words, but I felt my consciousness slipping as each second passed.

He lifted my body up and carelessly tossed me into the wagon, but I couldn't feel anything.

"My mate," I tried to whisper.

And then infinite darkness claimed me.

Jace

I could faintly hear my name being called from the distance, and then felt a light tapping on my arms and legs. My neck twitched slightly, causing a sharp pain to course through my face. My entire body ached and throbbed with an intensity I had never experienced before.

"Easy, Jace, easy! Don't move too quickly." I heard the voice, now sounding as if it was next to me.

I carefully opened my eyes, blinking away the blurriness, and allowing my sight to adjust to the sun that was now beaming down on me.

"There he is. I thought we were going to actually lose you for a moment there, brother."

Gage.

My body shot up, but Gage caught my shoulders with both hands and gently brought me back down to the ground.

"You can't move too fast, something...awful happened to your face. I don't want your body to go into shock," Zaela said from beside him.

My eyes were darting back and forth, trying to get a sense of my surroundings. "Where is she?"

Zaela sucked in her bottom lip as she brushed my blood coated hair away from my face. "Just relax."

My hand shot up without warning, and gripped her wrist tightly. "Where. Is. She."

Her eyes flew to Gage.

He audibly gulped. "Brother." He hesitated for a long moment. "She was gone when we got back here."

My vision was blurring again, but this time with silvery tears. "You're...you're lying!" I barely recognized my own voice.

Gage let out a whisper of a sob. "I wish I was," he breathed, as he sat back, no longer hovering over me.

"There was nothing we could do," Zaela chimed in. "It's only been a few hours since dawn, but by the time we got back here once the survivors were safe, we found you unconscious and...mutilated on the ground, and all signs of them had disappeared. We thought you were dead until we felt your pulse."

I wish I was. I would give anything. *Anything* to trade places with Elianna right now. I gladly would've taken her place if it meant she would be here, safe.

But they never would've let that happen. They left me for dead, and for all I knew, she was dead now too, or as good as.

I slowly sat up, putting my hand up, halting the two of them from mothering me once more. I then took that same hand and attempted to feel the gash on my face.

"They just missed your eyes. You're lucky. But why does it...look like that?"

She asked me as if I could fucking see the thing, but I answered with the only guess I had, "Wyvern's blood."

"Come again?"

"Kellan. That bastard captain. He poured wyvern's blood on the blade. It apparently melts through skin. If I was fully human, I wouldn't be alive right now. I think I blacked out from the pain and lost consciousness."

They both let out a loud gasp. "So wyverns actually exist? I thought she had been...fibbing about that," Gage admitted, and honestly, that hadn't even occurred to me when everything had been unfolding.

"It appears that they do."

"Damn, that is, that is something."

I eyed him but was too stressed to address him.

He placed his hand firmly on my shoulder and met my stare. "We'll get her back."

"We will," Zaela quickly agreed, and I arched a brow. "She saved me. I can put the rest of the shit behind us. She saved me, and now she is captured because of it."

I tried to not get irritated with her again over it.

I stood up on wobbly legs, clutching the side of my stomach as a phantom pain radiated from it, when I noticed a green glimmer out of the corner of my eye in the dirt. I slowly stumbled my way over to it to see that Lia's dagger, the dagger that sliced through my face only hours prior, was snapped in half on the ground.

I bent down to pick up the pieces. My hands shook with fury as I clutched the severed blade and its hilt, the sharpness of it slicing into my fingers. My body didn't register the pain, though, not over everything else I currently felt.

"We leave for Ellecaster now," I announced, as I pocketed the dagger's pieces. I turned back to them. "We leave for Ellecaster, gather everyone we can and then head beyond the mountains, to Alaia Valley. We assemble our full fucking armada and then we storm Isla and take our lives back." I hesitated from the ache in my chest. "We take Lia back. And then we end this shit once and for all."

They both met my gaze with menacing smiles.

FORTY-EIGHT

Elianna

My heavy eyes fluttered open to see I was locked in a dark, empty cell aboard a ship. How long had I been out for? The last thing I remembered was Kellan dumping an unknown, tangy substance down my throat, and then nothing.

I sat up from the floor too quickly, making a faint dizziness return. I lifted my still bound hands in an attempt to rub the headache from my temples, when I heard a slight stir of commotion coming from the corner of my cell.

"Jace?" I spoke out softly.

A sharp, deep snicker sounded from the dark corner. "I bet you would like that, wouldn't you, princess?"

Kellan.

"What have you done with him?" I said through my teeth, my voice hoarse, yet deep with the promise of vengeance. He stepped out from the shadows and into my view.

He eyed me and cocked his head to the side. "Perhaps I did give you too much ruefweed. You've been asleep for nine days, after all. We will be docking in Isla by sundown." My eyes widened in disbelief. He...he had drugged me, and I was out for *days*. "Your beloved human has probably already been picked apart by the crows by now, if there was anything left of him after the wyvern's blood seeped through, that is. His stench is still clinging onto you somehow. It's almost unbearable to be next to you."

It had just occurred to me now that what Kellan had scented at the village, and even now, was the mating bond. Jace's scent had mixed with my own. Could that mean he was still alive? I sniffed the air sadly, and my eyes flared as I realized it myself. Had I never scented it because I was always with Jace, assuming that what I smelled was just...*him?*

A roaring formed in my ears and my vision suddenly clouded in a crimson haze at the thought of what he had done to my mate, and I went to lash out once more when I remembered he had ripped the arrow from my body. My eyes shot down to my side, where I could see a minor infection clearing up with a layer of salve spread across it.

"Who did this?" I gestured to my side.

He smirked. "I did. I took it upon myself to snatch up the remaining hidden salve before we came for you. Can't have you dying on me yet. Not before I'm done with you." The look in his eye pledged torture. Had he touched me in my sleep? I wouldn't put it past him.

The thought of anyone touching me now aside from Jace made my skin crawl and bile climb up my throat. Especially thinking about it being Kellan.

"And what do you plan to do?" I asked in a tone that was less than polite.

"I bet you would love to know. For now, the plan is to sneak you back into Isla. Nobody outside of this crew, the queen and soon-to-be crowned king know of your treachery."

"Will I not be hung upon arrival?"

"Not immediately. The plan is to make an example out of you. Someone of such high rank betraying the crown...tsk tsk, Elianna." He started shaking his head. "But you will wish that a hanging is what you received by the time we are all through with you."

His grin promised an excruciating death, but I refused to let him see any fear...even though it was consuming my entire being.

Kellan had dragged me up to the deck of the ship as we docked in Isla. The setting sun nearly blinded me after being unconscious for days and then locked in a dark, rotting cell. He threw a sack over my head so no one could see who I was as we left the ship. With my hands now in iron cuffs, any civilians near the dock would assume I was a random prisoner being escorted into royal custody.

I felt someone's large hand as they shoved me head first into a horse-drawn carriage to bring us back to the castle. Nobody removed the bag over my head.

As I felt the carriage stop, I was aggressively dragged about once more and guided down multiple flights of stairs and winding tunnels that reeked of musky dampness. It wasn't difficult to assume that I was being led beneath the castles to the dungeons below.

Once we came to a stop, I could hear large chains rattling amongst the room, confusing me regarding my whereabouts. That was until the sack was finally ripped from my head.

As my eyes adjusted yet again, now in the shadows of the prison cells, my eyes flared wide when I noticed that I wasn't in a cell at all, and standing before me...was the wyvern. Imprisoned still in his chains, the creature wrapped himself up in a tight ball, the only way it could probably protect itself.

"Nox," I said on a loose breath. The enormous beast eyed me then, its thin, vertical pupil narrowing in on me, a stark contrast to his glimmering golden eye.

Kellan then tugged on my chained wrists and undid the locks connecting them together, confusing me further. "What's going on?" I asked. "Won't you be putting me in a cell?"

"Eventually," he answered, as he picked up a rather heavy looking chain from the ground. I followed the length of it with my eyes to find it was attached to the far wall. He locked it onto one of my cuffed hands.

"Kellan, what is this?"

He raised a brow at me. "So much like you, princess, to think you are in any position to demand information."

I rolled my eyes. "Stop, calling me that."

He let out a rough laugh. "Old habits, love," he said, as he went to my other side, picking up an identical chain that was attached to the opposite far wall.

Once both chains were attached to my wrists, my stance was spread wide, forcing my arms to remain straight out in the air at my sides. I had a sinking feeling roll through my gut.

I glanced around the enormous, almost empty space at the back end of the dungeons. Bones were piled up in corners of the cavern, and the only source of light was from the few lit torches strung along the rocky walls.

"What, are you going to have Nox roast me?" I mouthed off to him.

"That dumb creature wasted all of its fire it had recuperated once more yesterday. Callius walked down here and it unleashed its entire supply. It'll be a few days before he can do it again, and I'm sure he will."

While I was relieved to hear Nox wasn't going to rain hellfire down on me, I couldn't help but feel sorry for the creature. He constantly felt the need to waste his best defense he had, just in hopes of a moment of peace.

I then heard another set of footsteps come from behind me, where we had entered. My chains wouldn't allow my body to turn, so I was forced to remain staring at a very curious Nox, who I hoped wasn't eyeing me as his next meal.

"Callius, how nice of you to join us. I believe this is what you requested," Kellan said.

My stomach dropped.

"Yes, thank you, Adler. That will do." Callius then appeared in front of me, taking very large, tormenting steps, circling me. "Hello Miss Elianna." My brows furrowed, and I bared my teeth at him. "It appears you have gotten yourself into trouble yet again. I am sure you remember the first round of punishment for naughty little girls."

My eyes narrowed in on him and my jaw clenched as the satisfying vision of me slitting the fuckers throat crossed my mind...until I noticed he had been unwinding a long, leather whip in his hands.

My whole body stiffened. "Shit," I whispered.

His grin turned feral. "You remember your old friend, don't you?" He began to twirl the whip around his feet, forming swirl-like patterns along the dirt floor of the cavern. "I had to dig this out from within the stables, but I'm sure you two will become quite acquainted by the time I'm through with you this evening."

Before I could even think of a response, I felt a tug on the back of my shirt, and as I tried to turn my head enough to see what was happening, a blade cut up through the back of my shirt, tearing it wide open, revealing the entirety of my scar covered back. The front of the torn shirt began to slip down, slightly exposing my bare breasts to the despicable males before me.

Kellan walked around me again, ducking under the chains to stand next to Callius. He reached out and cupped one of my breasts with his rough, calloused hand. I reached my leg out to kick him, nearly losing my balance. All it did was cause the males to chuckle at my attempt.

"Don't ruin her tits yet, I'd like to enjoy them a few more times," he said sinisterly, as they both let out yet another laugh.

"Don't you *fucking* touch me," I hissed.

Callius tsked at me. "Still so mouthy, this one," he said, as he ducked back under the chains to get behind me.

"Not planning to take turns on the whip?" I snapped at Kellan.

He shook his head slowly in a sneer. "I want to watch the pain ignite in those pretty eyes of yours."

Gods, he was serious. How had I not seen this male for who he truly was all this time?

"How does seven lashes sound to start?" Callius' voice boomed from behind me, amusement and sick anticipation flooded his tone.

He didn't even give me a moment to brace myself before the whip cracked, slicing my back open. A scream tore from my throat from the soul consuming stinging that now vibrated through my entire being. My limbs trembled within the chains as my nostrils flared, trying to catch my breath in an attempt to keep myself calm.

Nox's head whipped up, his long neck trying to move closer to get a better look. I swore I saw sympathy in the beast's magnetic eyes. Sympathy for *me*.

Another lash followed, and then another five more, forcing me to vomit up the bile in my stomach. I hadn't eaten in days. The constant, burning ache was too much to bear. My back arched as I frantically tried to contort myself into a position to get out of reach of the whip. My body then sagged on the chains, barely able to hold myself up any longer.

I counted seven lashes. It was over. My head was bowed, and my body trembled violently from the torture it was just put through.

"How about one more for good measure?" He cackled.

My eyes flew open and my head snapped up as he lashed the whip at my back once more, but the tail end of the whip had maneuvered its way around to the front of my body, cutting across my chest, tearing open the flesh. Blood rose to the surface instantaneously as a sob ripped from my throat uncontrollably.

One of them walked up to me a moment later and undid the locks on my bloody, cut up wrists, and my body dropped to the floor.

Nox let out a monstrous growl as I hit the dirt with a loud groan.

"Shut up you beast, or you're next!" Callius barked at the wyvern. "Throw her in a cell. I will tell the royals she is here," he ordered Kellan, as I heard his footsteps walk further away from us.

Kellan nudged my shoulder with his boot, and let out a long whistle sound. "That sure just did a number on you huh?" He picked my body up and aggressively threw me over one of his shoulders, and I let out another deafening shriek of pain as blood from my wounds started to drip down my neck as I hung upside down over his body.

"So dramatic," he grumbled out as I whimpered, watching the floor move past as he made his way back to the cells with me.

He tossed my body down onto the floor of a cell and I anxiously moved as fast as the pain would allow, trying to cover my exposed breasts as I sat there hunched over in the center of my new prison.

He slammed the cell's door shut and locked it as I watched with heavy, swollen eyes from the tears that refused to stop coming.

"See you later, gorgeous," he said, as he walked away from the barred, iron door. The promise of more punishments to come hidden beneath the surface of his tone.

Sometime later, I heard a pair of footsteps approach my cell. I didn't know if it had been hours, or even days, since Callius whipped me. I lost all sense of time, too focused on trying to breathe through the unbearable burning caused by the numerous open wounds stretching across my chest and back.

Out of the corner of my eye, a shadow appeared beneath a lit torch and had halted directly in front of my door.

"Whoever you are, you can fuck off." I was barely able to rasp out.

"They thought they broke your spirit, but I knew better than to believe that." My heart stopped dead in my chest at the sound of Kai's voice.

I lifted my head slowly to meet his stare. "Come to enjoy the show?" I let out a lifeless chuckle.

He stared at me for a moment. "I heard you were able to witness firsthand the effects of wyvern's blood. Fascinating, isn't it?" he snarked. "How it just simply melts away the skin slowly, painfully." He was trying to get a rise out of me, and I was desperately trying to not show that it was working. "Such a shame the king had to die under such conditions."

I clenched my teeth as my hands balled into shaking fists. My breathing became harsh, staggered. "Excuse me?"

"Ah yes, I wasn't sure if Captain Adler had filled you in on how exactly he received the wyvern's blood. It was gifted to him by orders of the queen."

My heart was racing, and I couldn't catch my breath.

"This next part will be our little secret. I need to tell you something else about your king, something Kellan wasn't even made aware of." Kai's tone was venomous. "You see, Mother couldn't have you in the king's ear any longer regarding ending the war. So she was forced to take matters into her own hands." He couldn't be suggesting what I thought he was... "Just three drops in his nightly wine. That's all it took to bring down a king completely undetected."

"You lie!" I shouted, even though I knew within my soul that he spoke the truth. The queen had killed the king. My favorite person in the entire realm, gone. "That is considered treason. You all should be hung for what you have done. Not ascend the throne! The people will learn of what you have done!" I spat, my voice still hoarse from before, cracking as the thought of what my father had gone through plagued my mind.

He took a few steps closer to the cell and placed his face between two of the rusted bars. "See, that is where you're wrong. They will never know the truth, Elianna."

I bared my teeth at him in response.

He was silent for a moment before he continued. "Or should I call you...*sister*?"

To Be Continued...

end of book one.

Acknowledgements

THANK YOU SO MUCH to every single person who has believed in me, and my story, from the very start.

Celia and Tory, the dedication section of this book doesn't even begin to cover how grateful I am for you both. Between the constant, and I really do mean *constant*, daily discussions, plot planning, bouncing ideas off of you, and so much more, this never would've been possible for me without your unwavering amount of support. Thank you for being my first readers, biggest fans, and the greatest friends I could ever ask for.

Thank you to my parents, brother and the rest of my family for supporting this and cheering me on the whole way. Your words of encouragement when I doubted myself kept me going.

Thank you to my amazing editor, Makenna Albert, for teaching me the ways of how all of this works, and for being extremely patient with me and my thousands of questions. Also, she's a kickass hype-woman.

And lastly, to my love. Thank you for supporting me and this dream from the very start.